The Cross and the  Tomahawk Series

LONGSHOT

A NOVEL

mark ammerman

RIVEROAK®
Good News in Fiction

COOK COMMUNICATIONS MINISTRIES
Colorado Springs, Colorado • Paris, Ontario
KINGSWAY COMMUNICATIONS LTD
Eastbourne, England

River Oak® is an imprint of
Cook Communications Ministries, Colorado Springs, CO 80918
Cook Communications, Paris, Ontario
Kingsway Communications, Eastbourne, England

LONGSHOT
© 2000, 2005 by Mark Ammerman

This story is a work of fiction. All characters and events are the product of the author's imagination. Any resemblance to any person, living or dead, is coincidental.

First Cook Printing, 2005
Printed in the United States of America
1 2 3 4 5 6 7 8 9 10 Printing/Year 09 08 07 06 05

Cover Design: Two Moore Designs/Ray Moore
Cover Art: Ed French

Unless otherwise noted, Scripture quotations are the author's paraphrase of the King James Version of the Bible. Scripture references marked KJV are taken from the King James version of the Bible. Public Domain.

ISBN: 1-58919-047-5
LOC Catalog Card Number: 99-080158

The Cross and the Tomahawk Series

LONGSHOT

A NOVEL

mark ammerman

"An Indian ... came to me and said that their
great men, the Beaver and Captain Oppamylucah
(these are two Chiefs of the Delawares), desired to
know where the Indian's land lay, for ... the French
claimed all the Land on one side of the River Ohio
and the English on the other side."

—Christopher Gist

This story is dedicated to the memory of

Rich Mullins

whose recent, short life among the Navajo of Arizona
was a bright light and a strong song.
His voice is still clear in the ears of those he left behind,
and the heartbeat of his undying passion for God
and his children can still be felt wherever his music plays.

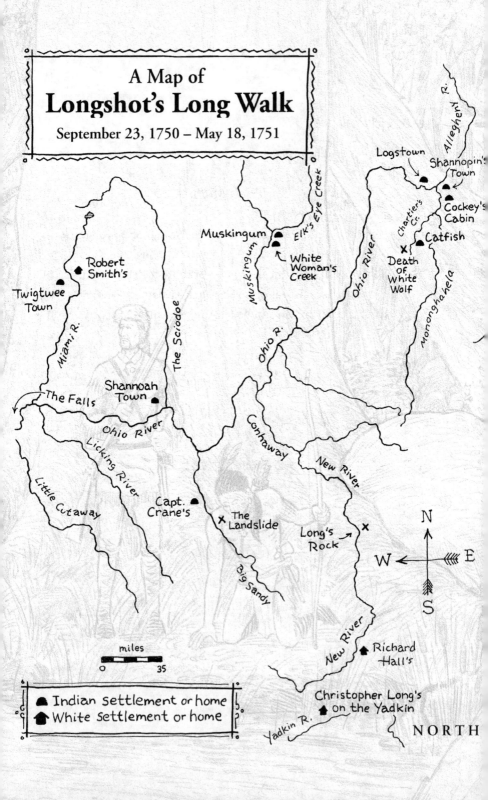

A Map of
Longshot's Long Walk
September 23, 1750 – May 18, 1751

Allegheny R.

Logstown
Shannopin's Town

Chartier's Cr.

Cockey's Cabin

Catfish

Elk's Eye Creek

Muskingum
White Woman's Creek

× Death of White Wolf

Muskingum

Ohio River

Ohio R.

Mononghahela

Robert Smith's

Twigtwee Town

Miami R.

The Sciodoe

Shannoah Town

The Falls

Ohio River

Licking River

Conhaway

New River

Little Cutaway

Capt. Crane's

× The Landslide

Long's Rock

×

Big Sandy

N

W ⫸ E

S

miles
0   35

New River

Richard Hall's

● Indian settlement or home
♠ White settlement or home

Christopher Long's on the Yadkin

Yadkin R.

NORTH

PENNSYLVANIA

NEW YORK

Susquehanna R.

Gnadenhütten

Bethlehem

New York

Hudson R.

Juniata River

Harris' Ferry

Delaware R.

Conestoga

Conestoga Cr.

Susquehanna R.

Lancaster

Philadelphia

Conewago (Connie Joe's Ferry)

Pequea Cr.

Bainbridge's

Great Hill's (Moses)

NEW JERSEY

Wright's Ferry

Vill's Creek

MARYLAND

Cresap's (Old Town)

Potomac R.

Baltimore

Delaware Bay

The Old Narragansett Country
(Southern Rhode Island, Sept. 1750)

miles 0 1 2 3 4 5

Providence (15 miles)

VIRGINIA

ATLANTIC OCEAN

Caleb's Island

Robert Hazard's (Joy Kattenanit)

Kingston

Red Cr.

Great Swamp

Old Capitol of Canonicus

Aquebapaug Pond

Netop's

NARRAGANSETT BAY

Narragansett Indian Church

Charlestown (Big Bill Moose)

Rhode Island Sound

Block Island Sound

CAROLINA

Map by Mark Ammerman

Contents

Part One: A Once Awakening

Part Two: A Narrowing Way

Part Three: A Westward Wandering

Part Four: La Belle Riviere

God Never Sleeps

By the end of the seventeenth century, the political presence and the military "medicine" of the southern New England Native American was gone. The once plentiful and powerful tribes of Massachusetts, Rhode Island, and Connecticut—principally the Nipmuc, Pequot, Narragansett, Wampanoag, Massachusetts, and Mohegan—had been subjugated or dispersed by war.

Surrounded by a growing English population, they were continual victims of the colonial lust for land, and they suffered from even the most innocent expansion. English law and English culture consistently chipped away at the ancient, now impotent rock of Indian tradition, while English society crawled over that same rock like the wooded vines of the thinning forest. What land the Indian had left was often sold out from under him by his own sachems, and he could do little or nothing about it.

With the loss of the open forest—that great, green, and once boundless world that had called the Indian from his bed each morning since his forefathers first walked eastward to the sea—the New England Indian was a man without a soul. His bowstring grew limp, his arrows lay bent and broken in the browning ferns of the autumn of his race, and his tomahawk (long since made of English steel) rusted in its scabbard. Banished from the eastern seashore by the sons of the English isles and cut off from the northern forest by unfriendly tribes of free and sovereign Indians (the Mohawk of New York and the Abenaki of Maine), some pushed west to make new lives among distant tribes.

But most simply lingered on their dwindling lands, slaves to the rum jug, servants to the English, and increasingly dependent upon the gleanings of English civilization. A voiceless fringe minority, many married interracially with the growing black slave population—especially in southern Rhode Island where the remnant of the Narragansett nation was huddled upon the last of its ancient lands.

But they were men. And the spirit of a man will not lie dormant forever, no matter how many seasons of darkness and despair have laid it low—especially when that spirit is pursued and quickened by the Spirit of God himself.

Our tale begins in the middle of the eighteenth century, a decade after the Great Awakening has swept like holy fire throughout the colonies from Massachusetts to Georgia. The divine flame of revival has burned brightly even upon the lands of Canonicus, Miantonomi, and Katanaquat, irrevocably and eternally marking an ancient people with the brand of a holy God. But some still run the old and shadowed paths of their forebears. Some still have not bowed the knee to the Love that tirelessly pursues them. But no man can run forever, and God never sleeps.

Mark Ammerman, November 1998
South Duke Street on the Conestoga,
where Indians once ran.

To learn more about the historical background of this book, see "Historical Notes: Under the Sun," pg. 269.

ACKNOWLEDGMENTS

Merci Beaucoup to a Whole Lot of You

First thanks go to my wife, Terri Lynn, who—in such a very busy season of our lives (okay, so when have we *not* been busy?)—released me to the world of the past and to my imagination. Without her support, this book—and the series that it is a part of—would not have been written.

And piles of hugs and kisses to my children—Jandy, Bethany, and Jonathan (sorry, Brooklyn and Micah, but you weren't in the family yet)—who patiently waited, for hours and hours on end, for Daddy to come out of hiding.

Also thanks to:

My father, Clifford S. Ammerman (editor and publisher emeritus of "The Nation's Largest Rural Tri-weekly," *The Wayne Independent*), whose personal library (and impeccable memory, though he claims to be suffering from "Partzheimers disease") has been a handy, helpful, and pleasurable resource of historical materials. And for once again opening his house as a writer's hermitage in my hour of need.

Lancaster County Public Library (especially Sharon Gordon and Interlibrary Loan) for being my main supply line to the materials most needed in walking the path to the past.

William Scranton Simmons (Dean of Anthropology at the University of California, Berkeley) for his continuing commitment to research, interpret, and chronicle the cultural, spiritual, and social evolution of the New England Indian (the Narragansett in particular). Bill, though now a West Coast university professor, was born (and in his heart will always be) a Providence, Rhode Island boy.

Jim Rennick (former missionary to France and die-hard

Ammerman book fan) for his encouragement and help in promoting the historical message of redemption among the American Indians.

Richard Sensenig (humorist, poet, and sometime German linguist) for his role as consultant in finding the proper historical German word for "fool."

Janet Hixon, David Fesenden, Pam Taylor, George McPeek, Bill Goetz, Dr. K. Neill Foster and his wife Marilynne (the mid-1990's editorial crew at Horizon Books/Christian Publications) for believing in The Cross and the Tomahawk in the first place, and for doing all they could to launch this literary arrow from their corporate bow.

Jeff Dunn and all my new friends at River Oak Publishing and Cook Communications, for believing that a resurrection of this series can inspire, bless and challenge a new generation of literary fiction readers.

John Mort at the American Library Association's *Booklist* for being my Number One Fan (and for listing *Longshot* as one of the top ten best Christian books of the year 2000—even though I found out about the award months after the fact while doing a Google search of my own books!).

Roland Mars for taking me on a wonderful walk in the Rhode Island woods.

Jesus Christ—Lord, savior, brother, and friend—for giving up Heaven for a season in order to walk the dark trails of this forest of humanity in search of lost souls like me. And for the incredible love which drove him to a Roman cross of wood on our behalf. The grave could not hold such love down.

PART ONE

A Once Awakening

"After the war, they were soon reduced to the condition of the laboring poor, without property, hewers of wood and drawers of water."

—The Reverend John Callender of Providence

One Walk in Autumn

Sunday afternoon, September 23, 1750

The old willow was a massive, gnarled, and kingly corpse, standing thick and tall and evermore leafless beside the dark, wandering waters of Red Creek. Caleb knelt at its bark-bared feet and chanted in the rolling Narragansett tongue of his forefathers. And though I didn't believe in ghosts, the bank of that misty, muddy, reeded creek had the feel of a heavy haunt upon it.

"The spirits still linger," said Caleb, lifting his painted visage from the frost-browned ferns. His hands swept long, black locks from his hard-featured, sun-darkened face. "They linger, though the moon has walked the heavens a thousand times since my people last lit their fires beside this river." His large black eyes peered cleanly into mine, as if searching for my thoughts, then rose to the clouded skies and squinted at the veiled brightness of the midday.

"Over there," he breathed, standing to swing his greased arm in an arc that led my gaze across the creek to the balded heads of a stand of giant, withered pine. "They dance over there."

Caleb stepped upon the end of his bow with a moccasined foot, and the weapon rose from the ground to meet his calloused hand. With one last glance at the old willow, he plunged up to his knees in Red Creek and soon had reached the far side. I followed, bridging the waters upon the slippery, vine-covered trunk of a fallen sycamore. Its mottled bark broke off in brittle sheets beneath my leather-booted feet and floated downstream upon the whispering waters.

A thorn-entangled thicket of fruit-bare blackberry sprawled before us beneath a bent stand of white birch, blocking our way to the pines. "The earth has done its best to guard the sacred places," Caleb mused quietly. "But I must see for myself. And your eyes must see it too, Christopher Long." He unwrapped his fringed shirt from about his waist and buried his arms in its protective sleeves. Into the thicket he strode—as easily as he had forded the chilly waters of Red Creek—ignoring the sharp-taloned branches that clawed at his clothing and sought his flesh. I came on behind, bowing the bushes before me with the long barrel of my rifle. Ahead of us, and on both sides of the brambled birch, rose an ancient palisade of pine.

Suddenly, the Narragansett halted. Hanging his bow from the boughs of a lone ironwood, he pulled his tomahawk from his belt and began to lay the bushes low. "Here!" he declared. "Cut with me here. We must clear this grove in a circle—ten paces all around us. Trees and all. The birch will fall easily."

"Far more easily by English steel than by the chiseled stone of your ancestors!" I laughed, easing my hatchet from its sheath.

Caleb shot me a sharp glance.

"Just a jest!" I grumbled, putting my arms to the task beside my companion.

In a little time, we cleared away a quarter acre of the blackberry, felled a score of saplings, toppled two rotted old birch, and—after Caleb moved his bow to safer haven—joined our axes to down the stubborn young ironwood that had set itself up as prince of the birch stand. Quite a piece of work for a Sabbath afternoon! Sweating heavily, in spite of the unusually cool winds of the new autumn, we stood at last in the midst of our clearing, surrounded by a circle of large, flat, half-buried stones.

"The Council Rocks!" declared Caleb.

I had first met Caleb—and his brother Netop—three decades past on a surveying trip with my father, Richard Long. Pop had been hired to lay out some land for Robert Hazard, a wealthy farmer in Rhode Island. Caleb was a lad my own age, fourteen years and running toward twenty, the only other member of our party—besides Netop—under thirty. Netop was eighteen, and though his features and his height declared him the older brother, yet by his bearing he seemed to me the younger. But that is only because the true younger seemed wilder than the woods we walked. Netop, though as dark of skin as his Indian parents, appeared to be merely a young Englishman amid his elders. Caleb was undeniably an Indian.

I had seen Indians before, young and old, often and many. Some carrying water for their masters through the streets of Providence. Some in their poor homes along the banks of the many ponds and rivers of the colony of Rhode Island. Some fishing in their canoes and boats upon the Narragansett Bay. Some hewing wood beside the paths that I had walked with my father through the wooded flats and hills that he surveyed as he laid out tracts for the farmers and planters who moved more and more into the former country of the Narragansett. Occasionally, an untamed contingent of natives wandered into town from the distant north, but I thought them more a fantasy or a novelty than anything real of flesh and blood.

And once, a silver-haired Indian named Old Toby Smith came to call at our house to beg a few shillings—for he heard that my father was liberal in such things—to pay off a lender who threatened to take the old man to court and cast him into servanthood. Father entertained the poor fellow for some time, and I listened in fascination as Old Toby told tales of his childhood before King Philip's War. Toby had become a Christian just prior to the war, he said, and had fought with the English against Metacom (for this was Chief Philip's true Indian name). But now Old Toby was destitute, having been brought to ruin by the rum that became the companion of many Indian soldiers after the war. The church had pursued him with tears and prayer, he said, but the rum was the victor. Father paid his debt upon the promise that Old Toby come round each Sabbath and join us at worship. He came for a fortnight, dressed shabbily in his Sabbath best, and then we never saw him again.

But Caleb! He was as different from Old Toby as the noonday sun is from the new moon. He was no shadow of a lost race clothed in poor English wool, sneaking apologetically through the muddied streets of Providence. He was a wild and clear-eyed Narragansett son of a bright past that I thought lived only in the tall tales of toothless old warriors and the dreams of white-headed soldiers. He wore no English clothes. He didn't carry an English rifle or an English hatchet. He had an Indian longbow slung over his shoulder and a deer-hide quiver strapped to his back, full of brightly painted arrows. His bared arms and chest and his sharp-featured face were painted also. His hair was longer than my mother's, tied back in braids with beaded thongs and the feathers of hawk and turkey. And though he spoke English as well as any Boston schoolboy, he chattered with Netop in a tongue that was theirs alone.

When first I saw him set an arrow to his bow, I thought he would never hit anything with that feathered stick. And when he bent the bow full to his cheek, I thought it would break, sure thing. And when he aimed it at the grazing stag that my father pointed out in the clearing beyond the woods, I thought, *Why is Pop letting him scare a good meal away?* But when Caleb let go of the bowstring, that feathered dart flew so swift and straight and quiet that a bird couldn't have followed it! The buck fell dead on the spot, a flint-tipped shaft of dogwood within its heart. Caleb let out a holler that made my hair jump up, ran nearly as fast as his arrow to the fallen animal, flopped to his knees, chanted something heathen, slid his knife into the belly of the beast, and laid open its bowels upon the meadow as easily as my mother cut a fresh loaf of bread. I knew from that moment that I wanted to be like Caleb.

"You're a Christian and an Englishman," my father counseled me as we walked the woods together, "and not a savage who worships false gods and paints himself to look like the Devil. But the king needs young Englishmen who know the forest as well as the Indian does. Who knows but that you may grow to be one of those men?"

"Do you remember?" I asked, as the cold wind sang in our ears.

"My soul remembers," replied the Narragansett, thinking I spoke of the Council Rocks.

"Not the stones, Caleb," I offered. "I'm recalling the days when we first met."

The Indian turned his hard gaze upon me, and his eyes softened, though his lips remained as straight and tight as they ever did when his heart was considering a right answer. His hand rose to let his fingers play with the ring of blue shells that hung from his right ear.

"In those days, my medicine was weak and my anger was strong," he replied at length, his eyes holding mine. "My brother, Netop, was a slave in the house of Hazard. My mother is still."

"By choice, good friend," I replied. "And no slave," I added carefully but surely, for Joy Kattenanit Hazard was comfortable and well cared for at the Hazard estate, more a part of the family than not. When her indenture had run its days, Netop's still had several years to go, and so she asked to stay on as housekeeper and kitchen help, as much for Netop's sake as to prevent herself from being thrust out upon the poverty of her own people. And she requested the servant's room with the window to the east. She was Narragansett, she quietly declared, and would face the rising sun each morning as her people had done from time beyond memory. She was a woman quickly liked and soon respected, but hardened deep within, sadly embittered by a past that she could not forget and would not forgive.

"These stones," said Caleb, pulling us once more into the world at our feet, "they are like the true ways of my people, strong and wedded to the earth, but long hidden from the eyes of men." He began to pace within the circle, singing quietly in the rhythmic tongue that I had come to understand nearly as well as my own:

> In the Dawning of the Morning
> Just before the World's Beginning,
> Cautantowwit sat a-singing,
> On the silver moon a-shining,
> Songs of joy and songs of sorrow
> From the dreams within his bosom
> Of a World Beyond Tomorrow,
> Of a land of his deep longing,
> And a home of his own making
> Just beyond the gray horizon ....

My painted companion halted his chant—an ancient myth of the creation that the Narragansett had passed down from father to son—and peered again to the tops of the dead and yellowed pine. "I have come here only a few times," he said, "because I was afraid that the longer I walked this land, the deeper my moccasins would sink into the soil. I was afraid that Chepi would hold me here and that I could no longer walk the woods or ride my horse beside the wind." And he turned to look me in the eyes again. "But I am no longer afraid," he said. "My medicine is strong. My spirits walk with Chepi in peace. My anger is reined. Come! Let me show you about."

We left the stones and walked beside Red Creek, crossing back and forth many times, passing beneath lightning-torn maples and half-rotted elms, pushing through thickets of hard, wrinkled chokecherry and the rough, dangling vines of wild grape. Caleb stopped often, sometimes to bow his face to the ground and chant, sometimes to hold his head erect and snort like a buck. Sometimes he laughed, but with little humor in his heart. Once he wept. Always he spoke, ofttimes in the Narragansett tongue and a little in English.

"Our feet walk this creek bank where dusty streets once wandered within the city of the great Canonicus and his strong son Miantonomi. Wigwams by the hundreds stood beside these waters. Men danced for war. For peace. For rain. For harvest. For joy. For sorrow. For life. For death. The spirits danced too," said Caleb. "They dance still," he declared, calling to my eyes with his. "But you don't wish to hear of such things.

"My great, great grandfather was Katanaquat, The Rain From God," he continued. "His grandfather was the mighty Askug, powwow of the Narragansett. Askug commanded the spirits and they obeyed him. He bade the winds to blow and they blew. He begged the sun to shine and it opened its eyes wide upon the earth. He cursed his enemies and they died. But you don't wish to hear of such things."

I did not, as he knew, but I said nothing. I would listen, as he knew, and so he spoke.

"Our great god Cautantowwit smiled upon us in those days," he said further, "before the English and the Dutch and the French and the German and the Scot ..."

"And the gospel of the Lord Jesus Christ," I said, finishing his thought for him. It was not an interruption, just the period on the end of a sentence he had oft rehearsed before me through the years. "But I love you still," I said, unashamed of the sentiment and rather glad to cast it upon him at the moment.

He continued his lecture. "Before the Baptist and the Quaker and the New Light and the Old Light and the Jew and the Presbyterian ..."

"And the Episcopalian," I said, speaking for him once more.

"And the Episcopalian!" he declared, piercing my defenses with his arrow-sharp eyes.

"God save the Church of England," I shouted, with a hearty laugh and a leap into the air besides.

"God save us from the Church of England!" he countered roughly, and any who did not know him would think he was primed for a fight.

"You are an incorrigible savage, Caleb Hobomucko!" I cried, not a bit angered but more than a little sorrowed in my soul. "And I declare my own faith weak before the shield of your heathenous contentions."

"Your faith is not weak," countered Caleb.

"I would give up all that I own to see you in church on the Sabbath!" I declared.

We crossed Red Creek once more in silence and found ourselves again within the sunken fortress of the Council Rocks.

"I am a red man, you are a white man," he said at length. And I thought I could hear the howl of his ancestors in the chill wind.

"It matters nothing to me what colour you are," I replied, running my fingers through my short growth of beard. "I once dreamed of being as you are. And the forest is my second home because of you."

"If my colour matters nothing to you, then you are more a son of the forest and a truer child of Providence than all of your people!" Caleb blurted. "Roger Williams loved my people. Few have loved them since."

"The years have joined our hearts, Caleb—yours and mine," I said, clapping my hand upon his muscled back. "And I speak for my father as well when I declare my love for you. Though my times with you have been fewer than the seasons that have passed since our first meeting, I count them among the best of my life."

The tall, dark, oft-lonely man pulled his lips even tighter and purposely furrowed his already wrinkled brow. He had shed tears once today—and once was enough for any man, his pride declared within his soul.

Those closest to Caleb hardly knew him. Susanna, his Narragansett wife of many years—"the squaw," he simply called her—was more a bed-warmer, a childbearer, and a fieldhand than an intimate companion of the heart. She carried his children in the womb, cared for them after they were born, and wept when they were grown and gone. She hoed his corn and harvested it, shucked it and cooked it and laid it on his plate.

She dried his tobacco and packed his pipe. She kept his fire burning even now. And what he did around that fire, civilized folks would like to know!

Caleb was no longer "that wild Indian boy" who had grown up naked and painted in the woods near Charlestown, chasing down deer like a wolf, hunting with the archaic wooden weapons of his aged elders, running the forest to round up stray cattle for the citizens of Charlestown. He was no longer that "young savage" who crafted canoes from the bark of birch and sold them to the English for the wampum that his fathers once made (which no one used as money anymore). He was no longer that playful recluse who built little wigwams—which the children of Charlestown loved to discover—in any wooded acreage large enough to hide one. Caleb was now "that sorcerer in the swamp," "that witch doctor" who dwelt somewhere on a godforsaken island in the middle of a cedar bog with his squaw. An island guarded by great snakes, some folks declared. And hidden from the human eye by Satan, others said—though few actually believed it.

Apart from the Hazards, most whites never saw Caleb except when he rode into town upon his "black demon of a horse" to doctor up some poor member of his race. "If ever we catch that witch conjuring up devils," the folks of Charlestown declared behind his back, "we'll slap him in irons and ship him away to work the sugar fields in Jamaica!" There were many Jamaicans and Caribs, and some Africans too—blacker than the sun ever baked an Indian—working the cornfields of the English planters of Narragansett. Caleb's brother Netop had married one.

Netop was more English than Indian, raised in the house of Robert Stanton, converted to Christ about seven years past under the enthusiastic preaching of the Reverend Davenport. Now he was himself an exhorter in the New Light Baptist Narragansett Church of the Indian pastor Samuel Niles. An amazing revival of religion that we came to call the Great Awakening swept like fire through the colonies in the early '40s. It also burned a cleansing path through the Narragansett country. Much of the tribe was won to the gospel. I was won too. Though I was raised in and cling still to the rightful doctrines of the Church of England, God used the Awakening to stir my own heart against the foulness of my sins, and I was greatly shaken in my soul to follow Christ. But not Caleb. He had other gods, more deeply rooted in his soul than any of us knew.

"I treasure these times with you as well, Christopher," sighed Caleb, "for you are my closest *netop*. Closer than a brother." *Netop* is a Narragansett word. It means *friend*.

Bidding me to follow with a wave of his arm, Caleb led us from the sacred place and back across the creek once more. Following our own path through the overgrown capitol of old Canonicus and Miantonomi, we shortly came upon a wall of stone that was only lately lain upon the land. "My brother Netop's sweat and blood," Caleb remarked, as we climbed over the skillfully built boundary. "A tribute to the English pharaohs of the Narragansett country," he quipped. I was used to his jibes at the English, but I was always taken aback by his reference to the Scriptures—though I knew full well he had learned to read and write his letters from the Bible.

Our way opened now into a wide pasture, and the autumn skies seemed to take it as a cue. A curtain of clouds rolled westward, pushed by the salt winds that flew from Narragansett Bay a few miles to our east, laying bare the bluest heaven I had seen in weeks. The late afternoon sun lit up the field with yellows and greens, casting the far and low horizon into silhouette. Upon that shadowed hilltop, with their dark and glistening heads raised to the salt breeze, stood a species of creature as close to Caleb's heart as the heritage of his people: *naynayoumewot*—horse.

A sharp whistle crossed the field from Caleb to the silhouetted beasts. A loud whinny answered, and a stunning black pacer separated itself from its fellows and trotted toward us. Caleb walked to meet it.

"*Metewis, netop! Black Earth, my friend!*" cried the Narragansett to the splendid animal. Metewis tossed its grand mane and nuzzled the Indian's chest. "*Tawhitch aunakean? Mat pitch cowahick Manit keesiteonckqus! Why do you paint yourself? The god who made you will not know you!*" The horse was covered with mud, having rolled with its brothers in the fields where the cows graze. "*Cheskhosh! Wipe yourself off!*" commanded Caleb playfully, and the lighter side of my dark friend shone brightly in the meadow while the sun looked on.

"He's only living up to his name!" I jested. And Caleb laughed.

"Climb on!" my friend ordered. "Climb on and ride the midnight wind!"

I hesitated. A horse was a fine thing to sit upon when travelling the distance from town to town. A great blessing and a quiet kind of companionship upon the forest paths from Baltimore to the hunting villages of the Six Nations. And I wouldn't have been with Caleb now if a few good horses had not brought me wearily the hundreds of miles that stretched between Rhode Island and my new home along the Yadkin River in the woods of North Carolina. But this Metewis seemed suddenly a wild, unbridled thing. Indeed he was neither saddled nor bridled! I hesitated—but only for a moment.

Metewis took me well, though not without the spoken assurances of his master. *"Christopher nemat. Wunnaumwaw ewo,"* Caleb repeated in the pacer's ear. *"Christopher is my friend. He speaks true."*

We started off across the pasture, the black pacer and I. With only my hands in its mane, I rode the midnight wind. And it was more like sailing a fair sea than straddling the back of a horse. A marvelous runner, a beautiful beast!—Metewis carried me over the fields like the shot of a gun. He leapt a wall as gracefully and as effortlessly as a deer. He seemed to know my pleasure and sense my joy in the ride, and soon I felt as safe at his neck as if I were a boy upon my father's back. And so I shut my eyes—with neither a thought for the moment nor for my aging, aching bones—to breathe in the salt from the bay and to feel the wind in my locks and to let this splendid beast fly me through the skies of old Narragansett.

A pulsing thunder grew loud in my ears, and I opened my eyes to find myself in a raucous race with the brothers of Metewis. The ground shook, the planet trembled. Like one giant animal, the herd careened across the open pasture. Caleb was somewhere over the hill, lost to sight and nearly to mind. I was Adam, alone, astride the Black Earth in the midst of a great, grassy Eden.

Caleb's whistle sought us, found us even in our deafening stampede— and swiftly but gently the great pacer turned. The thundering shadows that followed him turned also, and together we ran, our faces to the wind, as the soft earth of Eden sank beneath our hooves.

"Heaven!" I declared, as I tumbled from the sweat-steaming animal. It tossed its head once more to the breeze and, with a last nudge against the chest of Caleb, sauntered off with its brothers, looking for some mud to roll in.

"Though all the animals of the earth can be tamed by man," Caleb said with a smile, "that beast has medicine stronger than mine!"

We came out of the pasture upon a road with no grass, and I could see it held the tracks of horse and cattle, men and wagons. We stayed to the right to avoid the dung. Three Negroes with a wooden staff, two pitchforks, and an axe passed us going the other way—to what sort of chore I do not know.

Soon, in the fields on either side, great herds of milk cattle lowed in the grasses and wandered off beneath the trees. Stone fences kept the beasts from visiting a neighbor's farm or trampling a neighbor's garden. But neighbors were few and far between in this fertile land of the English "Narragansett planter."

"The cow makes milk and the servant makes cheese and the farmer makes money from the islands far away," chanted Caleb as we walked.

"And you help him win his fortune, friend Caleb," I reminded. "For your Narragansett pacers are sold even in North Carolina."

"You insult me, Christopher," said Caleb, looking away from me into a field of grazing cattle. I doubted it, and so I waited for his further discourse.

"You insult me, Christopher," he repeated, turning again to face me as we rounded a slow bend near an orchard of apple trees and a field dotted with brown-fleeced sheep. "My pacers are sold even in Jamaica!" he declared. "And what have you been doing in North Carolina anyway?"

I laughed out loud. It was Caleb's wild and Indian ways that caught my eye and called to my heart when I was young; it was his wit that won me.

"After Pop and I helped lay out Lord Baltimore's town, I had some money in my pocketbook," I said, knocking an apple from a branch with the barrel of my gun. I stooped, without stopping, to pick it up. "But money has wings!" I declared, biting into the fruit. It was tart and firm. "Very good!" I noted as I swallowed the bite. "Would make splendid cider!"

"Your apples and your rum, with your cattle and your fences, have done more to ruin my people than the war with Metacom," shot Caleb, who would rather start a fight and bet on it than hear an answer to a rational question. I decided to enter the fray.

"Your people don't have to drink our rum!" I argued. "You yourself have lived long enough without it. Though a little cider might sweeten you up!"

"The English don't obey their own laws forbidding its sale to the Indian!"

"Supply and demand makes even a parson sell poison," I admitted, coining a proverb, though not a very apt one—may all good parsons forgive me!

"The love of money ..." quoted Caleb.

"No man can serve two masters," I added. "For he will surely love one and hate the other."

"My people have no money, and so they love rum," muttered Caleb.

"Then let them love God and throw off their indolence and earn a shilling!" I countered.

"Carrying water for the English? Shoveling horse dung? Cutting wood—our wood—for the English? Carrying stone for the English? Making fences for the English?"

"Darn good fences, I've noticed," I said.

"Fences that cut our lands into pieces!" cried Caleb, suddenly heated beyond the normal fire of our little game. "Fences behind which the forest falls and the houses of the great planters rise like castles in their new English kingdom. Fences that walk right into the very swamps of the Narragansett!" Caleb leapt upon the wide stone wall that led down the ever-widening road that fronted the large wooden home of Robert Hazard. "And if Caleb Hobomucko crosses any of those fences to chase his lost dog or to shoot a deer to feed his poor squaw—assuming there are deer left to shoot—he hears a hearty, 'Ho, injun! Hey, blackie! Ho, Nigra! Hey, mustee! This is my land! Get back in your swamp, if you please, and ... oh, wait! Don't run away so fast! I forget my Christian duty! You are hungry, are you not? Would you like to sit at my table tonight for a bite and a sip of rum? Come! Come!'

"And if I go home with the good Christian farmer and sit at his table and sip just a little bit too much rum, I will probably wake with a headache in the morning, finding my poor, drunken 'X' scratched on some deed.

'Thank you so much, Master X, for selling me your little acre in the swamp,' the good Christian farmer will say. 'I am sure my cows will like it well after I cut down all the trees and build them a proper road!'"

"Caleb," I said, as we came to the yard of the house of Robert Hazard, "we are almost at the door."

"So we are!" he cried. "And hardly a minute too soon. For the hour is getting late, and the law will not allow the poor Indian or Negro to wander the woods after nine of the English clock. He might lose his way, being as dark as the night itself! It must be a great blessing to have such light skin that you need no lantern upon the road!"

"Caleb," I insisted, taking his arm and pulling him from the wall. "It is not nearly seven of the clock! And your anger will not serve the righteousness of God."

"Which god?" demanded the sorcerer from the swamp. "Whose god?" he fired. "My gods are angry often and it serves them well!"

Your gods are no gods, my heart rebutted, but I held my tongue and put my face to Caleb's. "Caleb, my brother," I said firmly, "the stronger man is the one on top when the wrestling match is done."

"*Npenowauntawaunen!*" shouted Caleb. "*I cannot speak your language!*"

Suddenly a door was flung open before us, and an ancient, white-haired, dark-skinned woman thrust her head out to see who stood yelling in the master's yard at dusk.

"Caleb Hobomucko!" cried his mother, Joy. "Stop cussin' your friend and bring him in here to see us this minute!"

Chapter Two

The House of Hazard

Sunday evening, September 23, 1750

Robert Hazard was a large, gray-templed man, older than I by at least five years, and quite hospitable. He was at his door behind the aged Indian as she called us in.

Caleb underwent a strained transformation as he strode toward the house. The fire went out of his eyes, and a determined sigh escaped his parted lips through his clenched teeth. He glanced at me only once before we passed through the stone-silled portal. It was a strange look, somewhat sad and pleading, but I couldn't read its meaning.

Hazard took the door from Joy and ushered us in himself, taking Caleb's hand warmly and passing him on to his mother. Caleb greeted his mother courteously, but they didn't embrace. They walked off together toward the back of the house where a small door led out to the servant's quarters and the old woman's room.

"Christopher Long!" exclaimed the great farmer. "Welcome to the house of Hazard. Come into the parlor and pull a stool up to the fire. I will tell Lorea that we have a guest for the night. She'll have Red Mabel bring us some drink, and she'll pull out the trundle for you in the boys' room. Oh, never mind the trundle! The boys are at Newport with their uncle. Their beds are made up already and you can have your pick!"

"Thank you, Robert," I returned, doffing my hat. I fumbled with it, suddenly feeling that a coonskin cap was out of place in the home of a well-to-do planter.

"I take it," said a sweet, hoarse voice, and a thick, dark hand reached for the coonskin. "Coat too," said Red Mabel. "You find it again on a hook in the hall over there." She grinned a wide, toothless grin and pointed to a narrow passageway through which I could see the warm light of an impressive kitchen.

We had been ushered into a castle indeed! Compared to my two-room, one-loft cabin on the Yadkin, the house of Hazard seemed a king's court. I didn't inquire into the number of rooms (it not being my place to ask such things), but I couldn't help noticing—before my stay was done—that the place had grown a bit since I'd been there a few years past. More quarters for the house servants had been added to the back of the mansion, and a servants' village of sorts, with a grassy courtyard, was set apart from the main house. New barns too. Stables. A carriage house. And glass at every window—which I wouldn't have even noted but that my own place had only oiled paper. I determined to pick up some glass for Sarah on my trip back to the Yadkin and to buy it as close to home as possible so that it made it back in the right number of pieces!

The pleasant odor of bayberry candles filled the house and smelled like money to me, but the main lights were old betty lamps. Even those smelled better than I was used to, and I figured Goodwife Lorea Hazard kept the servants busy setting sweet herbs in the little pans I saw over each betty.

Pictures on the walls. Paintings and some samplers and embroideries that were pleasant to look upon. A portrait of the family in the parlor, next to a big painting of the ascension of Christ. An engraving of London on the Thames hung in the dim hall where my cap was hid behind my coat. Wish I could have seen that one better, London Bridge and all.

The kitchen was a large affair, and Sarah would've thought herself a queen in it. Massive cabinets held more sorts of plates and utensils than I'd seen in most taverns.

A central chimney serviced the whole house, divided as it was into so many rooms (four on the first floor at least, including the kitchen). But even with a mighty blaze throwing its welcoming light into the parlor, it seemed to me—and maybe I'd caught a chill in Red Creek—that all that heat just said "good-bye" and disappeared up the flue. I thought then, as I'd thought before, that there must be some better way to keep a fire inside a house to heat it.

And a clock from Germany—of all things!—was ticking away as happy as a cricket in July.

Red Mabel brought the cider hot, in two big black leather mugs, and

I burnt my tongue at first draught and couldn't enjoy the rest. But it went down warm, and that was fine. I hoped that Caleb was as well taken care of, but then I remembered that Joy had full run of the kitchen—indeed, of the house itself. Caleb would sleep in her room for the night, no doubt.

"What brings you north, Chris?" queried Hazard as he settled his own stool before the fire.

"Well, I thought I'd be telling this story to Caleb first, but we toured the city of Canonicus instead," I said.

"The city of Canonicus?" puzzled the planter.

"My father surveyed it," I commented with a grin, draining my mug. Mabel brought me more. "And now you own it," I said. Hazard wrinkled his nose and glanced nervously at the fire. He was slow with any jest, so I helped him out. "Your plantation, as you well know—like all the other farms along the Narragansett Bay—is on land which was once the Narragansett's. Their principal city was out there along the Pettaquamscutt and the Matatucket. Down by Red Creek, especially. We found the old Council Rocks today, about a mile east of the fields where your pacers run."

"Oh!" said the planter. "Council Rocks, eh? Gives me the shivers."

"Kind of spooky, I'll admit."

"But you didn't ride north to excavate Indian villages!"

"No, not intentionally," I said. "I came to ask Caleb to follow me west."

Hazard sipped his cider and nodded for me to continue.

"I had a business deal go bad in Baltimore," I said, which was an understatement that will be forgiven, God knowing my circumstances, my heart, and all things. "And I was in danger of prison on account of my debts." I stared into the crackling fire rather than take in the planter's eyes. It's not easy telling folks your failures—but confession is good for the soul, and so I did my soul one bit more good. "'Course Pop bailed me out. It's no small shame for a full-grown son with a family of his own to be calling on his old man to pull him out of a dry well."

I saw Hazard nodding still, from the corner of my eye. I thought he might be nodding off altogether, and so I looked at him straight. But he was quite alert. Just then Red Mabel's extraordinary ear heard me jiggling the empty mug upon my knee, and she waddled in with more cider. I thanked her with a smile and took up where I left off.

"I've a friend," I said, "a trailblazing companion who hiked a good distance of Maryland woods with me while I surveyed some wilderness for Lord Baltimore. He has some ground on the frontier of North Carolina, along the Yadkin River. I begged him for a few acres, because I had a plan for making some money to pay back Pop. He liked the idea. And Sarah was game. And the children—the boys especially—were itching to get closer to the big trees. So …"

I stood up and paced the room to illustrate the fact that we moved a long way, and then sat down again. Hazard's blue eyes followed me.

"Well," I said, "I figured I'd put away the surveying for a bit and try my hand at trapping and tanning and trading." Hazard winced. I put up my hands and cocked my head, because I knew what he was thinking. "It's not real respectable, I allow, Robert," I said with some resolve, "but God has given me grace and wisdom to know the forest and to walk it in peace with the natives. My own father once said that I might grow to be a man whom the king could call upon to walk the woods. …"

"This is no service to the Crown!" returned the good farmer suddenly. He leaned toward me, raised his mug as though it were the gavel in a magistrate's hand—and then thundered forth his judgment. "You were called to your father's trade! You have carried it well for decades! You have had the privilege of helping an English lord lay out a colonial capitol! Walking off into the wilderness to trade with the savages and catch beaver by the tail is a ridiculous scheme and a disgrace to the name of Richard Long of Providence."

"Formerly of Providence," I corrected meekly. "And you haven't heard the full tale."

The planter regained his composure and sat back upon his stool. Red Mabel brought him another mug, but he waved it away.

"A group of reputable men—Governor Dinwiddie of Virginia among them—have incorporated themselves as the Ohio Company," I continued. "The king has granted them 200,000 acres along the Ohio. But to make the grant stick," I said, blowing on my cider to cool it, "they've got to settle fifty families there and build a fort within the next seven years. 'Course first they've got to find someone to walk the woods, to discover the good ground and lay it out."

Hazard nodded, more knowingly now. "And you're the man for the job?" he asked.

"Got my contract and instructions from the Company just two weeks past," I said. "They're paying me well enough up front that I can give Pop a good piece of his cash back. And they'll cover other expenses as needed. I want to get onto it before the autumn's too far gone."

"And Caleb?" asked the planter.

"I want to take him with me," I replied.

We talked on into the night, the good farmer and I, about Caleb, whom Hazard didn't want to lose. "My pacers love him," the planter declared, "because he loves them. Never have I had a man, or heard of one elsewhere, who could train horses so well as this wild Narragansett. But Caleb is a free man who has never been a servant. It is up to him where he wanders," Hazard resolved.

"As long as he's in by nine," I reminded the planter.

"He's a clown!" declared Hazard suddenly and strongly, though not without affection. "A very intelligent one, I will admit, and I doubt very much that he hides himself at home after nine! He plays his games with us all."

"Games?" I nudged.

"Wants to be an Indian," judged the good farmer, "but he's not. Not a dangerous one, I mean, though people talk. They say he's a witch doctor. But I can't believe it. He's perfectly content when he's here on the plantation and behaves himself as well as any man should. Works hard for the small wage I pay! I love the man, really I do, though I find myself treating him poorly sometimes. He is a red man, after all, who has never truly opened his heart to me. And his paint and his costume—when others point it out to me, because frankly I'm quite used to it—are offensive and quite barbarous.

"But his brother is another story. Netop grew up in this house, learned his letters and his catechism here. Caleb learned them here too, of course, though his Narragansett uncle housed him and clothed him and raised him up heathen." The planter sighed. "He calls himself Caleb Hobomucko. He could have carried the name of Hazard, but he'd rather play the clown!"

The farmer laid another log in the fire.

"Caleb is no clown, I beg your pardon," I countered. "He's an Indian indeed in every way," I affirmed. "He plays the Englishman only when it suits him—and that's when he plays the clown, more often than not! His jests are subtle when he walks with the white man, and sometimes bitter, but they are not false. I've walked the woods with him, hunted, fished, fallen asleep beside him beneath the stars. His waters run deep, but I—if I might speak at liberty with one who sees him season in and season out—probably know him better than any man."

"And you wish to take him over the Ohio," Hazard sighed.

"I can think of no better companion in the forest," I declared. "His heart beats with the earth. When the Ohio Company hired me, they really hired the son of my father—and Caleb Hobomucko."

"You speak little of yourself where others speak large of you," chided the planter.

"The Scriptures admonish us to consider others as better than ourselves," I reminded him. "'Let another man praise thee and not thine own lips,'" I quoted old King Solomon.

"You are a good Christian, Christopher Long," said the planter.

"I hope to hear One other say as much one day," I answered quietly.

We talked about Caleb's mother, Joy.

"She's been staying much to herself lately. And reading," noted the good woman's keeper. "She has shown an increased interest in religion since Netop has embraced Christ, though I don't know her heart in the matter. She has an old Indian Bible, the one John Eliot made in the last century. It hardly holds together, and she reads the pages in leafs like a letter.

"And she begs to look over the books in my library," said the planter. "I lent her Bunyan's works and some other writings," he continued, "and I do believe she has read them. But she has two large volumes, handwritten manuscripts, that she looks upon the most. I asked once if I might see them, but she refused.

"I was rather surprised and at first offended, but then she told me they were personal accounts of family history and the like, and that she preferred to keep them to herself at this time. I believe her father wrote them. He could read and write his letters, Joy has said, and he spoke English well. I think he helped Eliot translate the Indian Bible and was one of the preacher's favorites. He was an Indian spy for the English during King Philip's War. Job Kattenanit. Up at Natick, Massachussetts. Have you heard of him?"

I said I had, and that Caleb had spoken of his grandfather though he never knew him, for the man had died nearly a decade before Caleb was born.

"Sad thing," said Hazard absently, "that the natives take to religion one day and discard it the next. But it seems to have stuck with Netop. Six years now, or seven. Of course he was brought up in it, and in the right way of it, the Episcopalian way! Ah, but now he is a New Light, a Separate!" troubled the planter. "He thinks himself an ordained and anointed exhorter, the poor fellow!"

We talked of the Great Awakening. Of how it had first revived the churches in the land, then split them into factions of Old Lights and New Lights, Established and Separate.

"In North Carolina, the Presbyterians call them Old Way and New Way," I said. "And the itinerant exhorters are labeled Hot Gospelers by the Anglicans in Virginia."

"Hot indeed!" fired Hazard. "Why, that crazy preacher Davenport had a book-burning over in New London! Made a bonfire of some of my favorite classics! I could show you identical volumes in my library," he declared, rising to lead me to his shelves.

The bettys were all but out, and the house was dark. But from the smell of leather, ink, and parchment, I knew when we'd entered the library.

"Here!" said Hazard, warming to his tirade. "Is this so heretical as to deserve the fire?" he asked, handing me a book whose title I could not make out in the dim light. But he didn't really want an answer.

"Whitefield was wild enough, though his doctrine seemed sound," the farmer declared, "but Tennant and Davenport, and even that Parks fellow over in Westerly … well, at least Parks has a church of his own. It's the wandering ones, the itinerants, who are the worst. 'Enlightened!' Enlightened idiots! They make inspiration and the Spirit of truth to be the vehicles of nonsense and contradictions. They declare the established churches to be dead, and that book-learning and seminaries are all of the flesh and the carnal man. They say written sermons and prepared prayers are from the corrupted mind and not of the Spirit. And so they declare themselves preachers of the Word—men, women, children, servants, white folks and red folks and Negroes alike—anyone who gets the fire lit under him long enough to run about shouting and shrieking!

"Their behavior at service is shocking! Groaning and crying out. Leaping and laughing and slapping each other on the back as if they were all drunkards watching a fight! And some of them lying on the floor as though dead. Perhaps we should bury them where they lie!

"The plain truth, Christopher," the Episcopalian planter concluded, with his own hard-reasoned slap upon my back, "is that an enlightened mind—and not riled-up emotions—ought always be the guide of those who call themselves men!"

I wasn't going to walk back through that riled-up sermon for a Spanish gold dollar! I didn't need a betty to see that the farmer had his own enlightened mind made up. Sure, it disturbed me to see book-learning thrown in the fire. And I'd been troubled in my own mind with the sort of ignorant folks who ran about preaching that ordination by a bishop was a sin and the invention of men.

But I couldn't deny that some of those "enlightened idiots"—friends of mine and relatives of Caleb and Joy and Netop—were changed overnight from drunken heathens into sober Christians, and that they'd set about since to live their lives responsibly, piously, and in the fear of God. Netop himself—and I was there and saw it—had fallen to the ground under the exhortations of the Reverend James Davenport. He lay there all night long. I couldn't rouse him, and to tell the truth, I didn't want to. I figured he was wrestling with God, and that was one fight I wasn't going to try to break up! Meanwhile, I was having my own fight. God won with Netop, and God won with me. No, I wasn't going to rail against the New Lights. I was half one myself—a spiritual "mulatto."

"Christopher," I heard the planter say, drawing me back from my theological musings. "You'll need some godly sustenance out there beyond the Ohio. Your only human contacts are likely to be the heathen native or the papish French."

"I thought I might hire a Jesuit priest to come along," I said, straight-faced. But when I saw the planter's eyes widen in puzzlement and disbelief, I quickly added, "Just a jest!" With an embarrassed snort, he passed me a small volume that he'd pulled from a shelf filled with religious works.

"This'll keep me orthodox," I admitted with a smile. "Thank you, Robert," and I gripped his right hand in mine. "I'll carry it with me while I'm out there among the unenlightened, and I'll read it morning and evening."

It was The Book of Common Prayer of the Church of England, and I was honored to receive it from the good planter's hand.

CHAPTER THREE

Joy Comes
in the Morning

Monday, Early Morn, September 24, 1750

I woke much later than I intended. Perhaps it was the cider. Perhaps it was the exhaustion of so many words the night before. It must have been seven of the clock when I finally rolled off my bed. I hadn't bothered to get into my bedclothes. I hadn't slept in them since leaving home, though Sarah insisted I pack them.

The view from my window showed the same blue skies from which the sun had descended the preceding day, and I thought the air was warmer. Autumn was playing its marvelous magic as far as my eye could see. The ground was covered with a brilliant carpet of lately fallen leaves, and Hazard's servants-of-many-colours could be seen going about their duties in the yards and fields below. Black men and women of various hues, from islands and continents I had only heard of. Red men and women, most likely Narragansett, Pequot, or Nipmuc. An occasional white—mostly young men. And the confused blur of the young offspring of mixed races.

"A rum stew!" declared a familiar tongue. I turned to find Caleb behind me. "There they are!" he said, gesturing to the activity in the yard below. "The children of the Great God *Ankapi—rum*."

"Morning, Caleb Hobomucko," I said, pulling on my shoes with a wooden bootjack.

"Molasses rides into Newport on the great white wings of the English trading ships," chanted the Narragansett. "And Rhode Island hums as it distills its rum from the sticky brown cargo.

"The great ships sail the rum to the hot, dry shores of Africa," Caleb sang, waving his arms about like the great sails in a fair sea wind, "where some Fat Black King sacrifices his indolent population to the Great God Rum.

"The Fat Black King's people are chained to each other and herded like cattle onto the great ships.

"The ships cross the sea where the Fat Black King's people are sold as slaves to the poor sugar farmers of the isles of the West Indies." The Indian hung his shoulders low in mock sympathy for the sugar planters. "The poor sugar farmers have families to feed—very large families to feed—and they can't be expected to raise all that sugar themselves! The poor sugar farmers buy slaves with molasses to harvest their sugar and to make more molasses." Caleb stared out the window and over the horizon toward the bay. "And then Johnny comes sailing home!"

"Have you ever tasted rum?" I asked rather stupidly, splashing my face from the water bowl beside my bed.

"My people have—and they swim in it too!—for Rhode Island's prosperous distilleries create a good surplus for its taverns … and for land deals with the savages," he replied. His anger had not cooled from the day before.

"What good are these words, Caleb?" I challenged, standing up to face him. "Do you think that either you or I can stop the ships from sailing, stop the rum from flowing, stop the slaves from being auctioned? Stop the Narragansett lands from being bought and sold? And do you think you must convince me of the foulness of it all? I love it not!"

But my own words didn't damp the fire.

"*Nmunnadtommin! I vomit!*" he barked. "*Npummaumpiteunck! My teeth ache!* My people are sick and lazy and drunken and dying and enslaved. The sacred places lie hidden under brambles and the dung of English cows. The gods of my fathers wail in the swamps and hide their faces beneath the earth because my people bow to the English and bow to the rum pot and bow to the …"

"Caleb," I said, taking him by the arm. "We are guests in this home. Your voice is loud and your words are ill-chosen. Is this how you repay the hospitality of an English household?"

"This house sits upon the throne of the Narragansett kings!" cried Caleb, his voice shaking and his dark eyes wide upon his paint-smeared face. "This land was taken in a war that my people swore not to fight until they were forced to it by the violence of the English! My words are drawn from a clean well, Christopher Long, and no man will ask me to close my lips upon the truth! Take your hand from me!" he roared, breaking from my grip as easily as a man pulls his finger from the hand of a babe.

I stepped back and stared at him. What had gotten into the man? From where had this rage arisen?

"Caleb, *weemat—my brother,*" I said to him quietly in his native tongue. "*Nowechusettimmin. We are together in this war. Nowetompatimmin. We are friends.*"

Suddenly, Hazard stood at the door.

"Outside with you," he said grimly, his eyes strong upon the Narragansett. "Outside—and don't leave the yard until I've had a talk with you."

I expected a great explosion just then, for Caleb had been a keg of powder with the fuse already lit. And who was Hazard to ask a free man to leave and to stay at the same time? But Caleb lowered his eyes to the floor, played for a moment with the ring in his ear, and walked from the room without a word or a gesture of defiance.

When Caleb had gone down the stairs and fully out the door, I blurted, "What spell do you have over the man, Hazard? And will he stay for you? And without violence in his heart?"

The planter looked at me in surprise. "I have no power over the Indian," he declared. "I simply asked him to leave my house. And of course he will stay."

"He was a mad beast with me, and I couldn't still him," I said, rubbing the back of my neck with the palms of my hands. My pillow had not agreed with me. I was used to meaner bedding and no pillow at all.

"You said last night that you know the man's heart. Perhaps he knows yours as well," offered the wise farmer. "The goodwife and I sometimes argue in ways that could start a war, but our love for one another never dims. Yet with those we love less, we would never dare to say such things in such ways. Caleb knows you will hear his anger, Christopher, and love him still. But I must go and speak to him," sighed the planter. "Have you told him of your employment with the Ohio Company?"

"No," I said. "We've been discussing politics."

Hazard looked at me blankly. "Oh!" he finally said, a wee bit annoyed. "A jest."

The planter and the Indian held conference under the chestnuts while Red Mabel called me into the kitchen to break the last night's fast. But Joy met me before I sat myself to eat.

"May I have some of your time?" asked the old woman. And I knew she wouldn't have asked me at that moment—with the corn porridge already hot upon the trencher—if it were not urgent.

I followed her back to her little room with its window facing east, and I saw that she was indeed making a scholar of herself. Two small shelves of books hung upon the wall, and several volumes lay stacked on the floor and upon an engraved chest of drawers. A reading chair was situated by the window to take advantage of each day's light.

Joy was dressed very simply in linen and petticoats. Her dark wrinkled face was framed by thick, silver hair and a white woven shawl that she had about her neck. She seemed to be chilled, and my heart went out to her at once. I could not help but take her small hands in mine as she settled in her chair.

"Do sit down, Christopher. There, upon the bed," she said, in a voice that was younger than her eighty-three years. It is a strange sensation for the ear to hear a voice unchanged by time while the eye looks upon the speaker's body bent and withered by the seasons. "I have a story to tell you, but I must get to the end of it before Caleb returns."

"I don't know if Hazard will let him back in," I cautioned.

"He'll let him back in," Joy insisted with a wave of her wrinkled hand. "Now let me tell my story."

I bowed my head in deference and bade her start.

A century passed within my imagination in the brief minutes that I spent with Joy Kattenanit Hazard. Indians and English alike lived out their lives in the carefully chosen and skillfully spoken words of this old Narragansett woman. Her own story was only a part of the narrative, but of all of the tale, it held me the most.

Joy had been born into the home of Job and Esther Kattenanit, two Indians who were converted under the preaching of the apostle to the

Indians, John Eliot. Job had been a Narragansett before he walked north to find God amidst the Praying Indians of Massachusetts. Esther was a Nipmuc.

When Joy was only four, her mother died, leaving Job alone to raise his daughter and his nearly infant sons John and Jacob. The loss of her mother was a tragedy, which Joy nursed mournfully within her heart. Though her father loved them all and comforted them always with words of cheer and faith and courage, still she missed her mother terribly. And though there were many others who loved Joy in the small Praying Town in which she lived, no one knew her private pain. The little girl determined she must be the mother now, and she put her small hands to the task.

When she was not yet ten, the war between King Philip (sachem of the Wampanoag) and the English broke out in the colonies. The Praying Indians were caught in the middle. Many were forced to move from their homes, and laws were made forbidding them to walk more than a mile from their towns to hunt or harvest their crops.

As the war continued, friends and neighbors among the English began to treat her family as if they had some great sickness or plague. They wouldn't talk to them upon the paths. They no longer came to visit. And when they did come, it was to ask for men to help fight against Philip. Some of her father's Indian friends became soldiers for the English and were killed in the war.

Joy could not understand why God allowed these things to happen, and she feared that God would take her father and her family as he had her mother. She often cried herself to sleep while begging God to bring peace. But peace did not quickly come.

Then one day, a band of warring Nipmuc—allied to Philip—came upon Joy and her brothers as they gathered corn in their fields with the people of her town. The warriors threatened to kill the harvesters if they did not go with them far away. And so her people were taken captive and marched a long way to a large village beside a great lake. Joy—though she spoke a mix of Nipmuc and Narragansett at home, and had learned English well—could not understand much of what these strange Indians said to her. She thought that the end of the world was near, and surely Jesus must rescue her soon. But he didn't come.

He answered her prayer in a different way. In the village of the

Nipmuc, she found a mother, a woman named Mary Widowed-Once, a captive herself, who cared for Joy and the boys. Though she had a young daughter of her own, she took them into her own wigwam, prayed for them, and comforted them with words and songs of faith. The pastor from Joy's village was with them too, and he did what he could to exhort the Christian captives to trust themselves into God's hands. But Joy's heart was in darkness, for her father was not among them. Now she had lost him too.

Mercifully, this adventure ended well, for the children were at last restored to their father. And though their sufferings continued until the war ended, the Lord wed Job Kattenanit with Mary Widowed-Once, and Joy at last had her family complete. This brought her a happiness that was strong—but not deep, for she never again could bring herself to love the Father in heaven. Though she knew he was there in his courts far away, she strengthened her own arm here on earth and trusted in it alone.

When she came of age, she married a young man who had fought against Philip, but they had no children. And at length he became a drunkard and couldn't work. He began to be abusive and angry with Joy, accusing her of barrenness and, finally, unfaithfulness. Though none of his complaints were true, at last he divorced her. And she was bitter in her soul.

Her brother Jacob moved to Rhode Island about this time to live with an uncle named Winaponk, brother of Job and youngest son of that warrior once famous among the Narragansett—Katanaquat, The Rain From God. It was at the death of Katanaquat (who converted to Christ late in life and died upon Martha's Vineyard among the Praying Indians of that island) that Jacob removed to the country of the Narragansett, the ancestral lands that he had never known.

Joy moved in with her parents, and within a few years her father passed on to his reward—and great it is, I'm sure! But the thought of heaven brought no hope to Joy.

She married again, a man named Poor Tom, and took her mother into their home. Children were born, three times, only to die in infancy, and Joy grew very sour against the Lord. She refused to go any longer to church, and because her husband was not a Christian, it mattered little to him. Poor Tom also drank, but at least he worked. And though they were poor, they got by—with the help of some spinning that kept Mary, Joy's mother, quite busy.

Finally, another son was born, and he lived. They named him Netop. Then another son, named Caleb. And at last a girl whom Joy named *Ntummattaquomen,* which means in Narragansett, "I have had a good dream." Her nickname has always been Tooma.

Netop and Tooma were given Narragansett names because Joy had decided that the Father in heaven was Cautantowwit after all, and not Jehovah. For she felt the Creator to be distant, unknowable, just as the Narragansett had always taught. Caleb was given a biblical name only because Joy knew it to be the name of an ancient warrior who was unafraid to stand against his enemies and their gods. Mary was greatly discouraged that Joy's faith had failed, and daily she wept for her stepdaughter's soul.

Mary's own daughter, Patience, died in childbirth on a hot July morning. Though Patience was in heaven, Mary wept the more.

John, the oldest of Joy's brothers, enlisted to fight against the French. He walked north with a contingent of Indian soldiers and never came home. His body was buried somewhere in the Oneida country, Joy was told.

Jacob came often to visit his mother and his sister and tried to convince them to move to Rhode Island among the Narragansett. Mary wouldn't go, for there were no Christian Indians on the Narragansett reservation. But then the good old woman died, and Joy decided it was time to follow Jacob. She moved with Poor Tom and their children to the reservation just north of Charlestown, Rhode Island. Netop was eight, Caleb four, and Tooma three.

But tragedy and sorrow were not done with Joy. One night, her husband was drinking with some bad companions in a house in Charlestown, and there was a fight. Two Indian men brought Tom home, unconscious and with a broken tooth and a bloody lip. In Charlestown, in the morning, neighbors visited the house where they had heard such a row the night before, and they found a man dead on the floor—a Negro servant of a family in town. An investigation led to the home of Poor Tom and Joy. Tom was arrested and tried for the murder. Witnesses of the fight—the same men who had carried Poor Tom home that night—swore that Tom had done it. And he had no defense for himself because he could remember nothing beyond his second jug. He was convicted of murder, and hanged.

After the hanging, Joy cursed Jehovah and asked her brother Jacob to take Caleb in and raise him Indian—more Indian than anyone had seen in those parts for a long time. Jacob reluctantly agreed to do so. Then Joy, determined that her other children would not know the poverty she had known, gave them and herself up to an indentured servanthood at the estate of Robert Hazard.

Here she had been ever since.

Netop married a Carib slave of Hazard when his own indenture was through. The planter released the woman from her servitude and gave Netop twenty acres of land besides. Netop built a small house on it and continued to work for Hazard at some meager wages and some of the produce of his former master's farm.

Tooma also married, and she moved onto the Narragansett reservation. Caleb became an Indian.

"But my poor Tom didn't kill that man," said the silver-haired old squaw in her chair by the window facing east. "'Cause he wasn't the fightin' kind, even when drunk. He always got happy when he drank. Happy and sleepy. Always!

"Poor Tom probably just fell asleep and smacked his mouth on the table. He was always hurtin' himself that way. Himself and nobody else. And the next day, he'd be back to work. Count on it!

"No, my Poor Tom didn't kill that Negro, but I know who did— known it all these years and never told no one. But Caleb knows too! That much, at least. Told me last night. I still didn't let on to him what I know— but he's found it out somehow himself. I fear for things, Christopher, and I wanted to tell you so."

"What will he do?" I asked. "How long has he known?"

"He hasn't known long," said the old woman, and she turned from her window and stared into my soul. "And what he'll do I don't know. But I know what he can do. That scares me, and I fear for his soul."

She sighed and reached for a tattered pile of papers that lay beside her chair upon the floor. "Can you pick up that top page for me?" she asked, her arm not quite long enough for the reach she needed. I lifted it from the pile, and I saw immediately that the faded print was not English.

"*Upbiblum God,*" said Joy Kattenanit Hazard. "The Bible in the tongue of the Nipmuc and the Massachusetts. My father helped translate it. I've been readin' it lately—and a lot of other things that I turned from long ago." She didn't speak for a moment as her lips pursed and her eyes misted over. Then she hung her head, wrapped her face in her shawl, and bawled like a baby. I hardly knew what to do, and so I didn't do anything. I half feared that the good farmer would show up at the door again, but he didn't. And at length, the old Indian raised her tear-streaked face and planted her reddened eyes upon mine.

"Never doubt the mercy, the forgiveness, or the faithfulness of God," she said quietly. And I sat transfixed.

Which God does she mean? I wondered, for her tale had been a hard and bitter thing to hear. Her life had been one dark turning after another away from the God I had trusted my soul to.

But in answer to my thoughts, she brought me to my feet by whispering, "Jesus Christ is the path and the truth and the life, and no man walks to the Father but by him. I know this now. I have known it for a little while, but I have said nothin', desirin' instead—for the joy of the Father's presence—to walk that way alone. He is no distant God to those who draw near to him," she said, her voice cracking, and then she could speak no more for the tears that returned like a flood.

At last, she was silent again, and she pointed to a leather satchel upon her wooden drawers. I retrieved it and laid it in her lap.

"In here are two journals," she said, her dark eyes shining with a seeming inner light, "written by my father, Job Kattenanit. One tells the tale of Katanaquat, his father, my grandfather. The other is his own story—and mine in part. I have read them through again and again these past months. They are a heritage—a godly one!—that I want my children to know and to own. But the time is not yet come to pass this on.

"I intend to show them to Master Hazard, though until now I would not let him see them," she said with a wrinkled smile. "I will ask him to have them copied four times—one for each of the children and one for my sad old brother Jacob. I started to copy it once myself, but my hand shakes too much." She motioned for me to return the satchel to the chest top, and then she asked me to sit down once more.

"I came into the kitchen late last night," she said in a low voice, "and I heard you and Master Hazard speakin' about your headin' west over the Ohio. I heard you talkin' about takin' Caleb with you." She motioned me to lean closer to her. "I want you to do everything you can to convince

Caleb to go," she whispered, "for if he stays in Narragansett ... well ... I'm afraid for things."

"Afraid of what?" I pressed her.

"Afraid that he might kill someone," she answered frankly.

I stared into her midnight eyes. "Kill someone," I echoed quietly.

"Do you believe in witchcraft, Christopher?" she said, suddenly sitting up straight.

"I ... " I began. *Witchcraft?* "I don't know ... really," I stuttered. *Witchcraft? Like Salem? Superstition and hysteria?* "I don't believe in witchcraft, ma'am," I said at last. "No, I don't."

"Do you believe the Bible, Christopher?"

"'Course I do!"

"Then you believe in witchcraft!" she asserted. "In the Devil and his little devils! And in folks who run with him!"

"Well, yes," I said, haltingly. "I believe the Devil is real and that there are folks who run with him. But witchcraft ..."

"Caleb is a witch," said the old Indian, and I thought she must be losing her mind. Surely folks talked about him that way, and I knew he knew his herbs and some old secrets of Indian doctoring, but ...

"Caleb is a powwow," she repeated. "A real powwow. He runs with the Devil, though he doesn't know it's him. Took his name, even. Hobomucko. That's the Devil's name, or one of 'em. Chepi is another name for the Devil. Satan's another name. Folks can have lots of names that other folks know 'em by. The Devil's just like that, and you gotta believe me, Christopher Long!" She took a deep breath and continued. "The spirits Caleb speaks of, surely you have heard him speak of his spirits!" she said. I just stared at her, and she was silent for a moment. Thoughtful. Peering at me curiously with those dark, clean eyes. I think she thought it was I who was mad.

"You have heard him speak of his spirits," she asserted. I nodded affirmatively, and she continued, "Those spirits are real, Christopher, and the power they have is real. They can kill. Any old Indian can tell you so. Any old English can tell you so too. What's the matter with your brain, Christopher? The spirits can kill! And Caleb will ask 'em to. He knows their ways. He knows they hear him, and they know he hears them." She stopped.

I was gaping at her in disbelief. She sighed, and her countenance fell sadly and suddenly. "I thought you could help. But I will pray. God is greater. God is faithful. And yet ..." she stared out her window into the blue autumn sky. "And yet his ways are not our ways, and so I cannot know what he will do. Faithful and good and merciful, but still I cannot know what he will do," she murmured half to herself.

"What do you want of me?" I said, pulling myself together enough to offer my befuddled best. "I can pray," I said. "And I will talk to Caleb about anything you wish me to."

Joy turned to face me once more.

"Tell him what you came to tell him. And nothin' more," she said. "I will pray."

I stood up to go.

"Thank you for listenin', Christopher Long," she said, staring out her window once again. "You have always been a good friend. Please do pray. And please go and see Netop before you ride home. Tell him his mother wishes he'd come more often. Tell him she says that our Lord commands us to love our enemies. Tell him that the merciful will be shown mercy. Tell him these words as I have now spoken them. He will understand."

I bid her farewell, and walked the dim hallway in a dream.

CHAPTER FOUR

The Sorcerer's Isle

**Monday midmorning to midnight,
September 24, 1750**

I shook it off, that dream of dread, that dirge of winter that threatened to settle in my unsettled soul. Although Joy's foreboding—and especially her almost incomprehensible revelation concerning Caleb—was a chill wind within me, nature's sudden choice of song was delightfully like summer. The sun was high. The wind was warm. The wooded, wide, and well-worn trail that wound through the old Narragansett country was alive with the shifting colours of autumn's bright display. A magnificent animal cantered beneath me—a gift of no small benevolence from the present English monarch at the ancient seat of Canonicus. A faithful friend rode beside me. And God's mercies were new with the morning.

"I can hardly believe this horse is mine!" I declared, jogging beside Caleb on my new mount. "When my boys see it, they'll raise a Yadkin yell, shoot all their powder at the sky, and scare every bush-tailed squirrel out of western North Carolina."

"Blood brother of Metewis," said the Narragansett, turning his gaze upon the ink-black horse I rode. "Almost as fast, nearly as strong, and one year younger." He patted his own mount on its thick neck. Metewis bent his ears in response.

"No name comes to mind for him," I said, certain that Caleb had named him long ago.

"Neeyesee," said the Narragansett.

"Two?" I echoed in English.

"Second son of his mother, the Mare Of The Moon Of The New Green."

"Neeyesee," I repeated.

"Two," Caleb affirmed.

"I think I'll call him Nightwing or Big Black or … "

"He'll answer to Neeyesee, even at a whisper," offered the Narragansett horseman, "but not to any other name."

Neeyesee showed his teeth, as if to grin, as he trotted.

"This way," Caleb suddenly announced, turning his mount from the road and onto a narrow path that pulled us westward into a thicker woods than we had yet seen that day. The trees were shorn, I noticed, just above my head. The way was wide enough for one horse and its rider—a lonely, grassy snake of a road that soon became fenced by a palisade of sky-tickling virgin oak and elm. Though the trail was remarkably clear as we traveled— someone kept the winding alley tidy—it was not worn or beaten bare.

The sun nearly disappeared above the thick ceiling of autumn foliage as we wound through the forest in the half-light without speaking. I forgot for a while—as the muted hoofbeats of our mounts kept time nearly as monotonously as Robert Hazard's German clock—that we were in Rhode Island. My eyes walked the woods, curiously searching this rare bit of New England wilderness. Mottled shades of nature's many colours shimmered dimly in the webbed shadows of a million outstretched wooden arms. An occasional uprising of dark, mossy rock. Birds that hopped and climbed and occasionally shot across our path at face level. The sounds of larger beasts beyond our sight—deer or bear or some lone elk. Perhaps a moose looking for water or a cougar prowling for a snack—the forest was thick enough, wild enough. Where were we? Where was Caleb leading me? I didn't ask. The mystery was delicious.

At length, the forest thinned and the path became wet beneath us. Hemlock and cedar began to replace the ancient, leafy giants that had hidden the sun. Now our way was intermittently sun splashed and shadowed, and Neeyesee balked at the rocky, sucking mud that paved the narrow road. Then the forest opened fully on our left, and we walked beside a natural fortress of high, waving bushes and grasses that stood guard at the edge of a massive, sparkling, reeded lake. I knew it had to be Aquebapaug Pond, though I had never come at it from this way. Geese, heron, ducks, redwinged blackbirds—the air was filled with the quiet song of lazy wings and gentle wind upon the waters.

Our path turned north here, and slightly east again, plunging us back into a young stand of cedar whose roots sank deep into the swamp we were traversing. Caleb was taking me home, I realized, to his island in the Great Swamp. As our trail grew darker beneath the evergreens, I had a sudden longing for the sun upon Aquebapaug. The urge to turn back was strong.

"I wish to be in Charlestown by sundown," I heard myself say, and it was a strange sound—the voice of man—in this shadowed, black, forsaken bog. No one answered, and we traveled on, fording the dark Patuxet about a mile above Aquebapaug.

Sometimes the sun found us, sometimes we walked in the dusk of deep shade. Sometimes the path wandered over rock and root, sometimes it lay in wide, wet beaver meadows filled with rotted, fallen trees. In some of these meadows, there was no path and I simply followed Metewis and his master. It was at the edge of one such stagnant stand that Caleb finally halted. Ahead of us, beyond the wide and trackless moat, rose a grassy, thinly wooded hill. I saw the stumps of hewn trees, and as the wind shifted slightly toward the south, I smelled smoke. *The sorcerer's isle*, I confessed within myself.

"Home," said Caleb with a grim smile, and he urged his horse into the water. It wasn't deep, but Caleb warned me—his first instruction since we had left the road to Charlestown—not to step to the left or to the right.

As we came out of the moat, my guide dismounted and bowed his face to the earth. I climbed off my own horse and let it loose to graze in the fine grass beneath the trees.

"Christopher Long," announced the Indian, standing up to look me in the eyes. This was his way of introducing me to his domain.

"Caleb Hobomucko," I said with a stiff bow, realizing then how tensed I had become near the latter part of our journey. I chuckled at myself, somewhat nervously, and leapt about in an effort to convince my legs that it was time for them to get back on the job. "I reckon you have to go into town for your mail," I said, staring back in the direction from which we had come.

Caleb had his knife out and was digging its point into a tree. Something fell from the thick trunk into his palm—a beetle or a small pine knot, I thought. He clenched his fist around it and turned to face me. His eyes were dim like the shades through which we had marched. He held out his fist, and I slid my hand under it to receive what it held.

Cold, hard, flat on one side and rounded on the other. A musket ball!

"This is the isle upon which the Narragansett died," said the son of his people past. "This is the isle upon which I live."

The Great Swamp Fight. Seventy-five years ago. On this island. Some say it was a miracle that the ice froze hard enough to allow the English to cross the moat and attack the fortress of their armed enemies. Others say it was a massacre of old men, women, and children. Some say the Narragansett—by far one of the largest and strongest tribes in New England at the time—had allied themselves with Philip and were preparing to fall upon the towns of the English. Others say they had come to this bleak island in order to wait out a war that they didn't want to fight. Some say this. Others say that. It all depends on who you talk to.

We were truly on an island, surrounded on all sides by a swampy ring of lazy green water. No need to tether the horses here, and no stranger around to lead them away. They would find their own food and drink. I stuck the bullet in my beltbag and followed Caleb up the hill. An old dog limped down the path to meet us, wagging its tail and barking hoarsely. As we crested the rise, I saw Caleb's Indian home.

The wigwam of my Narragansett friend was a marvelous construction, built in the domed style of his people, with long, bent poles covered over with bark on the outside and laid thickly on the inside with beautifully woven mats and the dyed skins of animals. The smoke I had smelled rose from a small fire that Caleb's squaw kept burning in the center of the house. Susanna greeted us both sincerely as we entered, but she made no move to embrace her husband.

"The wind told me you were coming," she said, stirring broth on a pot over the fire, "and I have a soup ready for you both." *What kind of wind whispers to this woman?* I wondered.

"The wind also told me you were here," I answered. And Caleb stared at me. "Smelled the fire," I explained with a smile.

Caleb excused himself for a moment and led Susanna outside. As I awaited their return, I took a look around at the home of my Narragansett friends.

Even among the Indians along the Ohio, I had not seen a wigwam so stripped of English influence. The cooking pots were iron, but beyond that all else was of wood or shell or clay or bone or bark or the skins of animals. Moosehide boots and deerhide moccasins stood beside a low bed covered with the skin of a bear. A colourfully beaded cradleboard was propped in the shadows against the wall, a reminder of children grown and gone. A cedar-bark mat lay within the door. Birch-bark mockucks—the old "Indian boxes" that my mother used to collect at market—sat in an extended row along the wall. The mockucks held Susanna's tanning tools: her flesher, scraper, wringer, beamer, and other items used only by a squaw in the hard work that made up her hard life. Basswood-bark cordage hung in strips upon the wall next to two pairs of snowshoes.

Beside the bed, in a barrel hollowed from a section of pine trunk, was a collection of weapons and tools such as no Rhode Island Indian ever used anymore. Ornately carved war clubs. Bows of ash and white oak and shag-bark hickory. Buckskin quivers filled with long, straight, feathered arrows of dogwood and viburnum. Stone tomahawks, axes, and knives. But the sheathed blade that Caleb carried was steel—Dutch steel, he said, one hundred years old and sharp as a captain's sword.

In a small room separated from the rest of the wigwam by a colourful mat that hung from the ceiling were bags of leather and bark, filled with herbs and dried plants, seeds and shells, belts and chains of wampum—Caleb was rich by Indian standards. One bag bulged with hand-carved tobacco pipes. Several other bags were full of tobacco. I saw boxes hanging with bones and skulls of animals, and one that held the bones of men. An expertly decorated canoe paddle rested against the wall. Beside the paddle, I saw the only other evidence of English influence in all the house. A curious collection of green glass bottles was arranged on the floor at the wall—and hidden in the shadows next to the paddle was an English rifle.

"A gun," I exclaimed.

"A warrior must speak the language of his enemies," said Caleb, stepping into the room. "Or how can he declare war with honor?"

"His enemies?" I questioned, troubled anew by this stranger-friend.

"All men have enemies," said Caleb.

"Can you fire it straight?" I asked stupidly, running my fingers down its cold barrel.

"Not so straight as you can," he replied.

"I will not stir this soup forever!" said Susanna from her fire. "Shall I feed it to the dog?"

I had four bowls of the savory hot broth—a rich mix of venison, corn, and such herbs and flavorings as were known only to the sorcerer's squaw. An old Narragansett tribal recipe, no doubt.

Susanna was ten years younger than Caleb and I, but she looked nearly ten years older. I was rather shocked at the change since I had seen her last. Wandering wrinkles lined her brightly painted face, her fingers were calloused and crooked, and what teeth she had left were yellow from years of chewing bark and reeds and leather and God knows what else. Her black hair, iced with scattered strands of silver, was tied back in two long braids that hung to her waist.

Wizened and bent from the ancestral existence that her husband insisted she live—in which the hardest and most incessant labor fell to the women, and the hunting and fishing and warring were undertaken by the men—her form seemed a shadow of the woman I remembered. Though beauty and youth had forsaken her, there was strength in her visage, a hopeful spark in her deep, midnight eyes, and eternal patience in her quiet sighing as she filled her husband's bowl once more.

"It has been more moons than I can count, Christopher Long, since we have seen you in the country of the Narragansett," she said, seating herself at last beside her man.

"Six years, Susanna," I guessed. "Maybe seven. You were on the reservation then, and Nip was still home. He's gone to sea, Caleb tells me."

"And how is Sarah?" she asked, holding me with her eyes.

"She was just fine when I left," I smiled, rubbing my chin that hadn't been shaved since I bid farewell to my own woman by the Yadkin weeks ago. "And the boys—Nathanael and Richard and Thomas—are all grown taller than their old man. Nathanael's married."

"The girls?" she asked.

"Anne and Violette are looking too good to last long at home! But they ain't old enough yet to set loose, so I dragged them off to the woods where no Baltimore brandybegger can anchor his eye on them." *She must get lonely, this poor squaw,* I thought. *No kids. No neighbors. Just Caleb—when he comes home.*

"And now you want to take him far away," said the Narragansett squaw.

"I beg your pardon?" I said with a start. Was the wind speaking secrets in her ear?

Caleb laughed, a warm laugh by the small fire. "Hazard mentioned you might want a partner to follow you into the wilderness," said my old Indian friend. "I told the squaw about it when we stepped out of the wigwam earlier."

"This ain't the way I wanted to ask you about things, Caleb," I said, holding up my hands in my defense. He waved them away.

"Tell me about it now," he said. "My tribe is here—the squaw and I. We have a full council. Tell me now."

Caleb reached for a bag hanging near and retrieved a long, wooden pipe carved in the shape of a wolf's head. Susanna raised herself to her knees to pull a pouch of tobacco from the same bag—and two more pipes. She filled all three with the crushed, dried leaves and then leaned toward the fire to extract a thin, smouldering brand. She lit Caleb's pipe for him, then mine. Then she sat back beside her husband and lit her own.

"*La Belle Riviere,*" said Caleb, in an accent as French as a Montreal merchant. "*Spaylaywitheepi,*" he said in an Indian tongue I didn't know. I was blank. He smiled. "The Ohio," he explained. "Three tongues, three peoples, one river."

"The river belongs to the king of England," I began, "no matter which tongue you say it in. And where did you learn French?" He waved it away. I swatted a mosquito.

"The river belongs to itself," said Susanna.

"And whoever else has the good sense to palisade it with men and arms—white men and the king's arms most likely, with flags from across the sea!" added Caleb, blowing a perfect ring of smoke into the air above his head. It rose for a moment and hung lazily in the already smoky room. Our conversation was heading down a thorny path, but Caleb seemed incapable of running any other.

"I've contracted with some men of Virginia," I said, attempting a smoke ring of my own. It failed. "I'll be scouting out suitable lands for a settlement of some fifty families."

"English families, of course," Caleb interrupted.

"Not necessarily," I said. "German, maybe. Irish. Scot. Doesn't matter, so long as they farm the land and ..."

"... build fences," said Caleb.

I ignored him. "I'll be crossing to the west of the Ohio and heading south down as far as the Great Falls," I continued. "King George's colonial council has given these Virginians a large grant under the condition that it be settled and fortified—palisaded and well-armed, if you will—within seven years."

"And will you be taking rum?" asked the Narragansett.

"No rum," I declared.

"And what of the French?" he asked. He seemed to know far more of the political realities of the distant wilderness than I thought he would.

"The French are too busy with their beaver and their forts along the Great Lakes," I lied. "The peace of Aix-la-Chapelle will keep the French from trespassing on English lands."

"*La Belle Riviere*," repeated Caleb, blowing double rings now. "The French say it is theirs."

"It belongs to the king of England!" I declared, failing again to produce even a semblance of a ring. "How do you do it?" I blustered.

"The tongue," said the Narragansett. "It's a trick of the tongue." And he produced a triple marvel that floated off toward the fire. "And what about the kings of the Onondaga and the Miami and the Twigtwees?" he asked.

"They welcome the English on their lands," I reminded him.

"I welcome you into my home," he reminded me. "But just because you stay the night—and you will be staying the night, Christopher, because we cannot make Charlestown before sundown—just because you stay the night does not mean you can raise your flag over my wigwam and declare it yours."

I was not in the mood for a debate.

"I wish you to come with me," I said plainly, "because you are my twin in the forest, and I can think of none else who could make the trip so pleasant—if you promise not to rail against the French and the English!

I simply want good company in the wild, and such that won't get lost every time I walk fast."

"Your legs are long," said Caleb.

"I traveled north to ask you to join me, Caleb," I said, starting again, "because I believe it will do us both good to go together." I stood up and began to pace around the fire. The afternoon sun entered the tent and lit the smoky room in a bright, white haze. "The trees, Caleb! The trees go on forever over there, and they are everywhere as old and older than those upon the path we walked to your island. And the forest is packed full of the beasts that once lived near these eastern shores. And the Indians, Caleb! Forgive me if I call them wild. Your Narragansett brethren are palefaces beside them. Even you ... But you must come and see!"

He drew on his pipe without speaking. Susanna leaned into his breast.

"There are birds and beasts beyond the Ohio that you have never seen, Caleb. Monstrous big elk and moose besides. There are mountains and hills unscarred by any path made by man. There are flowered green meadows that rival Eden! The skies are bluer than above Rhode Island, I swear it. The music of the earth is stronger and sweeter. Who gives a shilling that kings would fight for it! I just want to walk in it! And I want you with me."

I sat down.

"I have much business here," said Caleb, squinting past me into the sun outside his door. "I do not know if I can get away."

I sighed. "I had hoped ..."

"I wish to go with you, Christopher," Caleb interrupted, reaching out to touch my arm. "With all of my heart, I wish to go with you. And ..." He blew his smoke forcefully from puffed cheeks. "And the squaw could take care of most of my doctoring. The spirits have taught her as much." *But you don't wish to hear of such things*, I thought he was going to say.

"But," he continued, "there is yet one thing I must do." His eyes narrowed. His lips tightened. The sun found a cloud to hide behind, and the tent fell quickly chill. The room was uncomfortably silent but for the low murmuring of the scant flames. I yawned nervously.

"When must your journey begin?" Caleb asked quietly and suddenly, shaking his long locks as if to waken himself. Sunlight crept once more into the house.

"I leave before the fall is full upon us," I said. "And I don't expect to return until the spring of next year."

Susanna sighed deeply and looked into the fire.

"There is yet one thing …" Caleb muttered. Then he stood to his feet. "But we can speak more of this tomorrow. Let me show you around my island." With one arm, he swept aside the thick mat that hung at his door; with the other, he ushered me out into the afternoon sun.

Caleb's dog ran ahead of us as we walked the path—wide enough for two (did the Indian and his squaw ever walk it together?)—that wound uphill and downhill on this little Narragansett fiefdom in the midst of the Great Swamp. A small stream flowed across the trail at one point, the fresh waters of a cold spring that was hidden at hilltop beneath the tall, straight legs of a stand of old spruce.

A field of corn. An acre of tobacco. Squash, beans, pumpkins, gourds. Vines of grape weaving through a sprawl of fallen maple and birch. Apple trees. "I didn't plant them," said Caleb, "but the squaw makes a good pie with them. Mother taught her." We found our horses grazing in a field of grass that was sprinkled with aster the colour of rose. "No fences," said Caleb. "No walls of stone."

"Why have you moved from the reservation to this lonely hill?" I asked.

"Do you love Baltimore?" he answered.

"Don't you miss your people? Your family?" I asked.

"I see my mother often, employed as I am by Hazard."

"And Netop?"

"He will not fellowship with a son of Belial," said the Narragansett. "For how can light lie down with darkness?"

"He is your brother!"

"Tell him that."

We came to another brook. "The spring bubbles out of both sides of the hill," Caleb explained. I stooped to drink. Delicious and refreshing—I had not tasted water so sweet and clean for quite some time.

"A son of Belial," I sighed, resuming our walk.

"Netop walks with God," said Caleb. "And I walk with the Devil, or so he is convinced."

"Your spirits," I said through my teeth, aiming at the heart of my confusion. "Just what are they? Entities? Phantoms? Voices? Ancestral legend? I mean ... do you honestly believe they are real?"

"I thought you knew," he said, and we entered the shadows of a young cedar stand. "I'm a powwow, Christopher," said the sorcerer, my friend. "The spirits talk to me. They come to me. They live with me, in me—some of them. They give me power to heal. Power to bless. Power to ..."

"Kill?" I asked.

He didn't answer me. I didn't ask again.

"Superstition," said the powwow, rolling his eyes to the clouding sky. "You think my faith is superstition." He bent to pick up a stick in the path. He tossed it into the trees.

"Why did you bring us here?" I queried. "We were on our way to see Netop."

"Since we are going to Charlestown," said the Narragansett, "I must see to a patient of mine who lies in bed there. I brought us here first to show you my home and to mix some medicines for my patient. I have to earn my living. Hazard pays so little. We'll visit the patient, and then we can call on that brother of mine."

"The Devil is real," I heard myself say. But who was I trying to convince?

"I believe he is," said Caleb. "Why do the English think I do not believe it? He is real, and he is evil. I know this. I have seen him. I know his presence."

"You have seen the Devil?" I coughed, staring at the Indian stupidly.

"Are you a child?" laughed the powwow, stopping in the middle of the path and turning to face me. "You declare the Devil real and then you scoff at the reality! Is your God also no more real to you than empty words spoken by some preacher dressed in long robes? What is faith, Christopher Long, if it lies sleeping between the pages of a black-bound book? My spirits speak. They howl upon the wind. They touch me. They put medicine in my soul and power in the palm of my hand. Where is the power of Jehovah among his people? Where is the medicine of Jesus among his brothers?"

"His medicine washes the soul clean, Caleb!" I declared. "His power conquers death."

"Will he raise up my father from the grave?" cried the powwow suddenly and angrily. "The dead do not move from where men lay them, Mister Long, whether they are heathen or Christian!"

"Christ raises souls from the grave, Caleb," I pleaded. "He has raised mine. He has raised your brother Netop's. I was there when God's power struck Netop down. I watched him shake and roll and writhe upon the floor. I heard him moan and weep and shout as God's Spirit moved upon him. I saw him lying later like a dead man, silent, motionless, barely breathing. And I was there when he crawled to the pew and raised himself at last to his feet—a new man, eyes filled with wonder. His soul beheld heaven, he said. Visions of glory and light. Power and medicine, Caleb— plenty of it!"

Caleb dug a small stone from the trail with the toe of his moccasin. He mumbled something about his people that I could not hear.

"Most of your tribe was conquered by that power!" I said. "God is not sleeping. His preachers are not fools."

"My people are fools," muttered the wild Narragansett. "They dance and shriek and fall down upon the ground before Jehovah, but when they get up—what then? Do they paint their faces and take up arms and run the warpath to victory against their foes, as their fathers' fathers did? No! They go back to their wretched shacks where they hoe corn like women!

"Do they sharpen their arrows and run the forest after the elk and the deer? No! They smash the rum pot—for at least their God gives them strength to do that much—and set their hands to milking goats and cows! What good is the power of Jehovah if it makes men into women?"

"Love!" I pressed. "God causes men to love where they hated. To forgive where they lusted for blood. To live decently and honorably. To work with their hands responsibly where once they were drunken sots who begged for bread or stole their neighbor's goods."

"To what end, Christopher?" Caleb challenged. "To what end does God make lovers out of haters? So that the Indian will now love the Englishman and build his walls and tend his horses and carry his water and ..."

"Caleb!" I cried. "Your brother owns two houses! One next to Hazard's land and another among the Narragansett. He has a small farm. He is a respected stonemason, a faithful husband and father, an elder in the Narragansett Indian church ..."

"These are English things," the Indian scoffed. "English houses and English fences and English farms and an English church with an Indian name."

We had walked the island full 'round and were climbing the hill toward the wigwam once more.

"Perhaps I should ask Netop to journey the Ohio with me," I said disgustedly.

"Perhaps you should," shot the Narragansett, pacing on ahead of me without looking back. And my heart sank within me for my utter lack of patience and my foolish words.

"My anger has risen to the top of the cup since you have come to me, and I do not know why," said Caleb as we sat by the fire in the quickly cooling eve. Susanna laid fresh kindling on the flames. The wood quickly caught, and the good squaw set a larger log upon the blaze. Its warmth made me sleepy. "I am sorry for the sharp words that fly from my bow, Christopher," said Caleb. "And I wish to make amends for assailing you in such a way."

"And I'm sorry for the crack about Netop and the Ohio," I said. "I'll have no use for a stonemason on my trip!"

The fire rose comfortingly at our feet. It hummed and crackled before us in mesmerizing harmony with the chattering song that rose from the darkening swamp outside the warm wigwam.

"I believe in Jesus and Jehovah," Caleb declared quietly. And I looked at him with unbelieving eyes. "They are spirits also, are they not?"

"There is a vast difference," I said haltingly, "between the angels who fell and the Holy One of heaven."

"They are all spirits, are they not?" he repeated, spitting into the fire. Susanna brought us pipes. "I have asked them all in at one time or another. I take what they give. This is the way of the powwow."

"You have asked Jesus in?"

"When I was young. And sometimes since. But he seems not to come."

"He is a jealous God," I said.

And we smoked our pipes in silence.

"Read it to me," said Caleb in a whisper. And I sat up with a start. I had thought him asleep. I could hardly see him lying in his bed with his squaw in the dim light of the fading flames. I lay near the fire, wrapped in a mat, with The Book of Common Prayer open at my face so that I could read the evening prayers. "Let me hear the words of Jehovah," he said.

I held the book closer to the light.

"O sing unto the Lord a new song," I read quietly, "for he hath done marvelous things.

"With his own right hand, and with his holy arm hath he gotten himself the victory.

"The Lord declared His salvation. His righteousness hath He openly shewed in the sight of the heathen.

"He hath remembered His mercy and truth toward the house of Israel, and all the ends of the world have seen the salvation of our God.

"Shew yourselves joyful unto the Lord, all ye lands. Sing, rejoice, and give thanks.

"Praise the Lord upon the harp. Sing to the harp with a psalm of thanksgiving.

"With trumpets also and shawms. O shew yourselves joyful before the Lord the King.

"Let the sea make a noise, and all that therein is; the round world, and they that dwell therein.

"Let the floods clap their hands, and let the hills be joyful together before the Lord, for he cometh to judge the earth.

"With righteousness shall he judge the world, and the people with equity.

"Glory be to the Father, and to the Son, and to the Holy Ghost;

"As it was in the beginning, is now, and ever shall be, world without end. Amen."

I rolled another log into the fire. The night would be long.

"Shawms?" questioned the Narragansett.

"Don't know what they are," I answered.

CHAPTER FIVE

Big Bill Moose

Tuesday morning, September 25, 1750

Morning came early, as morning always does. Caleb was up before me and woke me with a nudge of his moccasined foot. Huckleberry corn cakes for breakfast. Parched cornmeal for the road— which folks in Rhode Island call "no-cake," from the Narragansett *nokehick*. Caleb had his corn cooked up and mixed up and fixed up for just about every meal and every occasion. Venison for meat—the man was a hunter. Turtle for soup—the swamp was his home. And tobacco for after every meal—the man was an Indian.

"I have not seen you smoke with your own pipe," Caleb noted.

"I didn't bring it with me," I commented. "Didn't think to. I don't smoke at home anymore. Sarah's never liked the smell of smoldering tobacco."

Caleb and his squaw looked at me strangely. Tobacco was sacred to them. Good for the soul. And any Narragansett worth his granddaddy's warpaint knows that the great creator Cautantowwit spends his Eternal Southwest afternoons sitting—and smoking—in his great green garden in Sowanniu. Caleb handed me a small pipe with a cleverly carved walnut bowl. "Keep it," he said. "Sarah will not smell it from here."

We came out of the forest at Aquebapaug and swung from our path into the untrodden grasses that lay along the lakeside to the north. Circling the waters toward the west, we crossed the Chipuxet and entered a pine wood that led us to a well-traveled road heading south toward Charlestown. This was the quickest route to our destination and quite a bit tamer than Caleb's little road. The day was warm again, and the scents of God's creation were delicious in the autumn air.

We talked little, and I didn't mind. Caleb's conversation was too easily bound to run the warpath. I preferred the peace of my own thoughts and enjoyed the contemplative sounds of the quiet countryside and the steady plodding of our pacers' hooves upon the wagon-rutted road. Sometimes, our way lay shrouded by overhanging trees. Other times fields opened up on either side, fenced by rails or walled by stone. Cattle stood in the pastures or trod the woods. The indolent beasts chewed their cud and followed us with their eyes as we passed. A side path wandered now and then from the main road, leading to solitary farms back in the woods.

Occasionally, we met a traveler coming the other way. Each came upon us with a tip of the hat, an English greeting, and sober recognition of the wild and painted horseman who rode tall beside me.

Loin cloth, bared legs, and open-chested vest of red-dyed rawhide. Hair tied back in one long braid pinned through with the feathers of turkey and hawk. Skull of a squirrel dangling from his left ear. Sharp stone tomahawk hanging from his waist belt. Bow slung across his back. Arrows strapped in a quiver at the right flank of his midnight black mount. An Indian. No doubt about it.

At the Shannock, we let our horses drink while we stretched our legs a bit and took some smoke.

"Forgot how much I like the pipe," I commented, renewing my miserable attempts at blowing smoke rings. Caleb relaxed, laying himself full upon his back and letting the morning sun caress his shining flesh. "Bear grease?" I asked.

"Keeps the mosquitoes away," he said, his eyes closed to the azure skies.

"Reckon it keeps the rain off too!" I said.

"Shookekineas!" said Caleb aloud, waking me from daydreams of Sarah and the home chatter along the Yadkin. Our horses carried us at an even pace down the winding level road. *"Shookekineas!"* he declared anew. *"Look here!"* My eyes swept the landscape nervously, curiously. Nothing but trees and fields. Some corn. Some crows.

"We have crossed the invisible border that separates the lands of the

English from the last legal lands of the Narragansett," the Indian continued. "We are now upon the *sachimaunonck*—the kingdom—of his royal highness King Tom, child sachem of the mighty Narragansett. He's in England right now, all of sixteen years old, and learning his English letters and his English manners so that he can come back and properly sign away his land to his English masters."

The border was indeed invisible, for the lands looked identical to those we had been traversing: stone walls, poled fences, cattle, sheep—even horses.

"Thirty thousand acres by English measurement," said Caleb, extending his arms to embrace the world that surrounded us. "Tenants. Servants. Silks and hoops and stays and dresses for the ladies in the royal sachem's family. And an English-style manor just down the road. Sits tall and pretty on the wide path. We used to call it King George's Palace when Tom's father, George Ninigret, was alive. Tribal lands! *Chickauta wetu! A burned-down house!* Who can live in it with any pride?"

"Only thirty thousand acres for an entire nation," I murmured to Neeyesee, "and the Crown has just given one small merchant's company two hundred thousand acres to the west of the Ohio!"

"The Crown," echoed the Narragansett. "At least the English crown sits upon the head of a man who is free to rule his people."

"Well, there is parliament. … "

"King Tom of the Narragansett—until he comes of age—is under the guardianship of his mother and a drunken Indian council."

"Quite a bit like parliament," I quipped, warming to the conversation.

"Yet even when Tom comes of age," Caleb continued, "all he will rule over is a broken people, an English farm, and a cedar swamp—surrounded on all sides by the children of his master across the sea."

"Can he vote in Charlestown elections?" I asked.

"He can," admitted the Indian. "But none other of the reservation Indians are allowed. They are not landholders. They are wards of the state. They can't buy any English properties as long as they live on the reservation, and they can't sell even a handful of that soil, because it is the sachem's land. They are children who will never come of age!"

Crows flew overhead in raucous chorus as our road took us onward through a golden forest of late corn. Caleb's eyes rose to the cry of the black-winged birds. "Kaukant laughs," he said of the crows. "He brought us our first corn from the garden of Cautantowwit, and now he rules the cornfields in our place."

Suddenly, he halted his horse and unslung his bow from his back. In a motion so swift I hardly saw it, an arrow leapt from his quiver and onto his fully drawn bowstring. A whisper and a hiss, and the long shaft shrank in size as it sped upward toward the mocking flock. A limp black form fell impaled from the heavens into the rattling, dry stalks of the field to our left. Caleb slid from his mount and vaulted the rail fence as gracefully as a buck leaps a wall. He disappeared into the corn, emerging in a moment with his bloody arrow in one hand and the corpse of a crow in the other.

"Kaukant will laugh no more," he said soberly, tossing the limp bird in the middle of the road. "And Cautantowwit will forgive me this massacre of his once-provider if indeed he has seen it at all—he has not looked east for many moons. I believe that our creator cares little anymore what happens in the once-lands of the Narragansett. But if my people are no longer under the protective eye of Cautantowwit, still I know that Chepi is near. And Chepi honors blood wherever it flows, be it the blood of men—or the blood of crows."

The Narragansett threw himself back upon his horse. In obedience to one short command, the splendid animal raised itself on its hind legs and brought its forehooves violently down upon the hapless bird. Then the horse and its rider pranced in an eerie ceremony around the mangled crow. "Medicine comes in many packages," said the powwow at last. "The spirits take delight in that which men despise. But you don't want to know these things." He spun his mount to the south and started back down the road.

Perhaps I had been mistaken to invite this strange man to walk the Ohio. Perhaps I should rejoice that his "business" would not allow him to accompany me. Perhaps I should bid him farewell at Charlestown instead of riding with him back to Netop's. I found myself praying for wisdom. God promises wisdom to those who ask. Figured I'd better ask.

Our way took us past King George's Palace, past the ancient cedar swamp, past the small wooden church built at the late sachem's request by the Church of England. Past the poor homes of the tenant Indian farmers. Past running children and barking dogs and scampering chickens. Past a few old wigwams and then beyond the road to Netop's house. We rode at last out of the lands of the Narragansett Ninigrets and into the streeted borough of English Charlestown in the colony of Rhode Island. And I was glad to see white men walking in the dusty lanes. And I was glad to get off my horse and walk there too.

"Come in with me," Caleb said as he stepped up to a warped plank door that hung on leather hinges at a house that leaned into the street on the far east edge of town. "I danced and shrieked and sweated and conjured at my last visit here. I won't need to do so this time." He rapped his knuckles against the rough wood. Was he jesting with me?

"Whoosit?" came the rough reply from inside the house.

"Hobomucko," replied the powwow.

"The Devil, you say! Open it yerself!" ordered the man inside.

We went in.

Though the afternoon sun was bright in the street, it had its work cut out for it in this dark little hovel. The windows were boarded all but one, which was too dirty to let a man look either out or in. There was no fire in the ash-piled fireplace and no wood to burn if anyone had wished for a fire. A single candle flickered, secured upon a small hill of wax on the only table in the place. A large, ugly, scar-visaged Indian sat at the table drinking. A movement in a shadowed corner caught my eye, and I saw that another man—an Indian too, I assumed in the dim light—lay upon a bed.

"The witch doctor's come callin'," coughed the man at the table, and I knew it was he who had answered our knock. He belched loudly. I smelled brandy.

Caleb ignored him and went directly to the man upon the bed. A sudden change came over my friend—his professional manners, I supposed. He immediately knelt and gently took the man's hands in his. I heard them exchange some low words in English as the bedded man, still covered by a tattered mat, raised himself to a seated position. Caleb carefully helped him to make himself comfortable with his back against a pillow at the wall. Then he looked about for a moment and motioned to the man at the table. "Moose," Caleb said to the drunkard. "Bring me some water."

Moose didn't move.

Caleb rose and fetched the dirty pitcher himself. He lifted it to the bedded man's lips.

"Thank you," the man sighed weakly. "Thank you, Caleb."

The powwow pulled a small bag from his pack and laid it on the bed. "Boil a little of this with your soup tonight," he said, "and a little each day until it's gone. It will settle your stomach."

By now, my eyes were fully used to the small light in the house, and I could see things as clearly as any could expect in this shadowed little shack. I saw that the sick man was indeed an Indian, and that Moose—who appeared to me to have some Negro blood in him as well—was aptly named. I saw filthy clutter in every corner, including the bones of chickens or some other fowl. Flies buzzed at the greasy windowpane. A couple of rifles leaned up against the crooked fireplace. An old Indian rug—expertly woven but hardly visible—hung on the windowless north wall beside the fireplace. A bow hung across it, secured with a bowstring to a limp, empty quiver. I wondered if it once had brought down game for its owner. Or if it had ever taken aim at man.

"Are you sitting often?" asked Caleb to his patient. "And have you walked outside at all?"

"Yesterday was warm," said the sick man. "And Moose walked me to the common and back. Felt good to be out. Today I'm wantin' to sleep. But I been sittin' some. And I ain't havin' no more nightmares since you danced." He smiled and nodded at me.

"My friend—Christopher Long," said Caleb, standing to introduce me.

"I'm Woody One-shot," said the bedded Indian, swinging his legs weakly onto the floor. "Help me up, Caleb." The doctor supported his patient as he stood. "Feels good to be on my legs!" said One-shot, stretching his arms to work the sleep out of them, lifting his legs slowly to march in place. Then he held his hand out to greet me. "That's Big Bill Moose over there at the bottle," said One-shot, pointing at his ugly companion. Moose raised his mug and snorted, avoiding our eyes. "He cain't breathe in the mornin' but that he has a drink first."

"Shut up, Woody," grunted the drunken Indian.

"And he wouldn't be near this pleasant if he was sober," One-shot added. Moose laughed roughly deep in his chest. "Now what do I owe you, Caleb?" asked Woody.

"You don't owe him nothin'," said Moose darkly. "You'd be dead if I wasn't nursin' you day and night."

"Why it's you that nearly killed me with yer nursin', you big animal!" blurted the sick Indian, standing to his full height and leaning toward the table. He was six feet tall and probably an inch or two more. Grey-haired and toothless, but with a strength in his aged eyes that belied the weak condition of his flesh and bones. Had he ever run a warpath? Probably. Perhaps against the Mohegan. Maybe against the French in King George's lately ended war. Maybe against the French in Queen Anne's war—he might have been a young warrior then. *He'll only fight death from now on,* I thought. *Is he ready for that one?*

"You don't owe him nothin'," repeated Moose, digging a sharp-bladed knife into the wax upon the table.

"But you owe me much," Caleb said suddenly in a voice as cold as the steel of Moose's knife. He was addressing the drunkard.

"Huh?" said the big souse. And he looked up at us fully for the first time. His eyes were red with brandy—and a fire I'd seen a few times before in men who'd kill if you'd give them half a reason. "I don't owe you nothin', witch doctor!" he spat. And then he brought himself reeling to his feet. Big guy. Well-named. Broad, burly shoulders. Thick arms. Twitching, thick hands that looked like hooves when fisted. And a knife. What would Caleb do? I fingered my hatchet. I asked for that wisdom.

"Now sit down, Bill!" pleaded One-shot. "Have a drink and let me go about my own business!" The tall, thin Indian moved toward the table, but Caleb's arm held him back.

"We'll take care of your business in a moment, Woody," said the powwow. One-shot retreated in a slow wobble and sat himself down on his bed. He crossed his arms, set his face in a disinterested frown, and settled back to watch the action.

"You owe me much," Caleb repeated to the drunken Moose.

"You think yer some kind of Indian!" challenged Moose. "Painted like a woman and dressed like a half-naked little girl!" He swung his knife in picturesque circles in front of him. Then he almost fell but caught himself quickly and steadied his legs—glaring at Caleb all the while.

"You ride thet animal of yers like you think yer some kinda English gen'ral! And you take poor fools like Woody for the fools they are by dancin' and stompin' and knockin' the glass outen their windows while tryin' to chase the shadows outen the house—and then you take their last beads of wampum or their granddaddy's bow or ..." He belched again, hiccupped loudly, almost lost his balance once more, coughed for a full minute straight (I'm sure!), and then leaned full across the table to point his blade at Caleb's chest. "The English want to run you outta here or rope you up by the neck," the drunkard continued, "and mebbe I'll do it fer 'em!"

"You can't even stand up," said Caleb quietly, pushing the blade to the side with his forearm. Moose swung it back.

"I've killed men," said the Moose.

"More than one," said Caleb.

"Killed a moose with my knife and my bare hands once!"

"Killed a man with a noose too," whispered Caleb. "When you should have been hung by it yourself!"

"You don't know that!" bellowed the Moose.

"You talk too much when yer drunk, Bill," muttered One-shot from the bed.

"Shut up, Woody!" snorted the Moose.

"You're a dead man," said Caleb.

"Yer a woman!" taunted the Moose.

And suddenly the table leapt at the drunken Indian. And Caleb followed it.

"Aw!" sighed One-shot, his arms still crossed and his face still frowning.

Moose was on his back against the floor. Caleb was astride him, the drunken Indian's knife in his hand. He held the blade to his adversary's chin.

"You're a murderer and a dead man," said Caleb grimly, and he slid the knife across Bill Moose's neck. I saw blood. Caleb swatted at a fly.

"Aw!" coughed One-shot from his bed.

"You've killed me!" cried Big Bill Moose.

Caleb got up and tossed the knife in the corner with the chicken bones.

"You're not a dead man yet," said the powwow. "Your mother could doctor up that scratch!" Moose ran his fingers across his neck. The cut was barely skin deep. A barelegged walk through blackberry brambles could produce worse wounds.

The drunken Indian scrambled to his feet again, lunging for his blade. Caleb tripped him, and the pitiful sot fell crashing to the rough wooden floor.

"I'll cut out yer heart!" he bellowed.

"Aw," moaned One-shot from his bed.

"Shut up, Woody," ordered the Moose.

The room was suddenly lit white, or so it seemed in comparison to the dark drama I had been privy to. The door was open. Caleb was gone.

"What do I owe you?" shouted Woody One-shot toward the shining portal.

"You don't owe him nothin'!" declared the Moose.

I figured it was time for me to leave.

Caleb kept one hand fisted as he strode ahead of me to where we had our horses tied. I didn't try to catch up. But when we got to our animals, he fumbled one-handedly to open the pack that was slung at Metewis's side. "Will you open it for me?" he finally asked.

"Is your hand hurt?" I wondered.

"No," he replied. I untied the straps at his horse's pack. He nodded his thanks and rummaged for a moment with his open hand. He brought out a small bottle of green glass with a cork stopper. He pulled the cork with his teeth and then carefully deposited something in it from his fisted hand. 'Course I was mighty interested in this funny business and I didn't attempt to pretend otherwise. Caleb handed me the bottle. "Don't open it," he cautioned.

There was a large brown fly inside, bashing itself uselessly against the green walls of its shiny prison.

"Bill Moose's soul," Caleb declared. "I'm going to take it home with me."

CHAPTER SIX

Netop

Tuesday midday until night, September 25, 1750

A man's soul cannot be touched or held by any other man," I lectured the Narragansett powwow as we rode toward the reservation of King Tom.

"You have touched my soul, Christopher Long," he countered. "Many times."

I asked for wisdom.

"A fly is no soul," I declared incredulously, "but only an insect. And a result of Adam's fall at that!"

"I thought that sin was the result of Adam's fall," said the Narragansett theologian.

I asked for wisdom speedily.

"That fly you have in your bottle is not Bill Moose's soul!" I argued.

"My spirits tell me otherwise," said the Narragansett medium. "And they should know more about such things than you and I. They live in both worlds, the seen and the unseen. They can touch men's souls."

"They probably can!" I said desperately, unbelievingly. "But that fly in your bottle is no man's soul! It is an ugly brown fly!"

"Then I shall kill it when I get home," said the Indian, "and rid the world of Adam's bitter fruit."

"Caleb, you are deceived," I cried, losing my patience with the man. "You are lost in a mad world that does not exist. Is it not enough to hunt and dress and dwell as your ancestors? That I can respect—and I do, you know that I do. But must you live in their dreams as well? Dark dreams! Dead dreams! Devilish dreams!"

"I run with the Devil, some say," Caleb replied. And then we were silent as our horses paced side by side upon our road, their legs rising and falling like the ever-turning spokes of two wheels on the axle of a wagon.

We crossed that invisible border again between the English world and the kingdom of the Narragansett sachem, this time heading north. And soon we found ourselves upon the way that led to Netop's door. Little black Indians ran to greet us as we dismounted—the young children of Netop and his Caribbean wife. They ran their hands over the sweaty horses, ducked beneath the tall mounts, tugged at Caleb's loin cloth, grabbed at the tail of my coonskin cap, and generally made a noisy fuss over us all the way to the house. A short Negro woman—less African in her features than I expected—came shyly to the door.

"Good day, Caleb," she said, her dark eyes peering out from beneath the long black curls that hung across her forehead. "Will you come in?"

"Thank you, Neeka," said Caleb, "but no." I was surprised, but I said nothing.

"Netop is not home," said the black woman.

"Then you may entertain his friend and mine until my brother returns." He nodded toward me. "Neeka," he said, "this is Christopher Long."

"Will you come in?" she repeated, this time with her eyes upon mine.

"Thank you," I found myself saying, "but I would like to wait for Netop in the sunlight, while it lasts. But I am thirsty," I added with a smile, "and would appreciate some water for myself and for my horse." She nodded and bowed and disappeared into the house. In a few moments, the children were carrying two wooden buckets of water to the horses while I stood with Caleb and drank gratefully from a deep wooden mug that I shared with him.

"You are going home after all?" I questioned my distant friend as he mounted his animal.

"I have business to attend to, Christopher," he said. "Narragansett business."

"Vengeance is nobody's business but God's," I said, shooting in the dark.

"Vengeance is as Narragansett as the blood that ran in my father's veins," said Caleb honestly.

"Will you not come with me instead?" I pleaded. "Will you not lay aside your 'business' for a season to walk in woods where no English bullets are lodged in the trees? Where the paths—when you can find them—are wide enough only for two friends to walk? Where fences are strangers. Where wild animals live as thick as ..."

"... flies on a brandy bottle," said Caleb coldly. "No, I will not go with you. Though my heart longs for such paths, I will not, because I cannot. The spirits plead louder. And I have given them my pledge."

"Your soul is a fly in their bottle!" I cried.

"I am a Narragansett," said Caleb. "And you are an Englishman. But you don't wish to hear of such things." He backed his horse up as he spoke. "I hope to see you again, Christopher."

I could think of nothing to say. He rode off down the road and out of sight among the trees.

Netop came running like a child when he saw me, a broad and free and welcoming smile upon his dark face. *What a contrast to his brother!* I thought. Tall like Caleb, strong in body and spirit, the difference was not in form or in flesh. Netop possessed a different kind of "medicine" than Caleb. A different eye upon his world. A different heart. And even before his conversion, I realized suddenly, his abilities had been no less remarkable than his brother's. Though tame by first comparison—as the family dog appears tame beside the rangy wolf—Netop nevertheless was a man to be reckoned with. The dog that sleeps at his master's side can rise up to defend a household, run in the hunt and take down the deer, and steadfastly serve for a lifetime. Netop was as good a man and as much a man—in circumstances suited to his gifts—as his brother. He had set his hands faithfully to his work during his indenture to Hazard. He had labored hard to conquer the forest and the field. He laid stone on stone to set the foundations upon which many an English house was raised to the comfort and pleasure of its occupants.

He knew the woods as well or better than most of his peers, could shoot a squirrel in the head at one hundred yards, and was no drunkard, no fool, and no debtor to any man. Did it matter that he wore English clothes—and what were English clothes anyway, if not sensible and practical? Did it matter that he couldn't shoot a bow and arrow? That he didn't live in a wigwam? That his hair was cut short? The man was a man and could stand tall by any man at midcentury in English Rhode Island. His brother was a warrior in a war that no one wished to fight. Netop was a man who wished to be your friend.

"What cheer, Netop!" I shouted as he trotted toward me. The greeting was a traditional Rhode Island proverb—and my own personal hello to Netop since we first had met. It is said that Roger Williams, when canoeing down the Seekonk on his way to the lands that would become Providence, was hailed by friendly Narragansett in that mixed language greeting: What cheer, Netop!

It was good to see him.

His children were a delight, and they made me miss my home—though my own little ones were no longer so little. His wife was quiet, pretty and pleasant, and a hardworking woman as could easily be seen by the tidy, well-kept home she oversaw.

The house was a simple dwelling, and the home was English in all ways except for the colour of the skin of those who lived there. The two hospitably large rooms and small loft were clean and warm. The marvelously built fireplace (twin chimneys in old Rhode Island style, laid stone upon stone by Netop himself) took up an entire wall, upon which hung a fair assortment of pots and kettles and cooking and cleaning utensils. The floor was carpeted with colourfully woven rugs that lay brightly about like so many lily pads on a lake. Well-crafted stools and benches were arranged around a heavy oak table. A spinning wheel and a lumpy-cushioned armchair sat near the southern window, with a small bookcase standing next to them. Children's toys peeked out of a box on the floor near the door. A cleverly carved candle-beam chandelier hung from the low ceiling with six candle holders on it. Only two of the candles were lit. I think they were whalewax because they were a good bit brighter than a tallow candle is. The sun of late afternoon shot through the house from the west, brightening the smoky kitchen, illuminating the far walls in exaggerated colours of gold and red and brown.

"How long will you be gone along the Ohio?" Netop asked as we drank the cider that his wife set before us in dented pewter mugs.

"Longer than I might have been if your brother had agreed to come," I said.

The oldest son of Joy Kattenanit stared into the low fire. I could see his own fire burning slow and steady behind his eyes. It was a lonely blaze, crackling sadly. It moaned in its private mourning, and I felt my heart touched by its song.

"Your mother says to come and see her more often," I commented, doing my duty by the old woman. "And she says that the Lord commands us to love our enemies." Netop turned to hold my eyes in his. "She also wanted to remind you that the merciful will be shown mercy," I said.

"Caleb," said Netop, a glistening of tears at the corners of his large, dark eyes.

"He's a powwow," I said to myself, aloud.

Netop blew a sigh out of his cheeks and turned to face the fire anew.

"I'm not a man," he said strangely. I let him tell the fire his woes. "I don't know how to talk to Caleb anymore. He will not hear of God. He will not sup at my table. He walks his own way and will let no one walk with him. He tells Mother that I am opposed to him, and I am. Opposed to the devils in his soul, at least! I … I don't know how to talk to him anymore."

Neeka sat down beside him and put her hand upon his arm. I let them sit.

"Did he say why he would not stay?" Netop asked his wife.

She shook her head.

"What is this business you told me he must be about?" Netop asked me.

I fumbled with my mug.

"Do you know? Do you have a thought?" he asked.

I whistled stupidly.

"Out with it, Long," ordered the brother of the powwow.

"Well," I began, finding the fire a convenient thing to speak to myself, "perhaps we should take a little hike to talk about this."

Neeka urged her husband off the bench and pushed the two of us out into the setting sun.

"Big Bill Moose," mumbled Netop as we walked the grassy lane. The first stars of evening winked in the dusk-laden sky. "I should have known. But nobody believes his drunken boasting! Reverend Niles will not allow him in the church. Few pay him any heed. Only old One-shot. They're related. One-shot's sister married Moose twenty years ago. She died in childbirth. The baby died too. Moose and One-shot have kept house together ever since." We walked in silence for a while.

"One-shot's all right, though," muttered Netop at last. "God touched him during the Awakening, just as he touched me. But Moose won't let him worship with us. Tells him we're all hypocrites and liars and thieves. So One-shot stopped praying and started back drinking. Now he's even trusting in demons to heal him of his ills! Caleb—my brother the powwow!" he said. "Big Bill Moose! Killer. Liar. Drunkard," he coughed. "And Poor Tom my father. Hanging from another man's rope," he said. "And mother's known the truth. How long? And Caleb too. How long? Doesn't matter. My brother the powwow!"

"I … I don't know," I stammered. "I don't know what to do with this spirit stuff, Netop. My pop taught me to think higher than such things. Demons and witchcraft are … well, they were for another day. For Romish priests back in the Dark Ages. For Irish hags in old fables. Children's stories. Superstition."

Netop sighed as we shuffled our way through the full-fallen leaves of a tall stand of black ash.

"You believe in the power of God, Christopher," said my dark brother in Christ. "And you believe the Scriptures to be the Word of God."

"I do," I admitted.

"Then you know that our war in this life is not against folks like you and me, not against folks at all," he said.

"Yes," I said. "Unless we have to defend ourselves and our loved ones," I added.

"And that we wrestle with powers and principalities and the unseen rulers of the darkness of this age," he continued. "Against fallen angels and demons. Against evil spirits like those Caleb entertains upon his island in that cursed swamp, where our Narragansett fathers fell before the bullet and the sword."

"Have you been there?"

"I have been there."

"Are your fathers' ghosts still there?"

Netop stopped and looked at me. I felt silly, and I almost attempted a jest, but I thought better of it.

"My fathers' ghosts are in heaven or hell, Chrisopher," said the Indian simply. And I knew it was so, but what of these spirits? Were they really demons? Did they really live, unseen, in trees and rocks and men who danced and shrieked and asked them in? Did they really fly and walk and run about this world invisibly? I didn't want to know, if it were so. I was raised to think higher than such things. And, after all, Netop and his brother—Christian or pagan—were Indians. This was their heritage—spirits and shadows and gods for every stick and stone and breeze and blade of grass. These boys were bent that way. Couldn't help thinking that way.

"So what will Caleb do?" I asked.

"He will ask the spirits to do it," said the Indian.

Do what? I wanted to say, but I didn't wish to hear of such things. And so I tried to change the subject, carefully, cowardly.

"Will you tell the church?" I asked. "Will they pray? Will anyone go and talk to Caleb?"

Netop motioned for me to follow him farther down the path. A half-moon rose above the treeline of an open pasture to our right. The sky had grown quite dark in the east. I saw a building rising up before us in the clearing, a black steeple against the velvet sky. Netop took me to its door, opened it, and led me into the darkness inside. He closed the door, and we stood there silently while the world outside began to sing its evening song.

"I have no fire," said Netop at last. "Our eyes must adjust to the moonlight." Mine had, and I could see two rows of long wooden pews that led to a small raised pulpit at the front of the building. "We finished this only last month," Netop said with obvious pride in his voice. "And we fill it with shouts and song and the strong Word of God each Sabbath morning and several nights out of the week."

"Built it yourself?" I queried, running my fingers along the smooth-finished pewbacks.

"Ever since Samuel Niles got kicked out of Reverend Park's church in Westerly," Netop explained, "a group of us have gathered our own church here on the reservation. After Niles was ordained—and some of the Old Lights say his ordination doesn't stick with the Lord, but I know that he's a called man of God—we knew we must have a building to meet in. So we put our hands together and we raised us one here!"

The moon shone unevenly through the bubbled-glass window panes, laying dim patches of gray and brown and blue upon the floor and across the pews of the simple sanctuary. The smell of fresh-cut spruce was strong and invigorating. I imagined the building full of praying Indians. Heaven touched my shoulder gently.

"Let's pray for Caleb now," I heard my friend say, "and for Big Bill Moose." And the room was suddenly shaken with the loud wailing of one soul in travail for another. I had not heard such prayer in years, and it entered me with a strength that both shamed and astounded me. But it unstopped a well deep within, and I found my tongue whispering with pleadings that my mind had been taught to think higher than. Groanings of the spirit of a man. Utterances that shut the door to reason and opened the door to truth—and power.

The weapons of our warfare are not carnal, spoke the Scriptures to my memory, *but mighty through God to the pulling down of strongholds.* A second set of eyes blinked within my soul, and I saw—as in a dream—a pow-wow dancing in a wigwam. He danced and danced and danced until there was no dance left in him. I saw a fly in a bottle, lying as though dead at the bottom of the glass. It had a man's face, an ugly, scarred face with a bloody line across its neck. I prayed—lost in the sound of Netop's loud intercession—until suddenly the room was silent but for my prayerful whistlings and the low, lazy hum of a fly against a window.

I lay by the low fire awake. A small child sighed in the far room. Netop snored. Neeka mumbled. I stared into the meager flames. They were dancing, dancing, dancing. I opened the pages of the small book that Hazard had graced me with. My gaze fell upon an evening prayer—the

Lord's Prayer. It was meant to be read by the minister, the clerks, and the people—with a loud voice. Being without a minister or a clerk, and seeing the time and the place were not appropriate for loud prayer, I prayed silently these words: *Our Father, which art in Heaven, hallowed be thy Name. Thy kingdom come. Thy will be done, on earth as it is in heaven. Give us this day our daily bread. And forgive us our trespasses, as we forgive them that trespass against us. And lead us not into temptation, but deliver us from evil. Amen.*

Thus I committed my soul into the Father's hands and fell asleep.

PART TWO

A Narrowing Way

"That it may please thee to preserve all that travel by land or by water ... We beseech thee to hear us, good Lord."
—from *The Book of Common Prayer*
of the Church of England

CHAPTER SEVEN

Conestoga Joe

The last days of September, 1750

I had often dreamed of the long trail homeward. The time and expense of my hurried northern trip had seemed a small matter in light of my expectation of Caleb's company in the wilderness. Anticipation of my old friend's companionship had filled my heart and entertained my imagination for months. But now he would not be riding beside me as I struck the southern trail, would not be walking with me along *La Belle Riviere*. "Hope deferred maketh the heart sick," wrote King Solomon so very long ago. My heart needed the powwow—but the doctor had other business.

In duty dull and drear, I sent word by Netop to his mother and to Hazard of my failure to enlist Caleb. In Charlestown, I purchased what supplies I needed for my return journey, including an old packhorse that I intended to sell somewhere along the way—in New York or Philadelphia or to some German farmer in Pennsylvania. I wanted the animal in order to loosen the load on Neeyesee. I couldn't envision the grand pacer carrying anything more than a man and his gun.

I tipped my hat to the old Narragansett country and wandered toward Westerly and then out of Rhode Island altogether. It's a strange sort of tug that the heart feels when a man's horse carries him across a river and out of his old homelands, but in crossing the Pocatuck into Connecticut I actually felt a weight slide off me. My time with Caleb had been a storm of trouble in my soul, and though my expectations were dashed, I felt that it must be for the best. I threw one last prayer over my shoulder and set Neeyesee's nose along the eastward-winding road.

Connecticut passed me by in a blur of ripening autumn and a tangle of wandering thoughts as the pacer stepped lively on the road and the roped packer trotted clumsily behind us. I thought about my boyhood at my father's side, treading the woods beside a wild Narragansett, learning to shoot a musket, watching Caleb bend a bow.

I remembered my growing years amid the confused bustle of Providence. Quakers, Jews, Baptists, Seekers, and Finders—all thrown together in one soul-free city. Indians and Negroes and Englishmen, preachers and planters and pirates. I recalled my mother's death and her burial beside the Seekonk. I could hear the minister mumbling his prayers, the wind whispering mournfully in my ears.

I remembered girls I had wanted to marry and the precious one who finally said yes. I could smell my Sarah's kitchen as I passed the country homes of the wives of Connecticut, and sometimes the air held the acrid sweetness of smoldering Yankee tobacco. I thought of the pipe Caleb had given me, and my fingers searched for it in my bag as I rode. "Sarah wouldn't want me smoking," I said to Neeyesee. The black horse snorted in agreement. I pulled the pipe out and tossed it into the bushes by the road. "I can cast out demons too," I said.

I thought of Joy Kattenanit Hazard sitting in her little room, reading the Bible in a tongue that no one else in the house could even understand. I felt her prayers. I tried not to think of Caleb.

But what of Caleb? What of his bitter business? Would he poison Big Bill Moose on his next doctoring trip to One-shot's dismal shack? Cut the ugly Indian's throat while he slept? Or dance like a devil upon his haunted isle until Satan appeared and said (like Herod after watching the daughter of Herodias dance), *Ask of me whatever you will, and I will give it to you.* "Give me the head of Bill Moose on a platter," Caleb might say. And would the Devil deliver? I shuddered. I was taught to think higher than such things.

My mind fled to the wilderness along the Ohio. I saw the tall trees, standing thick with their arms in the clouds. I imagined the forest empty of all the children of Adam, a garden undiscovered and untouched by man. Then I saw Indians running the woods, painted like the autumn, as much a part of the forest as the leaves of red and gold that blew upon the breeze. I saw rough, bearded English and Irish traders and trappers sitting on felled logs in Indian towns full of tall warriors, dark women, and naked children. The traders were cheating the Indians out of a hard day's work—but at least they cheated them more liberally than the French. I saw French soldiers in birch-bark canoes. French priests with crosses around their necks. French trappers with brandy at their lips. I heard French oaths and French threats. I saw English traders, bound by ropes, being led captive by French hunters and French-allied Indians on the northbound trails toward Quebec. I heard the guns of war.

I was not afraid of war, but I didn't want to think of it. How many wars had we fought with France since my mother first heard me cry? How many more would there be? I knew full well that the Ohio was the bullseye in the target for the empire, but what did I care for that? God bless the king of England! I had two hundred thousand acres to scout out for the Ohio Company, and I'd better be about my business.

The days passed with the miles. The nights passed as I slept—once in an abandoned cabin in the woods, once or twice in a farmhouse along the way, sometimes in a proper inn, sometimes under the autumn sky. I neglected my reading and my prayers—God forgive me.

In the city of New York, I sold the weary packhorse and walked my proud Neeyesee aboard a merchant frigate bound for Philadelphia. Perhaps I should have taken a ship out of Connecticut or Rhode Island instead of kicking up dust all the way to New York, but I'd coveted that time to walk around inside my own head. Now that we were at sea, the salt air awakened something new within me, and the uncluttered, clear Atlantic sky was a fine, bracing sight after all those brain-clouded New England miles. The passage was restful, straight, and pleasant, and we sailed into Delaware Bay on the second day.

Monday through Sunday, October 1 through October 7, 1750

Philadelphia. The City of Brotherly Love. Twenty thousand people packed into the cleverest town I ever did see. Some of the streets were brick— mighty nice to walk upon, but a little rough on a horse's hooves. Plenty of blacksmiths, though, to shoe the horses up. And all the streets were lit at night! Nothing fancy, just tallow candles or fat lamps set out at dusk by shopkeepers and householders. Lamplighters walked the streets every night to make sure the lights stayed lit. They earned three shillings monthly for their midnight vigils.

I spent a week in the city—longer than I had expected—lodging with George Bonham, an old friend of Pop. Philadelphia kind of grabbed at me and held on tight. I walked everywhere in that great town, giving Neeyesee a much-deserved rest. He had half an acre of fenced-in grass at Bonham's— with oats and hay besides.

I walked one morning along the docks, especially admiring the city's newly constructed battery, "The Association." A timber and plank breast-work, eight or ten feet thick and filled with earth that had been rammed down, the battery boasted of fifty cannons to guard the harbor against pirates or any ships belonging to our oft-time enemies, France and Spain. Only three years previous, twelve English merchant vessels were captured by pirates in a year's time. But the Quakers wouldn't contribute a penny toward anything that could be used in war or defense. So one of the city's most active and inventive citizens, Benjamin Franklin, founded an association of men willing to be armed and trained in order to garrison a fort. Then a lot-tery was announced and money was raised to build the fort. It was a fine battery, and at the time I couldn't imagine an enemy ship that would dare to face those fifty guns.

Franklin had busied himself with another project as well, proposing to bring drinking water into the city through a series of pipes, using gravity to move the water from a single source rather than relying on the ancient town pumps that pulled rancid water up from old wells. Folks were debating the issue everywhere I wandered. Franklin's idea won out soon after.

I went to visit Franklin to see his printing press, but he was out of town, and so I stopped by the printing shop of Christopher Sauer instead. Sauer had a whole room full of Bibles that he had recently printed in the German tongue. *The First Bible Printed in America,* read a sign in his window. I fig-ured it was my duty to correct the advertisement, so I told him about Reverend Eliot's Indian Bible, which preceded the Sauer Bible by eighty years or more. He didn't take too well to the news. Didn't even believe me at first. And declared at last that an Indian Bible is not a real Bible. This would-be Gutenburg couldn't sell his Holy Volumes, though—his price was too dear!

Bonham took me one afternoon by horse and cart to Bartram's Gardens at Gray's Ferry on the west bank of the Schuylkill. John Bartram was a botanist who had turned his estate into the prettiest garden east of Eden. He had trees and bushes from all over the Americas and from England too. I only wish I had seen it in the springtime instead of fall. And I wished that Sarah could have been there with me. But I've told her about it plenty, and we've since cleared several acres to experiment with some fancy trees of our own—some that I've bought here and there, and some that I've uprooted and brought home from my wanderings in the wilderness.

On the Sabbath, October 7, I worshiped at Christ Church on Second Street just north of Market Street. It was the only Church of England congregation in the city. They started building in 1727, and they hung their first church bell in the crotch of a tree. The structure still wasn't complete when I visited. Ben Franklin was managing a lottery to raise funds for the steeple and chimes—he's no Episcopalian, but he has his helpful fingers even in the sacred things of the city. It was a comforting thing to worship with the liturgy, but a confining thing to sit there in those pews. I felt stirred to renew my daily devotions, and I vowed to God that I wouldn't miss a morning or an evening in the book that Hazard had given me. I've kept that vow, knowing full well that it is better not to vow at all than to break your promises to God. Sunday was my last day in the City of Brotherly Love.

Twenty thousand people walking those brick-covered streets—but hardly an Indian among them.

Monday, October 8, 1750

Neeyesee was glad to be pacing once more, and—frankly—I was glad to be riding him. Though I generally prefer my own legs in the forest and the field, the streets of Philadelphia had made me wonder if I ought to visit the smithy for some iron shoes for myself! Now I was mounted once more, and though my week in the big town had been filled with exciting sights and sounds, I was not too sad to bid it "so long." With the bright trees of autumn rising before me and a fresh packhorse loping behind me (compliments of George Bonham the elder—thank the Lord for friends of the family), I set out westward upon the Great Conestoga Road. It was once called the Allegheny Path by the first sons of the forest before the sons of William Penn inherited their father's vast woodlands.

Penn's boys were one of the reasons Indians were so scarce in this corner of Penn's Woods. Thirteen years earlier, the Penn family decided to tie up the loose ends of a land deal made back in 1686 between the late governor and the Delaware Indians. The elder Penn had bought a tract of ground along the Delaware extending "back into the woods as far as a man can go in one day and a half." Well, that tract had never actually been measured off. As time passed, settlers just kept spreading out from Philadelphia, north and west. It made the Indians nervous. They wanted that day-and-a-half walk performed so things could be understood properly as to who owned what and who could walk where. But—and this is the kind of thing that would send Caleb on the verbal warpath—Penn's boys didn't play the game by the rules. A walk is a walk, after all, as any man knows, but the government of Pennsylvania employed three fast-running men. And they sure did run! One of the Indians chosen to accompany them commented later, "No sit down to smoke, no shoot a squirrel, just run, run, run, all day long." And the runners didn't strike a straight course along the Delaware as the Indians expected of them, but headed out—at the beginning of the second day—northeast to the mouth of the Lackawaxen.

My father did the surveying after the run. It took him four days to walk over the same ground, and the entire area covered not less than twelve hundred square miles. The Delawares cried foul—and no wonder—but they had little recourse. The Six Nations, to whom the Delawares bowed (though rather unwillingly), ordered the ancient river tribe to remove to Wyoming and Shamokin on the Susquehanna. So they no longer walked the old trails. They no longer fished the big bay. I wouldn't have been too happy about the way things came down if I were a Delaware, but I was no Delaware, and I didn't like to think about it. Nations rise. Nations fall. God sets kings up and knocks kings down. He has his purposes, and time treads on.

I was about half a day out of Philadelphia when I came on a wagon broken down by the road. The spokes of a front wheel had cracked and brought the whole thing down on its side. I could see it lying there ahead of me, its team of mules munching grass on the opposite side of the road.

"Ho, drover!" I hollered, pulling my mount up beside the wounded wagon. There was no answer, and I wondered if the drover had been hurt in the accident. Or perhaps he'd hopped on one of his mules and headed for the nearest farm. But the mules were still hitched together in their harnesses, and there didn't seem to be one missing. I jumped off Neeyesee and poked around in the bushes where the wagon lay. I climbed inside the topsy-turvy contraption. It was one of those Dutch or Conestoga wagons, German built, with a great white cloth roof. Kind of like a wigwam on wheels. It was full of boxes and barrels and bundles of merchandise—from Philadelphia no doubt—and headed for Lancaster probably. Lancaster was pretty near the frontier and saw quite a business in furs from the western wilderness. Lancaster's wagons brought furs into Philadelphia and then took store-bought goods on back. Lots of goods in this wagon, but no drover. I stepped outside.

"Ho, yerself!" came the hoarse greeting from the other side of the road. And I saw a black-haired, smiling face—dark and toothless—rise from the grass where the mules were feeding. Something mighty familiar about that smile.

"Old Joe!" I cried. And it was him, sure thing.

Joe was a Susquehannock Indian, an ancient fellow who had lived along the Susquehanna River all his life. I spent a month in the woods with him once, ten years past or so, hunting along the Juniata. He was an old man then—maybe he'd always been old—but his hair had never gone gray.

"Longshot!" declared the Susquehannock. He had given me that moniker himself because of how far I could shoot and still hit my target. I crossed the road as the Indian lifted his stiff frame out of the grass where he'd been napping. We embraced.

"My name's Conestoga Joe now," he said. "But I go by Connie Joe."

"You old son of a river snake!" I said. "You look awful, but I sure am glad to see you!"

"Look pretty bad yerself!" laughed the toothless, wrinkled man. "But not as bad as that poor wagon over there!"

"You driving?" I asked.

"No," said the Indian. "Mister Siegrist drivin'. But he's walkin' now! I'm just guardin' his mules and stuff." Just then, the old man's misty eyes narrowed and he jutted his chin southward down the road. His sight might be fading, but his ears were still better than mine. Then I heard it too. Horses. Three of them. Coming along at a fair pace. Connie Joe stood up straighter—as straight as his bent back would let him—and I saw that he had a longrifle in his hand. "Caught me sleepin' on the job, Longshot," he muttered. "Good thing you came along."

Around the bend came the riders, two men hauling a packhorse with a wagon wheel across its back. The man in the lead pulled up his mount at the sight of us. "Everything all right, Joe?" he asked, as he slid off his horse into the grass in front of us. Siegrist, I figured. He eyed me carelessly, but I could see in the way that he stood that he was ready to do what he had to if he found me to be a danger to his property or person. And he was a big fellow, round in the face and wide at the shoulders.

"Everythin's all right, yessir," answered Connie Joe. "I was just enlistin' this here longshooter to sit and watch wagon with me when my ears tells me somethin's comin'." Joe curled his lips in a wide grin and introduced me to his boss. "Mister Daniel Siegrist," said the Susquehannock, "this here's Mister Christopher Long—Longshot, folks call 'im. Old huntin' brother." I held out my hand to the drover.

"Pleased to meet you, Long," said Siegrist sincerely, taking my hand firmly, a smile of relief breaking on his portly face. "I've heard tell of you. Mostly from old Joe here. Says you can shoot the tail off a chipmunk at a hundred yards."

"Two hundred yards," Joe declared quietly. "Said two hundred yards, Mister Siegrist."

I chuckled, shuffling my thoughts for a clever answer, and then I saw the mounted fellow staring at us sourly. I figured I should address him instead.

"Let's get that wheel off that poor nag," I offered, moving toward the pack. "Chris Long," I said, holding my hand out to greet the man upon the horse.

"Yeah," he replied, nodding and shifting himself in his saddle. He turned his eyes to Siegrist and spoke to him, "Guess you have all the help you need. I'll be heading back. Just drop the horses off when you roll by. And you can pay me then too. Maybe a dress for the wife. You've got dresses in the wagon?"

"Dresses and plenty of fine cloth to make more," said the drover. "Won't you stay for a smoke and a drink?"

"Got work to attend to," replied the sourpuss. "See you when you roll by." And he turned his horse and headed back down the road. I saw dark clouds in Connie Joe's eyes.

"Good man, that Bainbridge," said Siegrist, fumbling with the straps that held the wheel to the pack's back. "Not much on socializing, though." The wheel came loose, and I helped Siegrist wrestle it to the ground. "Joe," said the drover, "make yourself useful, old black! Get me some drink." And the drover and I rolled the wheel beside the fallen wagon.

It took a good bit of muscle, some levering with a thick tree we felled, some help from the mule team, and a mess of axle grease to get the old wheel off and the new one on. The mules earned their oats by pulling the wagon upright, and Siegrist swore and drank all the while. He offered me his rum, but I declined. Connie Joe's eyes begged for the stuff, but Siegrist never passed it his way.

"Mister Siegrist," said the old Indian after hitching the mules back up so they could pull the wagon home. "You know that the Great Spirit, the heavenly Father who made all things, made everythin' for some use."

The drover nodded wearily, leaning against his wagon.

"And whatever he designed anythin' for, that's what use it oughta always be put to."

Siegrist sat down in the grass and lit his pipe. Joe lit his own. I sort of wished I hadn't discarded mine.

"Now, when he made rum," continued the clever Susquehannock, "he said, 'Let this be for the Indians to get happy with.'"

Siegrist yawned and smiled.

"And so it's gotta be," concluded the Indian.

Siegrist passed him the bottle.

"Thank you," said Connie Joe, with the glass at his lips.

I lit a fire as the sun was setting. The drover and the Indian were singing a song in German. I boiled some water to make us all a little corn soup, and I set myself down to read my prayers. When the moon rose, the labor of the day weighed heavily upon me. As I lay myself down to sleep, I saw Siegrist feeding the fire. "Longshot, they call him," mumbled the drover, his back silhouetted against the blaze. "Two hundred yards," he chuckled.

"Three hundred!" coughed the Indian. "Said three hundred, Mister Siegrist."

"Did not!" returned the big drover, as my dreams overtook me.

CHAPTER EIGHT

Longshot

Tuesday, October 9, 1750

I t was one of those sunlit autumn mornings when the wind blows clean and cool and easy across the countryside. I was glad to be riding in the company of the big drover and his Indian companion. I was glad to be heading west toward Lancaster and the frontier farther on. Siegrist let me unburden my packhorse and load my goods into the wagon. Then Connie Joe begged for my ear privately. He rode Bainbridge's packhorse bareback as we followed the wagon at a short distance.

"Yestiday you seen how that Bainbridge fellow was lookin' at me?" said the Indian, as our mounts trod the leaf-strewn road.

I nodded affirmatively.

"Well," continued Connie Joe, "he's a bad'un."

"What's he got against you, Joe?" I asked.

"He hates Indians most ways," said the old Susquehannock. "But he hates me special."

"You scalp any of his family?" I jested. Connie Joe threw me a dark frown. I had picked the wrong jest. I apologized.

"He'd like to scalp *me*!" returned the Indian. "I'll tell ya 'bout it." I kept my mouth shut as Joe unwound his tale. "Bainbridge and his brothers lived near Paxtang, where his father dug up a farm along the Susquehanna," said Connie Joe. "Friends came to settle with 'em. Cut down the trees. Built fences and a tradin' house for buyin' furs from the Indians. I lived in Paxtang when they first came into our country, five or six moons after I returned from huntin' with you along the Juniata.

"A man named Harris figgered he could make a barrel fulla wampum ferryin' people 'cross the river just north of Paxtang. He figgered right.

Harris's Ferry picked up a lot of tradin' traffic real quick. But most of the Paxtang Indians didn't like that traffic, and they moved west over the river or further south along the waters. I moved with 'em. But I saw that Harris had a pretty smart idea, so I built myself a real good raft—you shoulda seen it, Longshot, a real good raft! You know an Indian can build a better river raft than a white man!" Connie Joe's near-toothless mouth stretched wide in a wrinkled, cavernous grin. "You shoulda seen it," he repeated.

A massive flock of high-flying geese caught our attention for a few minutes, and we studied their well-ordered flight until they were out of sight beyond the southern treeline. Their rude song serenaded us a few minutes more, and then the morning was silent but for the twittering of birds in the trees, the squeaking of the slatted wagon, and the rhythmic drumming hooves of the plodding animals. Joe took up his tale again.

"I raised my wigwam at Conewago on the west side of the Susquehanna and offered all travelers good passage 'cross the river on my raft. Conoy Path meets the river on the west there, Old Peter's Road meets the river on the east—so my traffic was as good as Harris's, and I guess he didn't like the competition. Sent Bainbridge down to buy my raft. But I wouldn't sell." The old Indian sighed, pulling his lips so tight that his wrinkles vanished and his dark eyes flashed like midnight lightning. "Bainbridge is a bad'un," muttered the Susquehannock, and then he fell as silent as the cool, mute breeze that kissed our brows as we rode.

"You wouldn't sell," I said at last, nudging the old warrior out of his dark reverie.

"Nope," said Connie Joe. "Bainbridge went next down to Dekanoga," continued Connie Joe with a growl, "and went partners with a man named Wright to lay some rafts in the river where Monacasy Path meets Conoy Path at Captain Beaver's village. But folks still came to me for passage—I charged 'em less than Harris or Wright and Bainbridge. The Indians would rather cross with me, and a good number of white traders liked my price. And they all bragged about my raft, Longshot—you shoulda seen it! Bainbridge tried to buy me out again."

"And you wouldn't sell," I added assuredly.

"Started hearin' stories 'bout myself right after that," muttered the Susquehannock darkly. "Bitter, black lies—an Indian won't never tell lies like these lies. Even when he hates a man, he won't lie like these lies." The old man straightened his hunched shoulders and sighed heavily. "It was told all over the hills that I'd murdered a white farmer and his children 'long the Juniata," said the tired Indian. "That I'd taken his wife captive and lain with her 'gainst her will—this is a white man's sin, Longshot, and not never the way of a Susquehannock! These lies said that I abandoned the mother in the woods—leavin' her just 'nough food for one day. And the food they said I gave her was the boiled heart of her husband who I killed and cut up right in front of her eyes!"

The old Indian sagged heavily upon his mount. I could feel his pain, could see the scars that all the slander had left upon the old man's soul. I wanted to say something to cheer him, but my words are too often the wrong kind of medicine for heavy hearts. So I silently asked God to comfort the old boy.

"Wanted to kill someone for real after I heard these lies," admitted the Susquehannock. "Made me so dark inside that I truly wanted to cut out and eat the heart of the father of these lies—Bainbridge! Who else? But I knew the vengeful ways of my fathers should never again belong to the children. I's long heard and believed that the heavenly Father will punish a man who spills blood in vengeance. I's long heard that the Son of the heavenly Father spilled his own blood so that all may live in love. And isn't it said that he counseled us to forgive even our enemies? I swallowed my pride like bitter berries. I told the heavenly Father that I forgave even the liars who'd paint my name in blood. But people couldn't see my heart. They could only see the liar's paint, and they turned from the road that led to my house. 'Course my raft wasn't asked for as often after this. When Bainbridge came to offer to buy it again, I wouldn't speak with 'im. Couldn't bear to even look at 'im. I sang a song by the river to drown out his poison words, to quiet my own risin' fury. He rode off as stirred up as a hive of angry hornets.

"The next morning, I found my raft gone—cut loose from shore. Pieces of it washed up near the Pequea. I collected 'em and made a fire upon one of the islands on the Susquehanna. Took off my clothes and burned 'em in that fire. Then I chanted to the heavenly Father and the gods of the rivers and the trees. 'As long as these lies are loose in the woods, I will never hunt again along the Juniata or the Susquehanna or any of the rivers of this world, or beneath any of the trees that grow upon the hills and in the valleys.' That's what I told 'em, and that's what I meant. Then I went to live at Conestoga, where a German farmer let me raise a small hut in return for helpin' him in his fields. He taught me how to drive wagon, and I changed my name to Conestoga Joe. And then I met Mister Siegrist, and now I ride with 'im to Philadelphia and back. And sometimes the lies still follow me."

We rode on in silence.

Bainbridge's place sat along Old Peter's Road on the east side of Pequea Creek. He had a large plank house with some barns and sheds and a carriage house big enough to fit two or three German wagons. A smith's forge sat next to the carriage house, with a jumbled pile of rusted wagon wheels leaning at its walls. A small stone mill rested on the other side of the creek, palisaded on three sides by a field of dried, golden-leafed corn that had been planted right down to the water. Perhaps the man was a "bad'un," but he sure seemed a hard worker, judging by the way he'd tamed the land. Siegrist halted the mules in the road and gave a holler. "Bainbridge!" shouted the drover. "Here we are at last!"

The sour-faced farmer came out of his house with a gun in his hand and stood upon his porch, nodding his head slowly up and down. I felt blood rising in my face as I looked into his dull eyes and recalled the bitter testimony of my Susquehannock friend. I climbed off Neeyesee and helped Joe down from the Bainbridge horse. Siegrist was already leading the other mount toward the barn. Bainbridge never left his porch. He just stood there nodding, frowning, fingering the long barrel of his rifle.

Don't know what got into me, but the steam was rising in my kettle and I decided to take the lid off. I strode up to the house and mounted the steps that fronted the porch. Bainbridge stepped back and swung his rifle across his chest as if it were an iron bolt and he was the front door. His cloudy eyes darkened further, and his scowl dropped to show a bottom set of strong, straight teeth. But he still didn't speak. I walked to within a couple of feet of the man and stood there staring at him.

"You can leave," said the farmer through his teeth.

"I can," I replied. "And I will, gladly. But I got something to say to you first."

"Say it," said the man with the rifle across his chest.

But I couldn't think of anything to say!

"Long!" hollered Siegrist from the barn. "Bring that other horse along, will you?"

My hands were sweaty and my heart was pounding. Bainbridge's eyes bored into me like a smithy's iron into wood. I could almost smell the smoke.

"Say it and leave," said the man with the rifle across his chest.

"Not yer trouble, Longshot," croaked old Connie Joe from the foot of the steps.

"You shut your black face!" snapped Bainbridge, and I remembered my duty.

My hands leapt to the barrel of Bainbridge's gun, and with one quick jerk I wrenched the weapon from his hands and flung it at the muttering Susquehannock. Joe caught it and spun it in his arms with amazing agility. The barrel was now pointed at the farmer.

"Dang!" cried Bainbridge, his dark eyes flying open like two big windows. He stood still as a rock, the veins of his neck twitching like snakes going up a tree. "Dang!" he repeated, blowing his curse out of his cheeks like a dragon spits fire. I laughed, which wasn't the charitable thing to do, but I still could think of nothing to say.

"Long!" bellowed the drover from the barnyard. "What in the name of King George are you boys doing? Robbing the man? Put down that gun, Joe!" The trader was running across the yard now.

Connie Joe lowered the rifle—and Bainbridge leapt like a cougar, right off his porch and onto the Indian. Oaths in many tongues rose from the lawn as the Indian and the Englishman wrestled in the grass. Connie Joe's curses were much the more colourful and creative, and I'd love to repeat them for you here, but it wouldn't serve to edify. Siegrist tried to break up the dogfight, but you know what Solomon wrote about messing with a fight that isn't your own—it's like taking a mad dog by the ears! The drover got a fist in his eye for his trouble. I just sat down on the porch and watched.

Funny thing how one man can make an entertainment out of the pains of another—but you must understand that I hadn't seen a good fight for quite some time. Once, as the two men rolled around the yard, I was tempted to join in on Joe's side, but I thought better of it. Joe was doing pretty good for an old rheumatic warrior anyway. Finally, Missus Bainbridge and the boys came out to watch. She offered me some cider, for which I thanked her kindly. By then the mules were braying, and the Bainbridge hounds were howling, and the Bainbridge boys were all cheering their pop on to a dubious victory. Missus Bainbridge had picked up her husband's gun and was tinkering with it.

Bang! The fine conflict was brought to a sudden peace by Missus Bainbridge's purposeful finger on the trigger. Gunsmoke wafted blue across the yard while the Bainbridge boys stared at their mother like they were looking at a ghost. The bruised and bloodied wrestlers sat up in the grass, blinking at each other beneath the noonday sun. Siegrist stood up from where he'd been lying since crawling from the fray some time earlier. He held a hand over one eye and muttered something that I couldn't quite hear.

"We ain't done," said the farmer to his wife.

"You are," said the wife to the farmer, "'cause lunch is on the board."

"We'll finish up after we eat," declared the farmer to the Indian, getting up stiffly. Connie Joe couldn't get up at all, and so the farmer helped him to his feet. "You hungry, you blasted savage?"

"Sure am!" said the Indian, hobbling toward the porch.

The men sat at the table while the woman of the house waited on us. The boys ate standing, talking all the while about the punches their pop had landed and the armholds the Indian had constructed to hold their pop down while biting his back with all two of his yellowed, busted teeth. "Pop'll probably get the madness from those bites!" the boys laughed. The farmer scowled as he ate.

"A fair fight," I said while chewing the stringy venison that was laid before me.

"Most ways," admitted the German drover while emptying a mug of beer. "Wouldn't have thought it could be, but in most ways it was."

"We'll finish up the fight after we eat," said the English farmer.

"Fair fights are a new thing for you, Bainbridge," I said. The farmer's wife brought me another serving of meat. The farmer shot me one of his sour looks. "At least as far as your history in relationship to Connie Joe," I added.

"Not yer trouble, Longshot," said the Susquehannock as he shoveled corn into his mouth with his thick, wrinkled hands.

"What's this all about, Long?" asked Siegrist.

"Can I say my piece?" I asked the farmer.

"Say it," said Bainbridge.

I told Connie Joe's tale as he had laid it out to me that morning, adding all the good things I knew about the old Indian. It took a while, what with the farmer sticking in his own details, Siegrist chiding Bainbridge at each new disclosure of villainy, Joe talking to himself in Susquehannock, and the Bainbridge boys asking for things to be told twice. The farmer's wife brought out some puddings just as the story came to a final, raucous conclusion.

"All true," admitted the farmer proudly. "Especially the lies."

"Scoundrel!" declared Siegrist. "I've a mind not to pay you for this day's services—and to hire them no more!"

"Fix your own wagon from now on if you wish," said Bainbridge, picking his teeth with a splinter of wood from his tabletop. "I've got plenty of business without it."

"Bainbridge," I said, leaning toward him. "Your stinking dishonesty and lowdown ways have cost Connie Joe an honest vocation on the river, occasioned years of heartache and grief, and have blackened a good man's name even among his own people. Nothing could ever make up for what you've done, and in my book you owe this old Indian a good piece of what you now call your own."

"Not in this lifetime," said the farmer, spitting on the floor. His wife scolded him.

Connie Joe stood up—rather painfully, I thought.

"Sit down, old black!" Bainbridge ordered.

Connie Joe sighed deeply and sat back down.

"Let's go finish that fight," I muttered, "and then get out of here."

"Can I say *my* piece now?" coughed the old Indian.

Bainbridge continued to pick his teeth. "Say it," he said at last. "Say it quick."

"I never did none of these things you lied about, Bainbridge," said the Susquehannock. "The heavenly Father knows, and you know. Your lies has hung upon me all these years like the stench of a skunk. But I hasn't held it in my heart against you, though y'are the skunk hisself!" The Bainbridge boys howled at this kind of talk and urged their pop to throw the dog out, but the skunk let the dog keep on barking. "I's a better man than you are, Bainbridge," old Joe barked, "And if I's a younger man rollin' with you in the yard, I'd be wearin' yer scalp on my belt right now! But I's an old wolf and my teeth falls out when I eat meat—you can thank the spirits for that!" The farmer rubbed his shoulder where the wolf had chewed on him. "But I can still shoot straighter'n a crow can fly," declared the old wolf, "and I wanna finish our fight with a shootin' contest!"

"A shooting contest?" laughed the farmer. "Where's your bow and arrow, blackie? Shooting contest!"

"I'll make you a wager," I said to the farmer, "that the old man out-shoots you two of three times!"

"Name your wager!" said the farmer. "Whatever it is, I'll double it!"

"If Connie Joe beats you two out of three, Bainbridge, you tell every-one that rolls through here that those stories about him are untrue. And while you're setting the record straight, you confess to making up the lies in the first place. And you keep talking nothing but good about this old Indian till the day you die."

"Ha!" laughed the farmer. "Done!" declared the farmer. "But if I out-shoot him, I'll start the old rumors flying again and add two new ones to each of the old ones!"

"God'll be your judge," I said, taking his hand in pledge.

The farmer got to call the first shot. He set up a small wooden box—about as big as a man's hand—in the crotch of a tree. One hundred paces were marked off, and the contestants loaded their rifles. Both men were using longrifles that had been made in Lancaster County by German gunsmiths. Bainbridge's gun looked like a brand-new shooting piece fresh out of the gun shop, but Connie Joe's was the same faithful piece he had toted along the Juniata when we'd hunted together a decade previous. I knew what Joe could do with that weapon. Bainbridge's performance would be the sur-prise.

"You may fire first," said the farmer to the Indian.

"What you gonna shoot at after I blow that box to bits?" asked Connie

Joe. The farmer's cheering squad heartily jeered the Indian. Bainbridge just scowled.

Then old Joe cocked his hammer back fully, swung his gun up just as easy as if it had been hinged to his arm and well greased, and pulled the trigger. When the smoke cleared, that little box was kindling. The Bainbridge boys whistled in amazement. Siegrist chuckled. Bainbridge snorted, set up a second box, walked to his position, took aim, and blew his target in a couple dozen directions. "Tied," said the farmer.

"So far," said the Indian. "Now let's try somethin' worth braggin' about."

The old Indian, grinning toothlessly, limped to the side of the road and stood there. While his ancient eyes surveyed the plantation, his wrinkled hands loaded the gun all by themselves. Powder, liner, shot, ramrod in, ramrod out, powder in the pan, hammer half-cocked—all done in little over a minute! Connie Joe swiveled his grizzled chin and pointed a crooked finger toward the big barn. "'Bout three paces left of the busted window and four feet off the ground, there's a knot in a plank," said the Susquehannock. "See it? Darker'n the rest of the wood and 'bout as big as my thumb." I wondered whether Joe could see it himself!

"I see it," cried the youngest Bainbridge excitedly. "That injun'll never hit it!"

"He'll never hit it, will he, Pop?" shouted all the boys together.

"Not if yer pop hits it first," said Connie Joe quietly, his face a mass of dark, smiling wrinkles. "Right here," said Joe, drawing a line in the road with his toe. "We shoot from right here."

If Bainbridge was ruffled, his steady scowl didn't show it. Having reloaded his own weapon, he stepped onto the road and faced the barn. He squinted once, shot a sharp glance at his wide-eyed brood, raised his rifle and steadied it, then fired. Silence followed as the smoke drifted across the barnyard. Then the boys raised a shout and ran to check the results. From where I stood, I could see the ball nearly buried in the plank about an inch from the dark knot. "Good shot, Pop!" cheered the Bainbridge pups, and I agreed. The oldest boy started to dig the lead out with his knife. Missus Bainbridge sat down on the porch with her hands upon her lap.

"Get away from there!" the farmer ordered his boys. "Old black Joe's gonna break another window!"

As soon as the boys were safely out of the way, Connie Joe kissed the barrel of his gun, glanced up at the autumn sky, lifted his rifle, said "Watch close, Longshot," and pulled his trigger. I saw the ball fly. It knocked that knot clean into the barn!

Everyone gathered at the barn wall, peering through the knothole into the haystrewn stall inside. "There it is!" shouted the youngest one, and the boys poured into the barn through the side door. They returned with both the shot and the knot.

"Two to one!" said Joe to the farmer, dancing around like he was one of the boys. "Yer pick, now!"

Bainbridge shouldered his rifle and strode out to the road again. He loaded his piece and then set it up against a tree and ran his fingers through his dusty hair. His scowl sagged a bit, I thought, but he seemed more set on winning this last round than when we'd struck our wager. The wind rustled in the corn. A flock of crows nested in the trees beside the river.

"Bird on the wing," said the farmer at last. "And it's got to be dead when it drops." He nodded for his boys. They came across the road baying like a pack of hunting dogs. "Shut up, you ugly howlers," growled the farmer with sour affection, "and find me a couple of nice big round throwing stones." The boys followed each other along the road, kicking at half-buried boulders and scratching at dirt clods. Finally, they returned with a dozen contestants.

Bainbridge picked three and handed them to his oldest. "Toss one into that congregation of blackbirds, Johnny," said Bainbridge to the boy. "On the count of three. One … two …" And on "three," Bainbridge raised his rifle as the young man lobbed his missile into the uppermost branches of the crows' riverside rest. The black crew rose into the sky in a raucous chorus of discontent. Bainbridge fired. Dark feathers danced upon the breeze as a wildly flailing bird plummeted into the golden field. The Bainbridge hounds (including a couple of long-eared, four-legged ones) stampeded into the high corn.

"It ain't dead!" shouted the youngest pup.

"Shut your mouth!" cried the rest.

"But it'll be dead soon!" said the youngest. "Boomer's got it."

But the farmer's hound dog brought the bird back alive. Its leg and some tail feathers were shot off. It looked mighty sad, but not as sad as Bainbridge. He threw it into the field. The rest of the crows settled in a further tree, cursing us roundly from their new position.

"Can you throw one that far, Johnny?" asked Connie Joe.

Johnny, assuming an expression that mirrored his sour pop, didn't answer but swung his arm round and round as if he were David getting ready to sling one at Goliath. He loosed his stone in a high arc that brought it back down into the thick of the grumbling birds. They scattered again, squawking like hens running from a fox.

Connie Joe watched them circle, let them rally, let them settle in the trees again. Then he let loose a loud caw of his own, and the congregation rose once more from its perch. This time, old Joe hoisted his piece and pointed it at the sky. It barked and spat fire. A large bird tumbled from among its fellows, its head and its body falling separately. The boys ran into the field again. "Dead as a doornail!" announced the youngest and most truthful of the Bainbridge brood. He brought the head back in his hand. I thought for a moment of Caleb.

The farmer walked over to his porch and sat down beside his wife, laying his rifle against the steps. "Will they stay for supper?" the missus asked her man. He just scowled.

We stayed the afternoon. We stayed for supper. We stayed the night.

"That gun of mine," said Bainbridge as we ate, "is too new. Neither my hands nor my eyes is quite used to it. Otherwise …"

"Fair fight," I reminded the farmer.

"Fair fight," echoed the drover.

"Blasted new gun," mumbled the farmer.

"I'll buy it from you," I offered. I had looked the rifle over real close after the contest, and I thought it to be one of the finest shooting pieces I had ever seen. The barrel was longer than any I was used to, but it was a lighter gun than my own, and with a smaller bore. The butt was of cherry, finely carved, and curved to fit the shoulder comfortably. It felt almost natural in my hands.

"Longshot, they call you," muttered Bainbridge. "Like to see you try out my gun in the morning. Make you another wager. One shot takes all."

"No more wagers," I said. "But in the morning," I added, "I sure would like to shoot that piece."

Wednesday morning October 10, 1750

Before the cock crowed, I woke and pulled on my boots. Quietly, so as not to wake the household, I made my way past the dogs at the door and let myself out into the crisp autumn morn. The sky was light in the east, but the center of the heavens still looked like midnight—star-spangled and misted over with silvery clouds. I wandered out to the stables and looked in on Neeyesee. The black mount was still dreaming, so I walked a few miles along the lonely road that followed the Pequea. I hummed a morning psalm. And as the dawn chased the night, I thumbed open my prayer book and read to God. By the time I found my way back to the farm, men, women, boys, and animals alike had risen from their slumber. Pork was sizzling over the fire in the kitchen—I could smell that from the road.

After a breakfast of bacon and fresh eggs, with cider to chase it down, Bainbridge handed me his rifle and urged me out into the yard. Connie Joe had already hitched up the mules to the wagon, and Siegrist was trying to make a last-minute sale of dresses to the missus. The boys were doing their best to avoid morning chores until our departure. And I held a brand-new Pennsylvania rifle in my hands.

"This piece feels like it was born to rest in my arms, Bainbridge," I said, running my fingers over the newly oiled wood and the fine-tooled barrel.

"I just want to see you shoot it," said the farmer.

I tipped my powder horn into the muzzle of the barrel, set my patch and ball at the barrel's mouth, and rammed it in gently. It went down smooth and set itself firmly in place. I slid the ramrod back into its sheath beneath the barrel and filled the pan with powder. The hammer clicked into the half position so nice and easy. I liked that gun.

"Well," I said. "I been thinking about what to shoot at, and I figure that what's good for Connie Joe is good for me."

"Gonna shoot some crows?" asked the littlest Bainbridge. Johnny fidgeted, rubbing his arm. He'd thrown it out a bit the day before.

"Nope," I said. "We'll let God's creatures alone today."

"Gonna shoot out another knothole?" barked the little pup.

"Nope," I said. "Your pop's got enough holes to patch in his barn. And there's no sense in blasting any more boxes to smithereens, or your mom won't have anything to keep her thimbles in. Naw, I thought I'd try out this new gun on that new hole Connie Joe made yesterday."

With that, I walked out to the road where the men had stood for their second round. I lifted the rifle and kind of shifted it around a bit, to get the feel of it in my arms.

"Too close," I muttered, enjoying my jest and the attention of the Bainbridge pack. I walked to the other side of the road and aimed the rifle once more. Everyone was still, but the morning birds were cheering me on with their careless song. "Still too close," I complained, backing up into the field. "Now I can't see the knothole," I cried as I stood in the midst of the faded cornstalks.

So I strode to a lone maple that set in the middle of the field, and I hoisted myself up into it. Finding a fair seat upon a thick branch that let me face the barn, I sat down and pulled my knees up in front of me. "This'll do fine!" I shouted to the watchers on the road. Some of the boys came down into the field to the foot of the tree. Some stayed with their father at the roadside and out of shot's way. Connie Joe danced a little Indian dance on the lawn by the house, and Siegrist watched from his seat upon his wagon. The missus sat on the porch again with her hands in her lap.

"You're crazy, Long," said the farmer with a scowl.

I figured he was right, but I was having fun. Nothing to lose anyway.

I settled the rifle at my knees and stared out over the field and beyond the road to a small dark spot to the left of the broken window on Bainbridge's barn. "You teach my fingers to war," I whispered in the words of the psalmist as my hands gripped the rifle and my eyes focused in on that one small spot that hung a hair's breadth above the end of my barrel. I noted the direction of the morning breezes. I raised my rifle just a bit, obscuring my target, and pulled the trigger. As the smoke flew east, I laughed. Had I shot out the window as Bainbridge had predicted Connie Joe would do? Did it matter? The day was warming wonderfully. The morning wind was refreshing and brisk. My observation post was joyously red and gold in its shimmering fall coat. I thought maybe I'd sit there awhile longer.

"He missed!" shouted one of the boys. I think it was Johnny.

"Well," I said to wind, "it sure was a long shot, anyhow!"

"He missed the barn altogether!" came a chorus of young voices.

"Not so!" declared the Susquehannock. "Never so!" he insisted. And I saw him hobble on down into the barnyard. I slid from my perch and made my way back to the road.

"Ha!" laughed the farmer. "Can't even hit the broad side of a barn!" And that made me a bit miffed. Did the shot fly that wild? Couldn't have. Did I send the ball through the window after all? Didn't seem possible that the gun would shoot that far to the right. Siegrist was off his seat now and heading for the barn too. Connie Joe went in the side door with the boys right behind him. "Come in here, you white-faced foxes!" shouted the old Indian. "Come in here and see what Longshot's done!" I was mighty curious myself!

We crowded into the little stall where Connie Joe's knot had been retrieved the day before. And there, embedded neatly in the doorpost of the stall, was my rifle ball. "Right through the knothole!" Joe proudly declared. "Right through, clean as can be! Didn't come through the window—it woulda flown high into the hay. But there it is, straight shot from a tree clear 'cross the road and right through the knothole!"

No one was more amazed than I.

Bainbridge sold me his gun for fifteen dollars, the price he had paid (he showed me his bill). It was made by John Baker of Lancaster, son-in-law of a recently deceased gunsmith named Martin Meylin. I named the gun *Bainbridge*. The sour farmer actually smiled.

And he went one step further. He apologized to Connie Joe. Well, perhaps I'm stretching things to call it an apology. He hung his head an inch lower than his usual posture, shook the old Indian's hand, told Joe that he'd speak nothing but the truth about him from now on, and gave him an old tomahawk he had hanging in the barn. Joe was sober but grateful.

Sometime before noon, we pulled out of Bainbridge's acres and headed across the Pequea toward Lancaster Town.

"Longshot," said Joe from his seat at the back of the wagon. I was riding close behind. "I's a free man. The heavenly Father has answered my prayers and loosed me from these lies. And it's you that he used to bring it about."

"You did the shooting," I said.

"You called the wager," he said.

"I knew you could beat him," I declared.

"I asked for the shootin' contest only 'cause I's too worn out from wrestlin' that big moose!" cried the old man hoarsely. "I hasn't shot nothin' for years! What if he'd beaten me?"

"You beat him, Connie Joe," I said. "Fair as fair can be. Beat him real good."

"I's a free man!" shouted the wrinkled, toothless Susquehannock. "And I's gonna hunt again! 'Long the Susquehanna. 'Long the Juniata. And 'long the Ohio—with you, Longshot!"

"I heard that!" called Siegrist from the driver's seat.

"'Long the Ohio, Mister Siegrist, you ugly German!" laughed Connie Joe. "No more wagons to Philadelphia! This calls for a drink!"

"Take your nap, you wild old man!" cried the drover goodheartedly. "And leave my rum alone!"

CHAPTER NINE

Great Hill

Friday, October 12, 1750

Hardly pays bein' an Indian 'round here anymore!" said Connie Joe as our horses carried us west upon the Conoy Path. A light rain fell steadily upon us as we traveled, turning our road to mud beneath a slick and slippery carpet of fallen leaves.

"Paid you all right when you took up a white man's way of living," I said.

"Paid me all right when I *quit*!" Connie Joe corrected me. At our parting with Siegrist at Conestoga, the bighearted drover had given Joe a horse, a mule with a nice set of packbags, some gunpowder, a jug of rum—and the promise of a front seat on a Siegrist wagon if Joe ever wanted to come back. The German and the Indian had been working together for nearly three years, and Siegrist was more than misty-eyed when he bid the old Susquehannock farewell. But he told Connie Joe that the mules would miss him most.

"But now that I'm back to bein' a real Indian, like I was raised to be," Joe continued, "I don't think I like where the path is leadin'. English folk— most of 'em, I mean, and a big pack of those Irish kind—don't love real Indians. But maybe that's 'cause the real Indians aren't shoutin' for joy 'bout the English and the Irish spillin' over the Susquehanna and squattin' on Indian land without even a 'Hey!' or a 'Ho!'"

"An Irish friend of mine—George Croghan by name—led a group of magistrates and armed deputies to oust a bunch of squatters along the Juniata this past spring," I reminded Joe. "Threw all their belongings out into the woods and burned their cabins. Seems to me your real Indians have some white friends. Seems to me you're crowing too soon against the English and the Irish."

"Croghan's a sheriff, isn't he?" said Connie Joe. "He's just doin' his job. Most likely these squatters hasn't paid Croghan for a squattin' license! Just wait till the Penns run outta pasture for their cows; then we'll see whether Croghan kicks folks outta the woods or whether he builds a house there and names a town after hisself." Croghan already had a trading house or two in the woods. As a matter of fact, he'd built them smack in the middle of a couple of Indian trading towns.

"Now that you're a real Indian again," I said, "you're starting to whine like a Narragansett friend of mine!" And I wondered what Caleb was up to. And who he was whining to this morning.

The sky was a dismal, teary gray as we turned from the Conoy and headed southwest on a wider but less-traveled road of matted green grass and scattered leaves. This way had seen some wagon traffic recently, from Virginia and Maryland on up to Harris's Ferry on the Susquehanna, but mostly it was a lonely, dark avenue through the ancient Pennsylvania woods. Wildlife was plentiful. Men were scarce. But not so scarce as to be gone from the woods altogether.

"How much further to Great Hill's wigwam?" I asked, for we were planning to pass the night in the house of an old Indian friend of Connie Joe.

"We'll be there 'fore the sun sets," said the Susquehannock. "But his house is no wigwam. It's a longhouse like the Iroquois build."

"Isn't Great Hill a Delaware?" I asked.

"Yessir," said Connie Joe, "but not yer normal Delaware. He's a doctor, a medayoo."

"A powwow!" I choked.

"Strong one," Joe asserted.

I found myself arguing with God: *Can this cup pass from me?* But we needed a place for the night, and it was only one night, and the house of a powwow was better than a pile of wet leaves under the bare-branched forest. But ... "A strong one," I echoed weakly.

"Makes a lotta money with his conjurin'," said Connie Joe. "Built hisself a longhouse with three fires. Even has a Dutch stove with a stone chimney so's the house don't fill up with smoke when the wind howls."

"A medayoo," I moaned.

"Good one," Joe affirmed.

"Dances and shrieks and keeps flies in bottles," I chanted.

"Has a bearskin costume that makes 'im look more like a bear than a bear does," said the Susquehannock. "Without the costume, he looks like an English picture book! Tattoos all over 'im. The pictures tell of all of his conjurin'—his rain dancin' and his healin' and his battle blessin' and his dog silencin' …"

"'Dog silencin'?"

"He's real good at healin', but not so good at cursin'."

"You said 'dog silencin'.'"

"Comes from not bein' so good at cursin' Christians," explained the Susquehannock. And I wasn't sure I wanted any further explanation, but it was a comfort to know that Great Hill was not so good at cursing Christians. "Tried to send the pox plague 'gainst a group of Moravian missionaries once," Connie Joe continued, "but he only made hisself sick. And then he tried blessin' a war party that went out against the missionaries, but the Moravians had a buncha dogs that warned 'em so's they all got away from the war party. Great Hill sent a silencin' spirit into the dogs the next time, and they couldn't bark no matter how hard they tried. But that amazed the war party so much when they seen it—a pack of excited dogs with their mouths flappin' and no sound comin' out—that they stayed to watch and gave up their warrin'. Some of them Indians raised wigwams at the Moravian village and became Christians. But the dogs never barked again."

This was all nonsense, of course (I was taught to think higher than such things), but I wasn't going to argue with the old man. Besides, if Great Hill was good at silencing dogs, perhaps he could still wolves also, and we'd all get a good night's rest.

"'Course there's not much call for dog silencin'," thought Connie Joe aloud. "It's the healin' and the rain dancin' that makes a man rich."

I sort of wished we could dance to make the sun come out right about then, not because I couldn't take the rain—my pop taught me to take whatever God sends as from his hand and for my good—but a little sunshine would have cheered me up a bit. However, since the sun wasn't likely to make a sudden appearance, I figured maybe changing the subject might help.

"Those Indians you were talking with back at Lancaster," I said. "They

Conestogas?" We had spent an afternoon in Lancaster Town unloading most of Siegrist's goods. There were some Indians trading in the town, and Joe had some acquaintance with them.

"Cousins," said Conestoga Joe. "Somewhere back a couple of generations."

"Any news among them that we ought to discuss?" I asked.

"The price of brooms any interest to you?" he offered.

"Not much," I said.

"How 'bout the fishin' on the Susquehanna?"

"Not much, either," I grinned. Joe was a pleasant companion, and a clever one. I thanked God for the old fellow, and a sudden desire for his soul's eternal safety came upon my heart. I was struck by the instant change in my thoughts, and I decided then and there to talk more about Christ with Joe when the chance arose.

"How 'bout the doin's of the French upon the Ohio?" proffered the Susquehannock.

"Not much, even," I jested. And the old Indian chuckled.

"Tell ya anyway," said Connie Joe, "just to pass the time."

He filled me in on things I'd heard rumored while in Philadelphia and Lancaster. About the travels in the summer of 1749 of Captain Pierre Joseph de Céleron de Bienville. Céleron, with a large contingent of French and Canadian soldiers and twenty or so Abenaki and Algonquians, had journeyed by foot and canoe along the Ohio, declaring French friendship with the Indians, French enmity against the English, and French claims to *La Belle Riviere*. The French captain also buried lead plates along the way, at the junctures of rivers mostly, which declared *La Belle Riviere* and the lands on either side of it to be the rightful property of the king of France. One of those plates was confiscated by an Abenaki deserter from the French party. The plate found its way to the governor of New York, who was rather alarmed by Céleron's long hike in the woods, but what could be done? Our nations were at peace—on paper.

And then Connie Joe added some details that were inside information. About the reactions of the Indian tribes and towns that were visited by Céleron—most were for the English and against the French. About the English traders who were chased out of the Indian towns (for a day or two) by Céleron. About the talk in the woods concerning the French and the

English and the hide trade and the Six Nations—and about the fishing on the Ohio.

"The Treaty of Aix-la-Chapelle," I said. "Ever hear of that one, Connie Joe?"

"Might have," said the Susquehannock, goading his mount onward through a stream that had risen with the rains to spill across our road.

"It ended King George's War two years ago," I said, splashing along beside my companion. Our pack mounts plodded through the water behind us.

"If I'da been a young warrior, I'da fought in that war myself," said Connie Joe. "Not for vengeance, mind ya, but to help George club the French."

"George didn't even get his own gun warmed," I commented. "And he didn't send much help over from England for those of us warming our guns for him here! Actually, I wasn't too keen on giving George a hand, Connie Joe, and I can't say that I'd care to waste any more powder on the French if it came to war again. But a man's got to do for his country as much as his conscience bids him do. That includes fighting for it."

"Real Indians feel the same way about their own country," said Connie Joe soberly.

"I don't much care about the precise measurements of Nova Scotia," I declared to the Susquehannock. "Do you?"

"Never had to walk none of it," admitted the Indian.

"And I don't really care about fishing rights along Newfoundland," I continued. "Or who owns an island or two in the West Indies. All that's the king's business, of course, and he's my king, Joe, though I've never even seen him or heard him speak a word. But the Yadkin—that's a different story!"

"And those two hundred thousand acres along the Ohio," added Joe, tightening up the wrinkles around his lips.

"I just want to walk on it!" I declared, only half believing myself. "Nothing more." The old Indian rode silently beside me. Somehow, this change of subject hadn't quite cheered me as I thought it might. The rain fell loudly, more heavily now, stripping the maples and the oaks. The ash had shed their cloaks weeks earlier.

"The kings of the Indians don't compel men to fight for 'em," said the

Susquehannock at last. "And no man fights who doesn't will it hisself. Isn't right to force a man to fight. A man's gotta have the reason in his own heart. Honor. Vengeance—if he's never heard what the heavenly Father says about it. Protectin' his own if he must. But it isn't right to force a man to run the warpath."

"The Quakers agree with you there," I said, "much to the dismay of the governor of Pennsylvania."

"The Moravians won't fight for nobody, neither," added Connie Joe. "Not with guns, anyway. They pray. They sing. They love. They fight with reason and wisdom and spiritual weapons—like the medayoo do."

And the conversation was right back where it started!

"Listen!" Joe whispered suddenly, pointing his crooked arm into the woods upon our left. I heard the drumming of the rain upon the leafy forest floor. I heard the lone hammering of a woodpecker digging for its lunch in the storm. The percussive cry of a blue jay added song to the rhythm of the moment. "Lookee!" breathed Joe quietly, his eyes peering intently into the wet woods. Then I saw what the Indian saw.

A large buck stood still as the trees and almost invisible in the midst of a leafless thicket. His coat could have been the bark of the ironwood that stood beside him; his antlers, the branches. He stared at us, unblinking. *A gift for Great Hill, the powwow*, I said within myself, reaching to unsheath my rifle from the saddle bundle where I had wrapped it to keep it dry. But by the time I slipped it out, I saw that Joe was one step ahead of me. His gun was primed and cocked before I even found my powder horn. I saw the buck blink. Then the pattering drone of the autumn storm was momentarily drowned out by the thunder of the old man's rifle. The buck fell where it stood.

"I's a hunter," Connie Joe declared solemnly as the rain ran down his face. "I's born a hunter in my father's wigwam. My bow and my rifle laid meat upon my father's mats, my own mats, the table of my children, and the grave of my squaw. Wicked lies stilled my gun for a season. But now, I's a hunter once more. Praise be the heavenly Father and the spirits of the four winds!"

He slid from his mount and limped into the woods, pulling a glistening blade of steel from a sheath at his side. Shortly he returned, dragging the gutted animal behind him with some difficulty. I would have offered my arms, but this was Connie Joe's triumph. Outshooting Bainbridge was the old man's deliverance. Shooting this buck was his restoration. Only when I saw that Joe could not hoist the beast upon his pack mule did I dismount and help him to secure the spoils of his victory.

"I's a hunter," said Connie Joe as we started off again upon our way. "A real Indian," he declared. "Sort of," he added with a wrinkled grin. "Hasn't got no paint on my face!"

As the drenching gray skies darkened into evening, our path led us across the Conococheague Creek and through the small Indian town of Falling Spring. Only a mile or so more, Connie Joe assured me, and we would leave the path and follow the creek to Great Hill's longhouse.

"His path is a narrow one, but well-marked by bones upon the branches and by rocks painted red and black," said the Susquehannock.

We found the path, but the rocks were nearly washed clean of colour, and the trees held no bones that we could see. At last, we came into a large clearing, fenced in wood, as the English build fences. An acre of harvested corn lay on either side of our way, leading to the front door of an impressive longhouse set in the center of the clearing. The hard rain had turned the cornfields into dark rivulets of muddy water. Our path was like a shallow stream itself. A thick circle of dark smoke hovered over the house. I smelled the wood fire of the powwow.

"I wonder," puzzled Connie Joe, "if Great Hill lives here anymore." The old man's eyes ran through the muddy fields and crawled over the longhouse. "No bear's head on a pole at the door—that's his doctor sign. No scalps nailed to his walls—these're his war medals from his youth."

Just then, a dog barked. Even if the conjurer was at home, I mused, he wouldn't silence his own hounds. The door opened, spilling light out into the deepening dusk. I saw a massive form silhouetted in the door-frame, bearlike in its stance. "Great Hill?" queried Connie Joe above the patter of the rain. "That you, Great Hill?" he asked again.

"Red Eyes!" came the greeting from the doorway. (Red Eyes was one of Connie Joe's old Indian names.) "You old rumbag! What are you doing out there in the storm?" And the bear walked out into the rain himself to meet us.

Inside, the longhouse was massive, or so it seemed for the absence of worldly possessions. A small English table with a few wooden chairs. A couple of Indian beds with mats. The Dutch stove that Connie Joe had told me about. Some baskets with dried corn and tobacco. A bow and a quiver of arrows. A musket against the wall. The place didn't look like the home of a rich witch doctor. But here was the man himself, spectacular tattoos covering his flesh like moss upon a rock. And then I saw the book upon the table.

We shed our clothes and hung them near the fire. Our host brought out mugs and poured us each some soup from a pot he had simmering on the stove.

"I am no longer Great Hill," said the giant Delaware to the stooped Susquehannock as we sat at the table and sipped the hot soup. Connie Joe stared at the human bear, open-mouthed. "I am now Moses," said the Delaware soberly, "for God has climbed the Great Hill and carved his Word upon my heart." Moses pointed to the book I had spotted. It was a ragged Bible, in German, opened to the Gospel of Saint Luke. "God's Son is my doctor now," said the Delaware. "And his Word is my medicine."

Just then Moses' hound began to bay once more. We heard the noise of a horse galloping up to the house. Then a sudden pounding at the door.

"Enter!" shouted the Delaware, rising from his seat but making no move toward his weapons. The door swung open. Illumined in its dark frame was the drenched and panting form of a wildly painted Narragansett warrior.

"Caleb!" I cried.

CHAPTER TEN

Long Night in the Longhouse

***Friday night till sunrise Saturday morning,
October 12–13, 1750***

The night sky cried mournfully above the longhouse of Moses as four men thanked their gods for the solid walls, the well-laid roof, and the remarkable Dutch stove that burned warmly in their midst. That stove was the answer to my hopes for a smokeless home! Iron-plated, four-legged, and sitting just a foot or so away from the stone chimney, the fully enclosed stove sent its smoke up the chimney through a flue. Its heat was more than sufficient to warm the large room of the longhouse (especially near its center), and the fact that it didn't fill the room with choking clouds of smoke was an astounding blessing. I asked Moses where he had gotten the device, and upon hearing that it was a Lancaster German invention that could be commonly purchased, I promptly paid him to procure me one and have it sent to Mrs. Sarah Long at Longstown on the Yadkin, North Carolina. My Sarah would be so pleased!

But the stove was not my first concern. It was Caleb Hobomucko's sudden appearance in the backwoods of Pennsylvania that clamored for the attention of my reason and imagination. He would say nothing to satisfy me, however, beyond that his business in Rhode Island was done and that he'd been tracking me down for two weeks. "Your trail was not hard to follow," said the Narragansett, "until the rain."

"I wasn't trying to hide my tracks, Caleb," I said. I wished the two of us could excuse ourselves and take a short wander into some dark corner to talk things over. But I didn't feel free to make the suggestion, and Caleb made no move in that direction on his own.

For some time, the talk in the longhouse was made up of introductions and the kind of storytelling that accompanies getting acquainted. But after old friends had bragged a bit on each other in order to enlighten the whole gang of us, the conversation took a decided and not wholly unexpected turn toward spiritual things. Connie Joe shot the first arrow into the woods.

"I's about as curious as an old man can be, Great Hill—I mean, Moses—concernin' yer turnin' from conjurin' to prayin' to the heavenly Father and his Son," said the Susquehannock.

Caleb's painted face was grim. His eyes sought a fire to lose themselves in, but the blaze was out of sight within the iron stove. The lack of crackling flames made him nervous, and he crossed his arms and shot me a cold look that said, *I can sleep in the rain if I must.* I scolded him with my eyes, and he loosened himself a bit, sitting lower in his chair and fingering his mug of soup.

"Let us smoke together as we talk," said Moses, pulling a pipe from a bag near the table. Caleb relaxed visibly at the suggestion. Old Joe grinned wide enough to show both teeth, and he asked if he might pull a mat over to the stove instead of sitting at his chair. I apologized for having no pipe—at which Caleb turned to me quizzically.

"Lost it," I lied in answer to his stare, and my conscience stung more at that moment for my tossing aside a friend's gift than at my deceit in speaking of it. Worst of all, my promise to Sarah flew from me altogether. The fear of man is a snare, and it causes the soul to shrink. I told Caleb the truth later and—when I'd had the time to think better of it—resolved before God to smoke no more. For now, a pipe was found for me, and pretty soon—Dutch stove or not—we had filled that big house with smoke.

"You were a strong powwow," said Caleb to Moses suddenly, leaning across the table to engage his eyes. And I was cautiously glad that my old friend had decided to take the offensive rather than be beaten into quiet submission by his volatile emotions.

"I was," said Moses. "Strong and rich—and full of darkness and misery."

"Did the spirits turn against you?" asked Caleb.

"I turned at last against them," said the former medayoo, "when the Lamb whispered love to my soul."

"How strong were you?" queried Caleb, blowing those impossible smoke rings into the air above us. I wished I could do the same to impress the present company, but I didn't even dare to try.

"Strong enough to make the heavens weep as they do today," declared Moses. "Though it was the strength of the spirits and not my own. Strong enough, too, to send sickness and death upon my enemies—but God has forgiven me such sins."

"Your medicine struck down your enemies," Caleb said quietly, absently, as though speaking to himself.

"And healed many a friend!" added Connie Joe, sending smoke curling from his lips in a curious fashion. "Healed a few well-payin' foes too, I hear," chuckled the old man. "As well as quieted a few missionary dogs."

"The spirits can do many things," declared Caleb.

Somehow this talk of spirits, in the company of these three Indians, didn't trouble me as much as I thought it might. And I found myself rooting for—even praying for—the tattooed ex-conjurer as he continued his tale.

"They can do many things, indeed," said Moses. "But never for the good of the soul. And never—successfully—against those who trust the Lamb."

"The prayers of Christians are strong medicine," whispered Caleb.

"This is what made me first doubt my own medicine," said Moses soberly, setting his pipe upon the table and wringing his bearlike hands together. "It is what first caused me shame among my people—I could not harm the Christians!"

"Shut up their dogs, though!" declared Connie Joe anew. "Couldn't bark to save their own hides!"

Moses pushed himself away from the table and got up to pace a path from the stove to the far, darkened wall—and back again. His moccasined feet padded softly on the matted dirt floor. "When I knew that my Indian brothers who followed the Lamb were no longer coming to me when they were sick, and that they were counseling others against my conjuring, I knew that I must strike at these Moravian Christians. My business was failing. My reputation was in danger. But when I saw that my medicine was weak against them, I dressed myself as the bear and set out to the camp of the Moravians." Moses lumbered like a bear as he paced.

"When I arrived there," he said, "I went into the house of one of the preachers, frightening him greatly at first. But when he discerned me to be a man within a bear's skin, he looked me in the eyes and said, 'Out with you, son of Satan!' And I did not know what to say or do. When he asked me who I was, I growled, 'Great Hill, the doctor,' for I thought he would be frightened by hearing my famous name. Instead, he said calmly, 'Great Hill, you have been troubling your Christian brothers with your threats of sickness and disaster, and I wish you to cease troubling them.'

"At which my blood began to boil within me so that I growled all the more, threatening the missionary. I told him that he must leave off his preaching and go at once from our land or I would tear his house to pieces and cause him to fly up his own chimney like smoke. I prowled around the room, chanting curses so loudly that at last I raised the preacher's own temper and he laid hold of me so firmly that he pinned my arms behind my back and tied them with a belt! Then he lifted me up and hung me by a hook from his ceiling! I howled like a dog and kicked like a horse, but the spirits did not help me.

"There were many Indians in the village who had seen me enter the house, and they heard my threats and told me afterward that they expected to see the house come apart and the preacher fly out the chimney, but when all they heard was my howling from my hook, they came to the door and looked within. When they saw me hanging there, they were much puzzled and went to counsel among themselves concerning the Son of God and his power over such a great medayoo. The preacher would not let me down until I had promised to go home and cease all my threats against him and the Christian Indians. When I came back to my house, my wives could not console me, and my children could not bring me joy. I was filled with anger and confusion."

Moses sat back down again and packed his pipe with fresh tobacco. He lit it and drew upon it silently for a time. Caleb's eyes were thoughtful, troubled, behind his storm-smeared, painted mask.

"And what did the spirits tell you to do?" Caleb asked at last, his own pipe cold in his hands.

"They told me to kill the preacher, or I myself would die," said Moses quietly.

Connie Joe's eyes were wide, his lips pressed tightly against the handle of his pipe. Smoke shot out his wide nostrils as if they were twin barrels of a musket. Little piles of ashes lay on the floor near his mat. I felt strangely as though I were dreaming.

"And so I determined to kill the preacher," said Moses finally. "But I could not, and it was I who died instead—though not as the spirits had promised."

"You are not a dead man!" declared Caleb.

"I have died," said the Delaware simply. "And it is Christ who now dwells within me."

Caleb rose from his seat and paced the large house in the opposite direction of the Delaware. "You are not dead!" he declared, "even though Christ may dwell within you!"

"Great Hill is dead," said the ex-conjurer, "and Moses now lives."

"My brother, Netop, speaks like this," said Caleb as he walked in the shadows. "And the Bible speaks like this. But my eyes tell me and my heart tells me that Great Hill is alive and Netop is alive. You deceive yourselves to think that God has killed you and brought you to life anew. You give yourselves new names like those who wish to begin life over after some great tragedy or achievement. But you are not new men. You are simply men who have cast aside your father's ways to embrace the gods of the English!"

"Great Hill is dead," insisted the ex-conjurer. "Nailed to the cross of the Lamb, buried with the Son of God our Creator. Raised with Christ a new man—Moses. And God is not the God of the English. He is the God of all men. I heard of him from German lips, not English. And his language is love."

"Love!" cried Caleb. "That is not how I have heard him speak. I have heard him speak of judgment against all who will not bow to him. Eternal wrath against all who refuse to kiss the Son. I have heard him demand allegiance to One Spirit alone and promise death to any who look to other gods. I have read this in the Bible myself!"

"The heavenly Father isn't like this at all …" began Connie Joe, but Caleb was not finished.

"Cautantowwit is creator!" declared the Narragansett. "Creator of my people at least. And who is this Jehovah that he comes to take Cautantowwit's lands and peoples as if they are his own? How is it love to take a man's children away from him? For the Narragansett are the children of Cautantowwit, not of Jehovah! And the Narragansett lands belong to the Narragansett and not to the children of the god of the English or the Dutch or the German or …"

"The heavenly Father is the Father of us all—" began Connie Joe, but Caleb would not let him speak.

"Your teeth have fallen like the leaves of autumn, your wrinkles are more than the cracks upon a dried and fallow field of corn, and your years should have made you wise!" Caleb shouted angrily at the old hunter. "But you speak as a fool who has lost his way in the woods and cannot find his wigwam! Are you not a Susquehannock? Are you not a Conestoga? Are you not an Indian whose fathers have told you what is true?"

"Are you not a guest in my home?" Moses asked the Narragansett strongly. "And is this old man not your elder, whether he were a fool or not? And did not your own fathers teach you to never rebuke an elder or to hold his word in scorn?"

Caleb gaped like a mad dog, his tongue rolling in his mouth. He sputtered in his frustration, barely holding his anger in check.

"He gets like this lately," I explained, embarrassed for my friend and too weary to endure a fight.

"I understand this darkness and this rage," said Moses.

"You understand!" fired Caleb, and he walked to the shadows and stood there facing the wall. "*Musquantum manit! The gods are angry. Musquantum Chepi! Chepi is angry.* I feel him. He calls you all fools!"

"I feel him too, and I do not wish him here," said Moses firmly.

"He wanders where he will!" declared the Narragansett, spinning around to face us, his eyes frighteningly wild.

"A friend knocks at the door before entering," I offered.

"Chepi is no friend, but rather a thief and a separator of chief friends," declared the big Delaware. "And may the blood of the Lamb cover my doorposts to keep him out!"

I found myself echoing his words within myself, words which became a prayer I repeated in my heart. Caleb lurched toward us, then stopped. I felt a cold presence, as if a door or a window had been opened to let in the spirit of the wild, whining wind. The chill went up my back, my hair stood on end, and my hands went looking for my gun. But then the sensation was gone, and the room filled with a warmth that seemed as unnatural as the sudden chill had been. I shook my head to wake myself.

Caleb sat down hard upon his chair and held his head in his hands. When he raised his face to look for me, the fire was gone out of his eyes. His whole form relaxed, and a weak smile cracked his paint. What had we witnessed? Something hard and relentless, angry and evil, had gone from the powwow. He tried to stand up, but he was too weak. Yet his mind was still quick, and he started back into the battle as if nothing had happened. But his tone was different. The edge had been taken off his tongue. And his challenges fell on my heart as if he sought an answer and not a fight.

"Connie Joe … Red Eyes … whatever we are to call you—I apologize," said Caleb simply. "My anger rises quickly and carries me away. It is cool now, and I have many questions." He looked around at the rest of us. "Forgive me my foolishness," he demanded. "And let me speak."

He stood as though at counsel around his great grandfather's fire. Moses nodded for him to continue. Connie Joe simply frowned and wrinkled up his face. I shook my head and said, "You're a puzzlement, Caleb Hobomucko!" The Narragansett snorted and began anew to pace his former path within the longhouse.

"How is it that the Delaware forget their father's gods?" he asked. "How is it that the Susquehannock exchange their traditions for those of other nations? Shall we sell our own children for rum and buy sons and daughters from the French or the Irish?"

"May I answer?" queried the eldest among us, as though he were a child who needed permission.

"Stand, our father," said Moses, "and let the Narragansett listen to a wise man's words."

"Do I have to stand?" asked the old Indian. "My legs is liable to give out 'fore my tongue does. Just close yer eyes and imagine I's standin'!"

We laughed, and the humor further warmed the room.

"The heavenly Father," Connie Joe began, "is the Great Spirit of my fathers. He's the Great Spirit of all tribes and nations, though we call him by different names. The Delaware and the Susquehannock, the Seneca and the Narragansett, the Mohawk and the Mohican all call him by different names and think that he made only them. But he's the heavenly Father and he made us all. That's what I heard long ago. And that's what I believe. And he made the spirits of the winds and the sun and the moon and all the beasts in them woods out there. That's what makes sense to me. And he sent his Son to die as a ransom—like we's been told by the Christians—for all of his children everywhere. That makes sense too. So that we can all be brothers. I don't see the heavenly Father as somethin' different than what my father taught me when I was young, only somethin' more. Somethin' cleaner somehow, like a blue sky without clouds. That's what this old man thinks. And that's better'n fightin' about who's right and who's wrong! So there it is, from an old Indian. A real Indian. Sort of." And then Joe managed to stand up for a moment, in order to sit back down to show that he was done.

Moses sighed. Caleb stared at the shadows. Connie Joe coughed and relit his pipe.

"May I speak?" I heard myself say as an inner nudge urged me off my chair. Moses nodded. Caleb smiled grimly. Connie Joe sucked on his pipe.

"I'm a white man," I said. "A real white man. But my blood is red like each of us here, and my heart beats same as yours. When it stops, this body'll be laid in a wooden box and buried under the earth. There it'll rot, same as yours. A man's a man no matter where he's born or dies, no matter who his parents were, who his grandparents were. No matter what he believes. The Narragansett say that Cautantowwit made the first man and woman from a tree. The Delaware, the Susquehannock—in fact, all the Six Nations and many other tribes in these long-walking woods—believe that the Great Spirit made man and woman. The Bible also teaches that God created the first man, Adam, and his wife, Eve. As Connie Joe has said of the heavenly Father, no matter what we call him, he's the Father of us all. If we were to walk the path that leads back to the beginning of all things, we'd see that we share the same God, the same first parents, the same blood.

"But our first parents sinned against God, and they were driven from their home. As their children and their children's children grew and wandered to the east and the west and the north and the south, they lost one another on their separate paths in this world. Years went by, and they—we—forgot the truth about that first day in Eden, about the Creator God who used to walk with us as a brother walks. We became darkened in our hearts, slaves to our sin and to the delusions of Satan.

"It's a strange thing I've noticed, my brothers, that no matter how many differences there are in the traditions of the various tribes of Indians, there's always a good creator and an evil adversary. There's always a transcendent God and a skulking Devil. There's always a Great Spirit who is distant and unreachable, lost to our sight but present in the tales of our fathers and the dim memories of our souls. And there is a great evil—with lesser evils at his bidding—which seems never too far from our doors. This sameness of belief that is common to us all is nothing less than the truth grown dim with the years that have passed since Eden. The Bible throws light on those old memories, calling us all back to the way the story ought really be told.

"And the spirits that you fellows have been bartering with all your lives are written about in the Bible too. They're called demons, and they're lying spirits and evil spirits and ... ask Moses here about it! He knows more about it than I do—I'm ashamed to say—though I've had my face in the Holy Scriptures since I was knee-high to a woodchuck. And Caleb, you know more about demons than the Bishop of London! You know more about them and their crooked ways than you admit to yourself!"

Caleb sat stiff-lipped, grimly morose, arms across his chest, brow furrowed. Moses simply motioned for me to continue. And I was glad to carry on, because some sort of holy fire was burning in my bones, urging me to speak.

"One family, all of us," I declared. "One Father, whose kids are scattered all over the wide world. Lost! We're lost and wandering and fighting and dying, never knowing which way we're really going! The Delawares sweat themselves halfway through purgatory in their Sweating Rite, and if they can put themselves through that torture twelve times, then they figure they've won their salvation. But even then, the soul has to fly at death past eleven heavens before it finds its rest in the twelfth. And how many men among the Delaware do you know who claim to know for certain where their soul is gonna fly?

"The old Narragansett begged Cautantowwit to accept their sacrifices. They bowed to the spirits throughout their life on earth, and hoped against hope that the Great Dog which guards the Garden of Cautantowwit would let their souls enter upon death.

"The Delaware say that the Great Manitoo came down to earth once to show man how to worship, and this much is true—he really did come! When he came, one of his names was Emmanuel, which means 'God with us.' But folks know him best by the name of Jesus, which means 'The Lord Saves!' And he came to tell all men that they must worship in spirit and in truth. Jesus said that he alone was the way, the truth, and the life, and that no man could go to the Father except through him.

"We are one family from the beginning, with one heavenly Father, one path to eternal life, and one life in which to choose that one path. You can cling to the lies of the spirits who deceived your ancestors—my ancestors too, some of them—if you choose, brothers. But you'll walk right into hell with them! Ask Moses. Moses, tell us. Tell us!"

And I sat down.

The Delaware giant arose. He pointed to the center of his tattooed chest at a skillfully painted turtle, the sign of his own clan.

"I am of the Lenape tribe of Unami—the Turtle," he declared proudly. The Delaware have always called themselves *Lenni Lenape*—The Original People. It was some of us English folks who started calling them Delaware, after the river upon which they lived (and which we named in honor of Thomas West, Baron De La Warr, first governor of Virginia).

"It is said that upon the turtle's back the world rests," continued Moses, "for it was upon the turtle that the pregnant Mother of Our World's Creator took refuge when she fell through the sky in the days before The Beginning. And the world will never die so long as the turtle swims upon the Everlasting Waters with the world upon its back. But if it should dive, the world will drown as in the days of the Great Flood. These are the words of my father." The big Delaware lifted his eyes to the ceiling and turned his ear to the sound of the falling rain. "But the turtle will not dive," he said at last, "for the words of God declare that the world will end in fire. My father did not tell me this, but my father did not know the Lamb nor have the words of God in a Book upon his table. The Lamb walks these woods like a spirit," said the Delaware, looking into our faces as he spoke, "and he fears neither man nor wolf. His words are the only true and everlasting words, and he comes to give his medicine to all who will follow him."

"I do not need his medicine!" declared Caleb from his seat in the shadows. But he said no more.

"His medicine is strong, Narragansett," said Moses quietly. "It saves the soul from the fires to come. The fire that devours the forest and the earth, as well as the fire that burns forever in hell."

"I do not believe in hell!" declared the powwow.

"Do you believe in love?" asked Moses.

"Speak to me of love," Caleb challenged.

The Delaware seemed to ignore the Narragansett as he opened his stove to feed it more fuel from the wood that lay stacked against the chimney. Then he took our mugs out into the rain to wash them. He was gone for a good bit of time. When he returned, he gave us each our mugs, and they were filled to the brim with fresh water from the skies. "Drink," he said simply, raising his own cup to his lips.

"Speak to me of love," Caleb repeated.

"Love is the way of the Lamb," said Moses at last. "Love is humbling yourself to wash your brother's cup as a woman would do in serving her man. Love is blessing instead of cursing. It is doing good to those who do evil to you. It is forgiving your enemies, praying for your enemies."

"No man has such love," declared Caleb from his shadows.

"The Lamb has such love," said Moses, "for he laid down his life even for his enemies. I was his enemy. I am now his friend."

Caleb leapt to his feet. Moses gave him the floor.

"Where is this love among the followers of the Lamb?" Caleb challenged. "I see little! For they fight among themselves like children arguing over the colour of a bird that has flown suddenly over their heads! They divide into tribes and camps over disagreements on how to worship their God, and they build their steepled forts to keep each other out. They write books against one another. They make laws against one another. They stand up in their churches and preach against one another.

When God's Spirit comes among them to cause them to dance, they argue over whether God ever intended their legs to be used in dancing. And if one dances when another does not, they point the finger of shame. They throw dirt on one another's souls. How can they love their enemies when they have not learned to love their brothers?

"The Indian, even with many gods to argue about if he wished to, lets his brother dance as he will! The Six Nations—the Iroquois, your masters," said Caleb derisively, forgetting, as I began to suppose was his habit, that he was a guest in another man's home, "once fought with one another, but now they are united as one. Though each tribe has its own traditions and dances as it will, the whole of them are more united than all the white nations who crossed the Great Sea to tell us of their one great common God of love!"

My eyes walked the floor with Caleb. It was hard to meet his gaze. His words, as usual, were more than empty rantings. He spoke what he had seen, what any man with eyes could see. And for a moment—a fleeting moment, mind you!—I was ashamed of my race and its religion. But then I thought of the enemy of our souls, and I knew that it was not Christ who should be blamed. Nor was this great disunity of the Church to be laid at the door of every Christian. I despised theological wrangling myself.

And as I recalled how the Great Awakening had swept away—for a time at least—all sectarian labels among Christians, I felt sure that Jesus wasn't done with the work of bringing his children together in a common way. If men could devise a way to make a fire in a house without filling that house with smoke, surely God could cause his people to walk together in love.

Moses was on his feet again. It was turning out to be quite an interesting and enlightening evening. With such entertaining teachers, who needed Robert Hazard's library?

"The Moravians preach unity among all brethren," said the big Delaware. "We speak of it wherever God moves our feet. We do not believe that men must think alike to live in love—only that they must follow the Lamb together."

"Can I stick my toe in these waters for a minute?" asked Connie Joe, who had been puffing on his pipe silently for quite some time.

Moses nodded and seated himself again.

"My words won't last long enough for me to bother gettin' up," said Joe with a wave of his crooked arm. "I only want to ask about this Lamb. I's heard tell 'bout the turtle, of course. Used to pile dirt on its back myself to see if I could start up a small world of my own. Didn't amount to much, as you can imagine. But what's this Lamb that yer talkin' about, Great Hill? And what's it got to do with Jesus and the heavenly Father?"

Moses rose, lifting his painted visage like the proud warrior and strong doctor he once was, and said, "Jesus is the Lamb of God who takes away the sins of the world. Like the captive who is tortured by his foes, whose dying song brings an end to the blood feud between tribes, Jesus is the tortured Lamb whose death song brings peace between God and those who hate God. Like the sacrifices that we make—with or without blood—to honor and to satisfy the spirits, the blood of Jesus honored the heavenly Father and satisfied his heartcry for vengeance against a world at war against him.

"Though I have never seen a lamb, I have been told that it is a small animal once used in sacrifice by the tribes of God's own Original People. And that is why Jesus is called the Lamb. He is no animal, of course. He is a man. But he gave himself up to the Great Sacrifice, as a lamb to be slaughtered unto God. It was done long ago, with much strong medicine, and needs never to be done again. One sacrifice that pays for all the sins in each man's heart and every evil thing men have ever done. One death of one man so that many might live. So that many might know the Father in heaven. So that many souls might be saved from the fire. And this is what we tell our brothers in the woods. This is the message of love and the Lamb. One sacrifice forever, for all who will believe."

"God sends his rain upon the good and the evil alike," I thought aloud.

"And no man needs to dance for it, this rain from God," said Moses. "The blood of the Lamb rains freely down upon the forest, to cleanse the heart, to paint the soul in new colours. The colours of love—and not war."

"Love and not war," echoed Caleb strangely.

"My bow and my gun," said Moses, pointing to the weapons that lay against the wall, "will nevermore be raised against another man."

"Not even the French?" asked Connie Joe as a polite reminder of where the big Delaware's enmities ought rightly to rest.

"Not even the French," answered Moses firmly. And I found my own English heart growling against the big man's declaration. "As we have said here tonight—and Longshot said it well—one blood runs within us all," said Moses. "One man and one woman were the father and mother of us all. The Lamb died for all, to turn the hearts of all nations to the Father in Heaven. How can a man follow the Lamb if he raises his club against his brother? How can I say that I love my brother if I run the warpath against him?

"My Lord commands me to rejoice when men speak against me because I follow the Lamb. And if a man strikes me in the face, the Lamb commands me to turn my other cheek to receive a second blow if a second blow is coming. But if I rise up at the first blow and return that blow myself, I am like any other man who lifts his pride above the Lamb's command to love. I will not rise up against the Lamb. For I am no longer Great Hill that I must rescue my name from under the feet of my enemies. I am Moses, and my hope is in God."

Caleb stood, but only to pace, muttering to himself in Narragansett. We sat and watched him for some time. Then Connie Joe broke the spell.

"Vengeance belongs to the heavenly Father," he said. "That's what I's heard for many long years. And I's been around for many long years. I give up vengeance—yessir, I did—and waited on the Lord. Rode back and forth to Philadelphia while I waited. Hard thing, waitin' on the seat of a Dutch wagon! But I didn't rise up to fix up my reputation when I might have. No, I didn't. I give up on that eye-for-an-eye, scalp-for-a-scalp stuff. Vowed to quit killin' even the beasts of the woods! Told Longshot all about it just the other day, didn't I, Longshot? You've known about it, Great Hill—all these lies 'bout me. But God's right now dustin' these lies right off me, yes he is! Though they's clung to my name for more moons than I can count, I'm free from these lies! The heavenly Father's a God to be counted on. And I thank the spirits for that!"

"Not even the French," murmured Caleb in English as his circuit brought him back within earshot.

Not even the French, my thoughts echoed. And I marveled at the mighty change that God had wrought within this giant Delaware.

"My horse is standing in the rain!" cried Caleb, stopping suddenly in his march across the longhouse.

"I took him under shelter with the rest of the horses," said Moses, "when I washed and filled our cups. I gave him grain and water. He is a marvelous animal!"

"Thank you," said the Narragansett, his dark eyes glistening in the singular light of a candle that burned upon the table of the reborn Delaware. I saw through those eyes, for a moment, and into the heart of an old friend. Within that heart echoed the loud and fervent prayers of Netop from a clapboard church far away. Within that heart I imagined an old, dark woman sitting by a window reading the Holy Scriptures in an ancient language. Within that heart, I heard the voice of an Indian child crying—Caleb himself, I thought. Within that heart, I heard the guns of war—and I prayed for God to win.

We talked all night.

As the dawn raised light upon a still-weeping world, we vowed to close our eyes at last—for a few hours' sleep, at least. But Moses asked me first to read aloud from my prayer book. As nobody had any particular objection, I thumbed the book open. My eye fell upon the Prayers and Thanksgivings section for special occasions. The prayer for fair weather seemed rather appropriate, so I jumped right into it.

"O Almighty Lord God—who for the sin of man didst once drown all the world, except eight persons, and afterward of thy great mercy didst promise never to destroy it so again—we humbly beseech thee that although we for our iniquities have worthily deserved a plague of rain and waters, yet upon our true repentance thou wilt send us such weather as that we may receive the fruits of the earth in due seasons and learn both by thy punishment to amend our lives, and for thy clemency to give thee praise and glory; through Jesus Christ our Lord. Amen."

"Eight people lived through that old flood!" said Connie Joe, seemingly awakened by the revelation. "Noah and who else?"

"His family," said Moses groggily.

"Which iniquities we got to repent of," asked the Susquehannock, "in order to get the sun shinin'?"

"Search your heart," yawned the big Delaware, turning upon his bed-mats to face the wall.

"Can I wait till I get some sleep?" asked Connie Joe, sounding rather worried about the whole affair. But Moses was snoring. "The heavenly Father'll understand," I heard Joe mutter to himself. "His Son was a real man. Had to sleep also, I wouldn't wonder, what with all the work he was carryin' on."

The last thing I remember was the sound of waking birds mixed with the gentle patter of the rain upon the longhouse roof.

PART THREE

A Westward Wandering

"… They began to suspect me, and said I was come to settle the Indians' lands and they knew I should never go Home again safe…"

—Christopher Gist

CHAPTER ELEVEN

One Leg after Another

Wednesday, October 31, 1750

We set out from Colonel Thomas Cresap's, at the Old Town on the Potomac in Maryland, and went along an old Shawanese Indian path north thirty miles and east about eleven miles. The horses carried things quite well that day, one leg after another.

Caleb claimed the rear guard, preferring to ride alone more often than not. Connie Joe and I moved out ahead together when we could, but most of the time the path only let us pass through the woods in single file. The packhorses—three of them, heavy laden—plodded behind Joe and me.

A little over two weeks had passed since Caleb had found us at the longhouse of Moses. We'd stayed on with the Delaware for another day, dressing the deer Joe had shot and helping Moses pack up his few belongings on a small cart he had in a shed behind his house. We even loaded on that fine stove. The retired powwow was closing up his longhouse and moving to a Moravian Indian settlement at the forks of the Mahoning and Lehigh rivers, called Gnadenhütten. One of his wives (his first squaw, I believe) had converted to Christ through the Moravians and was already at the mission town with their children. Another of his wives left him when Great Hill became Moses. She apparently saw little future in being married to a doctor without a practice.

Just in case my own squaw was beginning to wonder if I was still in the country, I sent her a packet of letters from Cresap's—little notes and longer missives I had written over the past weeks (and one poem I'd scribbled while at sea from Connecticut to New York). Cresap also promised to have some window glass delivered to my house with that new Dutch stove that Moses was going to have sent on down to Old Town. All this stuff would be gathered and carried off by horse and wagon from the Ohio Company's new storehouse at Will's Creek, only a few miles from Cresap's.

I wouldn't be home for Christmas—or anytime soon after—and I wanted Sarah and the children to have these few gifts for their comfort and their pleasure. In one of my letters, I instructed Richard on how to hook up the stove, and I knew he and Thomas would get right to work on the windows. I sent along some Indian dolls for Anne and Violette— girls never get too old for dolls.

The day before Connie Joe and Caleb and I finally set out for the Ohio, we outfitted ourselves and our animals at Will's Creek. Then we spent the night at Cresap's and started out early the next morn.

Friday, November 2, 1750

"Can't go on any further, Joe," I said hoarsely, climbing weakly from Neeyesee's back. The fever forced me to find somewhere to lay myself down, and the Lord provided a dry, leafy bed beneath an overhang of rock that jutted from the wooded hillside. The evening was cold, but sweat beaded my face and arms. My eyes ached. My head pounded. For two days, I'd traveled sick, and I knew I had to bed down now and let my body fight this thing. Otherwise, my companions might have to tie my cold carcass to my horse and lead it home—that's how bad I felt.

Connie Joe gathered wood for a fire. "Good a place as any for the night," said the Susquehannock, rummaging the darkening forest for some decent tinder. "Water and some grass for the horses about two whoops west and plenty of cover for three men under that rock. 'Course Caleb'll probably sleep on top of the rock! Or maybe up a tree, this time."

The powwow, besides riding behind each day, had been bedding down apart from us. He shared our meals with us—providing two ducks for a feast on our second day out—but then he'd retire to some lonely spot to sit in solitude. "My eyes are younger eyes than Connie Joe's," Caleb told me. "And my ears are keener than yours, Christopher. I will be our watchman." And he'd find a high rock or an elevated spot upon some hill and settle himself right there. I decided to leave him to his privacy, not caring to stir up any hornets that might be wintering in his soul.

He still had said nothing of the situation back in Rhode Island. Sooner or later, as it pleased God, I'd draw him out. For now, I was glad just to have him along. And he seemed—in a very private way—to be glad of it himself.

I heard the snort of a Narragansett pacer in the woods beyond the hill. Not my Neeyesee.

Metewis and Caleb came slowly up the trail, dark and barely visible amidst the black, bared forest that stood between our camp and the dimly lit western sky. The powwow dismounted without a word and set his bow against the rock. He pulled the limp form of a dead animal from the back of his horse and lifted it by its hind legs into the light of our fire. A small gray wolf—shot through the heart.

"Bow and arrow!" Connie Joe grinned. "Like a real Indian!"

"We haven't run into any real Indians yet," I muttered from my bed among the leaves. Caleb shot me a dark glance. Connie Joe just laughed.

"Don't know too many real Indians anymore," said the Susquehannock as he examined the dead wolf. "But Caleb could run with any of 'em, if he had to!"

"If he had to," I said, half-delirious in my fever.

"I will dance for your healing," offered the powwow sincerely as he knelt beside me. He put his hand upon my brow and wiped the sweat from my cheeks.

"How much will it cost me?" I jested weakly.

Caleb knew my heart. He took no offense at my words. In fact, his countenance brightened a bit at the thought of an exchange of wit. Or maybe it was the fire that flared up just then—I don't really know. I don't remember the night all too clearly, just snatches of sensations. Fire and shivers and sweat. The odor of old leaves. The smell of wolf flesh over flame. The marvelous sensation of cool water at my lips. The night breezes in my face. Then the taste of some nasty broth that Joe gave me. Got sick to my stomach and threw it up.

"I will dance for you," came the chant from the center of the earth as my head spun round and round.

"What'll it cost me?" I mumbled repeatedly in my daze.

"It will cost your soul," Caleb answered. Or maybe it wasn't Caleb. Couldn't have been Caleb. Didn't sound like Caleb. I really don't know.

But Caleb never danced. I thanked God for that. Instead, the powwow read me my prayers. I asked for one for healing. The closest thing in my book was for "any common plague," Caleb said. That would do just fine under the circumstances, I told him.

"O Almighty God," read the powwow in perfect English, "who in thy wrath didst send a plague upon thine own people in the wilderness for their obstinate rebellion against Moses and Aaron—and also in the time of King David didst slay with the plague of pestilence threescore and ten thousand, and yet remembering thy mercy didst save the rest—have pity upon us miserable sinners who now are visited with great sickness and mortality. That like as thou didst then accept of an atonement and didst command the destroying angel to cease from punishing, so it may now please thee to withdraw from us this plague and grievous sickness— through Jesus Christ our Lord. Amen."

"Does the heavenly Father understand all them words?" I dimly heard Connie Joe ask. "Seems to me that when a man needs help, one loud wail and a good sacrifice ought to do it!"

Saturday, November 3, 1750

I grew better in the morning—thanks be to God—and we were able to move about eight miles to the north along the Juniata, a large branch of the Susquehanna. We stayed there all night.

Before reading prayers, I caught up on writing in my journal. The Ohio Company had instructed me to keep an exact and particular account of all my proceedings, and so I wrote down the doings of each long day in order to be able to make a true report of my journey at its end.

Sunday, November 4, 1750

Crossed the Juniata and went up its course southwest about sixteen miles.

Monday, November 5, 1750

Continued on the same course southwest about six miles to the top of a large mountain called the Allegheny Mountain. There our path turned and we went northwest six more miles before setting up camp.

Tuesday, Wednesday, Thursday, November 6, 7, 8, 1750

Snow fell thick and wet, with intermittent rain and sleet, for three full days. The trees on our mountain were quickly covered with a heavy winter coat of dripping white. Branches groaned and snapped under their burdens, falling to the forest floor in sudden avalanches of sliding snow and splintered limbs. The weather was such that we dared not travel from our encampment. But I wandered off into the cold rain one morning and shot a young bear, and thus we had provision enough while we waited out the storm.

"A bit wilder than Roger Williams's fenced plantation, eh, Caleb?" I commented during our first meal of roast bear. Our fire was a well-trained animal by this time, having been coached and encouraged and fed for over a day and a half. We kept a continually renewed stock of wood sitting close enough to the blaze that it would be constantly drying while waiting its turn upon the pyre. Our tent consisted of a canvas stretched over our heads upon the bottom limbs of a marvelous pine that—of itself—nearly kept the winter off our heads. It was not at all an unpleasant shelter from which to watch the heavens fall.

"My island, though it is only a small canoe in the middle of an English sea, is wild enough. But I do not miss it," said Caleb, who was warming up to our company at last. He stared into the fire, a tired light in his dark eyes. "It is good to walk where wolves run," he said, "and to lay myself upon the fallen needles of a pine whose head nearly brushes the cheeks of Keesuckquand the Sun. When this great tree looks down from its high hill, it sees no man at its feet, only the mountains and valleys and rivers that run out of sight beyond the horizon. This is a good land. A land as all lands should be, unfettered by walls of stone, uncluttered by barns or mills, untouched by the axe or the hoe of the white man."

"Real Indians like this kind of ground," grinned Connie Joe, trying awful hard to chew his meat to make it fit to swallow. "But real Indians have to swing an axe too. And their squaws gotta hoe the fields or there won't be no corn in the kettle!"

"Do you not care that the ways of our fathers have been wrenched

from our hands?" Caleb asked the Susquehannock. "Do you think so little of your ancestors that you hold them in jest?"

Connie Joe screwed up his lined face in a ludicrous frown, chewing
right along like a cow with its cud. His misty eyes narrowed as his
thoughts brewed. "Please don't think 'bout me that way, Caleb," said the
old Indian at last. "I've been around long enough to *be* an ancestor."

"Just how old are you, Connie Joe?" I asked, laying more wood on
the fire.

"So old I can't remember," Joe answered with a twinkle in his eye,
"and ain't nobody left alive who saw me slide out on my first born day!
Guess I'm not as old as this here tree we're sittin' under, but I guess I'm
not much younger."

I settled myself contently upon the ground, back against the massive,
ancient trunk that rose out of sight in the white squall above us.

"The river runs all day, Caleb," said the Susquehannock. "And when
the day is done, it keeps on runnin' all night. Sometimes the waters are
full of fish, sometimes they ain't. Sometimes they run warm, sometimes
cold. And sometimes the seasons tear through the forest and mess things
up so that the old river cuts itself a new path and runs off in another
direction entirely. I's knowed some streams that's changed their ways five
or six times. But they keep on runnin' all day, all night."

Caleb was silent, attentive.

"I see myself and my people like that old river," continued the wrinkled sage. "The seasons come and go, and the winds blow and the heavy
snows fall. The old ways bend over and pull up their roots—and down
they go! And the people have to tread a new path around the fallen trees.
And that new path might take 'em up a hill they hasn't never seen before.
They'll give that hill a new name. And then their world is just a little bigger than before. A little different. But they'll keep runnin' just the same.
The thing is to keep runnin'."

"Maybe there is a new god upon that hill," Caleb said absently.

"Prob'ly is," said Connie Joe.

"Real Indians drink rum," declared Joe the next morning, rubbing his
eyes in the whiteness of the new day. "Wish I had me some!"

"Rum drinks real Indians," said Caleb grimly, "and then spits them out in the dirt at its feet!"

"Caleb doesn't drink rum," I yawned, brushing the snow off my blankets.

"Real Indians drink rum!" asserted Joe anew, slapping his leathered hand against his crooked leg to chase the pain that always plagued him upon waking.

"Rum scorns real Indians," argued Caleb, rising from his thick bed of pine needles. The needles clung to his dark flesh like the quills of a porcupine. It was a humorous sight, and I almost commented on it, but the moment didn't seem quite ripe for a jest. I turned my head so that the men wouldn't see me smiling, and I coughed to cover a laugh. "Rum lies like an English trader!" Caleb railed. "It steals into your house like a drunken Indian! It takes your reason and your honor and your pride and burns them in its fire! Then it comes back again to take the whole house and all the land upon which it is built! Soon it steals the soul! *Ankapi!* I curse the brew! No real Indian should even look upon it!"

"I'd be happy to drink some *without* lookin', right 'bout now," said Connie Joe, ignoring Caleb's hot sermon.

"You are a fool!" cried the Narragansett suddenly, striding over to where the Susquehannock sat scratching his head.

"No doubt," said Connie Joe quietly, looking up at the tensed pow-wow. "But you can thank yer spirits I's an agreeable sort of fool. You can thank the heavenly Father, while yer at it, that I don't throw tomahawks no more. Used to be real good at it 'fore I was an ancestor, 'specially when folks called me names."

Caleb caught himself. I could see him soften. His head fell a bit and his lips quivered. He was fighting. I was praying. *Can I pray for wisdom for Caleb?* I wondered. *He sure can use some!*

"My people have been ravaged by rum," explained the Narragansett with a deep sigh that sent his breath into the air like a cloud. "It makes the fire of anger burn hot within me to hear a man speak of rum as you have, Connie Joe. I wish you would not do so in my presence. But I have been the fool this morning more than you, and I have dishonored myself."

"I forgive you," said Joe simply. "And I'll try to keep my mouth shut about this partic'lar subject in the future. But let me ask you somethin' first, Real Indian—you ever take a scalp?"

Caleb had not.

"Ever run a warpath?"

Never.

"Ever send an arrow or a bullet into a man? Ever lay a warclub to another man's skull? Ever seen it happen?"

Ever pull a knife across a man's throat? I wondered to myself.

Caleb shook his head, No.

Connie Joe shook his head also, sadly, thoughtfully. "I used to drink rum to forget," muttered the old Susquehannock. "Now I drinks it so I can remember."

Caleb sat down beside Connie Joe. I raised myself from my bed, fed some dry needles to our smouldering fire, and coaxed it to a semblance of life. The Indians were silent as they leaned into the waking blaze. Caleb absently brushed his porcupine coat from his arms and legs. Connie Joe rubbed his foggy eyes with his wrinkled fists.

I imagined the two of them sitting alone at the fire, chanting like real Indians, talking like real Indians, dreaming and thinking like real Indians. I remembered myself sitting at just such a winter's fire, a wide-eyed child who had followed his father into the wide, white, howling wilderness. I saw that strong smile that was Pop's constant companion, felt his gentle hand in my hair, saw my head leaning into his breast as the sparks of recollection warmed the cold forest.

"What do you remember?" asked the Narragansett to the Susquehannock.

"War," said the old hunter grimly. "Revenge. Torture. Hunger. Blood on the snow. Blood in the rivers. Heads on poles. Scalps on belts. The wailin' of mournin' women. Real Indians killin' real Indians. The way it used to be."

Caleb said nothing.

"And the games at harvest," sighed the old man wistfully with a bent and toothless smile. "The great councils. Long speeches and wonderful stories 'round the fire. The strength and the medicine of youth. The excitement of the hunt. The rattle and the chant of the medicine man. The joy of children bein' born into the tribe. Singin'. Gamblin'. Gamin'.

Runnin'. Dancin'. It's been a million miles of moons since these old legs really danced! Like an Indian dances—a real Indian."

Caleb looked to me suddenly, as if surprised to see me there. I kept nursing the fire.

"Love," said Connie Joe. "I 'member lots of love. My mother and my father. My brothers. The wife of my youth. My children. Where are my children? Gone south. Gone west. Gone to the English. Gone to the French. Or just gone. The pine drops its cones and God only knows where the seeds roll!" The old hunter spat into the fire. "Let's have us some of that bear for breakfast," he said.

"It's buried under that snow pile over there," I said, pointing to where I'd put the meat up in cold storage.

Caleb sighed.

"God only knows where the seeds roll," Connie Joe repeated. "Ough! These legs!" He slapped his chaps as he rose to his feet. "I's countin' on tradin' 'em in when I get to heaven, boys!" he announced. "And I *am* steerin' my wagon toward heaven, boys!" he declared. "'Cause the heavenly Father's Son wants to see me there! That's what I heard and that's what I believe—and that's why I forgive folks, and that's why I ain't throwin' tomahawks no more!"

"This God who sent his son," said Caleb, standing now beside the wobbling Susquehannock. "Does he not declare that rum drunkards will not see his face?"

"Rightly so!" declared Connie Joe. "But rum drinkers and rum drunkards are of two different tribes! I's a natural-born member of the former. And I haven't got no more use for the latter than the heavenly Father does. But let's eat!" And with that, he hobbled off to dig our breakfast out of the snow.

Friday and Saturday, November 9 and 10, 1750

Set out at last northwest and traveled eight miles in heavy rains. We crossed a creek of the Conemaugh and found an old abandoned Indian cabin where we stayed the night. The next day brought more rain and snow, which cleared at length by evening.

Sunday, November 11 through Saturday, November 17, 1750

Through the snow and over paths barely passable, we traveled slowly, one leg after another. The horses had a workout from one camp to the next. Though they had plenty of water to slake their thirst, the going was rough. The Narragansett pacers trod on like warhorses, but I saw them getting weary. The packs sometimes looked as if they'd like to mutiny, but they kept on coming up behind us. On our third day out of the old Indian cabin, Connie Joe's nag started wobbling like the old Susquehannock himself.

We crossed two forks of a creek of the Quemahoning, and I shot a turkey. If our mounts had been meat-eaters, I'd have shot them a turkey too, but we still had a fair supply of grain laid up in our bags for them.

We crossed a great laurel mountain so thick with the viney growth that if there'd been no path, we'd have had to turn back and find another way. I wished it were spring and the mountains were all in flower. John Bartram's celebrated gardens on the Schuylkill would look like a mere flowerpot compared to this acre of God's earth with the blossoms full.

The forest went on and on, and I dreamed I was a buck all wild and wandering, full of the natural strength of the earth and its "medicine." But then I reckoned that a buck might wander while never knowing the joy of wandering, only the pride of it, the constancy, the inevitability of it. I rejoiced that God had made man in his own image, not only able to walk the woods as the buck does, but able to dream about it too. To write about it. To sing about it. To tell tales about it around the campfire. And to leave it behind if he wished—for the city or the sea or the farm or the hearth of home and the laughter of those he loves. I missed Sarah awful sometimes, but not with the kind of longing that made me want to turn my horse around. It was the kind of longing that a redeemed soul has for heaven—deeply thankful for the promise of a bright day ahead, strengthened by that promise for the hard path at hand. I could feel my Sarah's prayers. I held her hand in my heart.

The trees. They rose higher than church steeples into the winter sky. Ancient, dormant towers of oak and maple and ash and elm. Pine and spruce, green at their heads and brittle and dry at their feet, stretched their arms nearly out of sight above us, trunks thick enough that six men could stand around one and barely be able to link hands. Giants that must have stood for a millennium. Beneath them, tiny saplings slept and dreamed of spring and a chance to begin their own slow, eternal journey toward the heavens.

Sometimes we traveled in silence. Sometimes we sang. Connie Joe knew songs in three languages and several dialects: English, German, Susquehannock, and a marvelous mixture of forest tongues. I led us in Anglican hymns and some Baptist tunes I'd learned during the Great Awakening. We all sang lullabies that we'd heard as small children. Caleb had us chanting in Narragansett. We smoked. We laughed. The winter fled our hearts, though it ruled the world around us.

And it ruled with an iron hand. The rain was frigid. The snow fell wet and heavy. I took ill again and knew that we must find a camp where I could lay me down.

On the wide bottoms of the Kiscominatis Creek, on the north side, sits an old Indian town. Like most old Indian towns, it has worn many names in its long day. Joe called it *Laurel-hanne,* which means "middle stream" in the Delaware tongue. The English called it Loyal Hannin Old Town. We passed by it on our course and traveled little over a mile more until we came to the hunting camp of an old friend of Connie Joe's. I was grateful to get off my horse and lie by a fire in a house made with hands.

The Indian to whom this camp belonged spoke good English, and he was as hospitable as I've always found the forested Indians to be. The red children of the woods open their doors more widely and gladly than the white children of the plowed field and the sidewalked city. It's a strange thing, and an embarrassing reality, that many who call themselves Christians live less like Christ—as far as hospitality and the willingness to share what is theirs with others—than the heathen of the wild woods.

The weather being bad and I unwell, we stayed with this good fellow all day, and he mapped out a way for us that would take us to his own town, Shannopin's Town, about sixty miles west.

After a good night's rest—thanks be to God—we set out southwest and traveled nearly ten miles. Another night and a fresh start took us by the same course fifteen miles farther to an Indian camp called Cockey's Cabin. But my sickness had traveled with me, and our arrival at the camp is but a sweaty, blurred moment in my memory. I climbed off Neeyesee, shaking and shivering, but that's all I recall of the night.

CHAPTER TWELVE

Confession at Cockey's Cabin

Sunday, November 18, 1750

He's dancin'," I heard someone say. And I saw Big Bill Moose whooping and high-stepping around a red pole. Netop was right behind him, naked but for a loin cloth and an English hat. Connie Joe was there too, much younger in his bearing and with a full mouth of crooked, yellow teeth. His face was painted to look like an eagle. A vulture's beak was tied over his nose. He was drunk. He had a tomahawk in one hand and a Bible in the other. More Indians joined them and the whole scene became a mad revel, with white men and black men suddenly dancing in their midst.

Then they started falling and convulsing and groaning. I could hear a dozen preachers shouting about the judgment of God and the mercy of Christ. Women appeared in the crowd, weeping and wringing their hands. The sound of loud singing seemed to rise from the ground, and it grew to such an overwhelming pitch that nothing else could be heard. It was a congregational singing of the psalms—but all out of tune! "He's dancin'," I heard someone whisper in my ear, and I turned and saw Caleb sitting next to me in a pew. He was pointing to a raised pulpit near the red pole. A man was whirling like a top upon the platform. It was Caleb also, dancing all alone as men lay sprawled upon the ground at the foot of the pulpit. I turned back to speak to the Caleb who had whispered in my ear, but he was gone.

"*Noonamautuckquawhe! Trust me!*" cried the Caleb who was dancing.

"Tahenautatu? What will it cost me?" I shouted from my pew. But it wasn't a pew now. I was sitting on Neeyesee in an open field. Caleb was dancing on the horizon, a strange, dark, darting form against a shimmering red sky. Was that fire beyond him?

"Tocketussinommin?" cried the dancing shadow. *"What do you think of the weather?"*

"Tahki," I replied. *"It is cold weather."*

He kept dancing.

"Nuckqusquatch. I am cold," I said to Neeyesee. *"Nummauchnem. I am sick."*

"I will dance for you!" shouted the leaping shadow from the writhing, red horizon.

"He's dancin'," someone whispered in my ear again. It was Neeyesee.

"I didn't know you could speak," I said to my mount.

"Cowweke," said the horse in Narragansett. *"Sleep, sleep."*

And then I woke. Connie Joe was sitting next to my bed, half asleep in a curious and clever rocking chair made of slats and bent branches.

"Joe," I said weakly, and the old Indian turned to me with a start.

"He's dancin'," said the Susquehannock, looking at me with a strange light in his misty eyes.

"Caleb is dancing for my healing," I said grimly.

"How'd you know that!" asked the Susquehannock.

"You—he—someone's been telling me that in my dreams," I muttered. "Can you get me some water?" He brought me a mug and offered to put it to my lips. I took the mug in my own hand instead and forced myself to sit up in the bed.

"Tell him to stop," I said, draining the cup. I could hear the Narragansett chanting somewhere outside the house.

"Are you well?" asked Connie Joe.

"Not nearly!" I coughed. "But I'd rather be sick than have demons dancing on the blankets! Tell him to stop."

"He's doin' it fer you, Longshot!" said the old Indian a bit sharply. "How we gonna walk these woods with you fallin' off yer horse half the time and sleepin' the other half in order to whup yer fever! Either let him dance, or do somethin' 'bout it yerself!"

"Tell him to stop," I insisted.

"You've got to promise me you won't dance for anything—healing, rain, snow, sun, anything—while you're with me, Caleb," I said, eating my supper at the table of Cockey the Delaware. "Promise me!"

"There are no English doctors in these woods," said the powwow.

"God is in these woods," I said.

"I haven't seen him," said the powwow. "Is not your God seated on a throne in the seventh heaven? That is a long way to go for your healing."

"Much too far," said Cockey, pushing his thoughts into the discussion. This was his cabin I was sleeping in. His town. He figured his cards should be on the table too. I reckoned that was only right. But I was too tired for a theological argument. I could barely pray for wisdom.

"Too far?" was the best I could return.

"If a man was to come into my house while I was gone and begin to beat you while you lay upon your sickbed, who would you cry out to for mercy?" asked the Delaware. "Would you send a messenger to your sons upon the Yadkin, or would you parley with the man who was beating you?" I really didn't have a ready answer for that one, so I waited for the Indian to play his full hand. "You would beg your attacker to beat you no more, of course!" he said. "And so we pray to the Devil to leave off affecting us with evil and sickness."

"Chepi is near," said Caleb.

"I'll get better as the Lord prospers me," I declared weakly to the Narragansett and the Delaware and to my own faltering soul. "I don't want what the Devil offers! He comes only to kill and to steal and to destroy!"

But what if I didn't recover? What if I limped along through the wilderness falling off my horse half the time and sleeping the rest, as Connie Joe said? What if I had to turn back from my assignment altogether? And did it matter? *Even if he slay me, still I'll trust him*, Job says of God in the Scriptures. God would raise me up as it pleased him. I would trust him. Nothing else made any sense. Certainly not this traffic with demons!

"The Devil," muttered Caleb, pushing his chair away from the table. "The Devil with you!" And he strode from the cabin, slamming the door behind him.

"Touchy fella," said Connie Joe. "But his dancin' was for you, Longshot."

"I'm going to sweat this fever out," I said, rising wearily to my feet.

"You been sweatin' all day!" declared Connie Joe.

"Indian style," I explained.

"*Pimook!*" cried the Delaware happily. "*We go to sweat!*"

Cockey's sweathouse—used by all the male Indians and some of the traders at the village—was dug partway into the side of a thick-wooded hill a short distance from the town. The exposed part of the house was covered with split plank and earth. A small door allowed men to creep into it on all fours. On the outside were piles of stones about the size of turnips, and some of the men of Cockey's cabin were appointed to keep the stones heated on certain days each week. Indians aren't as dirty as most folks think they are. In fact, in spite of their greasing and painting themselves all over, they keep themselves cleaner than some white folks I've known. Most Indians generally retire to their sweathouses once or twice weekly—not just when they're ill. It's their way of taking a bath, you might say. And the sweating cleans their flesh as well as any soap and water you'll get in any city of the English.

The men have their own sweathouse, and the women have a separate oven in a different direction. Some sweathouses fit no more than two men. Some, like Cockey's, accommodate as many as six. The women don't sweat quite as often as the men, and in that they differ from the English considerably. My Sarah and her girls take baths so often that I think I've cut an acre of wood along the Yadkin just to heat water to keep them clean!

Connie Joe and Cockey joined me in the hothouse. Caleb too. It was sweltering in there, but that was the point. The stones, once heated outside the house, were rolled into the middle of it, and we took our places in a circle around the hot pile. We carried our sweating potions in with us—

a strong-tasting concoction of roots and plants that promotes the most profuse sweating as well as quenches the thirst that a man gets while he's squat-
ting around all those steaming stones. I almost fainted at one point, but the
sweating gave me ease, and my fever abated. The powwow declared that the
spirits had moved upon me. The Delaware bragged about the natural
advantages of traditional Indian medicine and the peculiar efficacy of his
personal sweathouse. And I just thanked God that I felt better.

"If hell's hotter'n that sweathouse," said Connie Joe as we later lay
upon our mats in Cockey's cabin, "then I isn't even gonna go there for a
short visit!"

"Hell is hotter," I promised. "And there's no such thing as visiting the
place. Once you're there, you're a permanent resident—a captive who'll
never see home again. And there's no sticking your head out the door for
fresh air!"

"Is this so?" asked the Delaware.

"Ho, Cockey!" blurted Connie Joe suddenly, raising himself up on his
wobbly elbows. "You know Great Hill the medayoo?"

"Great Hill has strong medicine," pondered Cockey.

"Not no more!" said old Joe. "Not the devilish kind of medicine, anyhow! He's run away from this hot old hell altogether by followin' the Lamb
of God who takes away everybody's sins. That's what he said, and that's
what I believe he's done. I seen him. We all here seen him only a few weeks
back. He's Moses now. A Moravian. He can sure tell you about hell and the
Devil! Says he's whupped the Devil real good, and he's never gonna call on
his old spirits again. Moses! New name. New path in the woods. Happens
this way more now than ever—'specially when the Heavenly Spirit starts
blowin' in the woods."

I thought right then that Connie Joe—with a little theological coach-
ing—would make a great preacher. Better than Netop. Better than
Davenport. My heart went out to the old Indian. The heavenly Father
might have been smiling down on us all right then, the way I felt.
Something welled up in me, and I stood up to give it more room to move.

"Connie Joe's right," I said. "God is blowing in these woods. He's not
just sitting on some throne in heaven, waiting for folks to find their way
there. He's walking this land with a wampum belt in his hands. That belt
is called the Bible, and it tells every man about the love of God. Moses

has one of those Bibles, and I wish I had one to leave here with you, Cockey. You could read it for yourself or have some English trader read it for you."

"I've heard of it," said the Delaware. "Is it not a white man's book?"

"It is a white man's book," declared the powwow. "And it speaks of the white man's God. But are not our father's traditions good enough for the Indian? Should the Delaware give up his father's wisdom for the wisdom of a white tribe that lived beyond the great seas?"

"I do not want the white man's book," said Cockey with a wave of his hand. "I only want the white man's money, the white man's guns, and the white man's rum," he grinned. Cockey's town was a trading town, well-known by both the English and the French fur traders in their backwoods dealings among the Indians.

"Don't go talkin' 'bout rum 'round this Narragansett," warned Connie Joe cautiously. "He's got some kinda blood feud goin' with *ankapi*."

"And will you sell the white man your town when your rum jug runs dry?" Caleb challenged Cockey. Connie Joe threw up his hands in frustration.

"If he offers me enough," replied the Delaware businessman. "I can always set up a new town elsewhere."

"And how many times will you move your town while the English walk west into your lands?" asked the Narragansett. "How many times have your people moved already?"

"Many," admitted the Delaware. "More than we wished. But I am happy, and the forest goes on forever, does it not?"

"The Narragansett have nowhere to go!" Caleb said. "To the east is the salt sea. To the south is the salt sea. To the north are the Mohawk and the Abenaki and the French. To the west are the English and the Delaware and the rest of the Six Nations. Our lands are gone! Perhaps the forest goes on forever, but how can a man walk in it as his own if others walk there already? And what will you do when the English put their axes to the trees and dig up the earth to make fences that keep you out? You are a fool like this old Susquehannock! He would rather drive a wagon between the cities of the English than sing upon the shores of the rivers of his own people!"

"I give up wagons!" said Connie Joe painfully. "And here I am walkin' the woods like a real Indian. Doggone if this medicine boy doesn't make me want to sharpen my tomahawk!"

"Try it out on me, old man!" said Caleb suddenly, and I saw Connie Joe's eyes widen in surprise. I knew the Susquehannock was no coward. And Caleb was pushing him awfully hard.

"Settle down, Caleb," I said firmly, rolling over on my bed to reach out my hand to my angered friend. "You should have stayed in Rhode Island if all you're going to do is start a war before the French do!"

"Rhode Island," said the Delaware trader with a start. "Narragansett," he recited, as if the name had suddenly taken on new meaning. He sat up in his own bed and leaned toward the scowling powwow. "There is one who has been looking for you," he said.

"What?" cried Caleb, rising to his feet so violently that the Delaware's dogs started barking. "Who? Tell me! Has he been here?"

The night air was cold with that kind of icy stab that cuts right through your coat like a long, sharp knife. And even though I knew it wasn't the wisest thing for me to walk under that weather, I had to have the story from the Narragansett. I insisted. Caleb followed me into the frigid midnight like a dog afraid of being whipped by its master.

"Now spill it, Caleb," I said as we paced the hard-packed snow that lay upon the well-trodden path that encircled the village of Cockey's Cabin. "Tell me everything; I've got a right to know."

The Narragansett strode nervously, tensely, swinging his head from one side of our path to the other, raking the dark woods with his black eyes. Who was he afraid of? What could affect such a hardened man in this way? Did he imagine that some evil spirit followed him? I had never known him to fear any man. And why should he?

"Bill Moose is dead," Caleb said simply, tersely. "Throat slit so deep that his head was almost cut from his body." I winced. Something especially ugly about going that way. Caleb stooped to scoop some snow into his hands. He washed his palms like Pilate. "I didn't kill him," he said, "and I don't know who did." I believed him, for he was never a liar, though I'd more than half-suspected all along that he'd murdered the wicked Indian before chasing me down in the woods.

"Woody One-shot?" I suggested absently. But even as I said it, my heart said no. The old hunter was no murderer.

"Woody's dead too," said Caleb. "Killed the same way."

I was stunned. Who would slaughter these Indians? And why? They were harmless old drunks. Not a shilling to their names. No property besides a leaning, old shack that would fall down on its own if it weren't held up by the pitiful houses on either side of it.

"Someone wanted Moose dead," said Caleb quietly, no longer watching the woods, intent only upon his own thoughts and troubled opinions. "Moose had enemies. He deserved to have enemies. I was his enemy, and he was mine. I would have killed him myself—in fact, I tried. But my medicine would not work. The fly in my bottle escaped. Moose became ill, very ill—but that is all. And he blamed me. I vowed publicly, in my rage against him, to kill him with my own hands—but someone else got to him first. I do not know who. Woody just got in the way somehow, probably trying to help Big Bill."

Hungry wolves howled in the cold forest. I pulled my hat down over my ears to keep the frost from biting them.

"Your father didn't kill that Negro all those years ago," I said, opening the door to some thoughts that were knocking. Caleb stopped suddenly and looked at me with a strange light in his eyes. His lips moved, but he didn't speak. Were his thoughts headed down the same path as mine? "Why are you running if you didn't kill Moose?" I asked.

"The sheriff came looking for me," said Caleb, his breath like clouds in the air between us. "English and Indian alike were blaming me for the murders. I sent my squaw to Netop's, left a note for my mother at Hazard's, and rode Metewis across the Pocatuck to follow you. Nobody's going to hang Caleb Hobomucko for a murder he did not commit!"

"And you think that the magistrates have sent someone to track you down?"

"I thought so—foolishly, in my fear—until now."

"Charlestown is not going to send a man trekking the wilderness for a suspected killer. Not for an Indian who has killed an Indian."

"Of course not."

"Who killed that Negro?"

"Bill Moose …"

"And who else?"

"The man who is following me," decided Caleb on the moment.

"Hazard told me something before you and I left him to ride toward Charlestown," I said to the Narragansett. "He told me that your mother had convinced him to talk to the governor about reinvestigating your father's trial and the murder of that Negro servant. Hazard said she'd been begging him to use his influence to try and clear your father's name. She told me herself that she knew who really did it—I guess it was Moose she meant, and probably the other fellow who was there the night of the murder."

"The other fellow," whispered Caleb as he slammed his fist against his leg. "Don't know who ... I figured he was long dead by now, or ..." He cursed himself. "My mother is in danger," he whispered.

"Hazard'll take good care of her," I affirmed. "Whoever this killer is, it was no great risk to him to knock on the door of Woody One-shot, because nobody'll care awful much that two old red men were killed. But the killer's an Indian himself if he's the other man who framed your father—he won't take his evil intent into the house of an English planter."

"But why did he kill Moose?" said Caleb, pacing wildly ahead of me into the night.

"Perhaps Moose didn't kill the Negro after all," I suggested. "He'd like folks to think he's killed men. Maybe he has, maybe he hasn't. But maybe it was the other Indian who actually killed the man. Maybe he's always been around Charlestown somewhere. And maybe he heard somehow that your father's trial might be dug up again. And maybe he feared that Moose would turn him in to save his own skin."

"I must return," said the Narragansett. "Or I must prowl about the woods to find my pursuer before he finds me. Yes, that is what I must do. I will be the hunter now, and no longer the hunted!"

"But why's he after you?" I wondered aloud. "You've never threatened him. In all these years, you've never tracked him down. Why does he fear you now?"

"Because I vowed to kill Bill Moose," said the powwow. "This man, whoever he is, certainly knows that I am my father's son. All men know that I am my father's son. 'The powwow dances upon his island like his father danced upon the end of the rope!' is the terrible proverb some throw at me. Yet all men—but one—think my hatred of Bill Moose to be simply the hatred of one man for another. 'Indians!' the English say. 'They would kill each other today for an insult hurled in their direction twenty years ago!'

"But this other man would see my vow with different eyes. He would say to himself, 'Caleb Hobomucko has vowed to kill a man who framed his father.' And if I have vowed to kill one of the men who framed my father, then perhaps I intend to kill the other. Would you not think so if you were this other man? And if you were this other man, would you not sharpen your own knife—and put it to another's throat—to save your own neck?"

"Wouldn't this fellow be an old Indian by now?" I wondered aloud. "And are there any among your people able to run the woods in pursuit of Caleb Hobomucko?"

"Connie Joe is as old an Indian as I have ever seen outside a wigwam," remarked the powwow, "and he's running these woods with the rest of us. I really don't know what an old Narragansett can do if you set him loose in the real wilderness. But someone is looking for me, and who else can it be?"

We paced the path in silence. A bone-numbing wind walked the woods with us. We would have headed back to the cabin long before now, but the fellowship of our troubled souls kept us treading side by side.

"Perhaps your mother is not well and Hazard has sent someone to find you," I suggested, running my reason down a different road.

"No," said Caleb. "If that were so, Hazard would publish the news everywhere. If he sent a messenger to find me, then the message would be clearly told wherever he went, whether I were there or not. Hazard would not send someone to skulk about asking for me in private. He would order the messenger to shout in the forest if need be!"

"The planter loves you," I noted.

"He is a good man," Caleb affirmed simply. And I knew then that the heart of the Narragansett was indeed attached to the silver-haired planter, Englishman or not.

"What're you going to do?" I asked at last.

"I am staying with you," he answered. And I was amazed, but I waited to hear him further. "He has killed two men at once, and I am only one. He might find me before I find him, if I sleep alone in the woods. I will stay with you and walk the Ohio as we intended. We will let Connie Joe in on things, that there may be three sets of eyes open in the forest. I will continue to ride the woods wide, scouting for us as usual—but I will ask the spirits to walk wider still, to scout for me. I will know when this killer is near."

I wasn't so sure. "I don't dislike your idea entirely," I said, "but I can't say that I like putting Connie Joe in the line of fire. This isn't his fight. He didn't sign up with me to be shadowed by a murderer. He came along to hunt, to smoke, to walk where he might never walk again, and to have one last long tale to tell around the fire back home."

"Can we let him decide?" Caleb asked cautiously, almost pleadingly. "I will not ask him to play the shield—only to watch the shadows—and if he hesitates at all, I promise I will leave you both and find the man myself."

"When a man's had a lie painted on his face by someone else, there ain't nothin' worse could happen than that he dies with that lie still painted there!" bellowed the Susquehannock when he had heard Caleb's full tale. Connie Joe stood up and wobbled about the room. "Lightnin' oughta strike liars dead in their tracks! 'Course I can't wish for that to happen to any partic'lar liars, or I'd be takin' revenge. But I'd be shamed in my soul if I didn't do all I could to wipe that lie off of you, medicine boy!" declared the Susquehannock to the Narragansett. "Here I am beside you, and here you'll find me 'long as you need me!"

The powwow bowed before the old hunter, chanting his gratitude. When he rose, his eyes were close to tears.

"You are no fool," said the powwow to the hunter. "And may no man ever call you one again."

"That include yer own tongue?" grinned Connie Joe.

"You may cut my tongue from my mouth if it ever calls you a fool again," pledged the Narragansett.

"No thanks," said Connie Joe with a furrowed frown of twisted wrinkles. "Never had much taste for other men's tongues!"

Monday, November 19, 1750

We set out early in the morning on the same course we'd followed to Cockey's Cabin, traveling very hard about twenty miles to a small town of the Delaware—Shannopin's Town, on the Ohio. There we rested and purchased corn for our horses.

CHAPTER THIRTEEN

Logstown

Tuesday through Friday,
November 20 through 23, 1750

I was unwell, and we stayed in the town to let me recover. While we were there, I took an opportunity to set my compass privately, for it was dangerous to let a compass be seen among the Indians there (they liked such gadgets too much to let them remain long in the hands of their proper owners). I also checked the distance across the river.

The Ohio is seventy-six poles wide at Shannopin's Town, a village of about twenty warriors and their families. The town was named for an old Delaware chief who had died just the year before. The land (which I now began to note more particularly in my journal for the Ohio Company) had been generally stony and broken from the start of our journey until this place on the Ohio. Here and there upon our way, I'd seen some good spots upon the creeks and branches, but no large body of any land suitable for a settlement.

I was beginning to get almost used to being unwell—and it was a rather pleasant thing (when the fever was low) to lie around and get waited on. But it troubled me that I was such a burden on our progress. Connie Joe, who I would have thought most apt to drag on us, was the one who actually complained the most about our going slow. But he also made the best of it, lightening the hearts of all around him by his wit and good-natured conversation. And he didn't just sit around smoking and talking. He whittled little tops for the young children, gave rifle-shooting lessons to any hunter who was not out hunting, and he even took to throwing that old tomahawk that Bainbridge had given him. Said he had to test it out in case he might need it. Before long, he had challenged Caleb to a throwing contest! The old wagon drover actually outthrew the powwow in their first toss, but then his tomahawk arm gave out on him and he had to settle for throwing advice instead.

As the days passed, the Susquehannock and the Narragansett began to act more and more like friends, and it did my heart good to see them together. Caleb's independent spirit seemed to bow whenever he was around Connie Joe, and one day it struck me that the old, bent hunter hobbling next to the proud, tall powwow looked an awful lot like a father walking with his son.

Saturday, November 24, 1750

We set out from Shannopin's Town and swam our horses across the River Ohio. From there, we struck a well-walked path down the river and covered thirteen miles before stopping for the night. All the land from Shannopin's was very good along the water, but the bottoms weren't broad. At a short distance from the river, the land was tolerably level, quite suitable for farming, and covered with small white oak and red oak. There were fine runs for mills. In my imagination, I saw the turning waterwheels, heard the rolling millstones, watched the golden-headed young sons of English farmers pulling fish out of the river like they were picking berries from a ripe, full-laden bush.

Sunday, November 25, 1750

We traveled farther down the river about eight miles, heading toward the Shawanese trading camp of Logstown. These lands were very rich bottoms more than a mile wide on our side of the river, but on the southeast side they were scarcely a mile wide and walled in by high, steep, wooded hills.

Upon reaching Logstown, we found the place nearly empty but for a pack of reprobate white traders. The chiefs of the Indians and the main body of warriors were all out hunting. I didn't like the looks of this place—it stank of a den of thieves—and I imagined our packs being picked in our sleep. But we posted our horses where some grass had been cleared of snow, and we sniffed around for the captain of these backwoods pirates.

"Sean Doogan," said one particularly large and disheveled Irishman by way of introducing himself. He extended a broad and dirty hand. I shook it firmly, giving him my moniker in return. Then I introduced my traveling companions, purposefully mentioning their tribes as well. It was expected etiquette in the forest.

"We don't see very many small companies such as yerself in these parts," commented another trader as our circle began to fill up with the bored and the curious. Indian children pushed their way past the traders to stare at us and then run off to tell their friends of the newcomers. "Ya don't look outfitted for trappin' er tradin'. Just what's yer business, anyhow, if ya don't mind me pokin'?"

"Well, I guess I do mind," I said distrustfully, "until we get a chance to lay our things down and refresh ourselves a bit. It's been a hard push on the trail today, and we could use a hot meal and some good drink."

"Narragansett," mumbled one of the Irish traders as the company broke up to let us take some rest. "Never heered of 'em."

Caleb stepped after the man who had spoken and put his hand upon his back. The trader turned abruptly at the uninvited touch.

"You have never heard of the Narragansett?" Caleb asked in perfect English. "Have none of you?" he queried, looking around at the rest of the pack. They had wandered back to listen to the Indian.

"None of us," affirmed Doogan roughly.

"I had never heard of Ireland either," said the Narragansett without malice, "until an Irishman took the time to tell me of it."

The trader didn't know quite what to do with that comment.

"And I look forward to hearing more," continued the Narragansett, his face set in the sober, painted sincerity of his people at their proudest.

"Well," stammered the trader, wiping his hands on his pants, "I'd be glad to tell ya 'bout it once ya get fed and rested. Surely I'd be." And he grinned. *Good move, Caleb!* I said within myself. *A better move than mine!* And now we knew that no one had been nosing around for a powwow named Caleb Hobomucko.

After food and drink had been brought to us by some of the squaws in the town, we sought out a wigwam full of traders and sat at their fire to talk. I insisted that my Indian companions sit with us. There was a small discussion among the traders—heated at points—concerning my request, but at length they gave in and we settled down to drink and smoke.

They told us that George Croghan and Andrew Montour had passed through the town only a week ahead of us, on a mission from the government of Pennsylvania. Croghan, of course, is that Irish trader I have mentioned earlier, who ousted the squatters from the banks of the Juniata, and a friend of mine. Montour is a halfbreed Iroquois, son of a halfbreed Huron woman and her Huron husband. He looks so much like a Frenchman that if you stripped him of his wild garb and his paint, he'd pass as a full-blooded French gentleman. I had met Montour, for he traveled much as an interpreter for the English in Indian affairs, but I didn't know him well. Though his face and his name clearly spoke of France, his heart and his tongue spoke for England. Croghan and Montour had been dispatched by the governor to renew the chain of English friendship (Pennsylvanian, especially) with the Indians along the Ohio—particularly the Twigtwees and the Miamis—and to deliver them a present.

"Now about yer business in these woods," said Doogan at last. But I found myself no more ready to answer that question than when it was first presented.

"It's private business," I said. "And best kept private." But that didn't satisfy the Irish contingent, who considered themselves privy to any business carried through their established domain. After fumbling around a bit and realizing that neither Connie Joe nor Caleb could be of any practical help in this present situation, I decided to lie. God forgive me and may my mother never hear of it, I entirely invented an excuse for our journey in the wilderness. But not before the traders narrowed things a bit too close to the facts.

"You're here to settle these Indians' lands, aren't you?" said a short and swarthy young man who was seated uneasily next to the Narragansett pow-wow. Knowing Caleb's own convictions on such things, I half expected him to admit the truth and to stand and give a speech condemning English encroachment upon native lands. But he sat silently. I wondered what he was thinking, and my heart suddenly condemned me. The lie that I'd contrived stuck in my throat, and I sat numbly while the Irishman continued his musings. "If you're thinkin' about turnin' these acres into farmland, you'd better sneak out of here by night, Mister Long! Or you might not go home again safe!"

"To insure that I wake up in the morning," I said haltingly when he had finished, "I suppose I must give you what I'd rather keep in confidence with my superiors."

The whole lot of them leaned into the fire to hear me out. Connie Joe sat back and crossed his arms with a mixture of puzzlement and concern upon his wrinkled visage. Caleb's eyes walked the wigwam, purposefully reading each face before moving on.

"But first," I said, looking around at my audience, "is there any among you who represents Mister Croghan and Mister Montour?"

Several men pointed toward a rough-hewn fellow who had raised a hand to identify himself. I addressed my words to him.

"I have a message to deliver to the Indians from the king," I said, "by order of the president of Virginia. For this reason, we're following after Croghan and Montour, that they may take this message among the tribes to whom they've been sent. I hesitated saying so because of the nature of the message and the trust given to me in carrying it through these woods. Not every man who calls himself an Englishman is a true servant of the king. Some would like, for their own gain, to keep the king out of these woods. I don't know you men well, and so you must forgive me if I didn't empty my pockets into your hands so easily."

The troop of them began immediately to disclaim treason, to exclaim of their love for Merrie Olde England (though their first love must always be to that ancient, almost hallowed, emerald isle of their birth), and to proclaim their allegiance to the king. Some actually rose to shake my hand and apologize for putting me on the spot. The man whom Caleb had spoken to earlier got up from his seat to converse with the Narragansett about Ireland. And I was greatly relieved that my ruse had won us some momentary quiet and respect. I reminded my soul, not very successfully I must admit, that the harlot Rahab was commended in Scripture for lying in order to save the lives of the Hebrew spies who were hiding from their enemies within her house.

We made small talk and told tall tales into the wee hours of the night, and at some ghastly hour I excused myself to return to our appointed tent and get some sleep. Upon stepping out into the winter air, I saw that a great fire was burning in the center of the town, and I heard the loud sound of chanting and singing. I determined to have a look at this late-night conflagration before retiring. When I came 'round a wigwam into the full light of the bonfire, I saw Connie Joe playing snowsnakes with some Shawanese warriors! I joined them.

If you have never played snowsnakes or seen it played, you ought to set yourself to it next winter. The game is engaged by first making a level track in the snow by dragging a log or a boy (yes, a boy!) through the snow to pack it down. Then the "snakes"—long, smoothed poles of maple that are about an inch and a half thick at the head and tapered toward the tail—are slid by each player down the packed course of snow. Each snowsnake has a head carved marvelously like a real snake's head, and the tail is notched for the thrower's finger.

The object of the game is to try to slide your snake farther along the course than anyone else. The snake is commonly thrown underhand, and the winner gets to keep everyone else's snakes. Of course, all the watchers are betting on their favorite snowsnake sliders. Gambling is more in the blood of an Indian than of any other race I've known. Connie Joe had purchased a snowsnake for his own part in the games, and he offered to buy me one too.

"How will you pay for it?" I asked.

"With the goods I win when the games are done!" he replied. He had his own bets down.

"And if you lose?" I asked, gratefully accepting the fine snake that was offered to me by a grinning warrior with his hair greased straight up in the center of his fine, painted head.

"I'll cross that creek when I git there!" said the Susquehannock, and he slung his snake down the long track. Great cries went up as the snake rattled to a halt about two paces past the previous long-runner. A young boy lifted Connie Joe's pole from the course and stuck it upright in the snow beside the exact spot where it had stopped sliding.

"Yer turn, Longshot!" shouted the exultant Susquehannock. "And if you beat me, you'll beat us all."

Having played this sport only a few times before, and not for many years, I took my time in setting myself up at the start of the course.

"Baby needs a new pair of moccasins!" chanted the spectators from their seats beside the track.

"Sarah needs a new Indian broom!" I heard Caleb cry from somewhere behind me.

The humor and the simple joy of the moment caught me all of a sudden, and I imagined myself telling this tale at my own fireside along the

Yadkin. With a great laugh, I bent myself forward at a half-run, pulled back the snake in my right hand, and gave it the old Long shot! It ran fast as a dog after a hare and straight as an arrow from Caleb's bow. And when it finally rested its wooded head upon the slick path, it had beat Connie Joe's snake by an English yard.

"What am I going to do with all these idols made by hands?" I shouted to Connie Joe above the festive wailing as a great pile of snowsnakes was laid at my feet.

"Give 'em away!" said Connie, who was dividing the spoils of chance with the rest of the betters. "Give 'em all away to these good Indians!"

And that's what I did—all but for one, which I wrapped up to take home to the Yadkin.

It turned out that Connie Joe had bet on me! He won a wigwam, a drum, a belt of wampum, three pairs of moccasins, and a set of snowshoes. Also a canoe paddle and a jug of rum. He gave everything up but the rum. When I finally headed off to our tent, he was passing the jug around the fire (and taking a swig every time it came back to him).

Upon entering our tent, I halted just within the door. Something wasn't quite right. What did I hear? A quiet, slight movement on the mats at my feet.

"Caleb?" I inquired hesitantly.

I heard a soft sigh in reply. A woman!

"Dear God!" I pleaded aloud, and I backed out of the wigwam hurriedly.

"Sayin' yer prayers before retirin'?" said an Irish voice from the shadows.

"There's a squaw in my bed!" I explained.

"I sent her," he chortled. "It's a cold night, and the blankets are thin! Now don't play the Puritan and insult the poor thing. She wants to have somethin' to remember ya by when yer gone on yer way. These girls like white blood runnin' in their offspring."

"Call her out," I said grimly.

"She's gonna ketch her death of the cold if she comes out jest now," laughed the trader.

"Call her out," I repeated. "I have no desire to be unfaithful to my wife or to my God. Have you no wife of your own? Have you no morals? Have you no fear of the Lord? Call her out and tell her I love another woman. Tell her to go sleep in her own bed where she belongs!"

"Yer a sharp one!" grumbled the disgruntled trader. "A soldier who don't mess with civilian affairs, eh?" He stuck his head in the tent and spoke gruffly to the woman inside. She came out timidly, wrapped in a cloak, her head bowed and her eyes to the snow-packed ground, and quickly ran into the night.

"Neither I nor any of my men need company," I asserted as the Irishman turned sullenly and silently to go his own way. I saw that Caleb stood nearby. The Narragansett and I entered our wigwam together. I read my prayers, but my mind was not in them. Connie Joe came to bed shortly after, fairly sober and whistling a German tune.

CHAPTER FOURTEEN

On Elk's Eye

Monday, November 26, 1750

Though my fever dogged me, I preferred the woods to such company as the traders of Logstown, and so we lit out from there and moved down the river about six miles to Beaver Creek, where we met a man named Barny Curran, a trader for the Ohio Company. Being in the same employ, and finding him to be a rather agreeable fellow, we joined his troop with ours and continued on our way together.

The bottoms upon the river below Logstown were very rich but awfully narrow, and the lay of the high land looked pretty good for farming but the soil was not very rich. The acreage upon Beaver Creek was similar. From the place where we came upon Curran, we left the River Ohio and traveled southeast across the country.

Tuesday, November 27, 1750

We moved northwest about six miles and west about four miles more, up two water courses where the land was very good in the high places, not too broken, and quite fit for farming.

Wednesday, November 28, 1750

It rained all day, heavy and cold, so thick and furious that we couldn't see the trees more than an arm's length ahead of us. We couldn't travel. We stayed in camp and fought to keep our fire lit.

Thursday, November 29
through Thursday, December 6, 1750

We traveled through good land and bad land, land fit for wide plantations and land fit for quarries only. My fever fled entirely, and my appetite came back in full. Plenty of game crossed our path. I killed five deer during this time, and on one day, one of Curran's men and I killed twelve turkeys. Caleb combed the woods all around us but never killed a thing. Neither did he meet any man. He began to relax, and he pulled in his circuit a bit, so that we saw him more as the days passed. Connie Joe rode out with him sometimes now. The old hunter was better medicine for the powwow than anything ever concocted on the sorcerer's own dark island.

There were eleven in our combined company, and we ate well and enjoyed our travels. No snow fell upon us, and the rains—relentless and hard, when they came—washed the previously fallen snows clean from the forest and into the streams altogether.

On Wednesday the 5th of December, we came down the side of Elk's Eye Creek. There are three rivers in these parts known as Elk's Eye: the Muskingum (which means Elk's Eye), the Big Sandy, and the Tuscarawas. This particular Elk's Eye was so named—according to Connie Joe, who got the story from a Delaware friend—because elk were once so plentiful along that river that the Indians could get near enough to see into their eyes. We saw no elk at all. The land was good, but void of timber. Fine meadows lay along the creek, and there were plenty of runs for mills. It rained so hard the next day that we were obliged to remain in our camp.

Friday, December 7, 1750

About eight miles southwest of our last night's camp, across Elk's Eye Creek, we came to a town of the Ottaways, a nation of Indians allied to the French. An old Frenchman named Mark Coonce lived there. He had long ago married an Indian woman of the Six Nations. All the Indians were out hunting, and the old man received us very civilly.

"It is good to see a European face," he said. "I think myself an Indian after so long a life among them, and I have no mirror to remind me that my own face is French," he grinned. He thought that we were from Virginia, and he called us Long Knives. I wondered what life must be like for a man who had chosen to cut himself off from all the heritage that had been his father's and his forefathers' from time unknown. It would be like taking a tree from the forest where it has always grown in the midst of the thickest of trees and planting it alone in a city square surrounded by brick streets and three-story buildings. I have always pitied trees thus planted, though their presence in such places adds a natural song that otherwise would be sorely missed.

But a man—to take him from his own and give him utterly over to a land and a people not his own! It made me lonely and depressed just contemplating the mystery. I thought of the Africans and the Caribs on the plantations of Rhode Island. I thought of the slaves in Virginia. I thought of the Pequots and the Narragansetts and the Wampanoags who—after the Indian wars in New England in the past century—had been shipped as slaves to Jamaica. And my English soul felt suddenly soiled, and I had to take a walk alone.

There were only six or eight families in this town, and we stayed among them—I with Coonce, and the rest in other homes—for one more day.

Friday, December 14, 1750

"English colours!" shouted Barny Curran as our company came within sight of Muskingum on the Elk's Eye.

"And they're flying over the Wyendot sachem's house," noted another among us who was familiar with this prosperous Wyendot Indian town.

"And another one is flyin' over Croghan's," said a third, pointing to the log trading house of the Pennsylvania ambassador to the red man.

The Wyendot nation, sometimes called the Mingoes, was divided in its loyalties between the English and the French, but this town of nearly one hundred Wyendot families was firmly attached to the English. Even so, such a flagrant show of partisanship was rare in the forest. Upon our arrival in the town, I inquired about the reason for this high flag-flying, and I was told that the French had lately captured several English traders and that Croghan himself had ordered all outlying white men into the town. He had also sent messages to the traders in the towns south upon the river and among the Pickawaylinees. Many of the local tribes had sent out word to their people scattered along the Ohio to gather for a council about the French action.

"The war ain't never ended," Curran commented to me. "It's just taken a short vacation."

Saturday, December 14 through Monday, December 24, 1750

The Wyendots were called the Tobacco Indians because of their great fields of Indian tobacco. They wore this reputation like war paint. Acres of tobacco, in season, were rife and rich along the Elk's Eye. Every Wyendot warrior had a dozen pipes or more. They traded them like wampum, with tobacco in bags in tow. I was offered more pipes than I could ever honestly discard along my way home. I gave them to Connie Joe, who had decided that he was going into the pipe-trading business once he returned to the Conestoga.

"I can sell pipes to the Conestoga Indians, to the German farmers, to the smokers of Lancaster Town at market and in the tobacco shops, and to smoke shops in Philadelphia through the good drover Mister Siegrist! And I could suppl'ment my profits with a business in snowsnakes," he said. "You could arrange with Croghan or some other agent to have snowsnakes sent in to Wills Creek and then on up to Conestoga. I'll take 'em from there! I can just see them young German farm boys slidin' them long snakes down their daddys' snow-filled furrows!"

Caleb grew sullen shortly after our arrival in Muskingum. I told him our stay there would be longer than normal because of business I wanted to cover with Croghan and Montour, both of whom were currently in town. I told him also that our horses needed a good rest, and he didn't need my word on that. Metewis and Neeyesee were almost kin to the Narragansett, and he'd been increasingly concerned for them since we'd left Logstown nearly three weeks past. The mounts were overweary, greatly worn, haggard, and weak from carrying their masters over muddy mountains and across cold streams, and worst of all, they were much in need of proper nourishment. I didn't want to take them back out on the trail for at least three weeks more. Caleb agreed wholeheartedly for the sake of the pacers, but his fixation with the pursuing phantom from Rhode Island grew each day we stayed at Muskingum. He took to roaming the woods alone on foot.

"Spotted two white men today and followed them into town," said Caleb one afternoon.

"Traders who work with Croghan," I said.

"Yes," said Caleb, "I have heard."

"Then you've also heard the news they brought in with them?" I asked.

"About more traders being taken by the French," he answered.

"Yessir!" piped up Connie Joe. "Forty French and twenty French Indians took 'em. Marched the traders and seven horseloads of beaver skins to a new fort the French are buildin' up along Lake Erie." The Susquehannock pointed dramatically south until he realized his mistake and turned to thrust his shaking arm northward. "Forts mean soldiers and soldiers mean war," said the old hunter soberly but with a twinkle in his misty eyes. "My old father would be dancin' round the war pole if he heard this news! 'Course he got hit on the head with a warclub when he was just a papoose, and I've always contended that's what made him think of nothin' but war all the rest of his days. Why, he was so set on warrin' that he'd run the warpath by hisself just to keep it clear of less important traffic. He had more scalps than a cornfield has ears of corn. 'Course some of them scalps were animal hide—he cheated that way and made up some awful excitin' lies 'bout his exploits. He talked 'bout war so much that I couldn't stand it no more," said the wrinkled old hunter. "Still, I'd give my rifle right now and my left arm tomorrow to hear him tell those tales again." Connie Joe sighed, forced a toothless smile, then shrank back upon the mats where he was sitting. "Guess he's not in heaven," he said almost to himself. "Too much war. Too much vengeance. Folks told him so too. Wouldn't listen. Kept on warrin'. Died in his own bed with a war cry on his lips. Bad way to go. Bad way."

"He's out there," said Caleb as we walked along the river.

"Seen him?" I asked.

"No."

"Seen sign of him?"

"No."

I didn't want to ask how he knew. Or how he thought he knew. But I asked anyway. "Something just telling you he's out there?"

"Yes."

"But you haven't seen him or any sign of him?"

"No."

"If you keep looking," I said, "and he's really out there, you'll see him."

Caleb was silent. His eyes were walking the riverbank. First one side, then the other.

Croghan and Montour received me gladly. It was good to see them again, and I was happy to catch up on Croghan especially. We talked about our respective business with the Indians and about a regulation of trade among them. We talked about building trading houses in their towns and about purchasing lands from them to build some settlements of our own along the Ohio. We discussed the French and their trade, their forts, and their recent violent incursion into the territories of the English.

"Elk's Eye Creek," said Caleb as we walked in the rain beside the icy waters. "And no elk."

"If I were an elk," I said, "I wouldn't wander too close to this big town myself."

"If you were an elk," said the Indian, "where would you wander?"

"West," I said. "And north."

"West is where the English wish to wander," said the Indian. "And north is where the French are building forts."

"If you were an elk," I said, "where would you wander?"

"I would wander backward into a day now gone," said the Indian.

"And if you were a real Indian," I goaded, "where then?"

"Real Indians can neither walk backward to yesterday nor forward to the west or to the north," said my lost friend. "They can only walk with white men along rivers where the elk are gone and the houses of English traders fly English flags. That is all they can do. That, and dream."

"Christmas is comin'," said Connie Joe as he sat smoking by a Wyendot fire.

"What do you care for Christmas, old man?" asked Barny Curran, who had wandered in to pass the evening hours in small talk and pleasant reminiscence of a New England childhood.

"Why, it's the feast day of the heavenly Father's Son, isn't it?" said the Susquehannock.

"Some celebrate it so," said the Puritan-tainted trader. "Some disdain to give it any mention, bein' a papish holiday with heathen roots."

"I don't know nothin' 'bout paper holidays, but I know plenty 'bout heathen roots, havin' my own full share of 'em," commented Connie Joe, wiggling his bared toes before the fire. "I like to celebrate the day with eatin' and drinkin' and thankin' the spirits that the heavenly Father sent his Son to find me where I was hidin' from him. Better tracker than any Indian ever was, that heavenly Father! And I like to sing a German song or two. There's a lullaby that Siegrist taught me 'bout how the Son was born in a cow trough. Hardly believe it to be true—seein' how the Son grew up to be a King and all—but it's the prettiest melody I ever heered. Only sing it on Christmas, though, but I could hum it for you a couple of days early."

The old hunter started rattling down deep in his throat, and I recognized the tune right off.

"'Away in a Manger'!" I cried. "My momma used to sing it at night when she'd lay me down to sleep!"

"Martin Luther would be proud of you all," said Caleb, his face to the fire and his back to the rest of us.

"That Indian know who Martin Luther was?" asked Curran.

"I don't know," I shrugged.

Christmas Eve on Elk's Eye Creek

The moon was bright in a black and starry winter sky. Earlier in the evening, there had been a flock of Indians bleating in the streets. Now, in the absence of a proper choir of angels, the wolves sang in the bare, wooded hills. Plenty of room at the Wyendot Inn for sinners and saints—and the newborn Savior. Connie Joe hummed German hymns. Caleb paced back and forth before the fire. I entered the day in my journal. I read my Scriptures and my prayers. I slept.

CHAPTER FIFTEEN

Longshot's Christmas

Christmas, Tuesday, December 25, 1750

They won't come," I told Connie Joe. "It was a fine idea, but they won't come."

"Didn't tell 'em it was this old Indian's idea, did you?" asked the Susquehannock.

"No," I replied, "but I told them there'd be Indians invited."

"Some white folks just don't like sayin' prayers—or hearin' 'em neither—when there's Indians sittin' 'round listenin'," commented the old hunter simply. "You'll say these prayers to me though, won't you?" he asked timidly.

"Of course I will!" I declared.

It was Christmas, though the morning was near spent, and I had invited some of the traders to come to a reading of the Christmas prayers. But after they informed one another of my intentions, they came to the convoluted conclusion that because they were of so many different religious persuasions, they wouldn't come at all. The truth was that few of them wanted to hear anything good about God. I was determined to go ahead and read the prayers aloud even if the audience was made up of no more than a sometime-surveyor from Providence and a retired wagon drover from Pennsylvania. Where two or more are gathered in the name of the Christ Jesus, the Savior promises to be right there in the midst of them.

Someone knocked on the door and then opened it just wide enough to stick his head inside. It was Thomas Burney, a blacksmith who had settled in Muskingum to keep the trader's horses shoed and the Indian's guns tooled. Through the window, I could see that several traders were with him.

"You havin' church?" asked Burney.

"Of a sort," I said.

"I talked some of these here fellows into comin'," said the smith. "Shamed 'em into it, actually. We've all been raised up right to worship God, but some men get out in these woods so far from the church that they get to thinkin' they can walk the earth without sayin' 'boo' to the Almighty. I told 'em they could shoe their own horses if that's all the religion they've got!"

They filed into the house and stood around fidgeting, looking at the floor or the fire, at the walls or out the window, shuffling their feet and taking their hats off and putting them back on again. A wind-blown fall of sleet and winter rain drummed nervously upon the roof.

Another knock at the door announced the arrival of Monsieur Andrew Montour and a considerable contingent of well-disposed Indians who'd been wondering and whispering all morning about the prayer meeting at Longshot's shack. Pretty soon, that cabin was stuffed as full as a wigwam during a Wyendot family reunion.

I climbed up on a small table that set near the fire and addressed the crowd.

"Gentlemen," I said. "I've neither design nor intention to give offense to any particular sect or religion. But just as our king has given us the liberty of our own conscience, and hinders none of us in the exercise of our religious worship, so I hope none of you will be so unjust as to put a stop this day on the propagation of the king's own faith." I let my eyes wander over the unlikely congregation. Folks appeared to be listening. Nobody was talking with his neighbor. Nobody was heading for the door. The quiet cackle of the droning fire caught my ear. "All I propose for this meeting is to recite the doctrine of salvation, faith, and good works as I find it here in this prayer book of the Church of England."

I held my little brown book up to the light of the fire, and I proceeded to read in the best manner I could.

After I was done, most of the traders shuffled out in good church order, having done their duty by God and the blacksmith. Then Montour interpreted to the Indians the things I had read, telling them this was the true faith, which the great English king and his church recommended to his children. And the Indians seemed well pleased, and they came to me to thank me for sharing these things with them. They even asked me to stay and live among them, and they gave me a name in their language.

"You are now Annosanah," they said. Montour told me this was the name of a good man who had once lived at Muskingum. And the sachem of the Wyendots—who was among my congregants that morning—said that Annosanah must be my name from now on.

"No more Longshot," said Connie Joe with a wrinkled grin and a Christmas wink.

I thanked them very much for my new name, but I told them that I didn't know if the king would let me stay there. And that if he did, the French might come and take me away as they had recently done with other English traders.

"You may come with great guns and build a fort!" said their chief. "For we have left the French altogether, and our hearts will never return to them."

And they begged to know more about Christ, and they asked me to remarry them in the Christian way. They insisted over and over that they were done with the French and the French priests, for they loved the English more, even though they'd seen very little religion among the English. It began to dawn on me that my simple morning service might well have been the introduction of the true gospel to these parts of the woods. Within a very short time, the whole town was converging on my house, and some of the great warriors of Muskingum were asking me to baptize their children.

"I wonder if Whitefield started like this," I shouted above the rattle of Indian tongues to no one in particular. "Montour! Montour!" I cried, seeing the half-breed in the midst of the crowd. "Tell them I am not a minister who can baptize or marry!"

Montour called them into a circle to better explain the ways of the king's faith. I told him to assure them that I hoped the king would send a proper minister to live among them and to teach them more about God and Christ. This pleased them well again, and many of them left the house singing and chanting joyfully.

Later in the afternoon, a young Wyendot hunter came to me with a book that had been given to him by the French. It was a kind of calendar in which the days of the week were marked in such a way that by moving a pin each morning you could keep a pretty exact account of the time. He showed me this to tell me that he had understood the things that I had spoken, and that he and his family always observed the Sabbath.

I hadn't seen Caleb since the early morn.

"I was thinking of Netop today," said the Narragansett as he came into the cabin and threw himself wearily upon his bed. The rain had ceased, the sun had set behind a scattered crowd of emptied, broken clouds, and the moon was now high. "With all these Indians running around the woods talking about Jesus Christ, I thought I was back upon the reservation among the disciples of Samuel Niles," he mumbled.

"I was thinking about Netop too," I said. "He'd likely been jumping around here like a hot-gospel hare at the sight of these Wyendots drinking in the Word of God. He'd be shouting 'hallelujah' and exhorting everyone to cast aside their sins and trust in Christ."

"Is that what you were doing?" asked the powwow.

"Hardly," I admitted. "I was just reading prayers."

"You should take up preachin' when you get back to the Yadkin!" said Connie Joe from his mat by the fire.

"I'm counting on you to do that!" I said.

The Susquehannock was silent.

"Where you been, Caleb?" I asked.

"Walking," said the Narragansett. "Dreaming."

"Out there?" I asked. Alone, along the river, combing the woods, watching, waiting, hunting for the hunter.

"Out there," said the Narragansett quietly.

And we spoke no more until the dawn.

CHAPTER SIXTEEN

Waiting Out Winter

Wednesday, December 26, 1750

Caleb was outside the town upon his circuit when he witnessed this day's gruesome and unfortunate display.

An Indian woman of an enemy tribe, long a prisoner among the Wyendots, had escaped into the woods about a week past. She was recaptured and brought back into the town on Christmas Eve. I saw her herded through the streets with her hands bound behind her back. Caleb had especially been drawn to the spectacle, for the woman strikingly resembled Susanna, his wife, in her youth. The Indians of Muskingum had welcomed the parade with a good deal of unpleasant clamor, loudly jeering and violently threatening the poor creature with bodily harm and spiritual damnation.

Apparently, by the ancient mind of justice among the Indians, the nature of her desertion was considered worthy of death. The sentence would have been carried out immediately except for the fact that the chief executioners were all out hunting. They arrived home on the day after Christmas, and the miserable captive was led out of town to meet her fate.

"I was standing in an open grove," Caleb told us haltingly, "watching a small herd of elk—the first I have seen here—walk along the river. Suddenly they halted, looking downstream. Then they bolted as one, leaping into the forest, gone from sight and sound in a matter of a few heartbeats. I could hear voices by then, and I soon saw the crowd.

"They came up from the river with the woman in front—pushing her, pushing her, pushing her. It was the one they brought into town two nights past. She looked just like ..." He pulled his lips tight and forced a violent sigh through his flared nostrils. "I took some cover behind a young pine—I had not been seen—and I watched."

Connie Joe stared at the Narragansett silently. He swallowed heavily and cleared his throat hoarsely. He wrung his thick, wrinkled hands as Caleb continued.

"They let her loose. She ran. Right toward the grove she ran. Almost like she was running for me! I nearly stepped out to meet her. Her eyes … the terror was in them. The fear of death. The utter fear of death!"

He paced the small room, kicking at the hard-packed dirt floor with his moccasined heels, shaking his head so forcibly that the long black tail of his hair leapt about his face like a whip.

"They ran after her, four swift warriors. They were gaining quickly. And then she saw me. For one brief moment, our eyes met, and her lips parted as though she meant to cry out to me for deliverance. I swear she looked so much like my squaw—even in her running—that my heart nearly leapt from my flesh. I armed my bow—fool that I am!—and pulled it to my ear. I meant to fell the closest brave and face the rest myself. I would have, but they reached her first."

The powwow's voice cracked. He pressed his face against the cabin's sole, cracked, and smoke-stained window to stare out into the dismal, gray dusk. When he spoke again, his voice was as cold as the winter wind.

"A warclub is an awful weapon, Connie Joe," said the Narragansett.

Joe nodded numbly.

"One stroke to the side of her head laid her flat on her face in the mud," recited Caleb. "Then a second warrior thrust his spear through her back and into her heart. Stuck her five times—I counted. One man scalped her and threw her scalp into the air. Another cut off her head."

Connie Joe sighed. His eyes were moist, his wrinkled lips were set straight and thin as a razor's edge. He tried to get up from his mats. I'm sure that he meant to walk over to the window and hold the powwow in his arms. But he couldn't quite get himself up at that moment. So he coughed a few times instead, and then spoke.

"Wished you never seen such a sight," he said sincerely. "Wished I never seen these kind of things neither. But what you seen is the reason I don't walk in the old ways no more, son." And when he said "son," the word was pregnant with tenderness, right from the old man's heart, and full of real medicine—the kind no man can buy and no doctor can sell.

Caleb turned to look the old hunter in the eyes. I couldn't read him. He seemed simply lost. And he said no more, but walked past us awkwardly toward the door. Almost weakly, he pushed the portal open and stepped out into the blackening eve.

Barny Curran came round just after darkness had fully settled over the forest. His countenance was grim. His hands were raw and dirty. He and some of his men, with a few of the Indians, had just come from laying the poor woman's remains beneath the frosted earth.

"Dismal spectacle," he muttered as he sat at our fire sipping soup. "Peace on earth, good will to men," he toasted bitterly, raising his cup to no one in particular.

"Read us some prayers, Longshot," said Connie Joe quietly.

"Yeah," said Curran, leaning his burly form closer to the hissing blaze, "read us some prayers." And I didn't know whether he mocked or whether he meant it, but I got out my book and read.

Thursday, December 27, 1750 through Thursday, January 3, 1751

Nothing remarkable happened in the town. We went out and hunted some when the weather allowed; we sat around the fires and talked much when it didn't.

Friday, January 4 through Tuesday, January 8, 1751

"Annosanah?"

I turned at the sound of the word, and then I remembered it was my name.

An old Wyendot hunter stood at the opened door, snow whirling around him, waiting permission to enter. I gestured him into the room, and he shut out the winter behind him.

"The price of corn has been agreed upon in counsel," said the tall and weathered old man, his eyes upon mine. He greeted Connie Joe and Caleb with a nod of his scarred head. An ancient wound of chance, sport, or war lay across his scalp from the center of his forehead to the top of his left ear. A thin band of short, bristled hair—streaked with the silver of his years—ran front to back upon his dark, shaven head. A single turkey feather pointed toward the ceiling from behind the crop of hair. The lobes of both ears were pierced and carved in the fashion of his people—and torn from years of catching them on branches while running the woods. From his right ear, which was slightly better preserved than his left, hung three beads of wampum. Two wide lines of black paint ran from that ear to his long, sharp nose, where they stopped.

No smile softened this proud, bleak countenance. His legs were bare beneath a ragged leather cloak that was wrapped around his shoulders and which hung to his knees. What a contrast this wild and aged creature presented when standing next to stooped old Connie Joe. While the Wyendot looked like a mangy, wiry, wary wolf, the Susquehannock could easily be mistaken for a domesticated, well-fed, lazy old dog. Yet even an old dog can run when it must, and bite when it will. And given the nature of the two beasts, I'd rather walk with the dog.

The old Wyendot stepped nimbly to my seat, where I was cleaning my rifle.

"It is a new gun?" he asked.

I lifted the piece and set it in his curious hands. His eyes widened.

"It is a good gun?" he asked.

"Fine gun," I answered, without smiling. A smile at that moment might have been taken wrong. The Indians in these parts never smiled when talking business with strangers. And if a trader smiled while naming his price, the Indians took it to mean they were getting cheated.

"The price of corn has been agreed upon in counsel," the Wyendot repeated absently, delicately fingering the intricate carvings on the oiled wood of my rifle's butt.

"How much?" I asked. And when he told me, I wanted to wince like a proper Englishman. A strong and stinging jest came to mind also, but I held it in. The price was mighty high, but the horses needed to stay well-fed. The ride ahead would be long and hard, and I was determined to pay whatever was needed to sustain the animals. I only wished the weather would let us start out, but the winter pressed on us hard.

"Tell your sachem that Annosanah will pay his price," I said, leaving my gun in the hunter's hands for a few minutes more. "But ask the counsel if they will half their price for a dozen slain deer."

The hunter's eyes narrowed in thought, and he fought to hide a smile of his own. Looking around the room, the Wyendot addressed Caleb and Connie Joe.

"Annosanah boasts," he said in his own tongue—which Connie Joe understood better than the rest of us.

"Annosanah is called Longshot by most who know him well," said Connie Joe. "He shoots long and true always."

"No man can shoot a dozen deer while the winter runs the warpath," declared the Wyendot.

"Annosanah can shoot the eye out of woodchuck in the midst of a thunderstorm!" declared the Susquehannock to the Wyendot on my behalf. "And he can knock the wings off a fly if the wind isn't blowin'!" he added in English.

"Is this gun magic?" asked the Wyendot, fingering my rifle.

"Annosanah's eye is magic!" declared Connie Joe.

The warrior carefully handed me back my weapon and purposefully looked me in the eyes.

"I will take your words to the counsel," he said soberly. "A dozen deer would feed us well for much days."

And he left.

"I haven't seen that many deer since we have been here," said Caleb from his self-appointed post at the window. "And I have walked this whole woods round."

"Maybe I'm over my head with the offer," I admitted, "but I couldn't just sit here and let us get scalped—so to speak!"

"If we all three go out on separate paths," said Connie Joe, "we might just pull in that number. 'Specially if we go out for two or three days straight."

"Might," said Caleb. "But my medicine is weak. My heart is heavy. Noonatch the deer does not come when I call. The spirits are wary. They fly around my head like the snow in the wind. I am in a dream even as I walk awake. I have killed only one turkey in all my wanderings along the river. The only elk I saw were scattered by the terror of a young squaw's death. Where is my hope in this wild wood? Where are the gods who answer my pleas? They laugh at me! What have I done to them to make them mock? I am a fly in a bottle myself! Who will let me out?"

I leaned my stool back against the wall and set my gun upon the table. Words came up from my heart for the despairing powwow, but I sensed that his questions weren't directed to me. I held my peace while the wind sang mournfully outside our wooded walls and the winter danced madly upon the frozen river. The Susquehannock commanded his flesh to get up off its bed to join the Narragansett at his lonesome watch. And father counseled son.

The Wyendots accepted my offer, and I waited for some break in the storm in order to set out on the hunt.

"Vengeance is like a smoldering coal beneath a blanket," said Connie Joe to Caleb as they sat at the fire late at night. They thought I was dreaming. I had been, but my bed had bugs, and I woke up from the itching. Now I lay silently, shamelessly straining to hear their low words, which rose into the air with the smoke of the muttering, midnight blaze. "You roll over to sleep, but the vengeance is wide awake beside you," said the Susquehannock. "Then suddenly yer bed is afire, and then yer house is afire, and everyone runs screamin' from the wigwam!"

"Vengeance is justice," said the Narragansett. "Without justice, the world has no meaning, a man has no recourse, a people have no soul."

"Vengeance belongs to the heavenly Father," argued Connie Joe. "'Cause he sits in the highest tree and has the best view of all things happenin' down here. He knows it all and he knows best what to do 'bout it all. That's what I heard and that's what I believe. And since I give up my own vengeance—and a few other things I used ta think I couldn't live without—my own soul walks in peace most all the time. 'Course a man stumbles off the path every now and then, but I ain't never found a better path than the heavenly Father's."

"*Mayuo?*" muttered Caleb in his native tongue.

"Try it again in English," said Connie Joe.

"Is there a way?" Caleb repeated.

"I used ta think there was lots of ways to get through the forest," said Connie Joe. "And there are. But each of them ways comes out of the forest in a different place. What I been hearin'—and what I been thinkin' 'bout a lot lately—is that there's only one way to the heavenly Father's house."

"Cannot a man find his own way?" asked the powwow.

The fire hummed monotonously as silence fell upon the room. I almost drifted back to sleep. But then Connie Joe spoke again.

"Mister Siegrist has a big house on a little farm," said the Susquehannock. "And he lives there with nobody but his missus. All the kids is grown and scattered. So when Siegrist leaves to drive his wagon to Philadelphia, his wife goes to stay with her daughter 'bout a mile down the road. They kiss good-bye—I always seen 'em do that—and the missus locks up that house behind 'em—all but one little door that goes into a small basement and comes up into the kitchen. If Mister Siegrist forgits somethin' and has to go back home before his wife expects him, the only way in is through that little door. There's lots of paths and roads to get to his house but only one way into the house once the missus has locked things up.

"So," sighed Connie Joe, "a man can make his own way if he wishes, but he still won't get into the house unless he goes through the right door."

"*Pauquanamiinnea,*" said Caleb. I held my breath. I prayed.

Old Joe waited for the word to come again in English.

"Open the door for me," Caleb repeated.

"I think you gotta knock on it yerself," said Connie Joe, "and somebody'll open it from the other side."

"What if Jesus comes to the door?" asked the Narragansett meekly. "What shall I say?"

"I ain't sure what you oughta say," said the Susquehannock.

"*Unháppo Kosh?*" said Caleb. *Is your father home?* But he didn't say it in English, and if the two men spoke further I missed it, because the next thing I heard was the sound of snow sliding off the roof with the morning sun.

Wednesday, January 9, 1751

The wind came from the south, and the days warmed. We went out on the hunt, and though we scouted the forest for miles around, we saw nothing.

Meanwhile, news came into town with two traders who'd just come from the Pickawaylinees.

"The French have taken another English trader prisoner," they said. "But three French soldiers have deserted and come over to the English."

"Fair trade," said Connie Joe with a thin grin. Nobody else smiled.

"The deserters surrendered themselves to us English at Pick Town," said the messengers. "Indians there wanted to kill 'em in revenge for the French having captured our traders. But we wouldn't allow it, seein' how the enemy gave themselves up willingly."

"Those French fellas will soon be on their way here," said the messengers, "under the arms of three of our traders. Croghan can see to 'em after that."

An Indian from over the lakes came into town the next day and confirmed the same news.

Friday, January 11, 1751

The wind continued from the south, warm and welcome. We went out on the hunt again and shot four deer. The town was happy for the meat.

Saturday, January 12, 1751

The weather was agreeable again, and we took to the woods—I by myself, and Caleb and Connie Joe together. Brought down three more deer. The sachem and his people were so happy for the seven deer so far that they gave me extra corn and—under the influence of some liquor they'd been drinking—called the deal done. I accepted it as from God's hand, but Caleb didn't share my conviction. He talked me into going out once more for meat, and we killed two deer and two turkeys.

"It is less than you pledged," said the Narragansett fairly, "but more than the sachem now expects. I am satisfied." I thanked him for pressing me. He was right, after all.

That evening, we all went into the Wyendot king's house for a council that had long been scheduled. But some of the great men of the Wyendot were either not in town or were a little disordered with the liquor, and so no business could be done. We desired to come again the next day.

Sunday, January 13, 1751

The king said it was the Sabbath. The bottle declared itself worthy of the day's worship. And no business was done.

Monday, January 14, 1751

The sachem's large and smoky wigwam was filled to capacity with red men and white, close quartered all round the room. Croghan stood in the center (dressed in his backwoods best) with Montour as interpreter (painted every inch the Indian) and addressed the tribe. He presented them with four strings of wampum and, looking keenly all about him, said, "Your Father, the Great-King-Over-the-Water, has sent you a large present of goods which has recently landed safely in Virginia, and which is waiting for you there under the care of your Brother the Governor of Virginia. The Governor invites you all to come see him in order to partake of this gift, which your Great Father sends with his love to all his children over the Ohio."

In answer to this, one of the chiefs stood up (dressed in his own backwoods best and painted every inch the Indian as well) and said, "Our own king, in whose house we here meet, and all of us among the Wyendot, thank our Brother the Governor of Virginia for his care. And we thank you, our Brother Croghan, for bringing us this news. But we cannot give an answer about our walking to Virginia, for we must sit in a full council of all our peoples and nations. And we cannot sit at such a council until the Moon of the New Green."

The king and his chamber seemed anxious to return to their unfinished business with the bottle, and so we shook hands all round and took our leave.

"The forest—does it really go on forever?" asked Caleb as we walked the muddy streets of Muskingum.

"There's an ocean or two on the other side," I said.

"One like the Great Salt Sea of the Narragansett?" he asked.

"Pretty much like it," I guessed. "All oceans are pretty much the same."

"And what will become of the forest when it has been walked clear through by the English?" he asked.

"God only knows if that will ever happen," I offered, but I thought for sure that it one day would. I'd have walked the whole way myself if some wealthy company of businessmen would agree to pay me well enough—and if I weren't a married man. That Yadkin seemed a long way off sometimes!

"When it happens," said Caleb, "the Indian will have to either die or live within the fences of the English."

"Why talk like that?" I coughed.

"The big stone rolls down the hill and never sees the pebbles in its path," declared the Narragansett.

"People aren't stones," I argued stupidly and simply for the sake of argument.

"People's hearts can be like stones," Caleb replied, turning to face me as we walked.

"I can't change men's hearts," I pleaded quietly to my relentless companion.

"God can," said Caleb mysteriously.

And I chewed on those words as we checked our packs and fed our horses and said our final farewells to the folks at Muskingum. We'd be leaving them at last—Caleb, Connie Joe, and I—before the dawning of the next-coming day.

PART FOUR

La Belle Riviere

"Brothers, our hearts are glad that you have taken notice of us …"

—Twigtwee, Indian warrior

CHAPTER SEVENTEEN

White Woman's Creek

Tuesday, January 15, 1751

Only five miles on this day. West to White Woman's Creek. Small town. Quiet. No traders. Mary Harris lived there.

Her house was a simple wigwam. Her husband was a Wyendot hunter. They welcomed us in and then sent out for several of their children who—with children of their own—came to eat with us all. The husband was open-handed with his hospitality, but he seldom spoke. His woman gave him little time to conjure up any conversation—she spoke that much herself!

"I's taked from my father and my mother when I's only ten," she told us, in broken English, "by the Abenaki."

"The Abenaki," said Caleb with interest. "They live to the north of the Narragansett. Where was your home? And how did you come to live so far south?" His questions were exactly mine.

"Home was Deerfield, Massachusetts," said the white woman, straining for memories of a lost life forty years past. She looked much older than she was, bent and grayed and worn by so many decades spent as an Indian squaw and an Indian mother.

"Deerfield!" cried Caleb and I as one.

"Dear me!" muttered Connie Joe almost incoherently. His mouth was full of meat and his gums were working mighty hard to convince the stringy venison to slide down his throat.

"1704," I said to Caleb. "The Deerfield massacre. Just a few years before either you or I first wet our diapers."

"I did not wear diapers," said the Narragansett.

"Diapers, loincloths—what's the difference?" I jested.

Caleb ignored me. "Some of my people fought with the English against the French in those years. Fought for them and died for them. For what?"

"I was already an ancestor by then!" laughed Connie Joe, who had finally swallowed his food and was reaching for his cup.

"What do you recall of your life in Deerfield?" I asked the white woman. "If it's proper to ask," I added, with a nod to her husband. He just shrugged and gestured toward his wife. The rest of the family ate and listened. They were used to the social arrangement, I figured.

"Not much," she admitted after a moment's silence. "Only that people was very religious," she said. "We talked 'bout God alla time. We prayed to him alla time. Went to church alla time. God was in our midst alla time. I's happy then, and I should 'member more, but they's empty places in my mind 'bout these things. I doesn't 'member at all the days right after I's taked from my mom. My man says it's good to forgit, for those days was surely days of pain and sorrow. I's happy now again. God is here. God is everywhere."

"Who is God?" asked Caleb, and I wondered at the strange question. But the white woman quickly took up the chance to talk some more.

"God is a Frenchman who sent his son Jez Christ to tell us how to live," she said, "but the English kilt the son and hanged him on a cross. I 'member that white men in Deerfield was very religious. But they's awful wicket in these woods. I wonder how they kin be so wicket!"

"All men are wicked, Missus Harris," said Connie Joe between gulps of water. "Until they decides to give it up."

"You's an Indian," she said to the Susquehannock.

"A real one," he answered. "Sort of."

The husband shifted uneasily on his stool. How much he understood, I don't know.

"You's an Indian," she said again, shifting her gaze to Caleb.

"Narragansett," he said, and the word carried strength when he spoke it. Almost made me proud to hear him say it.

"You said that name earlier," said Mary Harris, frowning queerly. And I noticed for the first time that her eyes were blue. "Narragansett," she repeated. Her husband stood. Turned out it was his way of getting in a word sideways.

"Caleb Hobomucko," he said, and Caleb came up from the bench with a start. He had not spoken his full name on this side of the Ohio—not even at Muskingum. How did this Wyendot know who he was?

"He is out there!" gasped the Narragansett.

Someone had come through White Woman's Creek only two or three days earlier—there was no pinning these folks down to the sure day; they simply declared it was less than a week. This someone, an elderly Indian who called himself White Wolf (for his hair was white, Mary told us), had come out of the forest one evening with meat for the town, but had stayed only for the night. The town cooked up his meat that night and had a feast to which everyone was invited. White Wolf's conversation at the feast fire was continual, said Mary Harris (and if she thought so, it must have been so), and full of tales. In the middle of his tales, he had the curious habit of stopping suddenly and asking, "Do you know So-and-So? He is an Indian of the Such-and-Such tribe, and I have not seen him in the woods for many moons." And sometimes the people of the village knew So-and-So, and sometimes they didn't. One of the So-and-So's whose name was unknown to the village was Caleb Hobomucko of the Narragansett.

"I do not wish to die in my sleep," said Caleb quietly as we lay upon mats near the fire of Mary Harris. She and her husband were dreaming.

"That's exactly how I wish to die," said Connie Joe, yawning so widely that I could plainly see the only two teeth he had left.

"Not with a knife sawing your throat!" said Caleb harshly.

"I had somethin' more peaceful in mind, it's true," said Connie Joe patiently.

The fire settled, launching a flurry of sparks toward the ceiling. They burned themselves out before kissing the sky outside the house.

"An old white wolf," I said.

"One that still bites," warned Caleb.

"One old wolf 'gainst two of the best hunters in these woods," said Joe honestly. "And one old wagon drover," he added.

"*Three* of the best hunters," said Caleb.

"Exactly!" I declared. "Now go to sleep and stop worrying about the old wolf."

"Have you a prayer in your book?" asked Caleb.

"I might," I said. "But don't you have one of your own?"

"The spirits yawn when I dance," he muttered.

"I never moved 'em much myself," admitted the Susquehannock. "But I still think it's safe to tell 'em what's on my mind. Though more often lately I been takin' things straight up to the heavenly Father. When a man's got a moose in his sight, he pulls his bow—speakin' like a real Indian now—and lets the arrow fly. Straight and true, just like Longshot and his rifle. That's how it feels to talk to the heavenly Father. Straight and true."

"What's it feel like to run things past the spirits?" I asked the old hunter. He seemed puzzled to hear that question coming from my quarter, but he picked it up without hesitation.

"Feels like …" He paused for a moment, and his eyes opened wide as some new thoughts ran a course through his head. His thin eyebrows bent toward his nose, sending a ripple of deep wrinkles across his dark brow. "Like runnin' the gauntlet!" he loudly and suddenly declared. It was a revelation to the old man. "Like a dadblamed gauntlet, I do believe, yessir. And no fool wants to run one of them things, not in a million moons!" And he sat up, a twisted, twitching frown upon his fine old forehead. "Why, I been torturin' myself by runnin' this moonblasted—forgive my swearin'—gauntlet so long that I thought I had to run it forever! Caleb!" cried the Susquehannock excitedly, pleadingly. "It's a gauntlet, this spirit thing! You run and you run and you run, and they hit you and they hit you—and then they don't hit you once or twice and so yer on yer face thankin' 'em for bein' so kind!"

The old man struck himself in the head with the flat of his palm. "Idiot! I's an old fool and an idiot besides! *Dummkopf!* That's what Mister Siegrist'd say, and I won't tell you what Missus Siegrist'd say. And all along I could've been walkin' that one path without duckin' and grovelin' and thankin' the bangdusted spirits fer …" Connie Joe was up and pacing—cursing better than an English duke or a Susquehannock sachem. "Coulda been walkin' with my head held high. Lookin' into heaven!" said Connie Joe as he paced. "Least that's what I heard—though I thought it was just men talkin'—and now that's what I believe, yessir. Straight and true from now on. Straight and true."

"I've found a prayer," I said, holding my book up to the dim light of the low fire.

"Give it to us, Longshot," said Connie Joe, panting in his course. "Straight and true!"

"O Almighty God," I read, "who art a strong tower of defense unto thy servants against the face of their enemies, we yield thee praise and thanksgiving for our deliverance from those great and apparent dangers wherewith we were encompassed. We acknowledge it thy goodness that we were not delivered over as a prey unto them, beseeching thee still to continue such thy mercies towards us, that all the world may know that thou art our Saviour and mighty Deliverer, through Jesus Christ our Lord. Amen."

"Amen," said the Susquehannock, and he lay back down on his mat.

"Thank you," said the Narragansett.

I woke once to find the fire nearly cold. I fed it until it was warm enough again to last till morning. Dawn seemed still distant as I fell to sleep once more.

CHAPTER EIGHTEEN

Just a Jest

**Sunday, January 20 through the end of
the first month of 1751**

Six days out of Muskingum, in the newer country of the displaced Delaware Indians, the snow began to grow thin and the weather warmer. We reached the Delaware town of Maguck by evening. It sat on a small rise in the middle of a clear field that stretched about five miles northeast to southwest and about two miles either way in the other directions. The view from the rise was a fine one, looking down over the whole plain to a stream on the north side called Sciodoe Creek. All the lands from Licking Creek (where we camped on our second night out) to Maguck were rich and level, with large meadows, fine clover bottoms, and spacious plains covered with wild rye. The woods were chiefly large walnuts and hickories, mixed here and there with poplars, cherry trees, and sugar trees. I wished again that I could walk these lands in springtime or summer, though Caleb and Connie Joe agreed in their opinion that early autumn would be best.

We stayed at Muguck Town for two days and then set out southward about fifteen miles through a pleasant, level, snow-covered land to a small village called Harrickintoms. Five or six Delaware families lived there on the southwest side of Sciodoe Creek. The white of winter was melting steadily. The creek was very high and full of free-flowing ice. We couldn't ford it, and we were forced to follow the high waters down to Salt Lick Creek.

About a mile up Salt Lick Creek, on the south side, is a very large and briny lick. The streams that flow into it are extremely salty, and though their waters are clear, they leave a blueish sediment. The Indians and traders in the area make salt for their horses by boiling this water. When first boiled, it is blue and bitter, but once it's dissolved in clear water and boiled a second time, it's nearly as pure a salt as one could buy with Spanish silver.

Farther south and back again along the Sciodoe, we came to a small Delaware town of about twenty families. There we lodged at the house of an Indian named Windaughalah, a great man among the Delaware and chief of this town. His loyalty—as far as his pick of white nations—was strongly with the English, and he entertained us very kindly. He had a Negro servant—a rarity among the Indians in these parts and a sure sign of Windaughalah's social standing—who fed our horses well. Our first night there (and I really can't recall the name of the town, an embarrassment that you must bear with me) it snowed, and in the morning the ground was covered with a fresh white carpet six or seven inches deep. But the plucky wild rye poked up green and flourishing through the snow, and our horses had fine feeding.

Windaughalah called us to council before we left him, and presented us with wampum and a brief speech of brotherhood and friendship. We gave him our thanks, promised our love, and returned to our tent to ready ourselves to move on by the next morn. Windaughalah's town was the last town of the Delawares to the westward. From there, we would be leaving the Delaware country altogether. By the best accounts and by my best figures, the Delaware Indians were about five hundred warriors strong at that time and firmly attached to the English. They were under the long arm of the Six Nations, though not really a part of them, and were scattered about among most of the Indians upon the Ohio. Some of them lived among the Six Nations, however, and had that ancient league's permission to hunt upon their lands.

At the mouth of the cold Sciodoe, we fired our guns into the thin, winter air. Our thunder was soon answered, as some traders poled across the Ohio to ferry us over to Shannoah Town.

"Starting to look like civilization around here," I remarked as we walked the streets of the Shawanese trading town. A large English storehouse belonging to Croghan (and some other interested parties)

was standing, half-finished, beside a log cabin. Smoke-plumed wigwams lined the streets of slippery mud and newly trodden snow.

"Not hardly!" said Connie Joe. "Ain't no brick!"

"Nor fences," added Caleb.

"Just a jest!" I fired in my defense.

"Does the Bible not say," began Caleb mysteriously, "that a man who
deceives his neighbor and then claims it to be a jest is like a madman
throwing fire into another man's wigwam?"

"Where does it say that?" I demanded.

"I have mangled the words, perhaps," said the Narragansett confi-
dently, "but I believe I am true to the purpose of them."

"Where does it say that?" I asked again.

"In the Proverbs of Solomon," Caleb answered. "My mother recited
them to me often. Solomon frowned on jesting. And was he not considered
the wisest man who ever lived? And was it not God himself who made the
man wise?"

I thought of a fine jest on Solomon. *If he was so wise, then how come
he got himself hooked up with all those wives and all those children and all
that responsibility?* But it didn't ring right in my own heart. After all,
Solomon was also one of the richest men who ever lived, and he could
take care of the biggest family any man ever had. And if he wanted to
get away from all those nagging wives and all those crying babies, he
had a house so big that he could probably go hide in a dozen places. Or
he could just go hunting. So I left off the idea of jesting on Solomon.
It would likely just get me into deeper water. But I wasn't going to let
this powwow beat me with the Bible!

"Jesus jested," I declared, but if that was my best shot, my powder
was wet!

"Did he?" challenged the powwow.

And I thought of Christ talking about the camel going through
the eye of a needle, but I knew it wasn't a pure jest—it was spoken
with good purpose and not to make men laugh. I remembered how
the fish had spit up tax money for Saint Peter, but that wasn't a jest
either—that was an actual event, a miracle (though it must have been
a funny sight!), and a blessing to men who hadn't a shilling otherwise.
I recalled Jesus calling the Pharisees "white-washed tombs full of

dead-men's bones," but that wasn't really a jest—it was the truth, spiritually speaking.

I was stuck.

"He was a man same as you and me," I said at last. "Yet without sin. I'm sure he jested, though not with the kind of jest that sets wigwams on fire."

"And your own jests?" asked the Narragansett.

"Now, why are you wrestling with me about my jests?" I challenged. "You've never thrown this at me before! I've jested with you all over the country! Makes the time pass more agreeably. Connie Joe jests too. Lightens the heart!"

"Caleb's just jestin', Longshot!" said Connie Joe helpfully.

Caleb smiled. I was not in a smiling mood.

"Just jesting," I mumbled.

Friday, February 1 through Monday, February 11, 1751

We stayed on at Shannoah Town to let our horses grow strong and to gather information concerning the lands and tribes west of the Ohio. News of the French came in from time to time, but I didn't know how much of it to trust. At one point, we held council with the Shawanese concerning trade and friendship. At the end of the council, the Shawanese talked a good bit about sending a guard with us to the Twigtwees Town, a journey of some two hundred miles. But after long consultation, their king being sick, they came to no conclusion on the matter. It occurred to me at that time that my own health had held up quite well considering the long bouts I'd had at the beginning of our journey. I thanked God for restoring me, and I began to pray for my horse instead.

Even with the blessing of fresh rye, Neeyesee was weak on his feet. The long treks through ice and snow had taken a hard toll. Thus, on the eve of the 12th of February, I determined to set out from Shannoah the next morn with a fresh mount, leaving my pacer and my packs in the town for a longer rest. I would return in due time.

Caleb could not bear to part from Metewis, and I didn't argue the matter with him. His goods and his beasts and his life were his own.

Connie Joe was agreeable to ride anything provided for him. I got him a strong, rested mount, and we readied our provisions for the day to come.

"He is out there," said Caleb on our last night at Shannoah.

"Prob'ly," said Connie Joe.

"God's out there too," I said.

"Surely," said Connie Joe.

"He will find me soon," said Caleb.

"God?" asked Connie Joe.

"The White Wolf," answered Caleb.

"Who told you?" asked Connie Joe.

"I don't know," said Caleb. "Never heard the voice before."

That troubled me, but the hour was late. There was no sense worrying about tomorrow. Tomorrow would worry about itself. That's what I'd read and that's what I believed.

CHAPTER NINETEEN

The Bite of the Wolf

Sunday, February 17, 1751

Walnut, ash, and sugar trees. Cherry, oak, and pine. Well-watered lands with a multitude of scattered streams and rivulets. Beautiful, natural meadows covered with rye, bluegrass, and clover, abounding with turkey, deer, elk, and every kind of game. But most of all the buffalo, seen frequently in herds of thirty or forty head feeding together in one meadow.

From Shannoah Town south and west, across the Little Miami River and all the way to the Big Miami River opposite the Twigtwee Town, the country lacked nothing but the cultivating hand of the white man to make it the most delightful of gardens imaginable. The Ohio and all of its largest branches were said to be full of fine fish of several kinds, particularly a sort of catfish of prodigious size. But I wasn't there at the right season to see them for myself. I've seen them since, and I've eaten many.

Though the traders at Shannoah had estimated the distance to Twigtwee Town to be about two hundred miles, by my computation it was no more than one hundred and fifty. The Miami River was high, too high to ford, and we were obliged to construct a raft of old logs to transport our goods and our saddles. Our horses swam behind the raft.

On the other side, we were met by a welcoming party of warriors from Twigtwee Town. We spent our first moments getting acquainted to the sound of each other's guns (we fired a few rifles and pistols into the air according to the custom), and we smoked the warrior's pipe together until such a time as the Twigtwees were inclined to escort us into town. We entered with English colours before us (I gave Connie Joe a flag I'd brought, and he carried it on a pole at the front of our march), and the king of the town received us grandly and invited us into his own house. He set our colours on his roof, and the firing of guns recommenced all over town for about a quarter of an hour. All the white men and traders that were there came to bid us welcome as well.

You might forgive the comparison, but I wondered how Jesus must have felt marching into Jerusalem on Palm Sunday—especially knowing, as he did, what lurked just around the corner on the following Friday. I thought about Caleb's prophecy that the wolf would find him soon. And while burnt powder was blowing into the woods on the west-riding wind, I prayed that Twigtwee Town wouldn't be our Jerusalem.

Twigtwee Town was a small Indian city, consisting of nearly four hundred families, and constantly increasing. It was one of the strongest Indian towns in this part of the continent, the Twigtwees being a numerous people made of many different tribes under the same form of government. Each tribe had a particular chief or king, one of which was chosen indifferently out of any tribe to rule the whole nation. This Grand Sachem—as he would have been called if this were an old Narragansett setup—was given greater authority than all the other chiefs. The Twigtwees were accounted the most powerful people westward of the English settlements and much superior to the Six Nations (with whom they enjoyed a season of peace at that time). Their full strength and numbers weren't known to us because only lately had they begun to trade with the English.

Other tribes and nations from points farther west came into the town almost daily, and some of the traders in town thought the Twigtwees had influence and interest even beyond the Mississippi—if not across the entire continent. The Twigtwees were very interested at that time in an alliance with the English, finding our goods to be equal to those of the French, but at a quarter of the price. The French, who called these united tribes *les Miamis*, wanted desperately to win them back. But none of the beckonings of France had been able to recall them.

Monday, February 18, 1751

"An Indian fort," I mused, walking around the fascinating structure.

"Did you think only white men could build forts?" asked Caleb absently. His eyes were upon the woods and not the fortress.

"Not at all," I answered. "If Netop were here, he could improve this one much."

The palisade was in need of some repairs. The sound of axe and saw could be heard in the forest, and traders were helping some Indians carry logs up the hill. There were cabins within the walls, a few wigwams, and an especially long council house.

"Netop," sighed the Narragansett. "I would like to see his face again."

"Soon enough," I said, "we'll be done with this long walk of ours and you can head home."

"He is out there," said my distant companion.

"God's out there too," I repeated my litany.

Suddenly, the sound of guns crackled in the streets, and a great alarm arose among the Indians. Caleb froze for a moment, but soon relaxed as we watched the town run to and fro from house to house, stopping one another in their haste just long enough to confirm or pass along some sort of troubling news.

"We'd better ask the reason for this stir," I said, coming down the hill and into the main street. But I found I couldn't get a clear answer from anyone. At last I found a trader named Smith who understood the present distress well enough to give me an answer for the confusion.

"Six Indians, some Cutaways and some Shanaws, have come to war against the town," said Smith.

"Six against six hundred?" I asked.

"Where there's smoke, there's fire," said the trader.

And by evening, a report had spread through town that four Indians and four hundred French were marching into the country and were even now not far from the city.

"Four hundred against six hundred," said Caleb. "The odds narrow considerably."

"Four hundred French soldiers," I added.

"And four Indians," reminded Caleb.

"Can it be war?" I asked.

But soon after the news had been brought into town, the Indian messenger owned up to the truth. It was four French Indians only who were on their way, he said. They were coming to council with the Twigtwees, and they had bid him to tell the false tale in order to see how the English would behave. "Since the English did not run away like women, but behaved themselves like men," said the messenger, "I tell you now the truth."

"Just a jest," said the Narragansett wryly.

The town was much relieved and received the four Indians kindly when they marched into town the next day under French colours.

Wednesday, February 27, 1751

A little over a week had passed since the French Indians arrived. Having been welcomed with dignity, they were fed and entertained as foreign ambassadors should be and as well as the Twigtwees were able. They were invited to council and, amidst the smoke of four hundred pipes, their pro-French speeches were endured. Subsequently and summarily denounced as lackeys of the French, they were warned that if they wished to war against the Twigtwees, the Twigtwees would meet them gladly in the contest. They were shown the way out of town. And they presumably walked back northward to some new wooded fortress of the king of France.

Thursday, February 28, 1751

The town crier came by the king's order to invite us to the longhouse to see the Warrior's Feather Dance. The prospect of such an event encouraged Caleb greatly. Connie Joe was grateful for the invite too, but he'd been feeling especially weary lately, and he begged to sleep the evening away. He didn't pass this on to the king, of course, but he said as much to Caleb.

"Sleep, then," said Caleb sincerely. "The king will not miss you among so many. Sleep on and dance in your dreams."

"Only way I *can* dance," declared the old hunter.

We left our hut and joined the throng as it made its way into the fort. I could hear the music already, a constant rhythm of drum and rattle mixed with the intermittent harmonies of the wooden flute and the human voice.

Upon entering the longhouse, we made our way to a small group of traders—men of Croghan's I'd gotten to know—and Caleb and I settled ourselves in the midst of the smoking, sweating, humming congregation.

The dance was performed by three dancing masters, painted all over in various colours, with long, carved sticks in their hands. At the ends of each stick were fastened the feathers of swans and other birds, neatly woven in the shape of a fowl's wing. In this disguise, the dancers performed many antics, waving their wands and feathers about with such skill that they seemed like so many giant, flying, fluttering fowls. While they danced, in exact time to the music, warriors reeled about a post. From time to time, a warrior struck the post and the music and the dancing ceased. Then that warrior began an account, as good and as rhythmic a piece of oratory as an English poet might invent, concerning his achievements at war. And when he was done, he threw down some goods upon the dance floor as a gift to the performers and the musicians.

Then the show was fired up again in earnest, until another warrior struck the post. This went on late into the night, and though I enjoyed it at first, it soon became tiring. It was like watching men play chess when you don't know the rules of the game—though it's a fascinating thing to see two minds begin to war against each other on the board, after a while it becomes intolerable. You don't know what they're thinking and you don't know what they're doing—and worse, you can't join them even if you knew! With no understanding of the tongue of the Twigtwees, I grew impatient with the bragging sessions. Though Caleb was in his glory, things looked like they might go on till dawn. I was about to excuse myself for the night when I saw that Connie Joe was signaling from the door. He wanted Caleb, and so the Narragansett and I both made our way—as inconspicuously as possible in a crowd of spectators who were practically sitting on top of one another—toward the far end of the longhouse.

"A man is askin' for you," said the Susquehannock simply. His lips were pulled thin upon his troubled face.

"The White Wolf," said Caleb with finality.

"I think so," said Connie Joe. "A trader got me outta bed to tell me.

Whoever it is that's lookin' for you, he's an old man like me, but with more teeth and more paint. A friendly, talkative sort of fella, the trader told me. Asked for Caleb Something-or-Other, he said. Narragansett, he said. But the trader didn't tell 'im nothin' 'bout you bein' here and came right over to let us know. I ran over here fast as I could, what with this pain in my legs and all." He slapped his thigh, more out of habit than personal concern. His eyes were upon Caleb. His heart was with him too.

The Narragansett turned suddenly and swept the interior of the longhouse with his dark, piercing eyes.

"He is in there," he said.

"Say it ain't so!" said the Susquehannock wearily. "And I's called you out of the crowd to stand here a spectacle for his eyes to see!"

"He has seen me," said Caleb, "but it was meant to be."

I squinted into the smoky revel. Where was the White Wolf? I saw many silver heads, many painted faces. How could we know? Was he really there? Caleb said so. Something, somebody told him.

"He will bite tonight," said the powwow.

"You gotta leave town!" said the Susquehannock.

"I will not go," said the Narragansett.

"I'll put out the word," I said quietly, "and ask some of the traders to watch the house tonight. I'll stay awake myself. Connie Joe better get his sleep."

"A horse don't sleep when his colt is bein' stalked by a panther!" declared the old hunter.

Caleb didn't balk at being called the old man's colt. He stood a bit taller and actually moved further into the light of the longhouse. He was calling the White Wolf out. Silently but surely. Would the wolf come? My eye caught the sight—brief and blurry in the thick, writhing smoke—of an old man, dark and thin, slipping from his place against the far wall and out a door to his right.

"Did you see …?" I began to ask, but Caleb was gone. Connie Joe too. I stood transfixed by the moment, the loud chanting of the Warrior's Dance ringing in my ears, the dark of the night calling me to run into its arms after my companions.

A lone bark. It was not a dog. It was the harsh cough of a longrifle. I followed its eternal echo into the empty streets.

"Caleb!" I cried. "Connie Joe!" I shouted. Something had happened, I knew. And I feared the worst.

Rounding the longhouse to the far side where I'd seen the old man exit, I nearly fell over two dark forms upon the snowy earth. A man was lying on his back. Another was bent over him, weeping. Weeping like a baby. Wailing like a stricken child. I had never heard Caleb cry. The sound, released at last from the prison of his soul, chilled me more deeply than the coldest wind of winter.

CHAPTER TWENTY

A Dream of Vengeance

Thursday night,
February 28, 1751

You will not die!" declared the Narragansett to the Susquehannock. With eyes reddened by bitter and sorrowful tears, Caleb stared into the pained and paled face of the weakened, wounded old warrior. The powwow's arms and hands were dark and sticky with Connie Joe's blood. A hot fire licked our backs near the bed and chased the cold night from the small wigwam. A woman carried out a pan of bloody water while another brought a clean pan in. "You will not die!" demanded the Narragansett again. I prayed he was right, but the wound was very bad.

"We'll have to move him in a day or two if he tarries that long and is strong enough to travel," said a squat Irish trader named McGarvey. "Get him back up to Shannoah at least. There's better beds there and an old London fella that knows some doctorin'."

"Caleb is a doctor," I simply said, as the Narragansett carefully wrapped the wound in poulticed bandages of his own design. "And I'd rather send for help than move Connie Joe," I added. The bullet had struck old Joe in the left side, passing right through him. No bones were shot up, but the stomach had taken some awful damage, and the bleeding was profuse. Only after two hours had it finally stopped altogether. The old Indian still had some blood in him, but how many days he had left, only God knew. Infection was my greatest fear—inevitable, but for God's merciful intervention. When the blood was fully stanched and Connie Joe slept fitfully upon the bed, I purged the tent of all but the poor old man, the powwow, and myself.

"You will not die," said Caleb softly to the Susquehannock. I imagined that Joe could hear the Narragansett even in his sleep. Heart to heart. The two had touched more intimately at that level in their short time in the woods than Caleb and I had managed to connect in a lifetime. But I didn't envy them the bond—I was glad for it. I felt it was something that God had engineered, something that might be the salvation of them both.

Connie Joe moaned pitifully in his dreams. A stomach wound is as painful as any wound gets. I prayed for comfort and healing, but I had little faith for either. The best we could do, I thought, was sit it out with the old man until he slipped from us altogether.

"You will not die," chanted the powwow as he anxiously paced the small, smoky room. His pacing soon turned to dancing, and his chanting to the wailing of a powwow invoking his deities. Though my own spirit groaned as Caleb called on his demons, I hadn't the heart to ask him to stop. I determined instead to step outside the wigwam and to leave the heathen doctor to his business. But as I was putting on my hat, Connie Joe began to cough and moan upon his mats. His arms rose weakly at his side, and his feverish face twisted into one great cracked and gnarled frown. His lips opened and closed with rasps that resembled speech, and Caleb and I threw ourselves as one upon our knees beside his bed. We bent our heads toward his parted lips.

"Shthbyup. Shthbyup. Shthbyup," whispered the tortured old hunter over and over.

Caleb looked at me for help, but I couldn't interpret the word any better than he could.

"I will dance some more," said the powwow, rising to his feet. "Perhaps the spirits will move his lips further."

Connie Joe's right arm shot suddenly up to grab Caleb's loin cloth from behind. He coughed loudly, once, and began to speak again.

"Shutheboyup!" he said, more clearly than before. And he opened his pain-wearied eyes.

"Shut the boy up!" I laughed.

Caleb stood still as stone, soaking in the words. He carefully loosened the old man's grip from his clothes and, taking the hand in his own, knelt again beside the bed.

"Is he dreaming?" asked the powwow. "Are these the eyes of waking?"

"Shut the boy up," said the Susquehannock again.

"Who is he speaking of?" asked the powwow.

"You," I offered. And Connie Joe cracked a weak but affirming smile.

"Me?" said the puzzled powwow.

"Dancing," said the Susquehannock clearly now.

"I have danced for you," said the Narragansett.

"My body's one big mountain of pain," said the Susquehannock haltingly.

"I will dance more," said the Narragansett.

"I don't need a headache too!" said Connie Joe. "Shut the boy up, Longshot!"

"I will not dance," said the Narragansett, understanding at last.

"Thank you," said Connie Joe, squeezing the powwow's hand. He closed his eyes again. "Don't need no demons," he declared quietly. "Just hold my paw while I sleep," he said. "That'll be good enough fer now." He was silent for some moments, then he spoke again in a low, hoarse whisper, "No vengeance." Then he slept.

My eyes opened suddenly from slumber. The blaze was still warm, and the firelight and the shadows danced silently upon the wigwam walls. I was sitting against a pile of mats beside Connie Joe's bed. He was lying awake upon his back, Caleb at his side. They were speaking in low tones, but their words wandered clearly to my ears. I closed my eyes again, to listen to this father with his son, this son with his father. They didn't know I was conscious.

"Had a dream," said Connie Joe to Caleb. "A dream of vengeance."

"It is my dream," said Caleb grimly, "and it will be my meditation as I walk the woods awake."

"It must not be," said Connie Joe.

"You are a real Indian," said Caleb. This was no small compliment.

"I am," said Connie Joe, and I wondered at the simple declaration of the old drover.

"And yet you refuse to let vengeance entertain you in anything but dreams," puzzled Caleb.

"Don't want it even in my dreams," said Connie Joe.

"Not even in your dreams," repeated Caleb.

"It isn't in my own heart to dream these things," said Connie Joe. "For I sent vengeance runnin' from me many moons ago. It's the spirits who shoot these evil thoughts into me—like the rifle ball of that White Wolf."

"I will return the ball to the wolf," said Caleb. "I will send it into his heart."

"No, no, no," said the old warrior weakly and sadly. "The heavenly Father says we mustn't return evil for evil."

"Turn the other cheek, then," said Caleb coldly. "Let the wolf tear your right side to pieces also! I will not call you a fool. This I have promised. But he was a fool who wrote such words in the Bible!"

"Yer a fool yerself, you dadblistered mangy puppy!" coughed the Susquehannock weakly. "And I don't say it for any other reason than that I love you!"

Caleb was silent. I wanted so badly to open my eyes to see his face, but I let the moment forever alone for the two of them.

"You are a real Indian," Caleb said again at last.

"So're you," said Connie Joe quietly.

"I have prayed to be so all my life," said the Narragansett.

"You wasted yer prayers!" declared the Susquehannock.

"Your words hurt," said Caleb simply. "Am I a real Indian, or am I not?" he asked, as a small child might ask his father.

"'Course y'are," said Connie Joe. "Just let me talk. But get me some of that water first, will you?" I heard the old man slurping at a cup. "Splash some of it on my face too," he said. "Oh, that sure feels fine! And thank you, Caleb, for wrappin' up this mess of meat at my side. I wouldn't be lyin' here talkin' with you if not for yer doctorin'."

"And my dancing?" said Caleb.

"Not yer dancin'!" said Connie Joe.

"My spirits?" asked the Narragansett.

"Not my friends!" said the Susquehannock. "Not yers, either, I believe."

"You said I was a real Indian," said the powwow.

"Let me talk 'bout bein' a real Indian," said the Susquehannock.

"Please do," said the Narragansett.

"Bein' a real Indian," began Connie Joe, "isn't nothin' much 'bout the forest or the rivers or the spirits or the ways of our fathers, though I used to think that way. Not too long ago, I thought more that way. But I climbed a few new hills on this little trip of ours. Ever since you and I been walkin' the woods together, I been wanderin' some new paths inside this old soul of mine. Bein' a real Indian—and this is Connie Joe talkin', just Connie Joe, take it or leave it in the woods—bein' a real Indian is about blood and heart. Not sheddin' men's blood or cuttin' out men's hearts like our fathers' fathers—that isn't real Indian stuff, that's just plain wrong stuff no matter who does it! Blood and heart, as I'm thinkin' 'bout it, is what the heavenly Father puts into a man from the start.

"The heavenly Father made me an Indian, and I can't be nothin' else. A pine tree is a pine tree and an oak tree is an oak tree. Maple sap flows in a maple tree and birch sap in a birch tree. My blood is Indian blood. My face is an Indian face. My father was an Indian and my mother was an Indian. I's an Indian. A real Indian. Can't be nothin' else. Same goes for you."

I heard Caleb move on the floor beside the bed. He sighed. Connie Joe continued.

"A real Indian runs his own path, Caleb, but so does any man of any race or tribe. It isn't the path that makes a man an Indian or an Englishman, it's the blood and the heart. The blood is the sap that runs in the tree, and the tree is what the heavenly Father declared it would be. The heart is the roots that hold the tree to the ground. No tree can live without its roots. You cut the roots out of the earth and the tree dies. Once it's dead, it don't take too long 'fore it looks like any other dead tree in the forest. And finally it just rots itself down to dirt. Flowers and berries and other trees grow right up out of it, and nobody knows it ever stood there lookin' down on the moose and the elk and the skunk and the chipmunk. The roots keep it alive. That's the heart, Caleb."

"Blood and heart," chanted the Narragansett quietly.

"An Indian is an Indian by blood," said the Susquehannock, "and his heart keeps him rooted to the lands of his fathers."

"I do not understand," said Caleb slowly.

"Where'd I lose you?" asked Connie Joe sincerely.

"If the heart keeps him rooted to the lands of his fathers," said Caleb, "then being a real Indian is indeed about the forest and the rivers and the ways of his fathers."

"In the heart it is," said Connie Joe.

"Whether the land is there at all," said Caleb.

"That's right," said Connie Joe.

"Whether he lives his life as his fathers did or not," said Caleb.

"That's right," said Connie Joe.

"How can a bird fly if the sky is gone?" asked the Narragansett.

"It's gotta learn to walk," said the Susquehannock.

"Then it is no longer a bird!" said the Narragansett.

"Says who?" argued the old man.

"God made it to fly!" cried the powwow.

"And it will someday!" declared the old hunter. "Where the sky is new and the night never falls."

"How can you be sure?" asked Caleb.

"Somebody told me that the heavenly Father sees every bird that falls," said Connie Joe. "And it grieves his heart. Now if the heavenly Father is grieved when one small creature of his falls from the sky, surely he'll pick it up and let it fly again in heaven. That's what I figure, and that's what I's countin' on. If I don't never get out of this bed, I won't fret much 'bout it. If I don't never dance like an Indian or run the woods like an Indian or hunt like an Indian again, I won't cry none 'bout it. I know what I am, and I know what I'll be when I open my eyes in my wigwam in heaven. Fine day it'll be too!"

"You are not afraid?" asked the powwow.

"Just a little," admitted the Susquehannock quietly.

The fire chattered low as the wind whistled outside the wigwam. In the moments when no one spoke, it was hard for me to stay awake. But I didn't want to miss the conversation. I held one of my own with God in the meantime.

"If I worship the spirits in my heart then," said Caleb at last, "and give up the dance while I walk English streets, and even if I never dance upon my own island again, I am still an Indian."

"Yes."

"And I will dance in heaven," said Caleb carefully.

"Not if you worship them old spirits in yer heart," answered Connie Joe.

"Must I turn my back on the gods who have raised my face from the cowdung of English farmers? Must I bid the spirits to fly away like clouds upon the wind? Must I worship the God of the Bible only?" questioned Caleb. "Like Netop my brother? Like the Christian Narragansetts? Like Moses the Delaware? Like …"

"Like me," said Connie Joe.

"How have you come to this place in your soul, old father?" asked Caleb.

"Seems only right at last," said Connie Joe, "to worship the One who came first and made all things. The spirits are liars. Liars and sneaks. I see that now more'n ever. Feel it too. Don't want 'em. You can have 'em! And what good will it do you if they give this whole world back to the Indians— and you end up losin' yer soul?"

"These are the words of Jesus," said Caleb simply.

"A real Indian can believe in Jesus," said Connie Joe wearily.

"I wish to understand," said Caleb patiently.

"An Indian is an Indian, no matter what he believes," said Connie Joe simply. "His blood is Indian blood, and his heart can't help but be rooted to the past. It must be rooted to the past, but …" The old Indian sighed, digging around in his tired mind for some kind of fitting analogy. "If a man wants to go to heaven—and real Indians can get there same as anyone else and still be real Indians—then that man's got to be a tree that walks. A tree that keeps its roots in the ground while wadin' the earth like a man wades a river. The ties to the past are still there, but the path is new."

"The spirits do not make a man an Indian," said Caleb slowly.

"'Course not!" said Connie Joe. "A man's an Indian or he's not, and the spirits got nothin' to do with it and nothin' to say 'bout it—though they'd like to! They'd like to tell you yer not even a man unless you do this or that! Unless you dance this way or shout that way. Unless you howl like a wolf 'fore goin' to bed at night and drink men's blood for breakfast the next morn. But a real Indian walks his own path, Caleb. You know that. And a man does what's right when he knows what's right.

"Just 'cause some devils told my father to run the warpath like a mad-man don't mean my father's son has to bow to these same devils! I's an Indian and a man, and no man nor spirit can say so otherwise. Got no paint on and don't care neither. Goin' to heaven with Jesus whether the spirits like it or not. Goin' pretty soon too, I believe. And when the heavenly Father—

who made me an Indian to begin with—sees my ugly face at his door, he's gonna say, 'There's that old Indian, Connie Joe! Come on in, Joe.' And that's that!"

"You will not die," said Caleb.

"On my way already," said Connie Joe weakly.

"Your blood cries for blood," said Caleb.

"No, no, no," moaned the Susquehannock. "The blood of the heavenly Father's Son takes care of all that. And that's what I believe. No vengeance. None of it, Caleb. Or you'll have to pay for it yerself."

"Pay for it?"

"The Son's blood has already paid for my blood. And if you open this wound again, you'll have to pay for it yerself. With yer own blood and yer own soul. Such is vengeance. Such is the way of the Indian."

"Such is the way of the Indian," echoed Caleb.

"Such is the way of the Devil," said the Susquehannock preacher, painfully shifting upon his pulpit.

"The Devil," said Caleb thoughtfully. "Chepi. Hobomucko."

"Vengeance is sin," said Connie Joe simply. "And sin will keep you outta heaven 'less it's paid for with blood. Jesus paid for it with his own blood. Nothin' else ever worked for me. I don't think you've got a better way."

"Vengeance will keep me out of heaven," Caleb repeated.

"Yes," said Connie Joe.

There was silence in the room for quite some time.

"Follow me," said Connie Joe at last, quietly and almost to himself.

"Where are you going?" asked the powwow.

"Heaven."

"How can I follow you after you are gone? Will you lead me in my dreams? Will you appear in a vision in the forest?"

"Follow the Lamb."

"Where do I find this Lamb?"

"Find Great Hill—Moses—and he'll tell you. Then follow the Lamb through the woods all yer days. When the path ends, I'll be there waitin' for you. Promise. A real Indian keeps a promise."

Not like the English, the night could have shouted. But it was silent. No one else spoke either. I opened my eyes. Connie Joe was sleeping. Caleb sat at his side, his hand upon the old man's slowly heaving chest, his eyes upon the old man's wrinkled face.

"Get some sleep," I said to the Narragansett. "I'll watch him awhile."

Caleb didn't move. He didn't take his gaze from Connie Joe. He simply shook his head no. I rearranged my own mats and lay down upon them. No sense in both of us staying up all night. I fell asleep in the midst of my sad and silent prayers.

A Solitary Season

Friday, March 1, 1751

The sun rose warm in a cloudless sky, quietly convincing the winter to retreat. The Miami River ran high with the melted snows. A southerly wind whistled its welcomed song in the bare forest. Connie Joe lay sleeping, slightly recovered and having had a small breakfast of dried berries and warm broth. Caleb paced the wigwam, muttering to himself. A guard was set at the door, as there had been all the night, against the White Wolf. Warriors had run the woods around the village after the shooting, finding nothing, seeing no one. The wolf had bitten and fled. Did it think it had taken its prey? Or did the taste in its mouth betray the truth? Time would tell. I left the doctor and his patient to join the rest of the English traders—Croghan and Montour being once again among us on their ambassadorial duties—for a council meeting with the Twigtwees.

The tall and stately chief of the Twigtwees stood in full colours with two long strings of wampum in his right hand. His eyes walked the council house, passing first over his own people who were seated around him in tightly packed concentric circles of dark, painted flesh, and resting at last upon the gathering of English traders in the midst of the Twigtwee congregation.

"Brothers," said the Twigtwee chief as though addressing himself to the governor of Pennsylvania and his magistrates. "Our hearts are glad that you have taken notice of us. And surely, brothers, we hope that you will order a smith to settle here to mend our guns and hatchets—your kindness makes us so bold as to ask this request." I wondered which kindness he referred to. The kindness of sending traders out among them rather than soldiers, or the kindness of paying them more useless baubles for their goods than the French did. I was thinking like Caleb—God have mercy on me!

"You told us your friendship should last as long and be as great as the greatest mountain," continued the king of the Twigtwees, "and we have considered your word well. Therefore, all of our great kings and warriors are come to a resolution never to give heed to what the French say to us, but always to hear and believe what you our brothers say to us. We are obliged to you, brothers, for your kind invitation to receive a present at Logstown, but as our foreign tribes are not yet come among us, we must wait for them.

"You may depend on us to come to you as soon as our women have planted our corn in the Moon of the New Green, for we long to hear what you have to say to us. Brothers, until we meet again, we present to you this bundle of skins," and two young hunters laid hides at our feet. "Though we are poor and can offer you no more, we hope these skins will be shoes for you upon the path, and we thank you from our hearts for the clothes which you have put upon our wives and children."

We then took our leave of the king and his council, and Croghan and Montour prepared to travel down the river to Hockhockin in party with a small escort of Indians from the town.

Caleb and I crossed over the Miami to Robert Smith's house. Smith was a lone trader with a small cabin in the woods. He had taken our horses in to care for them while we stayed at Twigtwee Town, and he had cared for them well. They looked fine and fit, ready to run at our bidding. Connie Joe's mount was healthy as well, in much better shape than its master, and trotting rather like a colt within the fenced corral of the trader. The animals knew the weather had changed, and even the packhorses seemed eager to be out on the road again.

Caleb tied his bags absently upon his pack, missing his knots several times. His gaze was more often across the water than upon the work at hand.

"He is well," said the Narragansett doctor of his Susquehannock patient. "Well enough to be nursed to fuller health by someone other than myself."

"Well enough," I agreed.

Caleb secured his blankets on Metewis. No saddle for the pacer, and no bit. Just a thin covering between master and mount and a loose set of reins to urge the beast north or south.

"Where will you go?" I asked.

"Wherever the hunting trail leads," he answered, pulling himself up onto his horse. He adjusted his bow and his quiver at his back.

"And when you find the wolf?" I asked, for I had no doubt that he would.

"The gods alone know the outcome," he said.

"Go," said Connie Joe as I sat with him at his bed. "Go and take my prayers with you. That's the best I can do for you. Only wish Caleb was ridin' with you. Hate to see you go alone."

"I need a solitary season," I said to the old hunter. "A time to wander the woods and gather up kindling for my own fire."

"My wanderin' days are done, I reckon," said the Susquehannock wistfully. "But maybe I'll be wobblin' around a bit by the time you return."

"I mean to travel down the Ohio as far as the Falls before circling back," I said. "I still have my job to do, though it seems a rather empty piece of employment under the present circumstances."

"Circumstances are always present!" declared the old philosopher. "Either you gotta climb over 'em or go round 'em. Just so's you get to the other side—that's what pays, gettin' to the other side to see what needs to be seen and to do what needs to be done. So, go on and hurry back! The Ohio Company can't lay any brick streets until you find 'em a good piece of Indian ground to lay 'em on!"

"Maybe Caleb is going with me after all," I jested.

"Me and him both!" said the bed-tied Susquehannock.

Saturday, March 2 through Thursday, April 4, 1751

This land of the English King. This domain of the American Indian. This

contested ground wherein King Louis the XV of France had buried lead
plates bearing his name. This ancient Eden awakening from winter even
as I walked. This wild and untamed parcel of paradise. I thanked God for
the privilege of simply passing through it.

The lands upon the Great Miami were verdant even before the winter had
fully faded, rich and level and well-timbered, with some of the finest meadows
I had ever seen. Indians and traders that I met along the way assured me that
the land was as good and—if possible—better as far west as the Obache
(which they accounted as one hundred miles away) and all the way up to the
head of the Miami (sixty miles above Twigtwee Town) and down the same
river nearly one hundred and fifty miles to the Ohio. The grass grew to an
astounding height in the clear fields, of which there were a great number, and
the bottoms were full of white clover, wild rye, and bluegrass.

Being quite alone, and wary of French Indians, I left the path and
went southwestward down the Little Miami. The way was fine traveling
through rich lands and beautiful meadows in which I could sometimes
see forty or fifty buffalo feeding at once. At one point, the river ran a
good distance through the middle of a vast meadow, about a mile wide
and without so much as a bush in it. Buffalo grazed in the distance. The
entire country seemed laid out in sight forever before me as my mount
walked me through this grand, expansive field. I traveled about thirty
miles that day.

Gunshots disturbed nature's quiet concert on the following day, but I
was afraid to investigate their source lest they turn out to be some of those
French Indians I had no desire to meet. So I headed into the woods and
traveled nearly thirty miles more until nightfall. Just as the sun was heading to bed, I killed a barren cow-buffalo and took out her tongue and
some of the best of her meat. The trees I passed were oak, walnut, ash,
locust, and sugar trees. The ground was still level and quite rich.

My days went by quickly on my way back up to Shannoah Town, and
thirty miles was my average from sunup to sundown. I killed a fat bear on
one day and set out with my packhorse laden with bear meat the next.
Early in that afternoon, I came across a young trader, and we camped
together for the night. He had some bread with him, and I had plenty of
meat, so we fared rather well and passed the evening in quiet conversation.

On Friday the 8th of March, I arrived at nightfall in Shannoah Town.

All of the Indians, as well as the white men, came out to welcome my return. They were very glad to hear how successfully things had gone in the Miami country, and they fired upward of one hundred and fifty guns in loud and raucous celebration of an English peace with the Twigtwees. While at Shannoah, I took the time to lay down my trail from Twigtwee Town on a map I had been drawing. I also found a mirror, and—rather alarmed at the unusual length of my unruly beard—I shaved. Folks wondered who the stranger was after the razor had done its work, but we got reacquainted pretty quickly. Of course, my beard began to take back its lost ground almost immediately.

On Saturday the 9th, I met with one of the Mingo chiefs who had been down at the Falls of the Ohio when last I was in town. I told him about King George's present at Logstown and the meeting in the spring, and I invited him on down to Virginia. In turn, he told me of a party of French Indians who were hunting at the Falls. "If you go there, they will certainly kill you or carry you away as a prisoner to the French," he warned. "They will certainly not let you pass them by." Though I had no plans to part with my scalp or any great desire to travel under Indian guard all the way to Canada with my hands tied behind my back, I was still inclined to see the Falls and the land on the east side of the Ohio, so I resolved to venture as far as I possibly could.

I stayed two more days in Shannoah, preparing for my departure, and on Tuesday the 12th, my packhorses, my rested Neeyesee, and I were ferried across the Ohio—a journey of three-quarters of a mile over smooth and very deep waters.

"*Mauchase. Be my guide,*" I prayed to God in the Narragansett tongue as I struck a southeast path along *La Belle Riviere.* And I wondered where the powwow was. And if he had found the wolf. *Not yet,* I thought, and I wondered at the thought itself.

God walked with me through that Eden, as he had walked with Adam—a far greater and more humbling privilege than a personal audience with the king of the Twigtwees, the king of England, or the prince of any worldly domain. It caused me to think again about the earth and its many masters, and I remembered Roger Williams, the founder of Providence, the city of my birth. Williams believed the land belonged fully and rightfully to the Indians who hunted it, fished it, and dwelt upon it. It was given to them by God, he declared, and no English king across the sea could claim it to be his simply because an English fisherman had set his flag upon it. Williams lived what he preached, settling only upon those lands given to him by the Narragansett or paid for out of his own hand. But Williams was a lone voice crying in the wilderness, and—as Caleb had said—the big stone rolls down the hill and never sees the pebbles in its path. Williams's convictions were but mere pebbles in the path of an English avalanche. I didn't like to think so much about such things. I was only a pebble myself. What can one pebble do? I stopped to pull a small stone from the hoof of my hobbling horse. He paced much more freely after that.

"When the wicked man turneth away from his wickedness that he hath committed, and doeth that which is lawful and right, he shall save himself," I shouted with a loud voice to the birds and the beasts and the bushes and the trees. The Evening Prayers were meant to be recited loudly, and so I practiced them as loudly as I could. God, of course, did not require me to shout in order to hear me, but my soul needed it. "I acknowledge my transgressions, and my sin is ever before me. Hide thy face from my sins and blot out mine iniquities," I cried. And my heart bent itself before the presence of a mighty, holy, merciful, and loving God. The grasses beside the river bent as well, beneath the brisk, cool winds of March.

"The sacrifices of God are a broken spirit, a broken and a contrite heart, O God, thou wilt not despise." I thought of my wife and my children far away, and the weight of my absence from them lay like a burden upon me. I thought of Caleb running after the wolf alone, and my conscience struck me. I thought of Connie Joe upon his sickbed, and I wondered at the foolishness of leaving the old man while I earned a dollar wandering through Eden.

"Rend your heart, and not your garments, and turn unto the Lord your God, for he is gracious and merciful, slow to anger and of great kindness," I recited aloud. "I will arise, and go to my father, and will say unto him, 'Father, I have sinned against heaven and before thee, and am no more worthy to be called thy son.'" I remembered Pop and his great desire that my love of the forest be useful to the king and to his country. He'd be walking with me here himself if he were able, my heart assured me. And the river murmured its "Amen" as the words of Holy Scripture drifted with the wind across the broad Ohio.

"This is but one small tooth of the largest beast!" declared Hugh Crawford.

I stood beside the Ohio with three English traders who had just come up the river from a certain salt lick upon a small creek that runs into the south side of the Ohio about twenty miles above the Falls. The tooth I held in my hand weighed nearly four pounds. The traders had a larger one packed away.

"There were three beasts found at the salt spring about seven years past," said Crawford, a man of small stature with wiry blond hair and sky-blue eyes. "All bones and teeth. The biggest of the beasts had rib bones eleven feet long!"

"The skull is six feet wide across the forehead," said another trader, a man with no small skull himself, whose dark brown hair claimed every inch of his face below his nose and above his ears.

"Several teeth in the skull," continued Crawford, "and two which are horns, upward of five feet long! Quite a monster, it was. Like an elephant, more than not, though I doubt that Hannibal ever marched his army this far!"

"The fella that found the bones hid 'em so the French Indians shouldn't carry them away," said a third man, dressed half like an Indian and half like a French trapper, though his face was Anglo-Saxon and his name was Robert Richards.

"And speaking of French Indians," said Crawford, "there are about sixty of 'em camped at the Falls—according to some Shannoah Indians we met coming up the river in canoes. I'd steer clear, if I were you."

They let me keep the tooth, and I brought it in later for the Ohio Company. It was determined to be a jaw tooth, and it looked like fine ivory when the outside was scraped off.

I went south down the river about fifteen miles. The land on that side of the Ohio was chiefly broken, and the bottoms were narrow. Fifteen miles more brought me at dusk to a creek so high that I couldn't cross it until the better light of the next morn.

On the fifth day since my meeting with Crawford and company, I came to Lower Salt Lick, which some Indians had told me was fifteen miles above the Falls. The land was hilly, and I heard the sound of gunfire coming from downriver.

"Those red Frenchmen are still hunting and fishing down there," I complained to Neeyesee. "But they'll move out before long."

I apologized to the fine animal for torturing him upon this rocky trail, and I promised him that the aesthetic pleasures of the Falls would be well worth the hard labors of the present journey. But the closer I got, the more I despaired. I spied some newly set traps in the river and the streams, and that dampened my hopes that the Indians would be leaving the Falls shortly. Moccasin prints were now clear, fresh, and only a day old along the riverways. I considered leaving the horses under cover and descending to the Falls on foot, but I feared that the Indians might come upon the horses' tracks while I was gone.

"Guess we've seen enough good land by now to earn our keep," I told the horses begrudgingly, "but I sure would have liked to watch that river tumble over the rocks!"

Sadly assured in my own heart that the safest course was to leave the sightseeing to others, I pulled away southward until I was over the Little Cuttaway River.

The shaggy herd moved slowly through the high grasses as if it were Moses and the children of Israel out on a leisurely stroll through the Red Sea. I followed at a distance in its wake, marveling at the wide path so easily mowed in the vast meadow. The herd was out for its breakfast, and I for mine.

Bainbridge (my longrifle) nodded his head in front of me as I quietly trod the field behind the grizzly, grazing bison. What were these strange beasts, these monstrous plodders of the marsh and meadow? Their hinds reminded me of oriental oxen or English bulls, but their massive, misshapen torsos and heads seemed stolen from some classic myth and grafted on in place of God's original design. Bearded, brown, broad-browed, and horned, their faces alone might give a child nightmares. But I had found them mild in their behavior, more apt to wander quietly and appreciatively in their great green garden than to threaten their neighbors or to bother with the business of any other man or beast. Perhaps that was why they were so easy to bring home to the dinner table.

I slipped to one side into untrodden grasses and ran a distance in the direction of the herd. I had been watching a lame calf at the rear of the pack, and I thought it would feed me well for a few days. Wolves think the same when they spy the old and the lame and the halt. I thought of Caleb and Connie Joe and the White Wolf. I prayed as I ran.

Beside the herd now, near its rear but downwind and hidden in the tall green, I carefully made my way toward the low and constant noise of tearing grass and grinding jaws. I meant to poke my head out of my cover only long enough to find the calf and put a bullet in its brain. The herd might panic, of course, and run, but I was sure they would flee along their present course and not turn back on me.

Close enough to the clearing to see but not be seen, I spied my calf and then purposefully pushed forward into clear sight of the herd. An old cow looked at me curiously. Several shaggy, nodding heads followed her gaze in seeming disinterest and with little fear. But I didn't want to presume them all tame, and so I swiftly leveled Bainbridge's long neck toward the prey. The crippled calf was eating quietly alone.

A sadness struck me, a strange moment of regret in the heart of the hunter, as I pulled the trigger and let Bainbridge howl. The calf fell instantly, as if lightning had taken it down, and for a minute the startled herd moaned and shifted and bawled and stomped its feet. But it didn't run. It settled itself instead, and then slowly moved on, leaving the dead calf lying in the wet grasses. I imagined Caleb kneeling beside the still animal, pulling a gory arrow from its heart, giving thanks to the spirits in one breath and apologizing to the dead beast in the next. A sudden strong and steady wind blew across the field from the river, bowing it down so that the entire herd was momentarily within my sight. Did they know one of their own was fallen? What of its mother? Its father? Its brothers and sisters? Would they miss it? Would they mourn? But they kept on moving, slowly shuffling, quietly trampling down the back lawn of Eden, carelessly and unconsciously winding their way through their grassy, green sea.

Was Caleb right? Did I jest too much? I found myself jesting even with Neeyesee and the packhorse! There was no one else to joust words with, so I practiced fully with the rocks and the trees and the animals that bore my burdens and my saddle-sore, long-legged form. I laughed at myself quite often also—and that's a good thing. Keeps a man honest, if not entirely humble. And since there was no one to hide from, there was no need to hide, and I saw my faults quite clearly as I walked the wide woods in unfettered contemplation and communion with God. *Perhaps Romish hermits and monks have something to offer the worldly religious after all,* I mused. As my sins and my weaknesses walked increasingly naked at my side, I brought them continually to God's attention (to whom they were no revelation, for he saw them long before I did, poorly robed and insufficiently masked as they were).

I began to take delight in their uncovering, experiencing for the first time the fullness of those scriptural promises, *If we walk in the light, as he is in the light, we have fellowship one with another, and the blood of Jesus Christ his Son cleanseth us from all sin,* and *If we confess our sins, he is faithful to forgive us our sins and cleanse us from all unrighteousness.* My fellowship with God grew progressively stronger until I wondered that Adam could have been such a fool as to throw away the sweetness of the company of God in the cool of the Garden.

And then the Spirit reminded me that I was of the same dust as Adam, as free and as apt to fly or fall as the first man had been. Able to walk with God by grace and obedience or to turn aside in an instant to some forbidden fruit. Who was I to judge the world's first father? Though I walked beside the grand Ohio in the dim memory and the long shadow of that lost Garden, the serpent still slithered among men, and I was still a man. I was humbled further by the thought and led to pray more fervently for my own soul and those of my family.

Like high-coloured brass, the stones on the hill glistened in the light of the noon as the heat of the sun drew out of them a kind of borax or saltpeter.

I packed some away to take back to the Ohio Company, though I thought them to be nothing but some sort of sulfur.

I met some Indians in the woods and followed them to their town upon the Cuttaway. They gave me a pretty little bright-winged parakeet and a small wooden cage to carry him in. The woods were full of the birds, and the Indians liked to capture and tame them. Mine was perfectly tame, and I was happy to receive him. With his cage tied to the side of Neeyesee (I didn't trust the packhorses to carry him), he had a rather rattled ride through the forest, but the battering didn't seem to steal his song or lessen his pluck.

I killed a fat bear and grew sick the same night. With some difficulty, I dug a small pit into the side of a hill and heated some rocks to sweat in the Indian fashion. The sweating helped me and I was able to set out the next morn and travel twenty-four crooked miles to a small creek along the Cuttaway where I finally encamped, weary and with my head sorely aching. The feeding was poor for the horses there, but the banks of the river were so steep that it was impossible to ford it to better ground on the other side. Ledges of rocky mountain laurel made our way almost impassable, and I hoped that the next day would find us better ground to cover.

Dawn found me creeping over rocks and leading my horses through thickets that I had to cut away ahead of us. Two days of this incessant labor left me so tired—and the horses too—that I was obliged to camp within the laurel for a whole day in order to rest.

I left the horses staked in some good grass and went off on foot to find a way out of that cursed ground southeast of Eden. Great hills rose on either side of me as I wound through the thickets and climbed over rocks to push my way through the eternal tangle of bush and wood. Though I knew it to be nearing noon, the sun had not yet topped the rocky ridges that stared down at me as I stumbled through their thorny gauntlet. At length, the lay of the land began mercifully to transform, as the trail softened and the way ahead opened into woods of intermittent pine and oak. Beneath the pine, at least, the going was clear, and the way widened between the two mountains, showing me a passage through the hills. I followed my trail back to the horses and, after a night's rest, trod the same path once more, out of the clinging valley and into a wider land upon an unfamiliar creek where black slate and coal abounded. I packed some away for the Ohio Company. Meadows walled the waters again, and I killed a buffalo for supper.

Beaver. Bear. Buffalo. Wildcats and wandering wolves. Armies of geese and flocks of passenger pigeons so plentiful that they darkened the earth in their flight. Indian paths that led up the sides of crumbling cliffs and through watered gaps in great mountains. Salt licks and a thousand small streams. Blocks of coal, eight to ten inches square, lying on the surface of the ground as if some giant's child had been playing dominoes with them and had left them there when it was suddenly called to dinner.

And then a small creek that wound its way south then southwest, east then southeast, to a large Indian camp of seventy or eighty warriors. Captain Crane's town. His "coat of arms"—a crane standing on a rock within a pond—was painted on a tree, a practice common among war parties far from home and squaw.

"Will there be war between the English and the French?" asked Captain Crane, an Indian whose advanced age was well hidden by a mask of disordered paint, a history book of battle scars, and a well-muscled form that belied his true years. His English was remarkably unbroken. He took pride in the fact, I could tell.

"What do your men say?" I asked in turn, drawing deeply on the pipe we shared.

"They say that the sky is red each morning in the forest," he answered. "And that the trees bleed when a man strikes them."

"I walk the woods in peace," I declared. "I strike neither man nor tree. My home is upon the Yadkin, and my feet are sore upon their long walk home."

"You are an Englishman," said the war chief.

"You are a Wyendot," I remarked in the big man's own language, and the old warrior grinned. To be identified truly for who you are and to hear your own tongue in the mouth of a stranger are two of the greatest delights an Indian knows. Monsieur Montour would have been pleased with my diplomatic and linguistic progress.

"I have heard of you," said Captain Crane. "You are called Longshot by some. Longknife by others. Christopher Long by a few of your own. And, lately, Annosanah of the Wyendot." It was my turn to be flattered. I returned the grin.

"The river runs faster than a man can ride beside it," I remarked. And we talked and smoked and chewed on bear steaks late into the night.

I stayed all the next day at Captain Crane's to rest my horses, to catch up on my journal, and to plot my course thus far upon my map. As dusk was settling over the town, and as I was settling down to a bowl of the captain's soup, the door of the wigwam was pushed aside to reveal a breathless, weary traveler.

"He is gone," said the gasping shadow of a Narragansett.

"Were you with him?" I asked, rising anxiously from my meal.

"I was with him," he said, staring past me into the mourning flames of the captain's fire.

Though my mind impatiently demanded every detail of Caleb's wandering odyssey—from his hunt for the White Wolf to his return to the bedside of the dying Susquehannock—my heart would hear nothing of it until I walked alone beside the captain's creek and wept.

My tears were two streams that flowed to the same sea. One was a turbulent river of sorrow for the loss of a precious friend—lost to my own heart and to a world that sorely needed men such as good old Conestoga Joe. The other was a clean-flowing river of joy for a soul set free—for I knew with an inexplicable certainty that Joe indeed had already heard from God's own lips the very words he had prophesied: "There's that old Indian, Connie Joe! Come on in, Joe." And for a brief minute, I wanted to shed this flesh and fly to his side by that heavenly ocean. But the flesh has a tight and jealous—and not unjustified—grip upon this world, and once my eyes were emptied of tears and my soul was sated with prayer, I was ready for whatever work might yet be laid before me.

It was midnight when I returned to the tent. Caleb was standing outside, staring into the star-scattered sky that blinked down upon us from above the newly budded trees. A lone star shot suddenly across the dark expanse, and Caleb stumbled back into my arms, startled at its sight.

"He's waving good-bye," I whispered.

"I must follow him," said the Narragansett.

CHAPTER TWENTY-TWO

Of Fangs and Fury

Narragansett followed Narragansett through the greening forest, the powwow after the wolf. It was a long trail. The wolf doubled back, walked in rivers, stole a horse, crossed mountains, slept in caves and trees and meadows and a burnt, abandoned trapper's cabin. Sometimes the wolf didn't sleep at all, but ran all night. It knew—or at least suspected, if not feared—that it was being followed. Once it slew a deer and took its heart and tongue. Once it lost a claw upon a rocky ledge. The powwow found the knife and slid it into his own sheath.

"I will bite the wolf's neck with his own tooth," said the powwow.

No vengeance! argued the spirit of a wounded man upon a sickbed far away.

And then the powwow saw the broken branch, the slide of stones, the twisted entanglement of crushed and matted bush and grass at the foot of the steep hill. And the blood on the rock. The wolf was wounded.

The powwow slowed his chase. The trail was clear and fresh. The wolf was no longer running in circles, no longer climbing trees. It was scrambling, running, limping through the forest on the wide and well-walked Mingo Path that led to the Indian town of Catfish on Chartier's Creek.

Four whoops from Catfish, the powwow caught up with the wolf.

"I smelled him first," Caleb told me as we sat beside the fire in the crowded, tented headquarters of Captain Crane. "Then I heard him. Then I saw him, running lame along the trail midway up a high hill, white tail hanging low upon his bent and blood-scabbed back. *He is a weary, old, and wicked beast!* I cried within my heart. *Has he prowled the woods for seventy years? Eighty, maybe? The world will smell better when his stench is finally gone!"*

No vengeance! whispered the nagging spirit of an old Susquehannock.

The powwow armed his bow, tightened his moccasins, loosened the wolf's claw within its sheath, and turned his face to the treetops.

"This man killed my father," whispered the powwow to the wind. "As surely as if he had put the noose around my father's neck himself. As surely as if he had dropped the gallows floor from beneath my father's feet. And he has nearly killed my father once again, for Connie Joe is as a father to me. More of a father than the man they hung in Charlestown. More of a father …" Perhaps the wind carried his words up the road. Perhaps the spirits were speaking in the White Wolf's ears. It turned suddenly upon the hill. It howled—an anguished, angry, mournful, bloody sound that seemed to rattle the very trees. Then silence reigned for an eternal moment as the dark, glinting stare of the wolf crept into the soul of the whispering powwow. The powwow shuddered.

"Come and climb my mountain!" shrieked the White Wolf, deftly arming its rifle as the challenge rolled down the long hill. "Come and stick your crooked nose into my lair! Come and die!"

The powwow pulled his bowstring to his ear, licked his lips to test the wind, raised his weapon, calmly eyed his prey, and said his prayers.

"Come and die!" howled the wolf, forcefully hoisting its gun to its shoulder.

Birds sang in the branches. A gentle breeze whistled in the trees. Mottled patches of shadow and light scampered restlessly upon the late-greening forest floor. The sun squinted from its throne in the cloudless blue heavens. A sigh slid from the powwow's lips, but he did not move. His form was like rock upon the path, still and certain and with no dream of running either backward from the smoke of death or forward into its menacing face.

The weapon of the White Wolf roared. Its ball clipped the branches over the powwow's head. The powwow stood his ground.

"Come and die!" howled the wolf, frantically pouring powder into his gun's smoking muzzle. He fumbled with the weapon until it was once more loaded and primed. He lifted it again and aimed it at the still and silent warrior at the foot of the hill.

Once more, the rifle thundered in the spring forest. Once more, the ball missed its mark. Then the wolf turned to hobble up the hill.

The powwow disarmed his bow, slung it over his back, and pushed the arrow into its quiver. Slipping the wolf's claw from its sheath, he climbed the mountain behind the fleeing wolf.

"An arrow in his neck would not have paid the debt," said Caleb, fingering the White Wolf's claw. Its edge was chipped, its handle encrusted with dried mud.

Captain Crane leaned into our conversation. Warriors enjoy such tales. I sat on the edge of my stool, saying nothing, letting the tale find its own way out of Caleb's heart.

Upon the ridge at hilltop, the path spilled eastward to the waters of Chartier's Creek. The winding silver ribbon could still be seen through the budding, flowering trees. Upon the ridge at hilltop, the powwow faced the wolf at arm's length.

"Come and die," said the powwow. "Your own words fly back to you in Narragansett moccasins."

"You are no Narragansett," taunted the old wolf. "Nor was your father."

"Come and taste my blood," said the powwow. "And see if it is Narragansett or not."

"Blood is blood," said the old wolf. "It all tastes the same."

"I have lived thus far without the pleasure," said the powwow.

"Even on your island? Even in your sacrifices to Chepi?"

"My island …" said the powwow absently.

"No blood on your lips! No scalps on your belt!" coughed the wolf. "You are no powwow!"

"You killed my father," said the powwow.

"And so I must kill you," growled the White Wolf, "that I may yet run free."

"My father ..." said the powwow.

"Your father was a fool," said the old wolf. "A drunken fool. Just like Big Bill Moose, who couldn't keep his drunken mouth shut. Just like Oneshot. Just like ..."

"Connie Joe?"

"I meant the man no harm," growled the wolf. "You alone were in my sights, then as now. My bullets flew wide. Your medicine is strong, whether you drink blood or not!"

"Am I not a powwow and a Narragansett?"

"There are no more powwows among the Narragansett! You are the son of a drunkard and the slave of English farmers! You have had no vision from the gods! You have never eaten at Chepi's table! Your medicine comes from crawling naked among the ruins of the city of Canonicus. The spirits cling to you like the blackberry thorns beside my grandfather's wigwam. But you are no powwow!"

"What do you know of these things?"

"What do I know of these things? What do I know?" howled the ancient wolf, its fangs foaming. And it dropped its rifle in the path. "What do I know of these things?" it shrieked, tearing its vest from its wrinkled chest. And it started to dance upon the ridge at hilltop.

"He chanted his story as he danced," said Caleb, stirring the captain's soup as it boiled above the flames. "He sang of his father's father, who was a powwow in the days of Canonicus and Mascus of the Narragansett, in the days of Woipequand and Sassacus of the Pequot. He sang of his father, powwow in the dark days when Canonchet of the Narragansett was taken and killed during King Philip's War. He sang about himself, White Wolf the powwow among the Mohegan under Oweneco son of Uncas.

"When the gospel came to the Mohegan, and when Oweneco gave up warring and married the rum jug, White Wolf separated himself from that people. But Oweneco owed the doctor much for his powwowing, and he paid him with land upon the Connecticut. White Wolf raised his wigwam and his family there, and his medicine was strong—but he had many enemies. Once, upon returning from hunting, he found his wigwam burned and his fields plundered. His squaw and his children had fled to a nearby village. The sachem of that village came to him, offering protection for a price.

"'Give up your powwowing,' the sachem said to White Wolf, 'and I will see that your family is always safe and that no foe comes near your door.'

"But White Wolf refused. 'As long as this land is mine,' he said, 'I will hold it with my life and I will not give up my powwowing. But if any man can wrest it from me, then I shall turn from the spirits and live among the English.'

"Shortly afterward, Oweneco of the Mohegan fell drunk from a canoe and was hauled senseless from the water by two Englishmen named John Plumb and Jonathan King. Oweneco gave Plumb one hundred acres for saving his life. Those acres were the land upon which White Wolf lived. He protested in English court—and of course he lost. So he gave up his powwowing, as he had said he would, and moved to Charlestown among his Narragansett relatives. There he met Big Bill Moose. There he met Poor Tom, my father. There he killed a Negro servant in a drunken brawl."

The White Wolf spun like a whirlwind chasing its tail. It howled like a hurricane upon the Great Narragansett Bay. It spit and slobbered like a waterfall tossed in the winds of a summer storm. It rolled in the dirt. It shouted for all the gods of the earth and the sky and the seas to descend upon the hill and smite its enemy. It dashed its head against a large rock, causing its own blood to paint its face red. It tore its fur. It kicked and fumed and flung its thin limbs round and round in an effort to conjure the spirits from their own business and into the battlefield upon the hill. And then it sat flat down upon the path, staring hatefully for one brief moment into the powwow's astounded eyes, and fell over backward in a dead faint.

"A dead faint," repeated Caleb. "So much dead that he never got up again. With this knife and with these hands, I buried the old wolf beside the path."

"Did the spirits not come to him?" asked Captain Crane, his old eyes wide with the wonder of the tale.

"They came," said Caleb. "I saw them."

"You saw them," I repeated skeptically.

"I saw them come upon the poor old creature," said Caleb simply. "I saw them lay him on his buttocks upon the road. I saw them crawl into him through his eyes, his ears, his nose. I saw them stir up his soul in hot and bitter hatred. I saw them grip his heart, squeeze it, and burst it within his bowels. I saw them leave. There was nothing left then but to bury his carcass."

"The spirits did this to him?" asked Captain Crane incredulously, his voice cracking.

"Yes," said the powwow.

"Your medicine ..." Captain Crane began.

"Had nothing to do with it," Caleb finished.

"But you are a powwow," said the captain.

"I am an Indian," said Caleb. "I am a Narragansett," he said. "And I do not want to die upon a hill far from home with demons tearing my flesh from within."

Caleb bought a horse at Catfish and wandered the same twisted trail back to where it had begun. "Back to the bed of Connie Joe," said the Narragansett sadly as the two of us walked alone beside the captain's creek. "The old hunter was under a fever from his wounds, and nothing that I tried—I did not dance, I will not dance again—could make him any better. But he could hear me always, and sometimes he could speak. I told him what had happened with the White Wolf. 'Vengeance belongs to the heavenly Father,' the old man said, and he warned me strongly to turn from the spirits entirely and forever. I made him no such promise while he lived, but I vowed upon his deathbed to follow him."

"Follow him?" I asked.

"He is *nósh*," said Caleb cleanly in his native tongue. "He is my *father*. Somewhere, he lives. His soul lives. Sowanniu or heaven. In the presence of some Great God. Somewhere."

"Follow him, then," I said.

CHAPTER TWENTY-THREE

Holler toward Home

Friday, April 5, 1751

I am going home," said Caleb.

"To Rhode Island?" I asked.

"I must see that my mother is well," said the Narragansett. "I must meet with Hazard and tell him the story of White Wolf. I must face the magistrates with the truth in order to clear my father and my mother, my sister and my brother, my children and my own soul from the lies that have been our burden for so long. Hazard's word is strong, and his love is good. I will have to trust it, English or not. Netop, too, has gained the respect of many, and his word is strong in our old country. For as you once said, he has even made something of himself in the eyes of the English. If they trust his fences to hold in their cattle, perhaps they—some of them, anyway—will trust his word on my behalf. I must go back. I can run no longer."

"When your business is done?" I asked.

"I will sell my island," he said, "and bring my squaw westward into these woods. I will look for Moses Great Hill. I will ask about the Lamb. I will follow my father, Connie Joe."

"You're a powwow," I reminded him.

"I am an Indian," he said. "A Narragansett. But I am no longer a pow-wow."

"I'm heading home too," I said, diverting the discussion from spiritual things. Though my heart was unspeakably gladdened by Caleb's decision to forsake the spirits and seek after God, I was afraid that my big mouth might cough up some kind of stumbling block upon his path. *Best to let God—and the words of old Connie Joe—take things from here,* I thought. Joy and Netop too, I reasoned, would be better used by the Spirit than I to take their own by the hand and point the way.

"To the Yadkin?" he asked.

"I forget what it looks like!" I jested.

"No one there will recognize you either," returned the Narragansett, "unless you shave your face and cut your locks."

I watched him go, tall and dark upon the back of his Narragansett pacer, feather in his long, black hair. I watched him go, and I said a prayer for his safety on the road and his salvation at its end. I knew he'd say one for me, no matter who he said it to. And I was sure God would hear him, whether Caleb knew it yet or not.

Saturday, April 6, 1751

I went south and southeast along the Warrior's Road, alone with my horses, my journal and my map, my bittersweet reflections of the long path behind me, my prayer book and my prayers, my wilderness spoils and my parakeet.

Sunday, April 7 through Sunday, May 12, 1751

Though spring had fully overtaken winter, the rains were merciless, so heavy and dark that I couldn't travel for days at a time. The country rose rocky and mountainous before me, wrapped in laurel so tangled and thick that no progress was possible without the constant hacking of the hatchet and the sawing of the knife. It was the worst traveling I had ever seen, and at night I dreamed of Bartram's gardens by the Schuylkill.

I killed bears for my meat, and though there was plenty of water for the horses, good grass was scarce in the barren hills. My grain ran low.

The cliffside was treacherous, wet and loose from the rains of yesterday. No path lay before us on the mountain, and there was no other course but to go up and over. Neeyesee never balked, but I could sense the desperation in his wild determination to carry us out of this terrible country. I barely needed to goad him on; his own will drove him up the rocky slope in strong, instinctive hope of good ground and green grass on the other side.

The packhorses didn't have quite the same fire burning on the inside of their mangy hides. If they'd have been men, they would have been the murmuring and disputing sort, always mumbling behind your back, plotting some kind of mutiny, demanding some sort of unreasonable recompense for their unbearable labors. They despised running. They didn't like to swim the rivers. They hated the mountains. Indeed, if they had been men, I would have dismissed them from their positions long ago. I should have traded them both to Captain Crane for just one good mule in their place. But they were all I had at the moment, to my dismay and to their own hurt.

Neeyesee halted upon the slope, not out of stubbornness or rebellion—neither vice was ever in the heart of the grand animal—but from that keen sense of danger that all good horses have somewhere within them.

"What do we see?" I asked him quietly. "What do we hear?" But my own eyes and ears could discern nothing amiss. "What do we smell?" I asked further, for perhaps the mount had caught the scent of some man or beast. The packhorses shuffled uneasily behind us.

Then I saw it, a lumbering, dark form upon the horizon above us. A black bear—nothing to fear and good news besides. If a bear was wandering upon the ridge, then the ground above us and beyond held promise of fresh feeding for the horses and the cover of trees over our heads. I urged Neeyesee onward, but he wouldn't move.

"Snakes?" I questioned, scanning the slippery surface around us. But I saw none.

Then the hill began to move. It was not the bear that the pacer had feared. It was the earth itself! The storm-loosened hillside was shifting beneath the hooves of the horses, slowly but absolutely. Quicksand is no less frightening than a mountain that threatens to fall with you on it. I had no answer for my mount. Up or down, at that moment, was all the same.

The packhorses panicked. One most surely said to the other, "We're gonna die!" and that set them both to stamping in circles 'round each other. The ground beneath them crumbled under their hooves, releasing a slide of stone and mud that caused them both to fall upon their sides on the steep incline.

It was all I could do to hold Neeyesee steady as I watched the unruly animals tumble down the mountainside. Mud and stone came behind them in short and terrifying pursuit. Neeyesee and I followed, keeping pace with the sliding hill as well as we could, colliding at times with low-leaning scrub oaks and stubborn outcrops of rock that held on tightly as the earth flowed around them. We stumbled at last to a hard-panting halt at the bottom of the restless cliff. The slide ceased. The packhorses struggled limply onto their legs, their packs torn in places and spilled here and there upon the ground. I climbed off Neeyesee to check him first for injuries—and I saw the broken bird cage. My parakeet wasn't moving.

I took the small bird from its damaged house and held it in my hand. It was dead. This tore my heart up more than the spilled packs or the battered packhorses. It may seem to you a silly trifle, but that little bird had been such a brisk and happy creature even in the midst of thundering storms and choking laurel. To see it suddenly limp and lifeless was a hard and bitter blow. I buried the little fellow beneath a laurel bush. I even thought of praying over it, but I reckoned that a funeral service for a bird might just be going a bit too far. I found some small comfort in the fact that God himself takes sad note of every sparrow that falls.

I patched the packs as best I could, fed the packhorses the remainder of the grain, and let them rest a day or two while I walked along the creek in search of better passage. I found only such a wicked precipice and such stubborn thickets of laurel that it was impossible even to attempt the way on horseback. We must go back up the hill from which we had fallen—and when the sun had dried the mountain sufficiently, that's exactly what we did. Neeyesee, champion that he is, led us all the way up and over.

I cut a two-mile gulch through the mountain vines, climbing the rocks all the while. I fell once while on foot and knocked my ribs up sorely. Thunder and lightning and rain dogged me each step of the way. Creeks ran high, too high to ford, forcing me to go over their heads upon a continual ledge of almost inaccessible mountains of rock and laurel. If I were ever a king with a castle, and I wanted to protect myself from the armies of my enemies, I would dismiss the old idea of encircling my house with stone walls and moats, and I would plant laurel instead!

The sun rose in a clear, blue sky. I had nearly worn out the page in my prayer book that entreated God for fair weather, but by then I knew the words by heart.

East and southeast I moved, to a little river that fell into the Big Conhaway, called Blue Stone. The horses had good feeding, and my camp was dry.

I killed a buffalo at the foot of a very high mountain, and I ate well in lone and quiet contemplation of the remarkable peak that rose above me. A monstrous rock, sixty or seventy feet in height and with a cavity in the middle of it, sat upon the top of the mountain, looking to all the world like the home of some mythological bird or beast. I thought of the winged Roc of Ulysses and half imagined that I saw—within the cavern high above my head—the massive, yellow, blinking eyes of that awful, ancient bird. I unpacked the great tooth that I'd been given on the other side of the Ohio and wondered further about the gigantic beast in whose mouth it once lodged. With my curiosity piqued, I determined to climb the hill before me, to enter it through its high window, and to see what might lie inside.

I scrambled up the stony incline in a race with my imagination. And even if the distant cavern held no monster, no ancient tooth nor bleached bones, the height would still afford me a grand and useful view of the countryside around me. A crisp, cool morning wind blew upon the mountain, pushing giant white billows through the clean, blue skies. The sun played hide-and-seek above the rolling clouds, falling on me in bright intervals that made the rocky cliffside shine about me so brightly that I squinted as I climbed. Laurel and rhododendron crawled intermittently among the rocks. Some sparse bushes and small trees clung precariously to the hillside. At length, I found myself at the chin of the great rock, within the shadows of its cavernous mouth.

I rested there, taking the thin air into my lungs with long and grateful breaths. My horses, at the roots of the great mountain, resembled little mice. They were tethered in good grass and would be content to rest there much longer than I intended to allow them.

I entered the cave and quickly discerned that few men—if any—had found this shelter before me. There were no signs of any human habitation anywhere. Bears may have wintered here. Cats too. But the droppings of birds and bats were the only fresh signs of life. Certainly none of the smaller mammals of the woods would have any use for a holiday this high above their feeding grounds. I wandered farther in and discovered a passage, dry and stone-walled, that gradually ascended to the very top of the gigantic rock. At certain places along the way, cracks extended their airy fingers to the bright outside, letting in the light of day, illuminating dimly the black walls and dusty floor of my natural stairwell.

When I'd ascended to the top, where my final steps were somewhat slippery with the rains that had entered some cracks in the stone roof, I found myself up against a dark and dripping ceiling of quartz-like rock. To my one side was a thin stream of white light that lay against the wet side of the stairwell like a lone torch upon the wall of a damp dungeon. I had to crawl to it, but once within reach of that handful of light, I could look up and see the sky. A crack opened in the ceiling, wide enough to climb into, but narrowing to an arms breadth near its exit. I decided to brave it.

Within moments, my own arm was out of the cavern and pointing toward the blue. Pebbles rolled in upon me, bouncing from my shoulders and head. I pulled some more of the outside in and realized quickly that I could dig my way out without much effort. A few larger stones took longer than I thought they would—some fell in past me, others were pushed out ahead of me—but soon I was atop the highest boulder I had ever straddled, a dizzying and frightening experience.

From my chair in the clouds, I could see a prodigious distance, and I plainly discovered, to my great joy and with gratitude to God, where the Big Conhaway broke through the next high mountain. That was the path I must travel homeward. I pulled myself precariously upon my feet, buffeted as I was by the wind and with no support at the top of the world but my own weary and shaking legs, and I gave one big holler toward home. I was sure that my Sarah could hear me (thin air at such heights affects the brain!), and I meant to ask her about it when I reached the Yadkin. I climbed back into my mountain, descended its dim and dusty hallway, came out upon its shadowed ledge, skittered down its steep hillside, untied my horses, rode about five miles north and east, and camped for the remainder of the afternoon and all through the night.

It rained for two days, and I stayed in my camp to take care of some provision I had killed. The next day, the packhorses ran away, and it was nearly evening before I found them again.

"Perhaps you'd like to find your own way home?" I asked them, as Neeyesee looked down upon them with something like contempt in his dark, round eyes.

The Big Conhaway was high, but I got us halfway over onto a large island where I stayed the night. The next morn found me cutting logs to construct a raft in order to cross the remaining half of the river. The waters were wider there and much deeper. I wished Connie Joe were with me. Indians are better at making rafts than Providence boys like me. Maybe he could even have ferried the horses across. The packhorses—if they'd had the resources—would have paid him handsomely for the service.

Across the Conhaway and up it about two miles south, the New River ran laughing through the woods. I crossed it about eight miles above the mouth of the Bluestone. It's better than two hundred yards wide there, and very deep, but full of rocks and falls. The bottoms on it are rich but narrow, and the high land is broken.

My path beyond the New River led me to a large warrior's camp, where I came upon an Indian who had hunted with Connie Joe and me upon the Juniata. We sat around his fire late into the night, telling old stories and making up new ones. He was grieved to hear about the death of the old Susquehannock, but I assured him that the old man was in heaven. He wasn't so willing to accept my word on such unseen realities, but he seemed comforted by the possibility. We talked a bit about the Moravians, and I told him about Moses Great Hill. He'd heard of the medicine man, and was curious—though understandably skeptical—about the old doctor's conversion. I read to him some from my prayer book, and he expressed his desire to learn to read for himself someday.

It was a fine, fresh, clear lake, about three-quarters of a mile long and about a quarter mile wide. A clean shore of gravel wrapped around it, ten yards wide and framed in its entirety by a wind-swept grassy meadow. Six fine springs bubbled up out of the meadow to feed the lake. Set on top of a very high mountain, I imagined I could see the Yadkin from its blue, watered summit. But I didn't write my dreams down in my journal. I only penned facts—the rest I wrapped up in my memory for tales around my table.

"We're so close now that I can smell the kitchen fires of home!" I told Neeyesee as we wandered southward from that bright oasis. *And yet so far away!* I told myself.

Augusta County on the New River. The homestead of Richard Hall. Stuck way out at the wild and farthest edge of the frontier. I don't know of anyone who lived farther west on the New at that time. Hall's piece of the woods was a frightening, shadowed, and uncertain country to most folks in that day, but it was the bright and welcomed doorway of civilization to me!

I stayed for a day at Richard Hall's and wrote a letter to the governor of Virginia and the Ohio Company, letting them know that I would be with them by the fifteenth of June. I told Hall and his wife that it hardly seemed possible that I'd been out in the wild for over half a year. Missus Hall assured me that it was not only possible, but it was also rather obvious, and she bid me look in her mirror to prove it to myself. After a quick study of my figure in the looking glass—and egged on by a social conscience that had been dormant in the wilderness but which, in the presence of an English woman who kept a clean house, was now once more awakening—I promptly begged for some soap and a sharp razor. I even considered buying some fresh clothes from Mister Harris. But when I tried on one of his shirts, it was too small, and so I settled for a bath, a shave, and a trimming and a combing of my long, tangled hair. I even scrubbed the tail of my coonskin cap.

"Now, that's better!" said Missus Hall.

"Thought you were a magical talkin' black bear when you walked in here!" jested Mister Hall, grinning. "And I was thinkin' about puttin' you in a cage and chargin' folks money to hear you speak. But now I can see you're nothin' but a plain old white fellow like me. So I guess I'll just sell you a fresh packhorse and send you on your way."

CHAPTER TWENTY-FOUR

The Yadkin

Saturday, May 18, 1751

I crossed the line between Virginia and Carolina, and my heart started singing like a robin in spring. The robins, of course, were already dutifully (and happily, I believe) occupied with their natural melodies—so my heart provided harmony.

Neeyesee paced the homeward trail—narrow and little-worn—as if he'd run it all his life. Perhaps he had a compass of his own somewhere inside. Perhaps he'd read my maps. I let his reins fall at his neck and stretched my tired arms toward the heavens to embrace the Carolina sky. I closed my eyes to breathe in the Carolina air, to soak in the Carolina sun, to dream of home.

Home. Sarah, my blue-eyed sunflower. Anne and Violette, spinning and cooking and laughing in their sleeves together by the fire. What would they do, what would they say, when I came riding up to the front door? Richard would greet me with a Yadkin holler and run to pull me off my horse. Thomas would stand there grinning real wide and turning red—I'd wager he'd probably grown a foot since I had gone! Nathanael— tall and unsmiling, looking more like my father every morning that he wakes up—would take my horse by the reins and say, "Welcome home, Pop. Missed ya a whole lot." And Mercy, his wife—quiet and shy most times, but loud and laughing when surprises sneak up on her—would clap her hands and giggle. Maybe there'd even be a grandchild on the way by now. I could almost hear their voices, smell the pudding cooking in the kitchen. I imagined lying next to my Sarah in the late, late evening, holding her close, whispering things that were meant for her ears only, things

I'd rehearsed in my heart a hundred times while sleeping alone beneath the western trees.

I woke with a start. In all the long miles upon the back of my Narragansett pacer, I had never fallen asleep while riding. And here I was on the last legs of my famous journey, napping like a baby while my horse carried me down the road past Indian wigwams and the homes and lands of the few, scattered whites that I dared to call neighbors.

The first thing that broke through my dreams was the quiet rush of the Yadkin under the willows. Though a man may cross five thousand rivers in a lifetime of wandering, I will swear on my prayer book that no river sings so soft and so sweet and so low as that which runs past a man's own house, sunlight and moonlight, week into week, season after season.

And though a traveler may lodge comfortably in the castles of kings and the longhouses of great sachems, there is no earthly abode that so sets the heart at peace and the body at rest than a man's own home. And there it was, suddenly and at last, the House of Long, purposefully and carefully carved out of the wooded wilderness and laid lovingly log on log by scarred and calloused Long hands, sitting pretty as a painting in that hard-won clearing near the old pine stand. Flowers winding up the trellis by the front door. Spring grass growing so high I'd need a scythe to lay it back down low. But why wasn't it cut?

And where were the horses? The cows? The dogs? The boys?

No sound of hounds barking. No smoke above the chimney.

I slid numbly from my mount and tread the tall grass to the door. It was locked. The windows were shut. I remembered a weak shutter back of the house, and I found it no stronger than when I'd left. I pried it open, splintering the latch from the wood.

No glass at the window. Hadn't the panes been delivered? Was Thomas hesitant to put them in himself? Where was Thomas? Where was the family?

My mind was a hornet's hive of perplexity as I tore the paper from the window frame, unlatched the window, and hauled myself inside. The house was void of life, dusty, but not disheveled. Nothing was out of its place or broken. The fire was tidy, swept clean of ashes.

"God," I said aloud, standing in the middle of the small cabin, "where's my Sarah?"

Almost unconsciously, I closed the broken shutter, plunging the house into shadowed darkness. I fumbled with the useless latch, then let the shutter go, and it swung back open of itself, enlightening the room anew. I walked to the door, turned its bolt, and heaved it open. The sounds of the forest at spring leapt upon me from the riverside as the afternoon sun called me out into the unkempt yard.

"Sarah!" I hollered as I stood beneath the spruce. "It's me—Chris! I'm home!" The robins sang in the willows. The red-winged blackbirds answered their song. "I'm home," I muttered to myself. "God! Where is my family!" I shouted to the heavens. Was I dreaming? Was I still asleep upon my pacer, dreaming? "Violette! Richard!" I bellowed as I ran beside the river. "It's your father! I'm home!"

And I sat down at last beside the weeping waters.

I was not despairing. But I was weary, oh, so weary.

I wasn't really scared—somehow I wasn't. I was just a man too tired. Tired of searching for my home. Too tired to be a man. Too lost to get up and check my compass or set a course. Too aching of heart to get back on my horse and ride to the nearest settlement to ask the questions that thundered in my head like a battery of cannons.

I laid myself upon my face at riverside. I prayed myself to sleep.

"Long?"

I rolled over and stared into a dark and indistinct face. Where was I? Somewhere along the Ohio? In some Indian town? In the camp of Irish traders? I'd been dreaming of home. Disappointment pierced my heart.

"Long?" the face repeated. The moon lay the man's shadow across my eyes. Crickets played their fiddles in the tall grass.

"Yeah," I answered. "I'm Long. Who are you?"

"Josh Harris," said the face. "Your neighbor." And then I knew the voice.

I sat up and ran my hands through my dew-soaked hair.

"The Yadkin," I said, glancing at the waters near my feet. "I'm home."

"My old lady, Sally, saw ya ridin' by earlier this mornin'," said Harris.

"Said ya looked either wounded or asleep. She knew ya must be headin' here, headin' home. So when I got back to my place from huntin', she told me I oughta come over here to check on ya. I rode on over, and I saw the horses, but I couldn't find ya. That big black mount led me down to the river. He knew right where ya were."

"Does he know where my family is?" I asked.

"Yer family is safe," said Harris. And I sighed a deep and grateful, healing, restful sigh.

"Thanks be to God," I whispered, and I thought that the river murmured—like a congregation in answer to its priest—*Thanks be to God.* I stood up, taking the man's hand firmly. "Where can I find them?" I asked.

Indians had been running the woods, killing, burning, scalping. Five English settlers had been murdered during the winter not far from my place. Sarah was frightened for her life and the safety of the children, and she closed up the house and took the family to Roanoke, about thirty-five miles east and closer to real civilization. Harris and his Sally, a tough old couple with a little house up under a hill some miles back along the path, stuck it out in the woods by themselves. Harris was half Indian anyway, if not by blood then by instinct and habit. I thanked the old man for the news, and as I knew him to be a man I could trust, I begged him to care for my packhorses and their loads while I rode to Roanoke. He was quite willing, and I watched him lead them off into the moonlit eve. No sooner was he out of sight than I climbed back on Neeyesee, headed his nose east, and ran him as fast as his hooves could fly.

The lonely path became a wheeled road at length, matted down by the occasional traffic of the trader's wagon, the farmer's cow, the wanderer's horse, or some old Indian's mule. The way opened wide and clear as the midnight black mount and the weary white boy from Providence thundered down the dark, grassy avenue. We arrived at Roanoke the same night, blowing and sweating and as wide awake as the glassy, white moon that hung full and bright in the star-splashed sky. I found all my family there, hearty, happy, and well.

CHAPTER TWENTY-FIVE

One Morn in Late Summer

Wednesday, September 17, 1751

Both letters came the same day. Cresap brought them down to me from Will's Creek. He stayed two nights before heading east on some business with the government of Maryland. I read the missives aloud to Sarah as we sat one morn in the late-summer sun beside our whispering Yadkin.

The corn stood high at our backs, a ripening, tousle-topped palisade of gold and green that ran out of sight in both directions along the river. Richard and Thomas and I had sweated together and plowed together and sowed together for many a day before sitting back to pray together and watch Nature do her part as God has instructed her. Now the harvest was nearly full, and we'd soon be calling on our scattered neighbors to help with the reaping and the storing and the feasting and the giving of thanks. Having my hands in the soil for a season, my feet at my own fire, and the hum of my own kin around my small kitchen, the wanderlust had almost been plucked from my heart. But not fully, for God himself had planted it there.

"Read the one from New England again, will you, Christopher?" said Sarah, brushing her long, yellow hair from her tired blue eyes as the wind sought to wrap it around her thin, lined face. The summer grasses bent their necks northward with the warm breeze that rolled over us from off the running waters. "Read the whole of it," she said. "We have time."

"Time," I sighed, smiling, as I unfolded the thin parchment.

"My dear Christopher," it began, written in the simple but elegant hand of a Narragansett hunter and doctor who had learned his letters on an English plantation in Rhode Island. "The gods (and One in particular) have been laboring on my behalf along the salty coast that my grandfathers once called their own. English cheese still sells well, Hazard's pacers are more famous by the day, and my mother is well (she sends your family thanks and greetings), but that is not what my heart is bursting to tell you.

"My father's name (and my own as well) is clean once more! For Hazard (bless his white skin and his gray head!) opened his pocketbook and risked his reputation to have Poor Tom's case brought to court again at last. It is a longer tale than I care to scrawl on paper, but the outcome (after those battles of the kind that only English lawyers and preachers can wage or comprehend) is the total purification of my family's name. True friends and witnesses (both red and white) rose up without fear when it was noised about that the White Wolf was dead. The noose has been cut from my deceased father's memory, and it has been lifted from my own head in the slaying of Bill Moose and Woody One-shot.

"I have sold my island to Netop (on the condition that he build no walls around it!), and with some of the money I have bought half a dozen pacers from Hazard. Three are for your sons, and you will have them soon, for I intend to deliver them myself.

"Susanna and I are riding south before the next new moon. I intend to leave her at Bethlehem among the Christian Indians while I come to see you. Then I will follow Connie Joe into the forest in search of the Lamb. I have not taken leave of my senses, Christopher, and I ask for your prayers.

"I am, sir, your faithful and unworthy friend, Caleb."

Squirrels dropped acorns onto the far shore from the treetops across the waters as a painted turtle slid from his riverside bed into the lazy stream to avoid the shower of nuts and shells.

"Susanna will be staying with Moravian Indians," noted Sarah thoughtfully.

"And Caleb will be hunting for the Lamb," I added.

"I thank God!" sighed Sarah, looking into the cloud-streaked summer sky. "And he has left the Devil off his name," she added. I had noticed that. It was of no small significance. I was about to comment further, when she asked for the second letter to be opened again.

"I'm sorry about it, Sarah," I said, as I picked up the parchment that was marked with the seal of the Ohio Company.

"A man must answer his calling," she stated simply, forcing a smile that lit her eyes briefly with that light that had caught my own eye so many years gone (and held it ever since).

I took her hand and placed the letter in it.

"Won't you read it to me instead?" I asked.

She laid it back on my lap and mouthed a quiet, "No."

I opened it. "Which part?" I asked.

"Just all of it," she said.

"I'm sorry about it," I repeated as I began to read: "'To Mr. Christopher Long from the Committee of the Ohio Company, July 16th, 1751.

"'As soon as you can conveniently, you are to apply to Col. Cresap for such of the Company's horses as you shall want for the use of yourself and such other person or persons you shall think necessary to carry with you; and you are to look out and observe the nearest and most convenient road you can find from the Company's store at Will's Creek to a landing at Mohongeyela. From thence, you are to proceed down the Ohio on the south side thereof, as low as the Big Conhaway and up the same as far as you judge proper, and find good land. You are all the way to keep an exact diary and journal and therein note every parcel of good land ...'"

"'As soon as you can conveniently,'" quoted Sarah tersely in the midst of my reading. I set the letter down.

"Not till harvest is done," I said. "Early November, I think."

"I will close up the house as I was forced to last winter," said Sarah.

"Harris will keep an eye on the place as he wanders through," I added. "And I'll pay him in corn to cut the grass down in the yard."

"Did the Company lose your first journal?" Sarah asked sarcastically.

"There's more land to be seen than what I last discovered," I answered.

"How long, Christopher?"

"Till March or April, I reckon."

Sarah leaned into my breast, and I held her close. "Time," she whispered sadly, fingering the leather fringes of my shirtsleeve.

The wind tied her hair around my neck as we watched the river run.

A Glossary of Terms

Though most of the Indian terms (and many of the older English terms) that are used in the story are easily understood in the context of our narrative, several items may need some explanation. This short glossary will help you better enter the eighteenth-century world of Caleb and Longshot and their companions, and will aid you in understanding the history of their own past. In a few cases, pronunciations are included for those words that are most apt to be mispronounced.

Askug Literally "snake" in Narragansett. Askug was the name of Caleb's great great great grandfather, a Narragansett powwow (fictional) in the early/mid 1600s.

Belial A Hebrew word meaning "worthless," "reckless," or "lawless." Biblically, the phrase "a son of Belial" simply means "a worthless person."

betty lamp The earliest form of oil lamp used in colonial America, the betty was a small, shallow receptacle, two or three inches in diameter and about an inch in depth. Some were rectangular, some oval, round, or triangular, with a projecting nose or spout an inch or so long. They usually had a hook and chain by which they could be hung on a nail on the wall. Tallow, grease, or oil was their fuel, and a piece of cotton rag or coarse wick was so placed that, when lighted, the end hung off the nose. From this wick, which dripped dirty grease, rose a "dull, smoky, ill-smelling flame" (Alice Morse Earle, *Home Life in Colonial Days,* p. 43). But they provided light!

bottoms The low, alluvial lands along a river or stream; the floodplain.

Cautantowwit (caw-TAN-tow-it) The Narragansett creator-god, who lived in the Southwest and who oversaw the affairs of men and judged them at death.

Chepi (also *Hobomucko*) The Devil of the Narragansett pantheon of gods. Not totally evil, Chepi nevertheless was associated with doom and gloom. He was also the patron spirit of the powwow, appearing in visions most often as a serpent (a very old trick!).

Conestoga Literally "people of the blackened pole," Conestoga is an English corruption of *Gandastogues*, a name the French attached to the Susquehannocks. This nation of Native Americans once inhabited the lands of the rich Susquehanna River basin. By the middle of the

eighteenth century (the time of our narrative in *Longshot*), only a
small town of Conestoga Indians still remained upon the
Susquehanna, at a point along the river just south of the city of
Lancaster, Pennsylvania.

Conestoga wagon This hardy wagon of Pennsylvania German invention and
construction was the heavyweight hauler of the eighteenth and nine-
teenth centuries. Its broad iron tires rolled over tens of thousands of
miles during those years, first carrying goods to and from Lancaster and
Philadelphia, and then rolling west with the expansion of the nation.
The boatlike shape of the wagon's body was designed to keep freight
from shifting on hills.

Delaware Called Delaware by the English because they were first seen on
the Delaware River (so named by the English in honor of Thomas
West, Baron De La Warr, first governor of Virginia), these Indians
called themselves the *Lenni Lenape* (The Original People). At the
beginning of the seventeenth century, the Delaware inhabited a continuous territory from Delaware Bay to Manhattan Island and up the
west bank of the Hudson as far as Kingston, New York. By the time
of our narrative, the Delaware had been pushed away from their earlier lands and were gathered in the Wyoming Valley of the
Susquehanna and farther west along the Allegheny River.

Kaukant Literally "crow." In Narragansett mythology, the crow brought
the Indians their first corn seed from the gardens of Cautantowwit. In
gratitude, the Narragansett allowed the crow (but no other bird!) the
freedom of the fields. If only kaukant could repay them for his centuries of mooching!

Keesuckquand Literally "the sun" in Narragansett.

longhouse The Delaware, the Susquehannock, and the nations of the
Iroquois all lived in houses called "longhouses." Though the roof
construction among the Susquehannock and the Iroquois was
rounded (like a military Quonset hut), and the Delawares built their
roofs with a peak like an English barn, the inside of all their houses
was very similar. Unlike the Indians of New England who generally
built their wigwams for individual families (which often, however,
included many generations), the longhouse was more of an apart-
ment building, housing several families of the same lineage. The typi-
cal longhouse was thirty to a hundred feet or more in length, having
a door at each end, a corridor down the middle, and bunks lining
the sides. Each family (mother, father, and children) lived around a

fire in the corridor, with a smoke hole in the ceiling above it. Bark partitions separated the bunks of each family. The framework was of poles, and the covering—inside and out, walls and roof—was long bark shingles, which overlapped. Everything was held together with strips of the inner bark of the linden tree or with hickory twigs, and with a crisscross of light poles on the outside to secure the bark firmly.

manitoo General term for a god. Besides the specific gods for whom the Indians had specific names, this term was often applied to any object, person, or happening the Indians found extraordinary. The English and the Dutch, when first encountered by the Indians of New England, were considered manitoos.

medayoo Literally "conjurer" in Munsee Delaware. The medayoo was the medicine man—the shaman—of the Delaware people.

medicine Of Latin and Middle English derivation, the New England Indian borrowed this word from the European to refer to the supernatural powers and protection given to the Indians by the spirits.

Moravians The Moravian Church, once known as the *Unitas Fratrum,* or Unity of the Brethren, is the oldest international Protestant church in the world, having its origin nearly 540 years ago (1457) in Bohemia and Moravia. Vilified and persecuted for centuries, the Unity enjoyed a golden age of peace and spiritual prosperity in the late 1500s and early 1600s. Then another great period of persecution, which eventually included all Protestants, forced the church from Bohemia and into the surrounding nations and states. For years, the Brethren worshiped in separated pockets of faith. But in April of 1722, Nicholas Lewis—Count Von Zinzendorf of Saxony—a visionary and prophetic Protestant with a desire to establish a "fellowship of true believers as Luther himself dreamed of," invited a group of persecuted Brethren in Moravia to come and live upon his estate (Paul A.W. Wallace, ed., *The Travels of John Heckewelder in Frontier America,* p. 22). Soon, as other religious refugees (some were of the Brethren and some not) came to settle on Zinzendorf's lands, a small village arose that was named *Herrnhut* (the Lord's Watch). This community of believers, under the spiritual leadership of Zinzendorf and others of like vision, came to be known as the Moravians. From their midst, in 1732, the first two Moravian missionaries were sent out to preach Christ to black slaves in the Danish West Indies; it was the genesis of "denominational" Protestant world missions. In 1740, a group of Moravians (dispersed again because of banishment from Saxony) settled in

Pennsylvania where they soon established a colony called Bethlehem. The little town of Bethlehem fast became a mission center from which "teachers" went out north, south, and west into the wilderness of the American frontier to live with, to love, and to bring the gospel of Jesus Christ to the native sons and daughters of the forest.

Narragansett "People of the little points and bays," or "at the small narrow point of land." Inhabiting lands that encompass most of present-day Rhode Island, the Narragansett were the principal power among the New England Indians after the Great Dying—a plague that decimated the coastal tribes of New England a few years prior to the coming of the Pilgrims in 1620. Untouched by the sickness, the Narragansett were able to subject many previously independent tribes—including the Wampanoag, whose chief sachem Massasoit celebrated the famous first Thanksgiving with the colonists of Plymouth. The Narragansett remained a strong military power until King Philip's War in 1675, when they were nearly exterminated by the combined forces of the English, the Mohegan, and the armed warriors of the Praying Indians of Massachusetts.

nokehick The English called this pounded, parched Indian corn "no-cake" from the Narragansett *nokehick*. This simple food was the traveling sustenance of the hunter and the warrior. It was mixed with a little water, hot or cold, and made a tasty and fully adequate meal on the trail. Every brave carried a small basket of nokehick at his back or in a hollow leather belt about his waist—usually enough for three or four days. But forty days' provision could be carried by any warrior with little inconvenience. This practical food item was in wide use by tribes all across the Northeast. The Delaware, renowned for the culinary skills of their women (they fixed corn in at least twelve creative ways), called their version of nokehick (which they sometimes sweetened with maple sugar) *psindamoakan*.

Pennsylvania rifle This fine shooting piece—sometimes called the Lancaster rifle and most popularly (but erroneously) called the Kentucky rifle—was a development of gunsmiths in the Conestoga valley of Lancaster County in the 1720s. The "magnificently handsome and deadly precise" rifle reached a state of near perfection in the late 1700s and was highly sought after as a sharpshooter's weapon during the Revolutionary War (John Ward Willson Loose, *The Heritage of Lancaster*, p. 43). In the hands of the American patriot, it was nicknamed "the widow maker."

powwow Literally "wise speaker" in the Narragansett tongue. The medicine man or shaman. The term has since come to mean any great
tribal or intertribal gathering. In *Longshot,* "powwow" is used only to
refer to the medicine man.

run (noun) A small stream, brook, or creek.

sachem (SAY-chem) Chief, king, or prince; the head of a tribe or village.
There were traditionally two main sachems among the Narragansett,
one older and one younger. This co-rulership was unique among the
New England tribes, but every tribe had at least one chief sachem,
and all large tribes had many undersachems who ruled smaller groups
of Indians. Most often, these sachems were male, but occasionally the
wife of a deceased sachem would inherit his position in the tribe.
Among the Iroquois, the Susquehannock, and the Delaware, sachems
were always men, but they were chosen by the women.

snowsnake A winter game played with a long stick of maple that was very
smooth and tapered near its "tail." The head of the stick was carved
into some semblance of a snake. The game's object was to slide the
snowsnake down a long, level track of packed snow. Men took turns
flinging their snowsnakes, and the distances were marked. Whoever
slid his snake the farthest won all the snakes. There were also many
side bets.

squaw Literally "woman" in Narragansett.

wampum (from the Algonquian *wompompeague*) The small beads made
from the shells of clam and whelk. The beads were white and—more
rarely—purple ("black"). They were woven into belts or strung on
leather thongs. *Wompompeague* literally means "white strings."
Wampum was the major trade currency of the seventeenth-century
Indians of the great northeastern forest, both among themselves and
with the Europeans. It was also an integral part of all treaties, ran-
soms, and various ceremonies; wampum used in this way had "meaning" spoken into it, and people recalled the events by "reading" the
wampum. The Narragansett and the Indians of Long Island were the
principal producers of wampum. By the middle of the eighteenth century, wampum had become predominantly a ceremonial item, having
been replaced as currency by animal skins.

wigwam The principal home structure of the New England Indian. It was
built in two main forms: the domed wigwam (which was the most
common), and the conical wigwam (which is more like the teepee of
the western Indians). Constructed of poles and covered most often

with the bark of trees and mats of cattail rushes, wigwams could be moved from one location to another. Tribes and families moved several times yearly, according to the seasons and the need to be near the harvest, the hunt, the fishing grounds, or the shelter of a wooded valley in winter. Sometimes, wigwams were moved simply because they became infested with vermin and needed to be set up anew on cleaner ground.

Under the Sun

From the end of King Philip's War in 1676 to the dead center of the eighteenth century, European colonization of the eastern coast of North America—by England especially—increased continually, crawling slowly westward from the familiar shores of the Atlantic. Long-entrenched (as well as recently displaced) Indian nations filled the forest just a whoop beyond the western borders of white settlement, and New France (Canada) and her Indian allies held the lands to the north. By 1750, however, a tentative peace had been struck between the oft-warring nations of England and France—a peace that extended to the New World—and an adventurous few pushed south and west into the frontiers of New York, Pennsylvania, Virginia, Maryland, and the Carolinas.

German Moravian missionaries walked Penn's Woods with the message of the crucified and risen Lamb, soundly converting a significant number of the sons of the forest. Irish, English, and French fur traders built cabins in the deep woods and in the hunting villages of Indian tribes west of the Alleghenies, vying for the friendship and the furs of the natives of the land. New France sent soldiers on a stiff-armed ambassadorial journey up and down the Ohio River, while England sent its wilderness diplomats into the woods to parley with their Indian allies.

And the red man himself? He was no fool. He watched the growing encroachment upon his lands with wary eyes and a dull foreboding in his soul. He knew that his wooded homeland was the contested prize of two great kings from across the sea, but he stayed his ground as long as he dared and took what he could get from the colonial hands of both the English and the French. There was a kind of weary and unsettled calm before the storm in the middle of that eventful century, and for a few short years the forest opened its dark doors to any who cared to brave the ancient paths and break a trail upon the yet untrodden hills. Upon those paths and over those hills we have walked in our present narrative with Christopher Long, Caleb Hobomucko, and Conestoga Joe.

In the following "biographical" glimpses into the hearts of these three men (and others whom we've met within the pages of Longshot), I will attempt to examine the souls and summarize the histories of the tribes and the peoples of our narrative. Though many of the main players in Longshot are fictional, they are the children of much historical research and are representative of real people of their time. Where some of our cast were drawn directly from the historical record, I have done my best to let them play themselves truly.

Caleb Hobomucko

Second son of Joy Kattenanit (daughter of Job Kattenanit, narrator and principal character in *The Ransom*, Book 3 of The Cross and the Tomahawk series), Caleb's character is fictional, but he represents the true native heritage of his Narragansett people. Having been raised in purposeful rebellion against the Christianity of his grandfather Job, Caleb has chosen to become a powwow like his great, great, great grandfather Askug (powwow of the Narragansett in the glory days of the great sachems Canonicus and Mascus and Miantonomi; see Book 2 of the series, *The Rain From God*.)

Before the coming of the gospel of Jesus Christ, the natives of northeastern America lived under the constant dark shadow of traditional animism, and the role of the powwow (which means "a wise speaker" in the Narragansett tongue) was a critical one in the daily existence of the Indian. The powwow was an essential link to the unseen realities that played with each man's fate.

By virtue of his intimacy with the spirits, the powwow advised his people on all matters of life, and his role within the tribe was secondary only to the paternal influence and government of the sachem. By the aid of the gods—some of which were familiar spirits that lodged within the powwow himself—he read the times and the seasons and the causes and the outcomes of events in the past, present, and future. He identified thieves and murderers. He danced and prayed for rain, harvest, and hunt. He bewitched his enemies and the political rivals of his tribe, causing sickness and death by sorcery. He conjured sickness out of suffering friends and tribesmen.

He practiced scientific medicine as well, setting bones, dressing wounds, massaging, and prescribing certain natural cures through his knowledge of roots and herbs.

Sometimes, he accomplished superhuman feats, causing rocks to move, water to burn, trees to dance, and the dried skins of dead snakes to come alive. Few could match or withstand his amazing powers—until the coming of the white-man's God. At the time of our present narrative, the role of the powwow had greatly diminished in much of New England, and in many of the colonies, the practice of powwowing was recognized essentially as witchcraft and was consequently outlawed.

The ancient traditions and beliefs that Caleb embraced and sought to keep alive were somewhat unique to the Narragansett, yet they held much in common with the oral traditions of other tribes in the area. The New England Indians did not worship one Great Spirit, as is often conceived. They had a virtual pantheon of gods, called manitoos. They had gods for men, women, children, animals, sun, moon, fire, water, rain, snow, directions, seasons, winds, houses, crops, and even colours. Yet, remarkably, there is a distant memory of the One Great God in their mythology: a Creator and provider who made man and woman; a garden; a fall of sorts; a flood. The shadow of the truth often lies long upon the land even after the sun has fallen below the hills of time.

Of the spirits and the gods, the Narragansett had three who reared their heads highest:

1. Cautantowwit was the distant and unseen creator, whose great gardens and green courts lay to the Southwest. He was mostly benevolent yet often sent misfortune when angry with his human subjects, and was the final judge of each man. At death, the soul (if not hindered by the direct efforts of the spirits or of living men) flew to the Southwest. If it had been good during life, it would be allowed entrance into the courts of Cautantowwit. But the wicked soul was turned away and forced to wander in eternal restlessness.

The Narragansett originally communicated with Cautantowwit through sacrifice, prayers, praise, and dance. Yet none knew him, and his face was a mystery.

2. Weetucks (or Maushop, as he was known by most of the tribes of Massachusetts and north) was a benevolent humanlike giant responsible for the creation of various landmarks—islands in particular. He could walk on water and catch whales single-handed. The smoke of his great pipe gave rise to the early-morning fogs that hung upon the shoreline of the bays and

rivers. Weetucks was the subject of many tales and legends around the fires of the Narragansett.

3. Chepi (or Hobomucko) was the Devil of the Narragansett. His name was associated with death, the deceased, and the cold northeast wind. He inhabited the black shadows of the forested swamps. He brought calamity and illness. He appeared to men in visions as a man, an animal, an inanimate object, or a mythical creature. Most often, he appeared as a serpent. And this was the sign of the powwow. Though most were terrified by these manifestations, many desired such visions, for Chepi did not appear to everyone, but to those who were called to leadership, great wisdom, and spiritual power ("medicine"). Caleb, in declaring himself a powwow and allying himself with this chief spirit, took upon himself the name of Hobomucko.

By the middle of the eighteenth century—nearly seventy-five years since King Philip's War had broken the back of Indian military power in New England—the original inhabitants of New England lived a poor and marginal existence at the edge of a growing English society. Some lived together on reservations in a semblance of their traditional tribal families, while going out to do day labor among the whites. As Rev. John Callender of Providence, Rhode Island remarked in 1739, "After the war, they were soon reduced to the condition of the laboring poor, without property, hewers of wood and drawers of water" (William S. Simmons, *The Narragansett*, p. 56). But others, like Caleb Hobomucko, purposed to live their lives with the independence and dignity of their unconquered forefathers, and in this they were rebels to both English society and the sad contemporary state of their own people as a whole.

In establishing Caleb as a traditional (though unique) Narragansett character, I have put a good bit of real Narragansett lingo on his lips. The phrases and words that he uses are as accurate a use of this ancient language as is possible. Though the Narragansett language itself (in its conversational and practical use) died before the middle of the last century, we have a remarkable linguistic record of early Narragansett speech in the form of a book written in 1643 by Puritan preacher (and intimate friend of the Narragansett) Roger Williams. Williams's book, *A Key into the Language of America,* was my text for Caleb's Narragansett vocabulary.

It is an interesting fact (both linguistically and in relation to The Cross and the Tomahawk series) that many of the native phrases that have found their way into the popular Indian vocabulary of the twentieth century—and which many of us associate more with the Indians of America's West—are Narragansett (and generally Algonquian) in origin: i.e., papoose, squaw, wigwam, moccasin, wampum, powwow, manitoo. Some other terms—like sachem (an Indian chief)—though in common use in New England literature during the seventeenth and eighteenth centuries, have fallen out of use. Apart from Williams's *Key*, the modern Narragansetts (most of whom still live in the southern environs of Rhode Island) have little knowledge of their ancient tongue. But the strong tradition of oral transmission is still retained among a remnant, and there are those in the tribe today (like Narragansett ethnohistorian Ella Thomas Sekatau) whose life purpose has been to learn and to teach the orally transmitted history, language, religion, and medicine of her people.z

Joy Kattenanit

Our bridge from the seventeenth century to the eighteenth, Joy's life spanned more than the end of one century and the beginning of the next. Her days began in freedom in a small Indian-built house (of the English style) in the dreamworld of the Praying Indian of Massachusetts in the days of the Apostle to the Indians, John Eliot. They ended in retired servitude in the massive colonial mansion of a Rhode Island plantation in the days of the English aristocracy of southern Rhode Island.

Her life as a traditional Indian was minimal. Though her mother was Nipmuc and her father Narragansett (both had been born when traditional tribal life was fairly intact among the Indians of New England), Joy was born in Natick, Massachusetts, a "Praying Town" of Christian Indians. Natick was the first of fourteen Praying Towns established through the work of John Eliot, and Joy's life in that small town (and among the Christian Indians of Massachusetts) was one in which the culture of her ancestors had been largely shed in favor of one that emulated English society and followed biblical law.

Though her people still hunted and fished and farmed as their fathers had, they learned new skills, built English-style houses and churches and schools, planted orchards, constructed bridges, cut their hair, wore English clothes, and kept house much like the English. This remarkable wilderness counterculture, in which thousands of lives were eternally (as well as temporally) transformed, was a unique indigenous and evangelistic Christian community. Eliot poured the latter part of his life into these red children of the faith, first learning their language and then teaching them to read it. The first Bible printed in America was Eliot's translation of the Scriptures in the tongue of the Indians of Massachusetts. Joy spent her childhood poring over its pages.

The fictional daughter of a historical Praying Indian (Job Kattenanit), Joy represents—from her mid-teens until her old age—the tragic fruit of a racism born of war. In 1675, after nearly fifty years of a shared existence of mutual respect and neighborly trade, red man and white took up arms against each other in a sorrowful conflict known to history as King Philip's War. Philip was the English name of Metacom of the Wampanoag, son of Massasoit (the sachem who had shared the first Thanksgiving with the Pilgrims in 1621).

Once English society had stabilized itself on the New England coast, it began to push away from the shores of the Atlantic and into the endless forest. In a relatively short time, the Indian found himself a fenced-in (and fenced-out) stranger in his own country. After a series of political mishaps that soured relations between the sachem of the Wampanoag and the sons of Plymouth, Metacom could no longer stand by and watch his lands slip from his hands. His warriors attacked an English town at the foot of his mountain capitol, and King Philip's War had begun.

When it was over, Metacom was dead and those tribes that had sided with him were politically destroyed. Even the tribes that had fought with the English were greatly reduced in numbers and power. But among the most tragic victims of the war were the Praying Indians. Caught between two worlds, feared by the English (who began to distrust all Indians because of savage attacks upon their settlements from all quarters and even from Indians they had considered friends and neighbors) and despised by their non-Christian red brethren (who considered the Praying Indians to be traitors to the traditions and the gods of their fathers), the Christian Indians were first neglected, then persecuted, and finally forced to leave their homes and their towns to live upon a nearly desolate island in Boston Harbor.

Many of the old and infirm died upon that island, and only when the war began to go more fully against the English did the colonial authorities agree to let some of the Praying Indians off the island to scout for their troops. Finally, the colonies armed the Christian Indians and let them fight by their side. A Praying Indian (a Wampanoag) brought down King Philip with an English rifle, and the war ended.

But the Praying Towns had been decimated, the compassionate work of Eliot and other spiritual allies of the Praying Indians was in a shambles, and the Christian red man became the victim of a new racism and the dis-illusionment of a war that had all but destroyed his new way of life. He couldn't go back to the traditions of his fathers, and he no longer had the hope of that brave new world he had built in the image of the English. Rum took its toll, and many of the Christian Indians (especially those who had fought in the war) backslid. Among the natives of New England, some of the enemies of the English were sold into slavery, and many of the friends of the English were forced by poverty to indenture themselves to the colonists.

Tribal life continued, however, though it was restricted by the growing presence of a victorious white race that didn't view the land as communal territory to be planted and hunted and fished in season, but as the partic-ular possession of the individual, subject to cultivation, "improvement," and that ever-present mark of private ownership: the fence. The sachems among the existing tribes, robbed of their ancient right to roam the woods and subjugate and tax their enemies, had no way to extend their royal dominions other than to sell their people's lands to better furnish their own castles. And so the American Native lost even more land after the war through the continuous, foolish, and selfish financial maneuverings of the chiefs. Of course, the more unscrupulous among the English were all too glad to open up their rum jugs and invite the sachems to supper to talk over some small land deal.

Among the Narragansett (who were nearly destroyed as a people in the war and who joined themselves to their former vassals, the Niantic), land disappeared very quickly, and the traditional country of their fathers was bought up by an English aristocracy that farmed it to great profit and began raising horses that became quite famous and were known far and afield as "Narragansett Pacers." These plantation owners ran their farms with the labor of English servants, African and East Indian slaves, and nonreservation Narragansett servants. Much of the land along the western shore of Narragansett Bay south of Providence was farmed by these English "Narragansett Planters." Here it was that Joy Kattenanit offered herself and her family (all but Caleb) as servants in the house of Robert Hazard. Here it was that many of the Narragansett, both the indentured in the houses of the planters and the free Indians who lived upon the dwindling reservation and among the English in nearby towns, learned to work with stone, becoming expert stonemasons, a skill that is known among them to this day.

Finally, Joy Kattenanit, as a spiritual link to the days of the Praying Indian of Massachusetts, represents that gospel cord that—though hacked at by Satan and assailed by salvo—holds strong and crimson and true through the centuries. Of all the Praying Towns that once stood within the Massachusetts woods, Natick alone remains, its name and its legacy intact (though the latter is lauded chiefly in heaven.)

Netop

Netop means *friend* in the Narragansett language. The oldest of the children of Joy Kattenanit, our man Netop is a friend to all who have him for a friend. His story, the story of the Christian Narragansett, deserves a full treatment of its own one day. In our present narrative, we are given but a brief, bright glimpse of the salvation of the Narragansett nation.

Though Roger Williams had preached extensively to the Narragansett in his lifetime among them, his words seemed to have borne little eternal fruit. From his introduction to the tribe in the early 1630s until his death in 1683, his Christian witness was strong and consistent. But though the Narragansett loved and respected him (the land upon which he founded Providence was a gift of love from the Narragansett sachem Canonicus), there is no record that they opened their hearts to Christ during that time. This may be due to the tragic fact that their beloved Miantonomi (grand sachem after the natural death of old Canonicus) was unjustly executed by a rival tribe upon the orders of the Christian clergy and government of Connecticut. This travesty of justice, along with other foolish political moves on the part of the governments of both Massachusetts and Connecticut, probably played largely in Narragansett resistance to the "white-man's God."

Roger Williams did what he could, both politically and religiously, to help his Narragansett neighbors and friends, but when King Philip and his

Wampanoags began their terrorist war, the fate of the independent and largely neutral Narragansett was inextricably sealed. The Great Swamp Fight of December 1675 both devastated the Narragansett nation and pulled it fully and unwillingly into the war. When the war was done, the remnant of the children of Cautantowwit (perhaps as few as 200 survivors from a prewar population of 5,000 to 7,000!) limped south to find poor shelter among the neutral Niantic. Some were forced into years of servitude with Rhode Island families, and some were sold into slavery in other colonies.

The Niantic adopted the Narragansett name, and the tribe lived on in dwindling obscurity. In 1709, Ninigret II, sachem of the Narragansett-Niantic, ceded all of his lands to Rhode Island except for a sixty-four-square-mile reservation that became, in effect, the recognized legal property of the sachem himself. As he saw fit, the sachem and his successors could lease, rent, or sell these tribal lands to the whites—and that is what they often did.

Thus, the rich lands of southern Rhode Island (the entire former domain of the Narragansett people) passed into English hands. Forests were felled, fields were cultivated, dairies were established, and a widely sought-after breed of horse was raised and sold. Our friend Netop grew to manhood on one such plantation, where he learned to speak and read English, and where he was introduced to the gospel of Jesus Christ (in spite of his mother's hopes otherwise, for she had turned her back—for a long season—upon the Son of God). Here, Netop learned to farm and to work with his hands as a stonemason, building walls and laying the foundations of various buildings upon the plantation.

Beyond the stone-walled borders of the English plantations, little was attempted in the way of ministry to the spiritual needs of the Narragansett commoner. A church was built in white Charlestown, and its doors were opened to English and Indian alike, but probably few of the common folk bothered to warm its pews. It took a fresh and sovereign wind from God to blow the spiritual dust from the souls of the Narragansett.

The Great Awakening is so-called because it knocked the English-American colonial world out of its bed of religious apathy and antipathy. Beginning with the evangelistic preaching of George Whitefield in 1739 and continuing at its strongest until 1743, a hurricane of religious fervor and spiritual revival swept from Georgia to New England. In the winter of 1741-42, the storm blew forcefully through the white and black communities of southern New England, and early in 1743 the sound of this wailing wind attracted a large number of curious Narragansett to the revival services taking place in the congregation of the Reverend Joseph Park of Westerly, Rhode Island.

Once inside the doors, the Spirit of the Lord apprehended these soul-weary sons of the past, pulling them fully into the kingdom of God and forever changing their destinies. In the days that followed, large numbers (perhaps the majority) of the Narragansett tribe converted to Christianity, many of them joining Park's church. Park noted at the time that the Narragansett converts drank less alcohol than before, argued less, and requested the opportunity to be educated. In 1744, he wrote that "there is among them a change for good respecting the outward as well as the inward man. They grow more decent and cleanly in their outward dress, provide better for their households, and get clearer of debt" (William S. Simmons, "Red Yankees" in *American Ethnologist,* p. 262).

One of those who surrendered to Christ was our fictional character Netop. Upon conversion, Netop joined Park's church but withdrew with others of his tribe in 1746 to start a congregation of their own, led by a common reservation tribesman named Samuel Niles. The Narragansett affectionately referred to Niles as "Father Sam."

In 1750, Niles and his congregation built a wooden meetinghouse on reservation land. From that day until now, a body of Narragansett Christians has continued to worship on that spot, led from generation to generation by Narragansett ministers of the gospel. In 1859, Narragansett masons built a granite church that still stands upon the site of the original wooden meetinghouse. I've stood within its walls. On Sundays, hymns still drift from its windows to wander through the forest and over the hills, all the way to heaven.

In our narrative, Netop is one of that early congregation's zealous "exhorters"—a transformed, praying man who works honestly and hard to earn a living for his family. Historically, Niles and his followers became the political opponents of their tribal sachem and the political heroes of the common tribesman. Emboldened by their faith, the Narragansett church challenged the abuses of tribal and colonial authority and argued for the maintenance of reservation land in Indian hands. The conversion of the Narraganasett to Christ not only fit him for heaven, but it also turned his face more positively and assuredly toward the dominant English culture and the challenges of the changing times. In direct opposition to the spirit worship of his fathers, the Christian Narragansett set a course toward heaven hitherto untraveled by any of his own. The way was narrow, but it led to life.

Big Bill Moose

Bill Moose is the town drunk of so many American tales. He is also the tragic personification of the devastation wrought by alcohol in the lives of so many Native Americans. Though a fictional character, Moose is no mere stereotype, and all of Caleb's railing against *ankapi* (rum) is fully justified historically (and, tragically, even in our present day). The rum trade and the slave trade were blood brothers in sin, and Caleb's words and Bill Moose's actions speak to the matter quite eloquently in our earlier chapters.

The practical laws of colonial society often forbade the sale of alcohol to the Indian, and many of the most responsible among the Indians begged for a full compliance with that law. But just as the drug dealer of today plies his illegal trade to the ruination of his customers' bodies and souls (and society at large)—all for the expansion of his own pocketbook—so were there conscienceless individuals in colonial days who broke the law to make a dollar (or get a deed signed).

Ninigret II, sachem of the Narragansett-Niantic and a contemporary of Big Bill Moose, signed away many a square mile of tribal lands to support his own alcoholic inclinations. He died in 1723 from drinking too much rum.

Christopher Long

Some heroes make their mark in a big way, catching the camera's eye and the public's imagination in one big, bold, and bowl-'em-over moment of glory. But most heroes make history (even big history) quietly, simply, and in the daily line of duty. Christopher Gist, backwoodsman for hire (and the historical model for our narrator, Christopher Long), was that quiet sort of hero.

Gist was one of the first Englishmen to explore the American wilderness west of the Ohio. He climbed high mountains and forded wide rivers. He shot buffalo for breakfast. He made fires in the midst of winter storms in order to cook his lunch. He chased wildcats out of their dens in order to have a dry place to lay his own head at night. He hunted with Indians and Irish fur traders. He acted as an ambassador to the Indians on behalf of the governor of Virginia. He officiated (in a simple and unaffected way) the first Protestant church service west of the Alleghenies—a reading of Scripture and prayers from The Book of Common Prayer to a serendipitous congregation of Indians and English traders in the midst of the vast Pennsylvania woods on a cold Christmas morn in 1750.

He guided twenty-two-year-old Major George Washington through the wild woods of western Pennsylvania. He acted as scout for British Major-General Edward Braddock on an ill-fated march to the forks of the Ohio. He kept journals of his groundbreaking travels, recording his daily progress in an optimistic and matter-of-fact style. And for all of this, he earned a day's wage for a day's work (and was given a few acres of land in the wilderness besides). He was a family man, and—though often far from home for extended periods of time—a faithful one. His older sons sometimes accompanied him on his journeys.

Of his travels, he left posterity three journals: two that chronicle his pioneer excursions into the wilderness along and over the Ohio (a seven-month journey in the fall of 1750 until the spring of 1751, and a second odyssey from November of 1751 until March of 1752); and one that tells the adventurous tale of his backwoods journey with Washington in the deep winter of 1753–54. Washington also kept a diary of this adventure, which was subsequently published upon his return from the wilderness, catapulting the Virginia major into the public eye—where he ever after would remain.

Gist, however, served his world in relative obscurity, dying of smallpox in Virginia on the road from Williamsburg to Winchester on July 25, 1759. He was fifty-three years old, a pioneer to the end, who—in advance of his contemporary, Daniel Boone—was probably the first white American to explore the Ohio country and northeastern Kentucky. Those territories were, of course, inhabited by the natives of the land, some of whom had moved there as a result of English habitation on the eastern coast and French habitation to the north.

Though Gist was a trailblazer and a true Englishman with the empirical mind-set of a European, he did not despise the culture of the American Indian and looked upon them as equals in the sight of God. He treated them fairly—though he dealt with them carefully and shrewdly—in matters of business and politics, and appears to have desired their best in both temporal and spiritual matters. His uniqueness among his trader-trapper-explorer peers was his integrity, his reasoned faith, his education, and his cultivation. Like his father, who had laid out the plans for the present city of Baltimore, Christopher was also a mathematically minded fellow, a precise draftsman, and a faithful son of the Anglican church.

In *Longshot*, Christopher Gist lives again in the person of Christopher Long. Though I have imaginatively cast Long as a son of Providence and a friend of the Narragansett (something not true of Gist), his travels in the western wilderness follow—to the day in most cases—the first of Gist's journals. Based upon my reading of Gist, I decided to lay out Long's travels in a first-person (though much amplified) journal style, with dates preceding events throughout. I am very happy to resurrect the memory of that hardy and personable soul whom S. K. Stevens noted as appearing "truly out of nowhere to become a strangely remote figure determining the course of empire in the mid-18th century" (Sylvester K. Stevens in the introduction to a 1966 reprint of *Christopher Gist's Journals*, p. vii).

Connie Joe

Connie (Conestoga) Joe is a mid-eighteenth-century representative of that great nation of Indians—the Susquehannock —who once roamed and ruled the vast lands of Pennsylvania's Susquehanna River Valley. As early as 1608, John Smith sailed up the Susquehanna to the falls (Deposit, Maryland) and was met there by a party of sixty Indian warriors. He called these Indians "Sasquesahannocks," which is not the name they gave themselves but rather the name given to Smith by his Indian interpreter (who is believed to have been a Powhatan). The Delawares called the Susquehannocks Minquas, which means "treacherous." Whether treacherous or not, it is a fact that they were a politically strong and militarily expert nation of warriors and traders whose influence extended far. The French called the Susquehannocks Gandastogues (from which we have the English pronunciation of Conestogas).

As the European fur trade developed among the Indians, the Susquehannock—along with their northern foes in the Five Nations of the Iroquois Confederacy and the Huron nations still farther north—quickly took advantage of their position as middlemen between the tribes of the pelt-rich forests to the west and the pelt-hungry French and English settlements to the north and east respectively. At first, this trade seemed to enrich the Indian nations involved in it, but in reality it increased their daily dependence upon European goods and eventually turned their attentions away from their traditional balanced pursuit of agriculture and subsistence hunting to a frenzied and wholehearted devotion to the skin of the beaver.

As these tribes beat the bushes for furs, their own lands were soon depleted, sending them over their borders and into the hunting grounds of neighboring tribes. Conflicts arose, eventuating in the tragedy of national wars. History calls these conflicts the Beaver Wars. Ultimately, these wars led to the defeat and dispersal of the Susquehannocks at the hands of the Iroquoian Seneca (and their Maryland allies) in the year 1675 (the same year, ironically, that many of the Indians of New England rose up to follow King Philip—Metacom—to their own demise in a war against the Puritan colonies).

Some went sadly south, where they were treated contemptuously by Virginia and Maryland. Some went north and were adopted into the tribes of their conquerors in the Iroquois Confederacy. A small number set up house (with Iroquois approval) at Conestoga on the Susquehanna near the present city of Lancaster, Pennsylvania. It is here, nearly seventy-five years later, that our Connie Joe took up residence upon the farm of a German tobacco planter.

Like Connie Joe, many other Conestogas of his day were well-traveled river-riders and trail-walkers, speaking several Indian dialects besides their own, and conversant in German and English as well. Most of the tribe lived in their own village of Conestoga, farming, hunting and fishing, selling their excess produce and crafts of their own making in the city of Lancaster and around the countryside. Others, like Joe, worked on the neighboring farms of the Pennsylvania Germans or were servants in their households. Peaceably settled into a rural and self-sufficient life at the edge of Pennsylvania's white frontier, this community of Native Americans (most of whom were converts to the Quaker faith) would die almost in its entirety in a horrific massacre in December 1763 (during Pontiac's War). They were murdered at the pitiless hands of a mob of "Indian haters" from Paxtang (now Harrisburg). Though the massacre was widely condemned (Benjamin Franklin published the angriest and most scathing article of his life in condemnation of the "Paxtang Boys"), the men were never brought to justice.

Moses (Great Hill)

The history of the Delaware Indians of Pennsylvania is such a unique story in the annals of Native America—and the story of their own Christian heritage is such a fantastic adventure—that, Lord willing, I will one day chronicle it in full. But as Moses (Great Hill) has but a bit part in this volume, and as his people are not a focus in our present narrative, my comments here will be limited to Moses' role as a medayoo.

Just as the Narragansett had their powwows, so too did the Delaware (and all other nations of Native Americans). Among the Delaware, there were two types of medicine men: physicians, who were great practitioners of herbal medicine with skill in treating wounds and setting bones; and conjurers, who trafficked with the spirits and were privy to supernatural powers that enabled them to detect the presence of evil spirits and to cast them out of those who were afflicted by them. The conjurers were also wise in the ways of herbal cures. The Munsee Delaware name for conjurer was medayoo, but they also called themselves doctols (having borrowed the word doctor from the English, but being largely unable to pronounce the letter "r").

Great Hill, as a renowned medayoo among his people, was both a conjurer and a physician. And like our own doctors today, he was a fairly well-to-do man. The conjurers, especially, raked in the wampum. When a regular Indian physician failed to cure his patient, the sickness was deemed spiritual in nature, and the medayoo was then called upon. But the medayoo would not begin to work his cure until he had been "made strong" by the patient's family. The more the conjurer was paid, the "stronger" he became in his ability to identify and combat the evil spirit plaguing his patient.

Sometimes he succeeded in casting the spirit out, but often his wailings and his dancing and his magical potions failed to impress the troublesome demon. When this was the case, the doctor would declare that he must be made stronger still (which meant a hiked-up fee for his services). If, after repeated efforts, the medicine of the medayoo had proved ineffectual, the conjurer would declare his patient incurable, saying that the patient had applied to him too late or that the patient had not followed his prescriptions properly, or that he was bewitched by some great master of the science and therefore doomed to die or linger on in pain beyond the power of relief.

"Thus these jugglers," says eighteenth-century Moravian missionary John Heckewelder, "carry on their deceit, and enrich themselves at the expense of the credulous and foolish" (Paul A.W. Wallace, *The Travels of John Heckewelder in Frontier America*, p. 127). But that they wielded real supernatural power (and thus great influence among their own) is not to be doubted. The source of such power was, of course, demonic.

Some medayoo were not content to limit themselves to the healing arts and thus practiced witchcraft against their enemies. The Delaware hated such witches, and when it was discovered that one among them was sending spells against another, the punishment was death—usually a tomahawk to the sorcerer's head at a moment when he least suspected it.

Great Hill, like others among the Delaware, discovered that a greater power than his own existed within the hearts of the Christian Moravians who came peacefully among them to live much as the Indians did and to tell them the story of the Lamb of God, the Son of the Great Spirit in heaven. As Great Hill's people began to believe in the Lamb, they began to turn away from the medayoo as a source of healing in times of sickness. This was bad for business, so Great Hill tried his magic against the missionaries. When his sorcery failed ultimately to harm the missionaries, he forsook the spirits and gave his heart to Christ, changing his name to Moses.

In our narrative, Moses is representative of hundreds among the Delaware who were born again when they responded to the gospel message of the Moravians and cast themselves fully upon the Son of God. Christian Indian towns, somewhat akin to the Praying Towns of New England in the seventeenth century, sprung up across the Pennsylvania wilderness. But unlike Eliot's Indians, these Moravian Delawares maintained a great degree of their native culture, and some of the Christian Indians attained to high political status among the non-Christian tribes around them.

The Moravian mission's approach was a truly cross-cultural one in which Native American culture and tradition was affirmed in all ways except where it clearly conflicted with biblical truth. And unlike the English missionaries among the New England Indians who preached to the natives and then returned to their own homes and parishes in their English towns, the Moravian missionaries (most of them German) left the comfort of their German settlements to live fully among the Indians. Thus these Moravian Delaware towns had a resident pastor and teacher who truly understood them and their ways. Some of these teachers even married among the Indians.

George Croghan

Among the actual historical figures in *Longshot*, George Croghan plays but a small role culled from a real-life story that is filled with candor, courage, and a good deal of backwoods intrigue. A native of Ireland, schooled in Dublin, he came to America in 1743 or 1744. In 1746, he was living in East Pennsboro Township, Lancaster County (now Cumberland County), five miles west of Harris's Ferry (now Harrisburg). For nearly twenty-five years preceding the Revolutionary War, Croghan was intimately involved with the Indians of the American frontier.

Shortly preceding our narrative, in 1748, he built a trading house at Logstown on the Ohio and began a successful business of trade among the Indians of the forest, establishing himself in many of the principal Indian towns. As a walker of the woods himself, and a man who understood the politics of his day, he early saw the importance of winning the Indians away from the French by means of gifts and a more favorable trade. In the years that followed, his trading business gave birth to his role as an advisor to the frontier colonies on Indian affairs. He often acted as English ambassador and messenger to the Indians (sometimes in the company of the Huron half-breed and Indian interpreter Andrew Montour, as we see in *Longshot*) and played an important part in many of the English-Indian conferences and treaties of the time. During the French and Indian War (1754–1760), Croghan was commissioned a captain and commanded Indian troops against the French.

Though not an explorer in the class of Gist or Boone, Croghan—like so many other sons of Ireland who had come to America at the time—was quite at home in the woods. In 1766, he made a settlement four miles above Fort Pitt (present day Pittsburgh). Except for Gist's wilderness settlement, George Croghan's would have been the first within the county of

Allegheny. He continued to act as a peaceful mediator between the Indians and the English until the onset of the Revolutionary War in 1776.

Andrew Montour

Another member of our cast who was drawn from the annals of real history, Andrew Montour was a uniquely colourful and courageous man of his time. In his life, we can see the overlapping histories of the children of New France, the sons of the English colonies, and the original natives of North America.

Montour's grandfather was a French gentleman who settled in Canada and—like many of his displaced countrymen—fathered children by Indian women. Andrew's grandmother was a Huron, and she bore Monsieur Montour one son and two daughters. Of the daughters, one—Andrew's mother—is known conspicuously to history as Madame Montour.

Born in Canada about 1684, she was captured by warriors of the Five Nations when she was only ten years old. She was raised among them and married an Oneida war chief named Carondawana (Big Tree), also known as Robert Hunter. Hunter was killed in 1729 while at war with the Catawbas in the Carolinas. Madame Montour outlived him by twenty-five years, making a name for herself as an Indian interpreter to the English. She never remarried, lived always among English-leaning Indians, was well-known to the tribes in Pennsylvania and New York, and was respected by the governments of these same English colonies. As a result, her eldest son, Andrew, was a man of two worlds who, though French in ancestry, was loyal to the English and yet fully an Indian beneath the tall trees.

Like his mother before him, Andrew (sometimes called Henry) was sought after for his skill as an ambassador and an interpreter. Also like his mother, he commanded a great deal of respect both in the forest and in the legislative chamber. And though he was a counselor of peace, he was also a warrior. Like his Irish friend George Croghan, Montour was commissioned a captain during the French and Indian War, and led war parties of Indians and English Rangers against the French Indians.

How often he heard the gospel or how he may have responded to it is unclear. It is clear, though, that his mother was deeply moved when she first met the Moravian bishop Count Zinzendorf in the fall of 1742 and heard of his purpose in the forest. She had quite forgotten the truths of the gospel and, in common with the French Indians, had believed the story that originated with the Jesuits that Christ was a Frenchman who had been crucified by the English. Zinzendorf also met Andrew at this time, and his description of this fascinating man is worth repeating here:

> His cast of countenance is decidedly European, and had not his face been encircled with a broad band of paint, applied with bear's fat, I would certainly have taken him for one. He wore a brown broadcloth coat, a scarlet damasken lappel waist-coat, breeches, over which his shirt hung, a black Cordovan neckerchief decked with silver bugles, shoes and stockings, and a hat. His ears were hung with pendants of brass and other wires plaited together like the handles of a basket. He was very cordial, but on addressing him in French, he, to my surprise, replied in English.

I hope these historical notes will help you to better find your way through the woods with Longshot, Caleb, and Connie Joe, and to better understand the lives they lived in the gaze of God while under the sun.

The sources utilized for the writing of *Longshot* were many and varied—books written in every century since the sixteenth, wilderness journals written nearly 150 years ago, and research articles published as recently as 1997. For your own further study and reading pleasure, I have listed here the materials that I found most helpful.

Boissevain, Ethel. *The Narragansett People* (Phoenix, Ariz.: Indian Tribal Series, 1975).

The Book of Common Prayer (Oxford, England: Oxford University Press, reprint). This book is a reprint of the original text published in the late sixteenth century during the reign of Queen Elizabeth. It was the prayer book of the colonial Anglican church, and Christopher Gist carried a copy of it with him on his wilderness journeys.

Channing, Edward, *The Narragansett Planters* (New York: reprint, Johnson Reprint Corporation, 1973). Originally published in Baltimore in the March, 1886 issue of Johns Hopkins University Studies in Historical and Political Science.

Chapin, Howard M., *Sachems of the Narragansett* (Providence, R.I.: Rhode Island Historical Society, 1931).

Darlington, William McC., *Christopher Gist's Journals* (Pittsburgh: n.p., 1893). I held an original copy of this rare book in my hands just long enough to photocopy major portions of it. A complete reprint of Darlington's book, with a new introduction and bibliographical notes by Frank Monaghan, was published in 1966 by Argonaut Press Ltd., New York. See also Sylvester K. Stevens' introduction to this edition.

DeForest, John W., *The History of the Indians of Connecticut from the Earliest Known Period to 1850* (Hartford, CT: Wm. Jas. Hamersley, 1852; reprinted by Native American Book Publishers, Brighton, MI).

Earle, Alice Morse, *Home Life in Colonial Days* (Stockbridge, MA: Berkshire House, 1992). Originally published in 1898.

Eckert, Allan W., *The Wilderness War* (New York: Bantam Books, 1982).

Graymont, Barbara, *The Iroquois* (New York/Philadelphia: Chelsea House Publishers, 1989).

Hawke, David Freeman, *Everyday Life in Early America* (New York: Harper and Row, 1988).

Herndon, Ruth Wallis (University of Toledo) and Sekatau, Ella Wilcox (Narragansett Tribe), "The Right to a Name: The Narragansett People and Rhode Island Officials in the Revolutionary Era," in Ethnohistory 44 (3): 432–462 (summer 1997).

Hudson, Winthrop S., *Religion in America* (New York: Charles Scribner's Sons, 1965).

Loose, John Ward Willson, *The Heritage of Lancaster* (Woodland Hills, CA:

Windsor Publications and Lancaster Association of Commerce and Industry, 1978).

Lovejoy, David S., *Religious Enthusiasm and the Great Awakening* (Englewood Cliffs, N.J.: Prentice-Hall, Inc., 1969).

Mannix, Daniel,. and Malcolm Cowley, *Black Cargoes, A History of the Atlantic Slave Trade* (New York: Viking Compass, 1962).

Morgan, Ted, *Wilderness at Dawn: The Settling of the North American Continent* (New York: Simon & Schuster, 1993).

Simmons, William S., *The Narragansett* (New York/Philadelphia: Chelsea House Publishers, 1989).

Simmons, William S., *Spirit of the New England Tribes: Indian History and Folklore,* 1620–1984 (Hanover, N.H.: University Press of New England, 1986).

Simmons, William S., "Conversion from Indian to Puritan," in New England Quarterly, 52 (2): 197–218 (1979a).

Simmons, William S., "The Great Awakening and Indian Conversion in Southern New England," in Papers of the Tenth Algonquian Conference: 25-36. William Cowan, ed. (Ottawa: Carleton University, 1979b).

Simmons, William S., "Red Yankees: Narragansett Conversion in the Great Awakening" in American Ethnologist 10(2): 253–71 (1983).

Sweet, William Warren, *Religion in Colonial America* (New York: Charles Scribner's Sons, 1942).

Tunis, Edwin, *Indians* (New York: Thomas Y. Crowell, 1979).

Tunis, Edwin, *Colonial Living* (New York: Thomas Y. Crowell).

Wallace, Paul A.W., *Historical Indian Paths of Pennsylvania* (Harrisburg, Penn.: The Pennsylvania Historical and Museum Commission, reprint). Originally printed in the October, 1952 edition of the Quarterly Journal of the Historical Society of Pennsylvania. Includes a fold-out map of Indian paths.

Wallace, Paul A.W., *Indians in Pennsylvania* (Harrisburg, PA: The Pennsylvania Historical and Museum Commission, 1975).

Wallace, Paul A.W., ed., *The Travels of John Heckewelder in Frontier America* (Pittsburgh: Pittsburgh University Press, 1985).

Wilbur, Keith, *New England Indians* (Chester, CT: Globe-Pequot Press, 1978).

Williams, Roger, *A Key into the Language of America* (New York: Russell & Russell, reprint, 1963). This book is my continual source (and the best source available anywhere) for the ancient language of the Narragansett Indians. Key was first published in London in 1643. There was yet no printing press on the continent of North America.

Wood, Betty, *The Origins of American Slavery, Freedom and Bondage in the English Colonies* (New York: Hill and Wang, 1997).

Readers' Guide

For Personal Reflection
or Group Discussion

Chapter One: ONE WALK IN AUTUMN

1. The Pharisees accused Jesus of being a "friend of sinners" (see Luke 7:34). And so he was. "Folks who are healthy don't need a doctor," Jesus said, "but those who are sick sure do! I didn't come to convert the righteous, I came to call sinners to repent" (see Mark 2:16–17; 1 Tim. 1:15). In our story, Christopher Long, a committed Christian, maintained a lifelong friendship with Caleb Hobomucko, a practicing Narragansett powwow (witch doctor). Though the two could have no spiritual fellowship (2 Cor. 6:14), they shared a bond of filial love which opened a door for the gospel to touch Caleb's heart. As Jesus was sent to the world, so he sends us to be ambassadors of God's love (John 17:18; 2 Cor. 5:20). But how can we practically touch those we don't even know (Rom. 10:13–15). We must reach out to the lost who are all around, build relationships with them, and live our lives among them in a candid and compassionate way that opens their eyes to Jesus.

Personal Ponderance:

a. Who are my non-Christian friends? How can I draw closer to them, without compromising my walk with God, in order to impact their lives with the love of Jesus?

b. What non-Christian friends from my youth might I contact in order to reestablish a relationship that God can use to win them to Himself?

2. Anglo/European Americans have long looked at the historic Judeo-Christian culture of the United States as the norm of life, ignoring or disdaining the traditions and religions of other nations, tribes and tongues. Though this has changed in recent years, many of us still know little about the minority peoples who are growing in population all across our land. Our ignorance, apathy and prejudice often cut us off from those who have no witness of the gospel of Jesus Christ. Jesus died on the cross to make "one body" of people of all nations (Eph. 2:14–18). The apostle Paul was adept at cross-cultural evangelism, using his knowledge of varied cultures to "speak their own language" in order to present them with the claims of Christ. We, too, must step across the cultural divide to connect with those who don't

look, act, think or believe as we do. Our sincere interest in the lives of others is the bridge the Holy Spirit uses to speak the truth to unbelieving hearts.

Personal Ponderance:

a. Who can I befriend, of another culture, in order to learn more about them? In order to find some common ground for living life, for loving my neighbor, for engaging in discussion about God which may open hearts and minds to the gospel of Jesus Christ?

3. Alcohol (rum in particular) was an especially devastating substance among the Indians of New England. Introduced to them by Europeans who had known its "strong medicine" for millenia, the Indian simply could not handle it (and seldom drank it in moderation). Alcohol soon became the cause of much domestic and tribal violence, as well as senseless crime by Indians in and around English settlements. When the tribes of New England were reduced politically and militarily by war, and their ancient lifestyles were subjected to English colonial culture, many turned to alcohol to drown their sorrows and dull the ache of their defeats. This caused an even swifter fall into moral and societal decay. Even today, alcoholism and drug abuse are major social problems among the various Native-American peoples of America.

Because of what rum had done to his own people, Caleb avoided alcoholic drinks every form. In some colonies, it was illegal to trade or sell alcohol to the American tribes (though many broke that law for the sake of profit). Roger Williams, whose love for the Native-American was genuine and Christian, never trafficked in alcohol while trading with the Indians.

Today, though legally sold in all states—and even imbibed with a "clear conscience" by many Christians—alcohol remains a major national addiction, contributing greatly to crime, poverty, domestic violence, the breakup of the family, the corruption of morals, and untold deaths on our nation's highways through drunken driving.

The apostle Paul, inspired by the Holy Spirit, wrote a simple, powerful and convicting argument for self-control and self-sacrifice on behalf of others (in the eighth chapter of 1 Corinthians; see also 1 Cor. 6:12). He finished his reasoned words with this declaration (which can aptly be applied to drinking and other life habits): "Therefore, if meat [offered to idols] offends my brother, I will eat no meat as long as the world lasts if it will keep my brother from stumbling."

Personal Ponderance:

a). If I drink, why do I drink? Does my drinking glorify God or serve my flesh? When a brother questions my habit, what is my response?

b) What do I do out of "liberty" that might cause a brother or sister to stumble?

c) What habits or social conventions am I willing to set aside or change for the sake of the spiritual stability and growth of others?

Chapter Two: THE HOUSE OF HAZARD

4. Robert Hazard, Rhode Island planter and horse farmer, was a church-going Anglican of traditional doctrinal convictions who respected established religious practice and formal theological training among ministers. Christopher Long was a lay Anglican who had been touched by the Holy Spirit during the Great Awakening, and whose fellowship with other believers had crossed denominational and doctrinal lines. One of the results of the Great Awakening (and a sign of any genuine move of the Holy Spirit) was a "leveling" of doctrinal walls and a release of ministry among the laity, resulting in a grass-roots unity that reflected the oneness that Jesus prayed for on the night of his betrayal (John 17:23). Today, the church is nearer in heart and truth to that unity than at any time in church history. Even so, we still tend to look to the pastor, the prophet, the apostle, the teacher and the evangelist for ultimate leadership and significant ministry. Yet, these "big gifts" are given to the church to equip all of us for the work of the ministry. The "New Light" lay exhorters of the Great Awakening had a great impact upon the lives of the common people, and we must not disdain the visions and dreams, the gifts and yearnings that God has placed in each of us. And though theological education can be a good thing, it is absolutely nonessential to serving God.

We are ALL called to serve. In fact, Paul said, "Look at yourselves, brothers, and you can see that not many wise men have been called (according to the flesh), not many mighty, not many 'high born.' But God has chosen the foolish things of the world to confound the wise. He has chosen the weak things of the world to confound the mighty. Instead, he has chosen the plain, the despised, even the 'nothings' of the world, to bring to nothing those things that people think are 'something.'" (see 1 Cor. 1:26-28) We are all called to stir up the gifts that are in us and use them in serving one another, because God hasn't given us the spirit of fear, but of power, love and a sound mind (2 Tim. 1:6–7).

Personal Ponderance:

a) What is my principal spiritual gift? What are some of the dreams that God has laid on my heart to do for him?

b) What are some ways I can courageously and creatively stir up my gifts for God?

5. Christopher Long headed into the unmapped wilderness beyond the Ohio River with his horse, his gun and his Book of Common Prayer (a gift from his friend Robert Hazard). For Long, the book was a constant source of personal spiritual encouragement and a tool for evangelism and the encouragement of others. This official prayer book of the Church of England (still in use today with a few non-essential changes), contained the Christian calendar, morning and evening prayers related to the needs of life and the details of the Christian walk, readings from the Psalms and other portions of Scripture, the order of administering communion, and other sacramental instructions. Though it was meant to be used by the clergy in leading the people in united daily prayer, it became a beloved devotional tool for the English people. "I value the Prayer Book," says one of the Anglican characters in Newman's *Loss and Gain*, "for I have known what it is to one in affliction. May it be long before you know it in a similar way; but if affliction comes on you, depend on it [that] all these new fancies and fashions will vanish from you like the wind, and the good old Prayer Book alone will stand you in any stead."

Perhaps a certain popular devotional, inspirational volume, or book of the Bible has greatly impacted your life, encouraged you or equipped you in your walk of faith. How long has it been since you revisited that book? Perhaps it would be good to pick it up and let it speak to you anew.

Personal Ponderance:

a) What book or books have been foundational in my life and faith?

I will commit to re-read those books and let their truths renew my zeal and my faith in God and his calling on my life.

Chapter Three: JOY COMES IN THE MORNING

6. Joy Kattenanit Hazard had a spiritual legacy. Though her life had been hard, even tragic (tempting, and succeeding, to embitter her and lead her away from God), her Christian heritage and the faith of her youth finally called her home. "Train up a child in the way he should go, and when he is old he will not depart from it" (Prov. 22:6 KJV).

Though "God has no grandchildren" (we are all his sons and daughters through personal repentance and faith, and none of us is saved by virtue of our parent's relationship to God), yet God is "the faithful God, who keeps covenant and mercy with those that love him and keep his commandments, to a thousand generations" (Deut. 7:9). If we love him, we have a covenant right to say, "Not only am I saved, but my household will be saved too" (see Acts 11:14; 16:31). If there has been faith in our family tree, God desires to honor that covenant still, and answer the prayers long since prayed. Our lives and prayers, too, will affect the generations to come.

Personal Ponderance:

a) Who in my "family tree" has been a man or woman of God?

b) How can I learn more and pass the testimony of this legacy on to others in my present family?

7. Caleb was a powwow, a witch doctor in the spiritual tradition of the Narragansett Indians. This meant that, besides being a counselor and physician, he was in intimate communion with the spirits of his tribe and region. Because he didn't know God, he also didn't know the truth about the spirits he dealt with. He didn't know they were evil spirits in league with Satan and at war against the Creator. In essence, though Caleb was a thoughtful and intelligent man, he was a prisoner to the devil's deceit. Only the Spirit of God could convince him of his folly and bring him to a place of grace and faith where he could choose to renounce the spirits and cast himself upon the mercy of Jesus.

Today, there are many caught in the web of false spiritual practice and belief. Mormonism, Islam, Jehovah's Witnesses, Hinduism, Satanism, Buddhism, shamanism, holistic health philosophies rooted in eastern religious practice, earth worship, New Age thought in many forms: each of these is a deceptive, entrapping, demonically inspired philosophy "that exalts itself against the knowledge of God (2 Cor. 10:3–5). "As followers of Jesus, we have the authority, in the spiritual realm, to bind the spirits and cast down the strongholds which have trapped our friends and neighbors in these false religions. And we have the love of God (poured out in our hearts by the Holy Spirit) which enables us to connect with these folks at the heart level, pulling them toward faith in "the Way, the Truth and the Life" (John 14:6 KJV). Though it is good to know what others believe (i.e. Do you have accurate knowledge of what Mormons believe about Jesus Christ?), it is more important to know who WE ARE in Christ, to be able to "rightly divide the word" (2 Tim. 2:15) of God, and to "be ready always to give an answer to any who asks you a reason for the hope that is within you" (1 Peter 3:15).

Personal Ponderance:

a) Do I know the authority that I have in Christ to wage spiritual war? (Luke 9:1; Eph. 6:10–20; James 4:7; 1 John 4:4)

b) Do I know who I am in Christ? What Jesus did for me upon the cross? My gifts in God, my place in his family, my calling in his kingdom?

c) Have I taken the time to understand and biblically evaluate the world-view of those I know who are involved in false religious systems of belief?

Chapter Four: THE SORCERER'S ISLE

8. Caleb lived on an island in a swamp where a horrific battle had been fought (75 years earlier) in which a great number of his tribe (men, women and children) had died. Caleb made his home there out of choice, in order to identify with both the glory and the tragedy of his tribal history. This identification kept his heart, mind and soul strongly linked to his past. But it also embittered him against the English whom he blamed for the defeat and ultimate subjugation of the Narragansett people and their ways.

Sometimes we live in the past, build our lives upon the past, even worship the past in ways that keep us from moving forward in the will of God. The apostle Paul had good reason to boast about his own heritage and upbringing (Phil. 3:4–6), but he said instead that "forgetting those things which are behind, and reaching forward to those things which are ahead, I press toward the finish line to win the prize of the high calling of God in Christ Jesus" (Phil. 3:13–14).

Jesus said, "Let the dead bury the dead! You need to come and follow me" (Matt. 8:22).

Personal Ponderance:

a) What tradition, familiar religious practices or comfortable heritage may be keeping me from seeking new ways, new surroundings and renewed faith to serve others?

b) What is there in my past that causes me to judge others unrighteously?

9. "All men have enemies," said Caleb to Christopher. Are we as honest? Do we recognize that there are those who are opposed to us, to our good, to our faith, even to our life? Even if we do not know anyone personally whom we could call an enemy, the world is full of those who are at enmity (consciously and unconsciously) with God and the revealed truth of Scripture; and thus these people are our enemies too (if they hated me, they'll hate you; whoever is not for us is against us).

Perhaps there is someone in your family who is "against" you. Perhaps someone at work, in school, in your neighborhood, even in your church.

Jesus said we must love our enemies, bless those who curse us, pray for those who persecute us and do good to those who purposefully abuse us. He said that if we know of an individual who has something against us, that we must set aside our "religious pursuits" and do what we can to make things right relationally. We can do this because God hasn't given us a spirit of fear, but of love, power and a sound mind (2 Tim. 1:7). And he has poured out his love in our hearts by the Holy Spirit (Rom. 5:5).

Remarkably, Solomon said that if our ways are pleasing to God, he will make even our enemies to be at peace with us (Prov. 16:7). Sometimes that means we must first love our enemies in a way that enables peace to find a place to invade our relationships.

Personal Ponderance:

a) Who are my enemies?

b) Where is a need in my enemy's life that I can meet (and so do good to them)? What can I say to or say about my enemy that will bless them? Besides forgiving them in prayer and praying for their salvation, how else can I pray for God's goodness to come upon them to lead them to repentance?

10. "What is faith ... if it lies sleeping between the pages of a black-bound book?" Caleb challenged Christopher.

"Faith without works is dead," wrote the apostle James. "Show me your faith without your works, if you can. But I'll show you my faith by my works" (James 2:17–18).

Jesus said, "If you don't believe what I say, believe me because of the works that I do" (John 10:38).

It doesn't do much good to know about God if that knowledge doesn't produce the fruit of faith. And the fruit of faith is works that speak of God. Jesus healed people, cast out demons, taught people life-changing truths—raised people from the dead!

Where is the fruit of our faith? Are we all talk and no works? All three-point sermons and no power?

Personal Ponderance:

a) When was the last time I prayed for the sick and they were healed?

b) When was the last time I obeyed a nudge from God and saw him do a miracle?

c) When was the last time I shared God's word from the heart and helped change a life or save a soul?

d) When was the last time my faith moved me with compassion to meet another's need?

11. "I believe in Jesus and Jehovah," Caleb declared quietly. And I looked at him with unbelieving eyes. "They are spirits also, are they not?"

"There is a vast difference." I said haltingly, "between the angels who fell and the Holy One of Heaven."

"They are all spirits, are they not?" he repeated, spitting into the fire. "I have asked them all in at one time or another. I take what they give. This is the way of the powwow."

"You have asked Jesus in?"

"When I was young. And sometime since. But he seems not to come."

"He is a jealous God,' I said.

I have a Hindu brother-in-law who "has room" for Jesus in his pantheon of gods, but no room for Jesus as the only way to salvation. The Christian can have no other "gods" beside Jesus. He is not simply one god among many. He is the Alpha and the Omega (Rev. 1:8–18), the eternal Word made flesh (John 1:1–14), the fullness of the godhead bodily (Col. 2:8–9), the Way, the Truth and the Life—and nobody goes to the Father except through him (John 14:6). The first of the Ten Commandments that God gave to Moses was, "Thou shalt have no other god before me" (Deut. 5:7).

Jesus said, "No man can serve two masters" (Matt. 6:24). We must love the Lord our God with all our heart, all our soul and all our mind, and cling to him only. Apart from Jesus, we can do nothing (John 15:5)!

Personal Ponderance:

a) Do I know anyone who seems to honor Jesus but also honors other gods and religions?

b) Do I know the nature and character of Jesus as both God and man?

c) Am I fully convinced that Jesus is the only mediator between God and man (1 Tim. 2:5)? As the only way to the Father, the only road opened to humanity by which we may be saved (John 14:6; Acts 4:12)?

Chapter Five: BIG BILL MOOSE

12. **Caleb was a consummate smoker.** Smoking tobacco was a "big deal" among the New England Native American. Not only did the Indians enjoy it, but it held religious, ceremonial and relational significance in their lives and culture. In time, this habit was taken up by American colonists, becoming a major American habit and social pastime. Some claimed that tobacco was a medicine that could cure diseases! But many were opposed to the unsavory habit which stung the eyes, yellowed teeth, soured the breath, and filled rooms with its choking presence. Christopher Long's wife Sarah was one of those who didn't like smoking, and so Christopher finally gave it up altogether.

Over the years, an entire American industry grew up around the production and sale of tobacco for smoking and chewing—an industry which continues to promote this dirty habit to millions of Americans. Only in the past several decades has public opinion (backed by undeniable scientific proof of the addictive nature and the physically debilitating effects of smoking or chewing tobacco) brought about united action limiting the use of tobacco. Smoking is bad for us. Some Christians, in speaking against the "social sin" of smoking, have quoted 1 Corinthians 6:19–20 where Paul wrote, "What? Don't you know that your body is the temple of the Holy Spirit who is in you, whom God has given you, and you are not your own? For you are bought with a price; therefore glorify God in your body ..." Our bodies, our souls and our spirits have been bought with the precious blood of Christ (1 Peter 1:18–20). Abusing our bodies through bad habits is poor stewardship of the "temple" that God dwells in and which he bought on Calvary. We take care of our automobiles so that they can carry us where we need to go. God expects us to take care of our bodies so that we can carry his word and do his will wherever he wants us to go. To abuse our bodies through bad habits is—simply stated—sin.

Personal Ponderance:

a) What habits do I have which are harmful to my body? Smoking? Drinking? Improper eating? Laziness (resulting in an unfit body)? Busyness (resulting in no time for consistent exercise)?

b) If I were in shape, in what new ways could I serve the kingdom of God more effectively?

Chapter Six: NETOP

13. Christopher and Caleb parted ways, Caleb to carry out his plans for revenge, and Christopher to explore the wilderness west of the Ohio River. "I am Narragansett," said Caleb. "And you are an Englishman." But it wasn't culture that separated these friends, it was sin. Caleb was intent upon carrying out a plan that was opposed to God's ways and will, and he knew it.

We often justify relational separations because of differences of opinion, vision, doctrine or lifestyle. But sin and pride are more often the reasons why we cut ourselves off from one another. The apostle Paul said we divide ourselves into factional camps because we are "babies" in Christ when we should be mature believers (1 Cor. 3:1–3). In the church, we are called to strive "to keep the unity of the Spirit in the bond of peace" (Eph. 4:1–3 KJV), a unity which Jesus prayed for on the night he was betrayed (John 17:20–23) and bought with his own blood upon the cross (Eph. 2:14–16). Nothing, besides unrepentant sin, should separate Christian brothers and sisters.

Personal Ponderance:

a) Why do I separate myself from certain believers? Culture? Doctrine? Ethnicity?

b) Am I simply afraid? (I will repent of my fear.) Am I convinced they are wrong somehow? (I will repent of judgment and purpose to love them anyway.) Have I been taught to separate from certain Christians because of their doctrine? (I will seek to get to know them and better understand their beliefs. And I will bless them for their love of God regardless.)

14. Late one night, in the empty Narragansett church building, Netop and Christopher interceded for Caleb's soul. They labored long in prayer, and God met them there—strengthening their souls and renewing their faith. Christopher was especially touched and convicted of his need to be more of a praying man.

Too often we let the busyness of life crowd out disciplined prayer. We pray on the run, "popcorn prayers" which may be sincere but which hardly contribute to a healthy devotional life. Only the life rooted in habitual intercession will bear the fruit of answered prayer and bring the refreshing and the rest that God promises to those who "wait on him" (Isa. 40:29–31). If we want God's presence, we must take the time to "come boldly unto the throne of grace, that we may obtain mercy, and find grace to help in time of need" (Heb. 4:16 KJV).

Personal Ponderance:

a) What time of the day is best for me to spend undisturbed time in prayer and communion with God?

b) Can I make time every day for prayer and intercession? When? How?

Chapter Seven: CONESTOGA JOE

15. As Christopher traveled south from Rhode Island to New York City, he neglected his prayers again. Change in routine can lead too easily to a spiritual sidetrack where the disciplines of prayer and Bible reading get left at the rest stop. Vacations, business trips, even ministry trips can take us out of fellowship with those who know us best, away from the accountability of the familiar, and open us up for temptation and spiritual attack. Before traveling, we should plan Bible reading and prayer into our itinerary, as well as consistent communication with "home base," whether family or church. E-mail and cell phones make it very easy to be in touch with loved ones who can be praying for us (and with us); this helps keep us focused on the overall responsibilities and disciplines of our call in God.

Personal Ponderance:

a) When I travel, who can I stay in contact with back on the home front?

b) What are my greatest temptations when I travel?

c) How can I stay spiritually awake while "on the road"?

16. Benjamin Franklin was not a Christian, but he was a friend to Christianity. He believed in God, and he believed that faith in God was essential to making good citizens, good neighbors and good government. He was a friend of George Whitefield, the English evangelist whose preaching fanned the fires of the Great Awakening throughout the 13 American colonies. Though he would not bow the knee to Christ, he often helped the servants of Christ in their work and ministry. In so doing, he made himself the servant of all. Jesus said "whoever gives you a cup of water to drink in my name, because you belong to Christ, ... will not lose his reward" (Mark 9:41).

Today, do we give the Benjamin Franklins of the world a chance to serve us? Do we go out of our way to serve them? Do we take the time to get to know those in positions of public leadership and service outside the church? History doesn't tell us if Franklin surrendered to Jesus in his latter days, but we know that many Christians reached out to him in friendship and that he'd heard the gospel many, many times.

An aspect of our calling as "salt and light" (Matt. 5:13–16) is involvement in our communities, and this should include getting to know our civic leaders (and becoming civic leaders ourselves). In speaking about prayer for civic leaders, Paul told Timothy that "first of all supplications, prayers, intercession and thanksgiving be offered up for all men, for kings and for all that are in authority, so that we may lead a quiet and peaceable life in all godliness and honesty, for this is good and acceptable to God our Savior, who wants everybody to be saved and to come to the knowledge of the truth" (1 Tim. 2:1–4).

Personal Ponderance:

a) Do I know any of my locally elected officials? The mayor? The town or city council? The sheriff? My state representative or senator? Those on the school board? Do I keep them in prayer?

b) How can I get more involved in civic affairs in order to serve my community in the name of Jesus?

Chapter Eight: LONGSHOT

17. Connie Joe had a sad tale to tell, and Christopher listened to him without judgment or comment. It would have been easy to take his side and start badmouthing Bainbridge. It would have been just as easy to doubt the old Indian and think he'd made up or exaggerated his story. But Christopher let Joe talk until he was done, and then they rode on in silence. Joe knew Christopher had heard him fully, and this strengthened the bond of friendship and trust between the two men.

Too often, we don't let people fully share their stories, their hurt, their pain, because we think we have to have answers for them. We butt in on their tales, finish their sentences for them, offer a similar story of our own, give them advice (whether asked for or not)—anything but let them pour out the full dregs of their sorrow into our cup. And yet the Bible tells us we are to be "quick to hear, slow to speak, and slow to anger" (James 1:19). Even Job's friends, when they came upon their old comrade in the midst of his terrible tragedies, sat down next to him and were silent for seven days "for they saw that his grief was very great" (Job 2:13 KJV). They should have stayed that way!—because once they tried to figure it all out for him (blaming him for his own problems), it only drove a wedge between them.

We are to "rejoice with those who rejoice, and weep with those who weep" (Rom. 12:15). When Jesus said, "Blessed are those who mourn, for they will be comforted" (Matt. 5:4), he was promising comfort from God for those who are willing to be bear the sorrows of others. The Greek word translated "comfort" here is parakaleo, which means "to call near." This word, in another grammatical form, is used by John to describe the Holy Spirit as the "comforter" or the one who "comes alongside" (John 14:16, 26; 15:26; 16:7). When we mourn with others in a godly way, we are doing the work of the Holy Spirit, and God himself will comfort or "draw near" to us as we come alongside others.

Personal Ponderance:

a) Who do I know who has suffered a great loss or is going through a great trial? How can I come alongside as a listening ear and a caring presence?

18. Solomon said that "the words of a talebearer are as wounds, and they go down into the innermost parts of the belly" (Prov. 18:8 KJV). Telling tales out of school is always a hurtful thing. Telling lies about others, or even telling truths in order to defame another, is called slander, and it's a wicked thing which can destroy a person's reputation. Bainbridge had slandered Connie Joe intentionally, making up horrendous lies about him in order to draw people away from Connie Joe's ferry over the Susquehanna and increase business for his own ferry business. The lies cut Joe to the heart, and he gave up his business—and the life of an Indian—altogether.

Whether we mean to or not, we often hurt others by speaking about them when we shouldn't. Even when we have a real cause to be upset at someone, God doesn't give us the right to speak against them. Instead, Jesus commands us to go first and talk to them personally (Matt. 18:15). And when someone has a grudge against US (right or wrong), Jesus said to set aside the religious stuff we are involved with and go make things right with that person (Matt. 5:23–24). Right relationship is very high on God's priority list. Speaking well of others is very high, too. We are never to return evil for evil, but rather to overcome evil with good (Rom. 12:21). When someone curses us (speaks against us), we are commanded to bless them (speak good of them and speak good ON them). Just as the words of a talebearer can wound deeply, words spoken to bless can actually bring "health to the bones" (Prov. 15:30, 16:24).

Personal Ponderance:

a) Am I a talebearer? Do I speak about others when I should be praying for them and helping them to become more like Jesus instead?

b) Who have I been speaking against, and how can I make it right? How can I begin to bless them instead of cursing them?

19. Christopher Long was so moved by Connie Joe's tale of the slander that had been laid on him by Bainbridge, that when Long next met Bainbridge face-to-face, he confronted the man in a dramatic and courageous way that eventually led to contrition on the part of Bainbridge and long-overdue justice for Connie Joe.

God hates injustice, and we should too. When we see injustice, our hearts should be so touched that we get up and do something about it. Babies are being slaughtered daily in the womb in America. Drugs are being peddled to our children in our streets. Rich retail superstores elbow their way into small communities, underselling and bankrupting the mom and pop businesses of Main Street America. Morally aberrant lifestyles and antichristian philosophies are being forced upon our children in our public schools. The media makes light of sin and makes fun of Christians. Believers are being persecuted in other lands. Human slavery still exists in parts of the world. If we look the other way, or if all we do is complain about it to one another, we sin.

Write letters to your local editor. Picket the abortion clinic and pray for those who work there. Get involved in the local school. Turn off your TV or cancel your cable account (and tell your local cable company why). Pray, preach, protest and proclaim Christ. Stand up for those who need your help. Get involved.

Personal Ponderance:
a) Where are the downtrodden, the helpless, the poor and the persecuted in my community? What can I do to help them, to take up their cause in the name of Jesus?
b) How can I find out more about the persecuted church throughout the world? What can I do to help them?

20. "But a man's got to do for his country as much as his conscience bids him do. That includes fighting for it."
"Real Indians feel the same way about their own country," said Connie Joe soberly.

Patriotism. To some, it means taking up arms to defend house and home, neighbor and country, against a foreign antagonist. To others it means speaking up against injustice and tyranny within our own government. Either way, "pure patriotism" means taking a stand on behalf of the rights of others. Today, America goes to war in foreign lands—our justification is "freedom": to insure the freedom of our own people against the kind of horrific terrorist attacks that took place on 9/11, and to secure the freedom of others who suffer under tyrannical, expansionistic governments.

As Christians, we must seek God for the bigger picture, ask for wisdom, and be led by the Holy Spirit to take a stand for those who cannot stand for themselves. Some believers feel called to join the armed forces for the greater freedom of others. Some say that we should be fighting on our knees in prayer. This is a hard question, and I offer the following questions for deep reflection, not for the obvious answers that they might engender.

Personal Pondering:

a) Would Jesus fight for his country? What if the Father had bid him to (as God often did in the Old Testament)?

b) What was the cross? When the Father sent his Son to die a violent death on our behalf was it meant to be the last death for mankind, or does it justify us sending our own sons (and daughters!) to die on behalf of others?

c) I may be willing to lay down my life for another (John 15:13), but am I willing to take a life in order to save a life?

21. "I am no longer Great Hill," said the giant Delaware to the stooped Susquehannock as we sat at the table and sipped the hot soup. "I am now Moses, for God has climbed the Great Hill and carved His Word upon my heart." Moses pointed to the book I had spotted. It was a ragged Bible, in German, opened to the Gospel of Saint Luke. "God's Son is my doctor now," said the Delaware. "And His Word is my medicine."

Great Hill, the Delaware medayoo (medicine man) was now Moses, the Moravian Christian. He was a new man from the inside out, and had put aside the worship and work of the spirits of his ancestors. He didn't just believe new things, he was a transformed man (2 Cor. 5:17–28; Col. 3:9–10). He was "born again" by the Spirit of God, and was living an entirely new life (John 3:1–8). Once a violent man, he was now a man of peace.

The Christian apostle Paul had once been the Jewish rabbi Saul, a persecutor of the church and a murderer of the followers of Christ. But he was changed by the Spirit of God through the gospel of Jesus Christ, committing himself to compassionate service to those he once hounded and harassed. Risking his life countless times (and eventually losing his life for the sake of others), he traveled the known world proclaiming the power of God to all who would hear.

The gospel is a life-changing, revolutionizing gospel. That is its power. That is the hope it offers to a world stuck in sin.

Personal Pondering:

a) In what ways has the gospel changed me?

b) Who do I know that has been radically changed by God's Spirit?

c) How can use the testimonies of changed lives to point others to the love and the power of God in Christ Jesus?

Chapter Ten: LONG NIGHT IN THE LONGHOUSE

22. "As Connie Joe has said of the heavenly Father, no matter what we call Him, He's the Father of us all. If we were to walk the path that leads back to the beginning of all things, we'd see that we share the same God, the same first parents, the same blood."

Thus Christopher argued for an understanding of the bond that takes us back to Eden—and the fall. If it is true (and the Bible declares it so) that we share one blood from one set of original parents (Gen. 1:26–28), then "racism" is a lie. In essence, though the world is filled with men and women of many colored skins, diverse cultures and various genetic makeups, there is only one human race, made in the likeness and image of God. Though our sins (and God Himself) have scattered us across the earth (Gen. 11:1–8), we are all cousins with one bloodline that runs back to Noah—and ultimately to Adam and Eve.

So racism is a lie. The differences that make up the garden of humanity are not so different when we get down inside to the hearts that beat within us. We are all the children of one set of original parents, all created to know God, serve God, glorify God, and enjoy God forever. Sin has separated us from God and one another. Sin, with the fear and distrust of one another that it planted in our souls, bends us toward racism and prejudice. Sin, and the one who tempted us to it (Satan), are our true enemies—not one another.

Personal Pondering:

a) Since I am related to everyone I will ever meet, how should that change the way I think about them? The way I treat them?

23. While discussing the love of God, Caleb argued that he has seen very little love among varied Christian groups. "They fight among themselves like children arguing over the colour of a bird that has flown suddenly over their heads," he challenged. "They divide into tribes and camps over disagreements on how to worship their God, and they build their steepled forts to keep each other out. They write books against one another. They make laws against one another. They stand up in their churches and preach against one another. How can they love their enemies when they have not learned to love their brothers?"

Could any church historian say it better?

Jesus commanded us to love one another (John 15:12–14), and he prayed to the Father to make us one, as the Father and the Son are one, so that the world may believe that the Father sent the Son (John 17:20–23). If our manifest unity can actually cause an unbelieving world to believe, then that unity is the most powerful evangelistic tool we have—and our disunity is a shameful stumbling block to faith. Do we really love God? Do we really want His will to be done on earth as it is in heaven (Matt. 6:10)? Do we really want to see souls saved? Then we must obey Him—we must love one another (John 14:23–24). We must pray for, contend for, and walk in the unity of the Spirit which Christ died for on the Cross at Calvary (Eph. 2:14–16). When we are one, the world will see Jesus in our midst (He will thus be "lifted up" before their eyes), and God will draw all men unto Himself (John 12:32).

Personal Pondering:

a) Do I say I love God—whom I can't see—but hold back from loving my brother and sister who are right in front of me (1 John 4:20–21)?

b) Now that I see from Scripture that the Cross was not only for my personal salvation, but for the creation and unity of the church, Christ's body (Eph. 2:14–16; Rom. 12:5; 1 Cor. 12:12), how can I walk out that unity in relationship to my brothers and sisters in the faith? In my church? In my community? In my region? Throughout the world?

24. "My bow and my gun," said Moses, pointing to the weapons which lay against the wall, **"will nevermore be raised against another man.** One man and one woman were the father and mother of us all. The Lamb died for all, to turn the hearts of all nations to the Father in Heaven. How can a man follow the Lamb if he raises his club against his brother? How can I say I love my brother if I run the warpath against him?

"My Lord commands me to rejoice when men speak against me because I follow the Lamb. And if a man strikes me in the face, the lamb commands me to turn my other cheek to receive a second blow if a second blow is coming. But if I rise up after the first blow and return that blow myself, I am like any other man who lifts his pride above the Lamb's

command to love. I will not rise up against the Lamb. For I am no longer
Great Hill that I must rescue my name from under the feet of my enemies.
I am Moses, and my hope is in God."

Moses was a Moravian. Converted by German Moravian missionaries,
he had been taught to offer no violence to any man. His allegiance was no
longer to tribes or nations, but to the Lamb of God. His call was to love.
This politically-neutral stance was one shared by other contemporary
Christian movements of his day, including the Anabaptists and the
Quakers. Many Christians today hold to a "gospel of peace" which pre-
cludes fighting in any of the wars of men. Some of their arguments, like
Moses', are compelling. Are they biblically balanced?

Personal Pondering:

a) In the Old Testament, God initiates wars, sends his people out to war,
goes with them into war, wars on their behalf, and even commands the
slaughter of women, children and animals. Yet we know (from the revelation of the Old Testament and the New) that God loves mankind, and
indeed that God himself is love. Is God schizophrenic? Of course not! Then
how do I justify the wars that God commanded with the teaching and life
of the Christ who was born while angels sang "Glory to God in the highest! Peace on earth! Good will to men!"?

Chapter Thirteen: LOGSTOWN

**25. In the iniquitous backwoods trading village of Logstown, amidst
ungodly white trappers and unprincipled Indians, Christopher Long
was tempted to go to bed with an Indian maiden.** He met the test with
the moral commitment of a Joseph (Gen. 39:2–13), confessing his fear of
God and his love of his own wife. Furthermore, he declared that none of
his company would indulge in such sin. The very next morning, even
though he was still sick with a fever, he pulled out of Logstown to remove
himself and his men from the dishonesty and immorality that was so preva-
lent there.

In America, the popular culture is so filled with ungodliness that temptation grabs at us every way we turn. The culture is preoccupied with mate-
rialism, sexual gratification, selfish ambition, self-expression, comfort,
power, pleasure, perversion, and pride. As Christians, we are in this world,
but we are not of this world. We are commanded to offer our lives to God

for the sake of this world, but we are not to become like the world—instead, we are to let God renew our minds so that we think and act like Jesus. 1 John 5:4–5 states that "whoever is born of God overcomes the world, and this is the victory that overcomes the world: our faith! Who is he that overcomes the world? He who believes that Jesus is the Son of God."

King David asked the Lord, "How can a young man cleanse his ways?" And then he answered his own question with this advice: "By taking heed to Your word!" (Ps. 119:9) When Jesus was tempted by Satan in the wilderness, he met every test with a declaration of God's will as found in the Scriptures (Matt. 4:1–11).

Personal Pondering:

a) How do I "deny ungodliness and worldly lusts … live soberly, righteously, and godly in this present age" (Titus 2:12)?

b) How do I keep myself "unstained by the world" (James 1:27)?

c) What Scriptures can I memorize to give me "ammunition" against the temptations of the world, the flesh, and the devil?

Chapter Fifteen: LONGSHOT'S CHRISTMAS

26. The Christmas season has always been a God-given window of opportunity for Christians to witness to the grace and love of God. Christopher Long took advantage of that opportunity and invited his backwoods "brothers" to come to his cabin and hear Christmas prayers from the Common Book of Prayer. At first "few of them wanted to hear any good thing about God," but then an old blacksmith named Burney shamed some of the traders into coming and invited the Indians to come along too. The natives crowded into Long's cabin to hear what he had to say, and pretty soon things got downright evangelistic!

We must look for the "divine appointments" that God sets up in our lives—those times when, with a little courage, we can speak up for Jesus. Sometimes those we expect to listen will not listen, and we—like blacksmith Burney—may have to go out into the "highways and hedges and compel them to come in, so that the house may be filled" (Luke 14:23). Jesus wants us to be "fishers of men" (Matt. 4:19), so we must cast our nets and let them drag as the winds move us daily through the sea of life.

Personal Pondering:

a) Which holidays most speak of God and of Jesus? How might I use these traditional seasons to shine a spotlight on the gospel and the goodness of God?

b) Besides living a consistent witness among those I live and work with, what can I do to "go into the highways and hedges" in order to invite strangers to "come in" to the household of God?

Chapter Seventeen: WHITE WOMAN'S CREEK

27. On White Woman's Creek, on the eastern edge of the Ohio wilderness, lived a woman named Mary Harris. Born in Deerfield, Massachusetts around 1694, she was captured by Abenaki Indians when she was only 10. Nearly 50 now, married to a Wyendot, all she really knew was the life of an Indian. Her early years in Massachusetts were a dim and distorted memory.

She didn't know she was born a Puritan. She had no conception of the courageous and incredible Christian heritage that was hers through her natural parents. She had no accurate knowledge of the gospel or the person of Jesus Christ—she had been told by French trappers that "God is a Frenchman who sent his son Jez Christ to tell us how to live. But the English kilt the son and hanged him on a cross." Her only contact with other white men was with the rough and irreligious hunters and traders of the woods of Ohio. "But they's awful wicket in these woods," she said. "I wonder how they kin be so wicket!"

Many of us have been raised in the church. Those who were not probably still have a heritage of Christianity in their past. And our nation most assuredly has a rich and godly heritage (and calling). But it's far too easy to "forget" who we are. We spend too much time among the "wicket in the woods," and too little time in God's Word. Neglecting fellowship and attendance at corporate worship. Filling our minds with worldly entertainment. Immersing ourselves in the popular and overwhelmingly anti-Christian culture of our day. All this can dull our sense of who we are as God's children in a world that hates God. It can distort our vision of the power and purity of the person of Jesus Christ and the sacrifice He made for the sins of the world. If we don't know who we are, if we forget who He is, we will soon be backslidden in our hearts.

Personal Pondering
(Read Heb. 3:13, 10:25; 1 Peter 2:13–16; 1 John 2:15–17):

a) How can I keep my heritage, my personal salvation, and my calling before my face daily? How can I share this heritage with others in my family?

b) How consistent, honest, and deep is my fellowship with other believers?

c) In what ways am I obeying God through serving my brothers and sisters in Christ?

d) Do I encourage others "daily" as the Bible says is needed? Do I receive daily encouragement? How can I position myself relationally to give and receive daily encouragement in my walk with God?

Chapter Eighteen: JUST A JEST

28. Longshot was jester. Oh, not in the old English way in which a court clown would perform ridiculous and foolish antics to amuse the king or the lord and his ladies! But Long liked to joke. He played with words to get a point across or get a chuckle out of someone. He had a good sense of humor. But not all jesting is good.

Sometime we joke with people because it seems like a safe way to poke fun at them, or to air our grievances without really being open and honest about how we feel. Sometime our humor causes people to laugh at another's expense; we are made to appear clever while the person who is the butt of our joke is made to appear foolish. This is hurtful.

Humor is a wonderful thing. Laughter, when it is clean and free of malice, is a powerful medicine for the soul, and it can turn life into "a continual feast" of God's goodness (Prov. 15:15).

But we mustn't be found laughing as the world laughs—at coarse and careless things, at immorality and sin, at the mishaps and tragedies of others (Eph. 5:1–4). We are not cued to the world's "laugh track," as if we have to be tickled by every jab of the devil's elbow. We are to have "nothing to do with the worthless things … that belong to darkness …" or even to talk about them (Eph. 5:11–12). Instead, we are to speak to each other with psalms and hymns and spiritual songs, making melody in our hearts to the Lord, giving God thanks (always and for all things) in the name of our Lord Jesus Christ (Eph. 5:19–20). What a difference it would make in our lives if all our humor and our communication lifted our hearts in praise, joy, encouragement, and thanksgiving to God!

Personal Pondering:

a) What makes me laugh? Would Jesus laugh with me?

b) When I make others laugh, who is it for? Who is encouraged? Who is built up? Is anyone offended or put down by my humor?

c) Do my jokes, my stories, my comments give thanks or encourage thanks to God in the name of Jesus Christ? Do they encourage hope, faith, love, or praise?

Chapter Twenty-one: A SOLITARY SEASON

29. **"I need a solitary season," said Christopher to Connie Joe. "A time to wander the woods and gather up kindling for my own fire."**

Christopher took his leave of his friends to explore the forest alone. He wanted time to spend with God beneath the ancient trees and atop the wild mountain ridges. He knew that those who seek God will find Him, and he needed to find Him. He also needed to see the condition of his own soul, and so a "personal retreat" into the wilderness was just the right medicine. "And since there was no one to hide from [out there in the woods]," Long said, "there was no need to hide—and I saw my faults quite clearly as I walked the wide woods in unfettered contemplation and communion with God. As my sins and my weaknesses walked increasingly naked at my side, I brought them continually to God's attention (to whom whey were no revelation, for He saw them long before I did, poorly robed and insufficiently masked as they were). I began to take delight in their uncovering, experiencing for the first time the fullness of those scriptural promises, 'If we walk in the light, as he is in the light, we have fellowship one with another, and the blood of Jesus Christ his Son cleanseth us from all sin', and 'If we confess our sins, he is faithful to forgive us our sins and cleanse us from all unrighteousness.' My fellowship with God grew progressively stronger until I wondered that Adam could have been such a fool as to throw away the sweetness of the company of God in the cool of the garden. And then the Spirit reminded me that I was of the same dust as Adam, as free and as apt to fly or fall as the first man had been. Who was I to judge the world's first father? Though I walked beside the grand Ohio in the dim memory and the long shadow of that lost Garden, the serpent still slithered among men and I was still a man."

All of us need times apart from the routine of life—times with other believers or times alone—when we can examine our hearts and focus on the condition of our relationship with God. Jesus got up "long before daylight" (Mark 1:35) to spend time alone with God. And He often pulled His men away from the ministry in order to "rest" (Mark 6:31). This is healthy. This is good. This is needed by us all.

Personal Pondering:

a) When did I last go away on a personal retreat? Where might I go to pray and study and commune with God, where the distractions of life are few?

b) When did I last hear from God?

c) Read Hebrews 12:1–2. What are the "weights" in my life, which I tolerate without much thought, which keep me from running the race of faith with abandon? What are the sins which so easily beset me, which I have not fully dealt with, which hinder my walk with God? I must get aside, acknowledge, and confess my sin, refocus my eyes upon Jesus, and run the race!

Chapter Twenty-five: ONE MORN IN LATE SUMMER

30. Our story ends with Christopher Long and his wife Sarah sitting together beside the Yadkin River on their homestead in the frontier of North Carolina. Long had been home from his adventures for only four months when a letter arrived from the Ohio Company requesting he make another trip to finish his hunt for suitable lands for a white settlement in the Ohio country.

Sarah didn't want to see him go, but she knew that he would and believed that he must. "A man must follow his calling," she reminded him quietly (words that she also needed to hear herself say, for she dearly wished him to be home instead).

God may call us to pull up roots and to walk into untamed and unfamiliar corners of this world. Those corners may be thousands of miles from home or they may be across the street or on the other side of town. But when God asks, "Whom shall I send, and who shall go for us," we must be ready in our hearts to say, "Here I am. Send me" (Isa. 6:8).

And those of us who are called to stay behind must be willing to say, with Sarah Long, "A man must follow his calling."

In all this, we must never forget that our first calling—those of us who are husbands or wives, fathers or mothers—is to the families that God has given us. God will never call us to abandon our families, to put His work

before their welfare, to disavow them in order to commit ourselves to kingdom ministry. No! God clearly states that those who do not care for their
own, especially those in their own household, have denied the faith and are
worse than unbelievers (1 Tim. 5:8)! So our hearts must be open to obey
God in all things, go where He calls us, do what He tells us—but we must
never make His work an excuse to stop loving, caring for, and pouring out
our lives for the families God has given us. Even while dying upon the
cross, Jesus took measures to insure that Mary, His mother, would be cared
for after He was gone (John 19:25–27).

Faith lives at home.

Personal Pondering:

a) Is there a calling in my life that I have been fighting or ignoring? Have
I talked this over with a friend, a family member, or my pastor?

b) Am I hindering or holding back a loved one from their call in God?
What in me keeps me from releasing them to God?

c) Do I make kingdom work an excuse to avoid family responsibilities and
relationship?

d) What can I cut from my life that enables me to spend more time loving
and caring for my family?

Valor Christian High School
3775 Grace Blvd
Highlands Ranch, CO 80126

DATE DUE

The Word at Work Around the World

A vital part of Cook Communications Ministries is our international outreach, Cook Communications Ministries International (CCMI). Your purchase of this book, and of other books and Christian-growth products from Cook, enables CCMI to provide Bibles and Christian literature to people in more than 150 languages in 65 countries.

Cook Communications Ministries is a not-for-profit, self-supporting organization. Revenues from sales of our books, Bible curricula, and other church and home products not only fund our U.S. ministry, but also fund our CCMI ministry around the world. One hundred percent of donations to CCMI go to our international literature programs.

CCMI reaches out internationally in three ways:

· Our premier International Christian Publishing Institute (ICPI) trains leaders from nationally led publishing houses around the world.

· We provide literature for pastors, evangelists, and Christian workers in their national language.

· We reach people at risk—refugees, AIDS victims, street children, and famine victims—with God's Word.

Word Power, God's Power

Faith Kidz, RiverOak, Honor, Life Journey, Victor, NexGen — every time you purchase a book produced by Cook Communications Ministries, you not only meet a vital personal need in your life or in the life of someone you love, but you're also a part of ministering to José in Colombia, Humberto in Chile, Gousa in India, or Lidiane in Brazil. You help make it possible for a pastor in China, a child in Peru, or a mother in West Africa to enjoy a life-changing book. And because you helped, children and adults around the world are learning God's Word and walking in his ways.

Thank you for your partnership in helping to disciple the world. May God bless you with the power of his Word in your life.

For more information about our
international ministries, visit www.ccmi.org.

Additional copies of *LONGSHOT*
and other RiverOak titles are available
from your local bookseller.

If you have enjoyed this book,
or if it has had an impact on your life,
we would like to hear from you.

Please contact us at:

RIVEROAK BOOKS
Cook Communications Ministries, Dept. 201
4050 Lee Vance View
Colorado Springs, CO 80918
Or visit our Web site:
www.cookministries.com